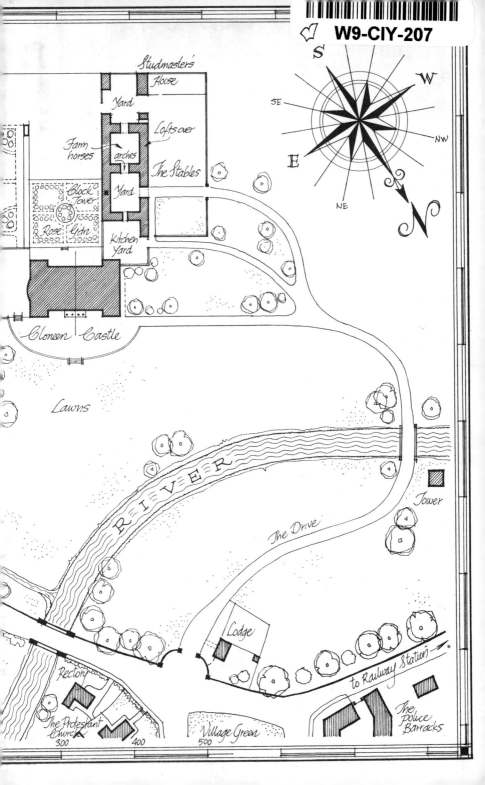

THE HERITAGE

Books by Frances Parkinson Keyes

The Heritage
I, The King
The Explorer
The Old Gray Homestead
The Career of David Noble
Letters from a Senator's Wife
Queen Anne's Lace
Silver Seas and Golden Cities
Lady Blanche Farm
The Safe Bridge
Senator Marlowe's Daughter
The Happy Wanderer
Honor Bright
Written in Heaven
  (Revised and reissued as)
  Therese: *Saint of a Little Way*
Capital Kaleidoscope
Parts Unknown
The Great Tradition
Along a Little Way
The Sublime Shepherdess
  (Revised and reissued as)
  Bernadette of Lourdes
Fielding's Folly
The Grace of Guadalupe
All That Glitters
Crescent Carnival

Also the Hills
The River Road
Once on Esplanade
Came a Cavalier
Dinner at Antoine's
All This Is Louisiana
The Cost of a Best Seller
Joy Street
Steamboat Gothic
The Royal Box
The Frances Parkinson Keyes Cookbook
St. Anne: *Grandmother of Our Saviour*
Blue Camellia
The Land of Stones and Saints
Victorine
Station Wagon in Spain
Mother Cabrini: *Missionary to the World*
Frances Parkinson Keyes' Christmas Gift
The Third Mystic of Avila
Roses in December
The Chess Players
The Rose and the Lily
Madame Castel's Lodger
A Treasury of Favorite Poems
The Restless Lady and Other Stories
Three Ways of Love
Tongues of Fire

THE HERITAGE

Frances Parkinson Keyes

McGraw-Hill Book Company

NEW YORK   TORONTO

Grateful acknowledgment is made to the following for
permission to quote from copyrighted material:
    The Dr. Douglas Hyde Trust, for verses by the
late Dr. Hyde.
    The Macmillan Company, New York, and A. P.
Watt & Son as literary agents to the Estate of W. B.
Yeats and on behalf of Macmillan & Co., Ltd., for
material from W. B. Yeats' *Autobiographies* and for
verses from "The Withering of the Boughs" from W. B.
Yeats' *The Collected Poems*.
    The Mercier Press, Cork, Ireland, for material
from *The Second Book of Irish Myths and Legends*, by
Eoin Neeson.

Contents

AUTHOR'S NOTE   vii

PRINCIPAL CHARACTERS   xvii

PART ONE The Irish Mail
Late June, 1882
[PAGE 3]

PART TWO The American Nephew
Late June, 1882
[PAGE 39]

PART THREE The Heir Apparent
Early July to Late August, 1882
[PAGE 75]

PART FOUR The Heir Presumptive
Late August, 1882, to Late March, 1883
[PAGE 133]

PART FIVE Peter Bradford of Boston, Massachusetts
Late March, 1883, to Early May, 1883
[PAGE 265]

FLOOR PLAN OF CLONEEN CASTLE   70–71

GENEALOGICAL CHART   322

BIBLIOGRAPHY   327

[THE ENDPAPERS SHOW A PLAN OF CLONEEN ESTATE.]

Author's Note

It is the pleasant custom of my publishers to give me presents, usually books, at Christmastime; and in 1965 my present from John Bright-Holmes of Eyre & Spottiswoode took the form of *Scenes from Edwardian Life,* by our mutual friend, Sir Charles Petrie. I started to read it with the delight which his brisk and charming style always inspires; but I had gone hardly more than a hundred pages when I was stopped short by an especially arresting paragraph. I read it over again several times and then I spent the better part of a night thinking about it. The next day I found myself impelled to write Mr. Bright-Holmes an urgent and totally uncharacteristic note of thanks. "Perhaps you won't agree with me," I said, "but I feel we should postpone the next major historical novel for a lighter story, with an Irish setting. The basis for the plot is contained in a single paragraph of Sir Charles Petrie's book which you were kind enough to give me. Will you let me know what you think?"

I identified the paragraph but said no more. The answer, written the day my letter had been received, came by air mail. "This is the best return I ever had for an inconsequential Christmas present," Mr. Bright-Holmes wrote graciously. "A whole extra novel for our list! And what an ideal subject for you to develop! Of course, you must write the Irish novel and, of course, the place for it is before the next major historical romance. I hope you will see your way clear to beginning it this coming spring in Ireland. I suggest the following terms."

I had not expected the response to be so prompt or so enthusiastic. I had made my suggestion on the spur of the moment and sober second thought led to some grave reflections: I had never been to Ireland and had never particularly wanted to go there. My knowledge of its history centered largely around St. Patrick and Charles Stewart Parnell —the former because Paul Gallico's wonderful book *The Steadfast Man* had led me to write about St. Patrick myself; and the latter because his maternal grandmother was Delia Tudor of Boston and I had grown up with another of her descendants by that name, whom I numbered among my best friends; I was therefore interested in her family's saga. As I have always been an addict of the drama, the movement which resulted in the foundation of the Abbey Theater and its subsequent success had thrilled me deeply; and as all my life I have been an avid reader, I was well acquainted with the works, as well as the names of Swift, Sheridan, Shaw, George Moore and W. B. Yeats; but I had always thought of them as geniuses rather than as Irishmen!

Aside from this, I had heard about leprechauns without visualizing them very clearly; I was familiar with shamrocks, tweed, Irish linen, Waterford glass, Irish greys and Irish crochet; and the term "Castle Irish," as used in Boston to denote a degree of prosperity beyond "Lace Curtain Irish," though not in general use elsewhere, as far as the United States is concerned. And that excellent drink, Irish coffee, had been introduced into our household as a result of a taste developed by my son John during World War II. This did not seem to be very adequate preparation for any kind of novel—I knew that much about Central Africa, which (happily!) it had not occurred to me I might try to interpret. Obviously, I was faced with a task very different from writing a book with a setting in France or Italy, where my personal acquaintance with place and people was lifelong and supplemented by a fair knowledge of their history; or in Spain, which had been my happy hunting ground, off and on, for more than forty years. Of course, there was still the chance that neither my American publisher nor my French publisher would agree with Mr. Bright-Holmes, in which case my ignorance need not be revealed. But both replied to my question about the possibility of an Irish novel with the same alacrity and the same enthusiasm that he had and I knew the matter was settled: it is pointless for an author to question the feasibility of writing a certain book when the scene and subject have declared themselves as the indicated task. I engaged trans-Atlantic passage for my secretary, Deanie Bullock, and myself, and set about reading hotel brochures and guidebooks and making inquiries about reservations from what I was told were the most reliable sources.

The first results of my investigations were not very encouraging. All the brochures from hotels outside of Dublin dwelt on the great opportunities they offered for golf and fishing, and mentioned no other special advantages. As golf never appealed to me, ever before I was so lame I could not play it, and as I went fishing just once in my life and hated it, I was not irresistibly attracted to any of these places; if they offered any more opportunity for learning about the history, culture and customs of a people unfamiliar to me, this was not mentioned. I do not usually have very good luck dealing with agencies, but this time I had been instructed to do so by an official whose authority I did not venture to question, and presently I received a long-distance telephone call from New York.

"I am happy to tell you I have exactly the right thing for you in Dublin," a jubilant voice informed me.

"At what price?" I inquired cautiously.

"A hundred and twenty dollars."

"A *week?*" I asked with almost equal jubilation, feeling that at last it would be possible to salvage something out of the sum allotted me for expenses.

"A *week!*" echoed the voice, no longer jubilant but horrified. "A *day.*"

With difficulty, I convinced my informer that authors, my kind of author anyway, do not earn that kind of money. I argued in vain that I thought fifty dollars a day ought to be enough without food, that that was a good deal more than I paid for a beautiful suite in Rome, double what I paid for a wholly satisfactory one in Madrid. At last, we compromised on sixty dollars, which did not include either taxes or service for accommodations, with so little closet (cupboard) space that we could never wholly unpack, no provision for heat in the bathrooms and none provided in the bedrooms during what we considered cold weather. Inquiries which I personally made at other hotels did not result in anything more reasonable; twice I paid twenty-five dollars for an overnight stay—once in Dublin and once elsewhere—for single occupancy of a room which had nothing in it but a large bed—not a dressing table, not even a chair.

Having resigned myself to the fact that two persons could not, apparently, live in any first-class Dublin hotel for less than eighty dollars a day, even though they required only one hearty meal in the course of twenty-four hours, I ventured to hope that I could economize on transportation. My lameness makes a car a necessity and, though Deanie has driven my station wagon without causing me a qualm through the Simplon Pass, across the Andes and—directly after World War II—over the battered remains of what were once excellent roads in France, I hesitated to have her do so in Ireland. The station wagon has, of course, a left-hand drive and that is exactly the opposite of what one should have in the Emerald Isle; and it so happens that several of my acquaintances, though excellent drivers by American and Continental standards, have come to grief elsewhere because in moments of crisis, they instinctively turned to the right. Quite aside from this, I had been told that most Irish roads were so narrow that a large car was apt to prove unwieldy on them; and the warning (contained in the one guidebook which dropped the subject of golf and fish long enough to speak of something else!) to the effect that American tourists would be well advised not to try motoring more than a hundred miles a day in Ireland convinced me that the roads were probably rough as well as narrow. (Their appearance is deceptive and roughness is actually not the right word to describe them; they produce an effect of undulation which does not seem bad until you have been bounced up and down on it for hours on end. Then you realize that you are pretty badly shaken unless your car has very good springs—and such a car is hard, if not impossible, to rent in Ireland.)

Dublin is the only capital with which I am familiar where it is not possible, almost at a moment's notice, to hire a comfortable chauffeur-driven car by the hour. There, as far as we could find out, rental had to be by the day at an astronomical price or by the week or season for one slightly less staggering—but in every case for a low-priced vehicle. The best rental bargain we were able to make, for a low-priced car, ten years old, was twenty dollars a day, whether it went some distance or was not used at all, with seven dollars extra for the driver's expenses when we were out of Dublin. As this came to a considerable sum the first summer, we tried to do better the second, with really sad results: the car put at our disposal had already been driven almost a hundred thousand miles and the charge was ten dollars a day, flat, with an allowance of twenty-five miles a day in Dublin and fifty miles out of Dublin; every mile beyond this represented a surcharge. The seven dollars a day for the driver remained the same, except that there was to be an extra allowance, even in Dublin, if he did not eat at home, which was apparently often his preference. However, this seemed an improvement, until we read the items for distances: fourteen miles from our hotel on O'Connell Street to our dressmakers' on Merrion

Square, which we clocked at a mile and a half; twenty-eight miles to the Horse Show in Ballsbridge and back, which we clocked at six miles. We then discovered that the charge for distance was computed from the time the car left the garage in the more remote suburbs and not from the time it picked us up; and, when we were out of Dublin, from the driver's preferred lodging to our hotel. Since he was a dedicated fisherman, the preferred lodging represented another ten miles extra per day. If we used the car before noon, we were charged double because, though what we were paying was allegedly a daily rate, ten dollars proved to cover only a half day, so that the car might be free for weddings in the morning. And the one time we kept it out a little after midnight, to attend a hunt ball, the surcharge was enormous on the ground that the driver had to be paid extra. All in all, the car hire the second summer came to $1,678, which seems pretty steep, especially when we discovered that the trade-in allowance on a car of that make and that vintage was two hundred dollars. For the first time in my experience as a travel writer, which has taken me to nearly all parts of the world in the course of the last forty-odd years, I was obliged to write my publisher that I did not have enough money to go on with my work.

I would not mention all this if it were not for the fact that many thoughtful persons in Ireland are taking fright at the tourist reaction to fantastic prices for inferior accommodations and transportation; and the mayor of one large city has gone so far as to say in a public address that Eire is in danger of killing the goose that lays the golden egg. Another official asked the cogent question, "But will they come again?" after outlining the enormous sums spent by certain British visitors who departed poorer as well as sadder and wiser than when they had come. His conclusion was that they would not. I feel this is all too true. I also feel that Ireland has so much to offer, not only to tourists but to students, scholars, musicians, authors and dramatists, that their tastes and needs might well be given the same consideration as those of sportsmen, and that they might be assured of this before they make their plans for a long sojourn.

Though it was in decrepit vehicles such as I have described that I was driven from one end of Ireland to the other, I am glad that I persevered. I got as far south as Killarney, as far north as Rosapenna, as far west as Galway and as far east as Howth. I took the Hundred Mile Drive, the Atlantic Drive and the Bloody Foreland Drive. I think I covered most of the "musts" for tourists and a good many places which tourists seem to ignore or for which they feel they cannot spare the time in the course of a pre-arranged itinerary. If I failed to get as much of a thrill as I was supposed to out of the lakes —after all, we have 350 of those in New Hampshire—or the cattle— after all, there are more cows than people in Vermont—I more than made up for it at the Cathedral in Kilkenny; at the salmon leap near Ramelton; at the view over the river as seen through a high window in the Yeats Tower; at the first sight of the magic mountain of Errigal at Gweedore; at the long stretches of roads bordered by peat, bog cotton and heather, with the mountains on one side, and the sea on the other; at the thousand-year-old church of Ballintubber, recently restored; at Killeen Castle, still standing four-square after nine centuries; at every sight of the swans, whether solitary in little coves on the rugged coast of Connemara, or in families—cob, pen and cygnets—from an inlet of Lough Corrib; at the wonderful unbroken spaciousness of the Curragh; and most of all at the Rock of Cashel, to me the most inspiring sight in Ireland and one of the most inspiring anywhere in the world. And everywhere I met with courtesy coupled with real kindliness. Irish cordiality is deservedly famous.

I was the beneficiary of this kindliness over and over again and, once I had made known my chief interests to the people I met, I had wonderful cooperation in my work. The name of Liam Miller, Director of the Dolmen Press, certainly leads all the rest on the list of those who helped me. I met this versatile, learned and accomplished gentleman, as I met several other delightful persons, through the good offices of Miss Ann Mahon, Assistant Cultural Affairs Attaché of the American Embassy. Mr. Miller's first love was architecture, but his fidelity to this underwent an acid test, first in the fascination held for him by the drama and then by the yen to establish a publishing house, which would specialize in poetry and *belles lettres* and he is one of the best editors, if not the very best, that it has ever been my good fortune to consult. And when I say best, I am thinking not only of the fund of information that is at his command to impart and share and the genius as to how best to adapt this information, both accurately and graciously to current needs; I am thinking also of the unfailing courtesy with which he gives advice and the faithfulness with which he fills all engagements for editorial conferences. Twice a week, month in and month out, despite the thousand and one demands upon his time from the publishing house and the theater, he arrived at the hour appointed and did not leave until he had scrutinized every word in the script I had written since he last saw me, and commented on it in a way that showed me how to make it better. It is no exaggeration to say that without his wise counsel, I never could have achieved *The Heritage* in its present form.

Mr. Miller's sixteen-year-old daughter, Maire, proved a very competent assistant when it came to locating data in old documents, newspapers and books and I was especially pleased when she found the account of "the reaping" at Avondale.

Next to Mr. Miller, my most authoritative source of information—though in a very different direction—was Mr. James Whyte, until recently Secretary and General Manager of the Londonderry & Lough Swilly Railway, and an authority on transportation generally. First through correspondence and then in the course of several productive meetings, I followed in his footsteps from one end of Ireland to the other. It is to him that I owe the priceless (to me!) story of "the other James Bond" and many more. In this connection, however, I must confess to an inaccuracy in my text. It appears with his knowledge and consent only because I promised I would set the matter straight in my Author's Note: the rule forbidding an engine-drawn train to cross a certain highway and obliging the temporary transfer to horse-power was abrogated long before the date of my story.

Another inaccuracy is that referring to the foot warmers. Actually, these were put on the Irish Mail in London; only the lunch baskets went on at Chester.

The poem by Yeats quoted on page 149 was written early in his career but not quite as early as the text would indicate, so this should be confessed as another inaccuracy. But since, like the other two, it was made with official approval, I do not feel too guilty about it.

The house, which Lady Susannah felt so fortunate as to find, was actually the so-called *hôtel* [private residence] of Jean Debray. According to Georges Pillement, this was "rebuilt" in 1650 by Bullet—Pillement does not say by whom it was built in the first place—and rightly describes its facades, ornamented with frontons, as having "harmonious simplicity." I owe my own acquaintance with it and one of the pleasantest afternoons of my latest stay in France—as I have so many other pleasures there—to my French publisher, Sven Nielsen.

The legend of the foxes is used by the kind permission of Lord Gormanston, on whose estate the phenomenon on which the story is based is reliably reported to have occurred. I am very grateful for the authorization to change the locale to my fictional Cloneen.

As usual, contacts which began with social occasions proved extremely helpful professionally as well as extremely pleasant personally. Among these were those with the Earl and Countess of Donoughmore, Knocklofty, Clonmel; their friends and neighbors Commander and Mrs. Thomson Moore, the actual owners of Barne, the first "fortified house" in Ireland; the Donoughmores' cousin Mrs. Michael Beaumont, of Harristown House, County Kildare; Henry McIlhenny of Glenveagh Castle, Churchill, Letterkenny; the Queen's Lieutenant, Colonel Sir Basil McFarland and Lady McFarland of Aberfoyle House, Londonderry; Captain and Mrs. J. Osborne of Milford; Mr. and Mrs. Robert Wheeler of Rathmullan; Mrs. Jack Boyd of Gweedore House; and all the McNutts of Downing in the famous Donegal firm of that name.

The Earl and Countess of Fingall no longer live at Killeen Castle, but at Corballis House, a charming house nearby; and the Earl is still in charge of the Killeen Stud. With his kind permission I used the plan of this as a guide in describing the stable, farm and stud at my fictional Cloneen. At the *Haras du Houlley* at Cour-tonne-la-Meurdrac I was kindly welcomed by its proprietors, M. et Mme. Marcel Labouré, and at the *Haras du Lieu Plaisant,* at Saint-Désir de Lisieux, by its owners, M. et Mme. Julien Derode. At both these superb stud farms, I was able to renew the acquaintance with conditions surrounding the breeding of purebred horses in Normandy, which I began more than twenty years ago; and I was especially delighted when the Derodes gave me permission to use the name of their *haras* in my new novel as if it belonged to my fictional De Briare family. My visit in and around Lisieux brought my summer to a very happy end and gave me hope that in some respects at least my readers may find *The Heritage* a worthy successor to *Came a Cavalier.*

The Horse Show was a focal point of my stay in Ireland and through the courtesy of Mr. John Wylie, Secretary of the Executive Committee of the Royal Dublin Society, I had seats in the Committee Box at the Horse Show both years I was in Ireland. And speaking of horses, my list of credits would not be complete if I did not mention my kinsfolk, Paul and Esther Hinman of Wells River, Vermont, the most reliable authorities on horseflesh of all kinds in my own part of the world, with whom I had several conferences on the subject and who loaned me various periodicals which were very helpful to me as well as the book entitled *The Morgan Horse.*

Questions of a legal nature were ably answered by Mr. James

Quirke, a friend of Sir Charles Petrie, to whom the latter commended me, and by Mr. Smyth of the firm of Fetherstonhaugh & Carter; and questions of a medical nature by my physician, Dr. Matthew White Perry of Washington, D.C., with whom I checked carefully both while drafting the story and after it was finished.

During the summer of 1966 most of the writing on *The Heritage* was done in Dublin, at Killarney and at Rosapenna; during the winter and spring of 1966 and 1967 the writing was done in Boston, Washington and New Orleans; during the summer of 1967 in Dublin and at Rosapenna; and during the autumn of 1967 on the S.S. *Paris* and in Washington.

FRANCES PARKINSON KEYES

Principal Characters

JAMES ARTHUR FREDERICK O'TOOLE, Earl of Cloneen

ANNE DE BRIARE O'TOOLE, his second wife

LADY SUSANNAH GLOVER, sister of the Earl and widow of Sir Michael Glover

PETER BRADFORD, her American grandson

EDWARD AND SUSANNAH BRADFORD, Peter's parents

SUE, ELIZABETH AND JANET BRADFORD, Peter's sisters

THE COUNT AND COUNTESS DE BRIARE, Anne's parents

CÉCILE DE BRIARE, Anne's sister

MAURICE DE BRIARE, Anne's second cousin

DERMOT, ALEC, AND SANDRA McKEEVER, Peter's Irish cousins

STEFAN WALEWSKI, a Polish prince in love with Peter's sister, Janet

GEORGE MacAULIFFE, solicitor to the O'Toole family

DR. DANIEL CAREY, doctor to the O'Toole family

FR. NEAL CARROLL, parish priest of Cloncoole

LAWRENCE DONOVAN, an Irish politician, strong supporter of Charles Stewart Parnell

BRENDAN DANAHY, land agent

Retainers of the Estate

BARNEY HEALEY, farmer

MARK FAGAN, gamekeeper

xvii

BART RIORDAN, studmaster

   MATT RIORDAN, stud groom

ANDY FARRELL, head groom

   NED FLYNN, ART NOLAN, stableboys

Servants at Cloneen Castle

MRS. BRENNAN, housekeeper

LIAM WADE, butler

JERRY RYAN, coachman

ANGIE CULLEN, cook

BRIDIE, parlormaid

TIM ROSS, valet

LETITIA, Lady Susannah's personal maid

Servants at Dower House

MAGGIE AND RORY DUNN, caretakers

SOLANGE, Anne's personal maid

MRS. HOGAN, monthly nurse

NORA MULHALL, 8th Earl's nanny

RUFUS, Peter's dog

There is not more desire, he [my father] had said, in lust than in true love, but in true love desire awakens pity, hope, affection, admiration, and, given appropriate circumstances, every emotion possible to men.

—*Autobiographies* by W. B. Yeats

PART ONE

Late June, 1882

The Irish
Mail

There is a Royal road to Chester. Even in the literal and unromancing eye of the law this fact has been conceded for 800 years. Norman chroniclers and Norman lawyers recognised four Royal roads in the Kingdom of England—Watling Street, Icknield Way, Ermin Street, and Fosse Way. The L M S route to Chester is so much identified with the first of these ancient roads that they run parallel, part and meet again, cross and re-cross each other through the greater part of the distance. Royal, in the older sense, meant the enjoyment of a special protection by the King. But in more modern times, and in more modern sense, the Watling Street has been a Royal road to Ireland. Since the days of Elizabeth Royal Deputies have travelled down it from London to Dublin, and for 200 years the Mail has gone that way. These memories are perpetuated to-day by a train that is the direct descendant of all historic communication between London and Dublin, and which is still called the Irish Mail.

—*The Track of the Irish Mail* (*Euston to Holyhead*)
L M S Route Book No. 1.

1

"There you are, sir, and time to spare, like I said."

The porter who spoke with such hearty assurance flung the miscellaneous gear, with which he had been unconcernedly over-burdened, into the compartment of a railway carriage, just as the guard, who had secured nearly all the other doors, was fast approaching the last one. It was a matter of both principle and pride to the Great Eastern Railway that the Irish Mail always left Euston Station on time to the minute; and the train was already in motion when Peter Bradford, who had leaped into the carriage seconds after his heaviest valises, stumbled over them while attempting to turn and toss a tip in the direction of the corduroy-clad porter, whose ruddy face, surmounted by a peaked cap, was wreathed in a triumphant smile. He hurled the last two pieces—a bag of golf clubs and a fishing rod—through the window and touched a grubby finger to his cap.

The train had begun to gather speed as it emerged, with surprising suddenness, from the enveloping gloom of the grimy station into the glow of the summer twilight, and its teetering motion was a further handicap to the passenger who had still not regained his footing. He fell backward and, struggling to his feet again, found himself face to face with an exceedingly pretty girl across whose lap the fishing rod had landed after sailing through the air. She was obviously very much amused, but she was making a valiant effort to smother her laughter; feeling somewhat chagrined, her fellow traveler brushed himself off and, realizing that he must indeed have cut a rather comic picture, laughed himself as she handed the rod back to him without any sign of embarrassment.

"Thanks very much," he said. "Perhaps I'd better put this on the rack before it gets away from me again. I never did know how to cope with fishing tackle and never much wanted to learn. But I

3

guess I'll have to. I'm an unenlightened American on my way to visit some Irish relatives I've never seen and, apparently, they spend most of their summers in pursuit of beautiful pink salmon. So I thought I'd come prepared."

The girl nodded pleasantly without speaking, smoothed her skirt and settled back with composure. It was still light and she was soon seemingly absorbed in gazing out at the pleasant countryside. As her head was now turned away from him, Peter could observe her carefully, without appearing to stare. She was quite as pretty, seen at leisure and in profile, as the first startled glimpse of her, full face, had revealed. Her coloring rather surprised him: he would have expected it to be rosier in an English or Irish girl, which she presumably was; her cheeks were delicately pink, her forehead and throat almost unbelievably white. He could not see her eyes, but her lashes, like her eyebrows, were dark, in startling contrast to her hair, which was a deep gold and beautifully arranged. There seemed to be a great deal of it and not a single lock was out of place. When she was a child it must have been flaxen and, instead of turning a dull brown, as was unfortunately so often the case, it had mellowed into a richer shade. He was rather surprised to find her bareheaded, especially as she was still wearing gloves, but decided that, in view of the long journey ahead of her, she had probably taken off her hat and put it on the rack in the neat bandbox, flanked on one side by a Victorian bottle bag and a tea basket and on the other by two portmanteaus. Her blue serge traveling dress looked simple enough, but the American —who had three smart young sisters and a style-conscious mother— knew that such simplicity was either deceptive or studied and that it was extremely expensive. She was tall and very slender, with the still-undeveloped figure of a girl, which was another source of surprise. He supposed that she must be at least twenty, probably more than that, or she would not have been traveling alone. Besides, everything else about her appearance and manner suggested this.

The deepening shadows on the landscape through which they were passing and in which his unknown companion seemed so entirely absorbed made him realize how long he had been studying this girl, who was a complete stranger to him, and with what fascination. It had taken him time, in London, to accustom himself to the length of the summer days. Now he was sorry to see the twilight end. He glanced at the small gas burner, which had not yet been lighted, and realized that when it was it would probably give only a very faint

4

gleam. But no doubt travelers were supposed to sleep, in any case, as soon as it grew dark outside, and not read—much less observe their fellow passengers to the point of analysis. He was trying to think of some remark which might serve as a suitable gambit for opening a conversation when he was providentially supplied with one: the train slowed down and gradually came to a stop. The next instant guards began to throw open the doors of the compartments, calling out, "Rugby!" as they did so. He rose, glad that he could do so steadily this time, and aproached the girl who had so greatly intrigued him.

"Are you getting off here by any chance? If you are, could I be of help with your luggage?"

She looked up without rising and smilingly shook her head. But it was still not too dark for him to see the color of her eyes and, though he could not have named it, he thought it was the only color that would go well with that burnished hair of hers—something between yellow and gray or between green and brown. Was it perhaps what was inadequately known as hazel? Most unreasonably, he wished he dared to ask her. Peter also wished that she would take off her gloves. They did not seem to be tight, for she moved her hands quite freely, but they fitted so closely that he could see the oval outline of her nails beneath the white kid. He did not know there was only one glove maker in the world who could achieve this outline, and that his gloves were correspondingly not merely costly but hard to come by. He only wanted them out of the way. He was sure her hands must be as white as her brow and her throat, long-fingered and very, very slim. He glanced down at them and almost instantly she did, too, giving him the uncanny feeling that she had guessed what was in his mind. But, if she had, she made no sign of it.

"Thank you," she said quietly, "but I still have a long journey before me. I'm going straight through."

"You mean to Ireland?"

"Yes, to Ireland."

"Well, as I told you, that's where I'm headed myself. It *is* a long journey. Don't you think we could make it seem a little shorter by talking to each other?"

"But you must wish to sleep."

"No, I don't wish to sleep. Do you—really?"

He had to wait for his answer and, meanwhile, new questions in regard to this girl were surging through his head. She spoke with a foreign accent, not a brogue, but unmistakably with the pronunciation of one to whom English was not a native language, though her speech was neither hesitant nor shy; in fact, it was as attractive as everything else about her—and as puzzling.

"I think we should both try to sleep, at least until we reach Chester," she answered, after due consideration. "Then we should wake, in any case, to receive the luncheon baskets."

"Luncheon baskets?"

"Yes—didn't anyone tell you? At Chester, luncheon baskets, containing wine, cold meats, bread and cheese, will be brought to all the first-class compartments. Of course, no one is obliged to accept them, but I find their contents so refreshing that I don't bother to stock my own tea basket for this lap of the journey."

"If I try to go to sleep now and don't talk to you until we arrive in Chester, could we share this feast?"

Again, she appeared to ponder. This time, he did not wait for her to be the first to speak. "I don't mean to be presumptuous," he said, "or to disregard the proprieties, but I've done a good deal of traveling on the Continent and some in England, even though I've never been to Ireland before, and I've noticed that people occupying the same compartment generally do talk to each other—just in a casual way, naturally, but still in a very friendly way. Isn't that so?"

"Yes, generally."

"Then is there any reason why we shouldn't?"

"Perhaps there isn't. I'll think it over and tell you when we're nearing Chester."

"How long will that be?"

"About three hours."

He thought he heard her give a little sigh, but he was not sure; it might have been merely a swift intake of breath. A plaid rug in soft shades of brown had been lying on the seat beside her and now she unfolded it and spread it over her knees, looking up with her pleasant smile and murmuring her thanks as the American hastened to help her with it. Then she turned her head away again. The guard, who closed the door as they were leaving Rugby, had lighted the gas burner; but as the young man had foreseen, it gave only a glimmer of light. However, the prints of Welsh scenes which surmounted the worn leather seats were not sufficiently attractive for him to feel disappointment because he could not carefully inspect the long row. He continued to gaze in the direction of the girl, whose eyes were now closed. He did not know whether or not she had gone

6

to sleep, though he somehow doubted it. He himself had never in his life felt less inclined for slumber. The fascination with which he had studied her had now mounted to exhilaration. The sensation was as surprising as it was stimulating.

When his Irish grandmother, Lady Susannah Glover, of whom he was very fond (much fonder than he was of his American grandmother) had suggested that it was high time he went to Ireland, he had accepted the idea complaisantly, rather than enthusiastically, partly because he knew it would please her very much if he did so and partly because he was not interested in the plans the rest of his family had made for that summer. Ever since the death of her husband, an Ulsterman by the name of Michael Glover, Lady Susannah had lived with their daughter, also named Susannah, the wife of a Bostonian, Edward Bradford, whom she had met when he was a young attaché at the American Legation in London the year she was presented at Court. Michael's outstanding success in promoting the weaving industry had earned him the title of baronet and, likewise, bolstered the fallen fortunes of Lady Susannah's brother, James Arthur Frederick O'Toole, seventh Earl of Cloneen, to such a considerable extent that his Georgian mansion could be restored before it had reached the stage of disrepair which had made his sixteenth-century castle uninhabitable. Lady Susannah and her brother had both been deeply grateful to Sir Michael for his succor; but neither she nor the Earl had been able to dismiss fully from their minds the knowledge that she had married beneath her station and this tinged their gratitude with regret. Moreover, she had never really enjoyed life in Donegal after the death of her husband and eventually welcomed an excuse for putting it behind her. She turned over the Glover estate at Rathmullan to Dermot McKeever, a nephew of Sir Michael's, who has always coveted it; and, as a further gesture of generosity, suggested that his son Alec should complete his education at the same institutions as her grandson Peter Bradford—an offer that was promptly accepted. Then she left with a happy heart for Boston, which, hitherto, she had visited only briefly with her husband for the christening of each successive grandchild and, when there were no more christenings, for an occasional birthday. Now she was astonished to find that Edward Bradford was also considered to have married beneath him in allying himself with her daughter. With tact and energy she set about to remedy this impression, and it was largely through her efforts that her grandchildren —Peter, Sue, Elizabeth and Janet Bradford—were not bracketed with other "Catholic Irish-Americans" and almost automatically excluded from the social circles of which her son-in-law and his family were an integral part. In order to do her difficult job more thoroughly, she seldom relaxed her vigilance to the extent of going home to Ireland or, indeed, any place where she would be too far away to control the situation; she was too much needed on Beacon Hill. Her moment of greatest triumph came when Sue, ardently courted by Robert Cushing, the scion of one of the bluest blue-bloods, was welcomed with open arms by his parents; the Cushing-Bradford wedding became the highlight of the season. But, even in the reflected glory of this achievement, Lady Susannah did not for one moment lose sight of the fact that her only surviving brother was childless and that, this being the case, her grandson Peter was the heir to an earldom. When he came into his own, *he* would really put Beacon Hill in its place.

Unfortunately, this viewpoint did not impress him or his parents with its advantages as keenly as Lady Susannah might have wished. Peter, having been graduated from Milton and Harvard, would now logically take his place in his father's firm and, in due time, become one of the leading lawyers in Boston. Edward Bradford's excursion into diplomacy had been limited to that one fateful year in London which his family had long felt was a mistake; since then, he had never strayed from the more circumscribed fold. He had no desire that his son should do so, and saw no reason for it. He knew several distinguished men who had fallen heir to foreign titles, but who had waved them aside, declining to give up American citizenship and living on contentedly in the cities where they were born, brought up and educated. As for Edward's wife, she had been so deeply in love and so young when she left Ireland that she had never been homesick. Though she and her husband traveled, periodically and elegantly, she went where he suggested—that is, regularly every other year to London for the Season; to Paris for the replenishment of her wardrobe and the girls'; to Baden-Baden for a conscientious cure and, intermittently, to Italy for conscientious sightseeing. (The alternate years they went to their suburban residence in Weston for May and June; to their seaside cottage at Beverly for July and August; and back to Weston for September and October, with an occasional fortnight in the White Mountains, where they went coaching between the Profile House and the Crawford House to vary the monotony of their established program.) It did not occur to either of them that any of their children, who were privileged to accompany them, might not enjoy and appreciate the same routine. Peter's unexpected declaration, toward the end of his last year at law school, which also happened to be the year for Italy, that he was tired to death of picture galleries, gave Lady Susannah her chance.

"Why don't you go to Ireland for a change?" she inquired, as they were finishing Sunday dinner.

"And do what?"

"Well, go first to Rathmullan for salmon fishing. And, afterward, to Cloneen for hunting."

"The boy can't hunt in midsummer," Edward Bradford reminded his mother-in-law, accepting a second helping of strawberry ice cream from the butler. The Bradfords always had ice cream for Sunday dinner; it was only the flavor that varied according to season and this was the season for strawberry. It was likewise the season for fresh asparagus, served on toast dripping with butter, so that had accompanied roast beef, Yorkshire pudding, browned potatoes, creamed onions and Parker House rolls; these were also invariable items, and most of the Bradfords were already so full of hearty food that they were beyond second helpings. But Edward Bradford never reached that point.

"He doesn't *have* to leave in June and come back in September any longer, does he?" Lady Susannah inquired rather acidly, as she waved the second helping away. She had never shared the Bradfords' predilection for ice cream; trifle and apple tart were both more to her taste. "After all, he's finished the part of his education which is bounded by dates," she went on. "That ought to leave him freer to learn some of the things he knows nothing whatsoever about. Heaven knows there are plenty of them."

"And you think he'd discover some of them while fishing and hunting?"

"Strange as it may seem to you, I do. Because he'd get his fishing with the McKeevers at Rathmullan and his hunting at Cloneen with James Arthur Frederick O'Toole. Whether you believe it or not, they are quite cultured people."

"I can see that you might like to have him go to the McKeevers, since your relations with them have always been pleasant and you've kept in touch with Alec's parents through him, even though you haven't seen them lately," Edward Bradford observed, glancing at his wife, who, he thought, might well have taken part in the conversation at this point, but who showed no disposition to do so. "In fact, I believe they have suggested more than once that they would like to have Peter visit them;

but I thought you'd been out of touch with your brother since his second marriage."

"I have," Lady Susannah replied calmly. "I agreed with you that it was most unsuitable for him to remarry at his age, especially a young girl none of us knew, but the fact remains that he did it and that, apparently, the girl belongs to a very good family. I've been thinking lately that perhaps I was too hasty, that I should get in touch with him again. Not that I mean to apologize, or anything like that. My position was understandable."

"Your position is always understandable, from your point of view, and you do not need to tell us that you do not mean to apologize," Edward Bradford said rather grimly. "However, I gather you are visualizing Peter as a sort of liaison officer."

"Yes—incidentally. But I wasn't thinking primarily about the advantages of this to myself. It's high time Peter went to Cloneen on his own account. You know it, whether you admit it or not. And, since he's tired of picture galleries and you are headed for Florence again, I don't see why he couldn't write to the McKeevers from here and to my brother from London and see if it would be convenient and agreeable—"

Peter, who had so far taken no part in the conversation, pushed back his chair and went around to his grandmother's. "Granny's right," he said, patting her on the shoulder, "it is high time I went to Ireland. I know all your relatives, Father. I ought to meet more of Mother's and I'd like to. I've always wanted to see the places where Grandfather Glover made his fortune and earned his title ever since he told me the fairy story about the *little people* who secretly helped a weaver finish his work, until he spied on them. After that, they never came back and he had to do it all by himself, which was what Grandfather had to do—and that was what his later stories were about. I've never forgotten how I loved listening to his tales or how kind he was to me. . . . I could go with the rest of you to London first, as usual, and then strike out for myself afterward, couldn't I? Isn't it high time I did that, too? After all, I'm twenty-four years old and, thanks to this fine old gentleman, I'm financially independent; yet, so far, I've never been on my own. I'd like to find out what would happen if I were."

There was a little further conversation on the subject, but when the Bradfords sailed the following week for England on a Cunarder—

French ships were regarded with suspicion—it was understood that Peter would soon be deserting the rest of his immediate family. The visit to London had followed its established pattern, except for the fact that Sue, now happily—and, oh, so suitably!—married, was not with them, but in Hamilton with her husband and their new baby, and Lady Susannah close by on Beacon Hill, sure to supply any supervision required by the *jeune ménage*. It was Elizabeth's turn to be presented at Court this year and there had been no change in the protocol since Sue's presentation two years earlier, nor would there be any when it was Janet's turn two years hence. As usual, the Bradfords were invited to innumerable luncheons and receptions; to dine at the American Legation; to attend the races at Ascot in the Royal Enclosure; to dance at the most important balls; and to spend the weekend at a ducal country seat. There was hardly time for the opera and a couple of new plays and for the fittings at the tailors whom the Bradfords, from father to son, had patronized for years. (Mrs. Bradford's dresses and the girls' were made, as usual, at Worth's and only those destined for Court wear were fitted in London; the others would receive attention in Paris.) A complication had arisen because Janet, who was occasionally left to her own devices, since she was too young for inclusion at major social events, had nevertheless managed to meet a young Polish prince, to whom she appeared to be attracted; and her parents were agreed that, even at the cost of cutting their stay in London short, their daughter must be saved from such entanglement. Janet, though sullen, seemed submissive, but unquestionably she would bear watching and Peter was kept busy with his share of this thankless task. Though he had heard from the McKeevers that they would be delighted to have him visit them, he had not written his uncle or begun his packing when he saw his parents and sisters safely on the train for Dover. Consequently, he himself had not even reached Euston Station early enough to witness the first part of a time-honored ceremony which his grandmother had told him he should on no account miss: the delivery of a watch to a guard on the Holyhead train, who, in turn, would relay the time to the Kingstown boat. (The second part of this ceremony was the return of the watch from Holyhead so that it could be adjusted to Greenwich time at the Admiralty the next day.) He caught the Irish Mail by the skin of his teeth and was literally catapulted into a life of his own, which he had announced it was high time he should begin. However, this had not begun, as he and his grandmother had planned, at the home of his cousins, Dermot and Sandra McKeever, at Rathmullan in Donegal; but on the Irish Mail between London and Holyhead, when a girl he had met only an hour or so earlier agreed to have supper with him when they reached Chester.

2

The night hours dragged on with unbelievable slowness. Once or twice before, Peter had had the vague and uncomfortable impression that there was never going to be an end to the journey he was taking; this time, the vague impression was gradually becoming almost a conviction and the stale chill air in the compartment added to his disquietude. He was cold as well as cramped. Only the stronger conviction that he would be defeating his ends if he tried to speak to the girl diagonally opposite him sooner than she had specified restrained him from doing so; but, eventually, his restlessness became a seething impatience. He was on the point of yielding to it, despite his better judgment, when he realized the train was, at last, slowing down again and, at the same moment, the girl turned and spoke to him.

"I told you I would let you know when we were coming into Chester," she said. "We'll be there in a few minutes now and, as soon as the guard opens the doors, the baskets will be brought to the train. The luncheon baskets and the foot warmers."

"*Foot warmers!*"

"Yes. They're a very welcome innovation on the Great Eastern, made just a year or two ago—in eighteen eighty, I believe. I've had my rug over me, so I've been very comfortable, but, without one, I'm afraid you must be chilled."

"I am. But it didn't occur to me I'd need a rug in June. Besides, I seem to have about enough baggage without adding anything more to it. Don't you agree?"

"Perhaps you'll learn to manage without some of the other things you brought this time and take along a rug instead—that is, if you are planning to travel much in Ireland."

"I'd be only too glad to leave the fishing tackle and golf clubs be-

13

hind. But, as I remarked before, my relatives seemed to feel those were even more important than a few extra shirts and socks. I never went fishing but once in my life and I've never played golf."

"You're not interested in sports?"

"Well, I play tennis. And I ride a good deal."

"Oh, if you ride—!"

Her eyes were suddenly shining and he thought she was on the point of saying that she rode a good deal, too, that she loved it, and then they would have, ready-made, a harmless and absorbing topic of conversation. But just then the door of the carriage was flung open by a guard and, as the girl had predicted, the purveyor of food followed close upon him. Peter hurried to meet him at the door.

"Two baskets, please."

"Thank you, sir. That'll be five shillings apiece."

Peter had taken the precaution of having change ready and handed over two crowns as the baskets were passed in from a trolley. But, having placed them with care on the seat, he looked around warily when another functionary appeared and the foot warmers were shoved onto the floor.

"Something more for me to stumble over," he remarked jocosely. Then, as the man who had brought the foot warmers looked at him with a puzzled expression, "Sorry," he added quickly. "It's quite all right. How much do I owe you?"

"Nothing, sir. Courtesy of Great Eastern."

"I'm certainly very much obliged to Great Eastern. But it doesn't forbid me showing my appreciation with a small coin of the realm, does it?"

When the man who had brought the foot warmers retreated, still looking very much puzzled, Peter saw that the girl was again trying to smother a laugh. "What did I do wrong this time?" he asked in a tone that showed his own bewilderment.

"Nothing. But Welsh porters don't take a joke as readily as Irish porters."

"Welsh porters?"

"Yes, most of the porters at Rugby and Chester are Welsh and practically all of them at Holyhead. You'll hear them wrangling among themselves about the luggage and not understand a word they say. But they will understand you and either they've less sense of humor than the Irish or a greater sense of the proprieties."

"Then please tell me whether or not it's safe to joke with you."

"Perfectly safe—within reasonable bounds."

"So you're Irish?"

"I didn't say that. No, I'm not Irish—except by adoption. . . . I have some serviettes and tableware in my tea basket. If you'll lift it down, I'll spread out our supper properly!"

"What a pleasant suggestion! I'll act on it at once."

She was taking off her gloves at last, rather slowly, again as if she understood that he wanted very much to see her hands and as if she wanted to delay this inspection. Then she began to busy herself with the contents of her tea basket and he, perforce, had his wish. Her fingers were as long and tapering as he had expected, but not as white; they were tipped with pink on the inside, the same pink as her nails—yes, and the same pink as her cheeks. On the third finger of each hand she wore a very large ring, heavily set with precious stones, though otherwise quite different; if there were a plain wedding band under one of them, it was completely covered and Peter decided, with an inexplicable degree of relief, that there was none. She was wearing no other jewelry, except for small pearl earrings and the pearl-rimmed cameo brooch which fastened her collar, and which he had not even noticed at first, as there was nothing in the least remarkable about them. But those rings were certainly very old and very valuable and, if he were not mistaken, something about their design suggested heraldry. But whether it did or not, the silverware she was now swiftly and capably arranging had a crest on it and so did the serviettes.

"Am I in the presence of royalty?" he asked lightly, picking up a fork. "I don't know why, but somehow it's easy for me to visualize you as living in a medieval castle, where peacocks strut over the grounds and you stroll about with a wolfhound at your side."

She shook her head. "That isn't my family crest," she said. "I think I have everything ready now." She crossed herself and sat down. "Will you pour the wine? The chicken looks very good. Suppose we decide on that for our first course."

He thought she had looked a little startled at his question, even that the delicate color in her cheeks had deepened, but in the dim light he could not be sure. The rings could account, at least in part, for her reluctance to remove her gloves; but evidently she had forgotten that the crests might arouse his curiosity, or else she took them so much for granted that it had not occurred to her anyone else would notice them. At all events, she had made the little spread look extremely appetizing and Peter was very hungry. He had left his packing until the last minute and, when it was finished, there had been no time for dinner; he had counted on a hearty tea to see him through and, since boarding the train, he had been so absorbed in his fellow traveler that he had forgotten all about the lack of the more substantial fare to which he was accustomed. Now that the girl was no longer withdrawn, but amicably sharing a meal with him, the situation, despite the crested silver and the ancestral rings, seemed far less tense, though no less provocative. He poured out more claret and proposed a toast.

"To my discovery of my ancestral country which you have honored by adopting!" he said. "You must love it or you wouldn't have stayed on there. I hope you think I'll love it, too."

She sipped her wine. "I was rather doubtful of it at first," she said demurely. "I mean, while you were worrying about the fishing and the golf. Since you've never seen these relatives you're going to visit and their tastes don't seem to be the same as yours, it didn't sound very promising, did it? But when you told me you liked to ride, I knew everything would be all right."

"I take it you're an enthusiastic horsewoman?"

"My father carried me around in front of him on his saddle when I was hardly more than a baby. I've been riding ever since."

"So that's what *you* do in Ireland?"

"It's one of the things. Yes, I suppose you might call it the main thing." Without further comment, she moved aside the plates and cutlery they had used for the cold meat and set out fresh tableware for the cheese and biscuits. Peter opened the second bottle of wine.

"You wouldn't care to be a little more explicit, would you?"

"No, I'd rather have you a little more explicit about your riding."

"Well, my sisters and I were lucky because our Irish grandmother, who lives with us, still has just as good a seat in the saddle as she did twenty years ago and that's very good indeed. She insisted on teaching us to ride herself. We went to Henri de Bussigny's riding school, like all our friends, to please my father and his family, because it's the thing for young Bostonians to do, just as it's the thing for them to go to Papanti's dancing school. But riding round and round in a ring isn't the same as getting out in the woods or even open fields, is it?"

"I shouldn't think so. I never went round and round in a ring— always from the beginning in the open. What kind of horses did you ride?"

"My eldest sister and I had ponies when we were very small and these were passed on to the younger girls when she and I were old enough for horses. I think we must have been about twelve and ten, respectively, by that time."

"I meant what breed."

"Those at the riding school would have been French, wouldn't they? I really don't know. My Irish grandmother always made a great point of having Irish grays for herself and for me. Nothing would induce my other grandmother to have anything Irish if she could help it. She has Morgans."

"Morgans?"

"Our first real American breed. There's quite an interesting story connected with it. A poor Vermont singing teacher, Justin Morgan, accepted two horses in payment for a bad debt, in no very cheerful frame of mind. One of them was a big three-year-old gelding. The other was a small bay colt which frisked along behind the gelding. No one has ever been able to prove anything about his lineage, but he proved himself that he could outrun, outwork and outget any other horse brought against him; and his descendants, under saddle, in harness or in the show ring have won prizes year after year. Their versatility is amazing, for they're equally good at work or pleasure and they're beautiful to look at, generally not quite as large as a Thoroughbred, but just as strong and swift. My Boston grandmother had stopped riding long before I was old enough to remember, but she goes for a drive every afternoon, punctually at three, with a fine pair of bay Morgans and two men on the box—a brougham in winter and a victoria in summer."

The girl shook her head. "Evidently there's an interesting story behind the creating of this American breed and I'd like to look into it. But I still don't understand why that grandmother wouldn't have wanted to have Irish horses when they've been considered by many the finest in the world for at least two hundred years and probably much longer than that. The stories of the Byerly Turk and the Spanish stallions are even more exciting than the one you've told me about Justin Morgan. Why, even the Empress of Austria comes almost every year to Ireland to choose her horses! We were terribly disappointed because she didn't come this year on account of the unsettled conditions."

"By 'unsettled conditions,' do you mean the assassination of Lord

Frederick Cavendish and Undersecretary Burke last month—what everyone in London was referring to as the Phoenix Park murders?"

"Yes, in part. Those had a good many ramifications."

"But when you said you were 'disappointed,' you weren't referring to those, were you? You meant *personally* disappointed."

"Yes, because the Empress always came to see us and our horses. Last year she bought two of them. We were delighted to have her as our guest and she and I always had some good rides together. She's a superb horsewoman and, in some ways, the most beautiful woman I ever saw. And very charming, though rather vain. That isn't strange. She can't help being vain, expecially of her hands and her figure."

"What's so remarkable about them?"

"Why, her hands are as small and as soft as a child's and her waist is only seventeen inches around."

"Is that supposed to be the ideal size? It seems awfully small to me."

The girl's answer was a little sigh, ending in a little laugh. "It is very small. But it *is* the ideal size. I'm ashamed to say I've never been able to attain it. Naturally, I'm about twenty. Every now and then I'm rebuked by my mother or my maid or my dressmaker and then I make an effort for a few days to please them by following the standard practice."

Peter had a vague idea that he had heard his sisters discuss the pros and cons of tight lacing, but hitherto he had found it a very dull subject. Now he was eager to hear more about it.

"I'm afraid I don't know what that is," he said. "Won't you explain?"

The girl shrugged her shoulders. "As I said, it's just standard practice. You say you have sisters, you must have heard them talking about it."

"I have, but I wasn't enough interested to pay much attention. Now I am."

"Then you'd better ask them to tell you all the dreadful details. I'm not going to do it."

Involuntarily, Peter's gaze shifted from the girl's face to the pearl-rimmed brooch which fastened her collar and downward over the discreet blue serge which covered and confined the curve of the girlish breast and was buckled at the trim and tiny waist. Whatever it measured, it looked to him so small that he was sure he could grasp it in his two hands and still find his thumbs overlapping. It was with the utmost difficulty that he resisted the impulse to ask if he might make the trial. Almost as if she guessed what was passing in his mind, the girl blushed, drew her plaid blanket more closely around her and reverted to the topic from which the Empress had led them astray.

"So one of your grandmothers liked Irish horses and the other liked Morgan horses and you had both kinds in your family stable. That must mean you had a good many."

"Not according to your standards. A carriage pair for each of the old ladies and also for my mother. Saddle horses for all of us except the grandmother who'd stopped riding. That includes my father, of course, so you add up to thirteen. That ought to be enough to make horses seem an integral part of everyday life. Anyway, they've been part of mine ever since I can remember and I'm looking forward to a lot of riding in Ireland."

"Do you hunt?"

"I don't, but my eldest sister does. She married a fellow who's very keen on it and, as they live in Hamilton where the Myopia Hunt has just moved from Winchester, I imagine she'll do a lot of it."

"I beg pardon. What did you say was the name of the Hunt?"

"I don't wonder you asked me to repeat it and that you're surprised—and amused. Four of the club's founders were very near-sighted, so a committee thought it would be a compliment to them to name the Hunt Myopia."

Peter and his traveling companion laughed together. The slight tension between them was gone. "But there are other hunt clubs, aren't there?" the girl inquired.

"There are several of long standing in Virginia. As a matter of fact, the president of the Myopia, who's not a Bostonian but a New Yorker, has a pack of hounds there, not to mention a cutter at Beverly and the fastest iceboat on the Hudson. I think he'd be called an all-around sportsman, even in Ireland. Then, a distant relative of mine has been fox hunting with his private pack of hounds at his country site near Middleton for almost twenty years; but I think Myopia's the first organized Hunt in New England. That way, we're far behind Old England, aren't we?"

"You certainly are—and further still behind Ireland. Hunting, as we know it today, probably originated there—as I said, the breeding of the hunting type has been going on for hundreds of years. However, you ought to get someone else to give you the facts and figures. You'll find any number of people delighted to do so. I'm not a hunter myself."

"But you said you'd ridden all your life!"

"I have. I ride in horse shows and I enjoy point-to-point racing, but I don't like killing things. I'm not enough of an Irishwoman for that."

"And I like you all the better for it, whether it makes you less typical or not, because I don't like killing things, either, and I'm sure there are lots of other things about which we'd agree."

His companion made no direct reply, but while they had been talking they had eaten their biscuits and cheese and drunk their wine in a leisurely way and had done full justice to both food and drink; now only crumbs remained on their plates and their glasses were empty. The girl brushed the crumbs from the plates into a serviette, wiped the glasses on another and replaced everything neatly in the tea basket.

"It's hardly worthwhile putting this on the rack again," she said, as she closed it. "Our journey's almost over. We're about to cross the Menai Bridge. In a minute, we'll see the lions guarding the entrance."

"The *lions!*"

"Stone lions—huge ones! Look quickly or you'll miss them and they're worth a glance."

Her warning came too late. The moonlight, which had made the landscape and its landmarks visible throughout the latter part of the journey, was suddenly shut out and the train was speeding noisily forward in the total darkness of complete enclosure.

"Are you sure you don't mean the Menai Tunnel?" he asked, conscious that he was shouting. "Though I never heard of that or the bridge, either."

He could barely hear the girl's answer, though he was aware that her normally soft voice had been raised to facilitate this.

"It really is a bridge—a covered bridge—and I believe it's supposed to represent a very remarkable feat of engineering. But there's no use in trying to talk while we're going through it. We'd have to scream to make ourselves heard and even screaming wouldn't be too successful."

It was quite true that the noise made conversation virtually impossible and to Peter the interruption was most unwelcome. Impersonal as the talk about horses had been at first, it soon revealed so many shared interests and shared standards that he felt he and this unknown girl were kindred spirits whose meeting was less accidental than portentous; and presently the feeling of harmony became so strong that he did not miss the spoken word. He was content to sit silent, because she was sharing the silence with him. If the tea basket had not still been on the seat between them, he would have reached for her hand and held it in his; but, probably, it was just as well that he could not do this. There was no way in which he could have made the gesture seem unintentional and she might have drawn away, not because she found his touch offensive in itself, but because she found it premature and ill timed, instead of finding it as natural as he would have wanted her to do. They were not children, afraid of the dark and instinctively seeking reassurance and comfort in each other. They were adults, drawn together by some mysterious force that was stronger than they were. . . .

The train rushed out of the bridge with the same suddenness that it had rushed in and moonlight lay around them again. "Didn't you know Anglesey was an island?" the girl asked in a tone tinged with amusement.

"I've already confessed to you my abysmal ignorance about a great many things," Peter answered. "You'll have to start giving me lessons."

"There isn't a great deal of time left. As I told you, our journey's almost over."

"Yes, but—" He had started to say, "but there are other days ahead of us," and checked himself. It was too soon for that, also; he should not rush his fences. "But there's still the boat," he went on, more cautiously. "It's only the train journey that's almost over."

"Yes—but three o'clock in the morning isn't a very good time for lessons, is it?"

"That depends. I'd be willing to take them from you at almost any hour."

"Nonsense! You will be tired and sleepy and so will I."

"You're sure?"

"I'm not sure of anything in this uncertain world. But that's what would be most natural and likely, isn't it?"

"Yes, but sometimes we find ourselves facing something that isn't either natural or likely. Just very wonderful."

She looked at him fixedly for a moment and he thought he saw her lips moving slightly, as if they were forming an answer to which she did not dare give utterance; but he was almost sure that, if she had, this answer would have been in the affirmative. Then, without speaking and as if bringing the conversation to an indicated end, she rose and, before he could do it for her, lifted down the bandbox that he had noticed at the beginning of the trip. Now he saw there was a crest on it, not the same as the one on the silver, surmounting the initials *A de B*, and he was tempted to ask her what they stood for, but wisely resisted the temptation; she had made it quite obvious that she wished to remain anonymous. Placing the bandbox on her lap, she raised the lid and took out a blue hat with a narrow brim and a soft feather curling over one side of it. She closed the box again and put on the hat without any search for a hand mirror to assure herself of its proper angle. Indeed, there was no need of one. The hat, which she secured with two long, dangerous-looking pins with amber and amethyst heads, was extremely becoming; its only displeasing feature, as far as Peter was concerned, lay in the fact that it hid a good deal of her hair. She next folded the plaid shawl into a neat bundle and secured it with a strap conveniently supplied with a handle.

"You seem to have everything very well organized," Peter remarked, wisely disregarding the lacking rejoinder to his last statement. "Isn't there anything I can do to help?"

She hesitated, in much the same way she had done when he first addressed her, suggesting that they should talk to each other; but, again, her answer, when it finally came, was pleasing to him.

"Perhaps you'd carry my bottle bag for me," she said. "Of course I can do it myself, but it's a little awkward with my skirt to hold up and a ticket to get out and all. I'm sure it would be perfectly safe with the porter, but I promised I wouldn't let it out of my sight. You see, there are other things in it besides perfumes and medicines."

"Certainly you shouldn't think of carrying it yourself or entrusting it to a porter. I'd be very honored to carry it for you. Couldn't I take your ticket, too? After all, I have to present my own and I could show yours at the same time. That is, I suppose I could. I haven't yet got used to all these British formalities about tickets."

"Well—thank you very much." She opened a silk reticule and handed him her travel ticket, which was separate from the train ticket already surrendered. "It's a nuisance to have so many kinds for one journey," she admitted, "and I can't help wishing sometimes that women could wear dresses that weren't quite so long when they're traveling. We need our hands for so many other things."

She was speaking again in the same easy, friendly way that she had before he mentioned wonders; the withdrawal of which he had been conscious then had passed. He smiled in return as he lifted down the bag—marked only by a small leather tag—that he felt sure must contain ancestral jewels—perhaps some that were not her own, but with which she had been entrusted for delivery. That would explain her promise to someone that she would take charge of the bag herself and, after all, she had said the crests on the silver were not her own, so his surmise was not without foundation. The train was slowing down again and, as it made a final turn, a lighted boat was visible beside the pier they were approaching. It loomed white against the starry sky and Peter saw that it was much larger and more imposing a craft than he had imagined it would be. But there was hardly time for him to express his surprise, much less to receive any comment on it, when the door of the carriage was thrown open again and porters rushed forward to seize the baggage. It was just as well, if his companion did not want to lose sight of her bottle bag, that he already had this firmly in his grasp; everything else in the compartment was hustled out of it and borne away with incredible speed to the boat, amid general confusion and much shouting, most of it in Welsh, though one voice rang out clearly in English, "First-class passengers this way! This way to first-class gangplank!"

Without making a futile effort to keep track of their belongings, they braced themselves against the stiff breeze and worked their way through the crowd to the gangplank, where they were called upon to deliver their travel tickets. It was fortunately not far and once inside the boat they found themselves almost directly in front of the purser's office. The voice and manner of this functionary betrayed his harassment as he assigned cabins, summoned stewards and dispatched passengers and their luggage in various directions, but his demeanor underwent a sudden change when he caught sight of the latest arrivals.

"Honored to have you with us again, my lady," he said, taking her cabin ticket. "I've set you down for Cabin 25—the one you had the last time and seemed to like—on Deck A right amidships, with Ellen, the same stewardess who served you before. . . . Dennis," he added, beckoning to a steward and holding out a key, "show her ladyship to her cabin." He turned politely to Peter, glanced at the bottle bag and instantly assumed that the personable young man, noticeably well dressed, who carried this was connected with his most outstanding passenger; very probably this was one of her foreign relatives whom he did not recognize. "Your cabin ticket please, sir. Number 27 for you. Your first crossing with us? I hope you will find it comfortable. The bar is open if you care for a drink and just leave your order for early-morning tea with your steward."

He nodded and turned to the other passengers who were crowding close behind. Peter started toward the companionway and stopped. "So my guess about a princess wasn't so far wrong, after all," he said lightly. "We seem to be through with tickets at last. Would you care to go into the lounge or to the restaurant before you go to your cabin, 'my lady?'"

"No, thank you," she answered, again disregarding part of his remark. "I found our supper on the train very sustaining. Besides, I'd rather get settled right away for what there is left of the night. But you really ought to see the bar. Please don't feel you have to take charge of the bottle bag any longer. I could carry it all right myself now."

"Over all those stairs? In all this crowd? Of course you couldn't— or, in any case, you shouldn't. It would be just as hard for you here as on the pier. I'm going to hang onto it until it's safely set down in your cabin."

"It's very kind of you. But I hate to make so much trouble."

"You know it isn't any trouble." *Of course she knows that,* he said to himself, *but no doubt she also thinks that, if I set the bottle bag down in her cabin this means I'd be there myself and she isn't sure I'd leave as quickly as I ought to. And she's quite right, to be thinking of that. I wouldn't want to leave; I'd try to think of some reasonable pretext for staying and there isn't any. You can't call what's in my mind a reasonable pretext. It's a deep and dangerous longing.* Increasingly sure that she could read his thoughts, he made a conscientious effort to cover the distance between the purser's office and the cabins as rapidly as possible and, when they reached the door of Number 25, he handed her the bottle bag without crossing the threshold and with only a conventional parting.

"Good night. I'll hope to see you when we get to Kingstown. Perhaps you'd let me carry the bottle bag again. And thank you a thousand times for making my introduction to Ireland such a pleasant one."

Standing just inside the open door, she took the bag from him with a murmured word of thanks. They were so close together that their nearness was like an embrace and, as he looked into her face, he could not doubt that she was as conscious of this as he was. Again, his glance strayed from her face to her figure and, as it rested on her waist, the impulse to measure it with his hands became stronger and stronger. But by now he was not thinking only of finding out whether or not his thumbs would overlap if he clasped his hands around that tiny tight belt of hers. He was thinking how it would be to encircle her with his arms when she was not wearing rigid garments, when he could feel soft yielding flesh. . . .

He turned abruptly and left her.

It was very cold in his cabin and Peter undressed quickly, hoping that he would be more comfortable if he were actually in bed, instead of merely stretching out on it, in a warm bathrobe, which at first had seemed the more sensible thing to do for a short crossing. But he could not seem to adjust himself to the hard pillow and the still harder mattress, let alone the damp sheets. He had expected to go to sleep at once, whatever the conditions of the voyage; he had been warned that it was apt to be very rough and that he would probably be seasick. But, despite the stiff breeze on the wharf, the channel seemed comparatively calm and he was normally a good sailor in any case. Yet, why should he be so wakeful? He had never minded hard pillows and mattresses before or damp sheets, either, for that matter. There was no reason why he should mind them now. And, being honest with himself, he presently admitted that they had very little to do with his restlessness. It was the girl on the train who was responsible for that. It was only seven hours since he had seen her for the first time, yet he desired her as he had never desired any woman before. What was even stranger, he believed that she had been conscious of this desire and that she had not resented it, that it would take very little to make her respond to it. Though she must at first have seen him as a rather comic figure, her manner soon indicated that this impression had been transitory, that she was inclined to regard him favorably. Otherwise, she would not have suggested the shared feast. But there had been no condescension in her graciousness. She had accepted him as an equal and, though she might not be a princess, she was certainly a very great lady. She had behaved with the utmost discretion; she had not even been willing to tell him her name, and yet, there had been an answering spark. He was sure of it, just as he had felt sure, almost as soon as he had looked at her, that she had never known love. Now she was ready for it.

He tried to rationalize his thoughts, but it was useless. Every moment found him more desperate, more convinced that he could not let the night go by without making an attempt, however rash, to possess this unknown girl. He flung back the bedclothes, slipped on his shoes and fastened his robe tightly around him. Then he went to the door and opened it cautiously. The corridor was empty. He took a few steps forward and tried the door next to his. The knob turned easily in his hand. He entered the adjoining cabin and paused just inside the threshold.

The cabin was in darkness except for the dim ceiling light, but this sufficed for Peter to see the girl in the bed. Her hair was spread out over the pillow, her white neck and arms were bare and her breast was only lightly covered with lace. Her eyes were open and she looked at him steadily.

"I didn't frighten you, did I?" he asked, wondering why it was so hard for him to speak.

"No," she said quietly. "Why should I be afraid of you?"

3

Her serene answer in reply to his agitated question emboldened him to cross the narrow strip of flooring between the door and her bed. "I tried to stay away," he said, looking down at her and still finding it hard to speak. "I couldn't."

"I know," she said quietly. "You had to come. I've known you would, almost from the moment we met. It was one of those things that had to happen."

"You told me you weren't afraid. But were you sorry?"

"Sorry?"

"When you felt sure it had to happen. Did you hope you were mistaken?"

"No. I hoped I wasn't."

He gazed at her in mingled joy and unbelief. "You might be sorry afterward," he said, still hesitantly. "If you were, I'd never forgive myself. Or if I hurt you."

"Aren't you the one who's afraid?"

"Not any longer," he said, accepting the challenge. And, as he spoke, he leaned over the bed and smoothed back the strands of golden hair that had strayed across her forehead. Then he bent lower and stroked the long waves that fell from her shoulders to her waist and rested his hands there before he kissed her, first with tenderness and then with passion. Almost instantly she raised her hands and clasped them around his neck, returning his kisses and drawing him down to her. Although she looked so fragile and slight and virginal, it was clear she did not need further casual caresses or murmured endearments to prepare her for surrender. He had not been mistaken in believing that she was ready for the full experience of love or presumptuous in hoping

27

that he might be her lover. And, as the wonder of this deepened, so did the compulsion, not only to take her, in the first flush of its glory, but to prove that he could more than meet her challenge, that he could be her master, as well as her mate. He forgot that he had meant to be gentle and patient, to help her as much as he could. His hands slid swiftly from her waist to her knees, parting them. His desire had become a driving force, his virility its spearhead. He locked her in an inflexible embrace and held her fast until she was so wholly his that it seemed as if some part of him must always be part of her.

He never knew how long it was before he spoke to her. He wanted to tell her how beautiful she was as she lay there; he wanted to tell her how much he loved her, more than any woman had ever been loved before, that he always would. He wanted to tell her that he felt doubly the man he had been before he had made her his, for now he was ready to believe that almost nothing was beyond him; but though the conviction was there, he could not form the words to express it. He could only hold her as if he would never let her go, adoring her more and more every minute.

At last she moved, ever so slightly, and he looked down at her with eyes of love and, though the light was so dim, he could see that she was smiling. "I'm very happy," she said in a glad voice.

"*You're* very happy! What do you think I am?"

"If you're half as happy as I am, you'd feel as if the whole world belonged to you, that you had nothing more to wish for, because you've already got everything that's worth having."

"Do you feel that way, too?"

"Yes. And something more." Surprisingly, she suddenly hid her face on his shoulder and whispered, "Now I know what it really means to be a woman. I want to thank you for making me one."

"You're *thanking* me for what happened?"

"There isn't anyone else I should thank, is there?"

He could not let her jest about it; he was too much moved. "You knew it was inevitable that we should become lovers. But I don't believe you thought it would happen the way it did. Sometimes that's called by a very ugly name."

"Not when a woman's already shown a man she wants him for a lover. Not when the only kind of a man a woman like me would want couldn't help taking her that way."

"I know I did hurt you—after saying I'd never forgive myself if I did."

28

"You couldn't help that, either. You won't the next time."

"The next time!"

She was smiling at him again. "You don't have to go yet, do you?" she asked anxiously.

"I hope not, but my watch is in my cabin. I wasn't thinking much about the hour when I charged in here."

"My watch is under my pillow in my money belt. If you move a little, you can get at it."

"I don't want to move, even a little, but if I must, the first thing I'm going to do is to satisfy my curiosity on a certain point."

"Yes?"

"I want to see if my hands won't go around your waist and still leave space for my thumbs to lap over. I've been dying to find that out for hours and hours."

"Then why didn't you do that first?"

"You know very well why not—because I was in such an ungodly hurry to get all the way through to you, which I wanted even more."

"And don't you still want to, even more?"

"Yes, but now I want to take time for some other supplementary pleasures as well. You'll have to move a little, too—that's fine. And I was right, wasn't I? They lap by a good two inches. . . . Darling, will you do something that would please me very much?"

"If I can."

"Stop lacing yourself in. I cannot bear to think of your being hurt that way, bruising your beautiful white skin, constricting this beautiful soft flesh. It is all so lovely just as it is."

It was her turn to be greatly touched. "If you really feel that way. . . . But I'd hate to be big and clumsy."

"You'll never be big and clumsy. And you'll be even more graceful than you are now if you can move with more freedom. You'll see. That's what my sisters decided. I remember now and I'm sure they were right. Will you promise?"

"Yes, I promise."

He straightened up and then bent over to kiss the place where his thumbs had so triumphantly overlapped. As he smoothed out the shift he had displaced, he said, "Is it all right for me to tell you how much I admire your nightgown?"

"Yes, if it's all right for me to tell you it isn't a nightgown."

She was not only smiling now, she was very close to laughing. "Didn't you guess?" she asked. "My nightgowns all have long sleeves with ruffles around the wrists and collars that button close to the throat. Just the same kind, I'm sure, that your sisters wear. But you see, when I undressed, I was only as far as my chemise when I thought I heard—something—someone—coming and I leaped into bed just as I was. Actually, you didn't come until some time later, but meanwhile, I had decided—"

"That I would like the chemise better than one of those hideous nightgowns you've been talking about? And you were right, of course."

They were laughing together now with the sense of happy companionship that comes to true lovers, already assured of physical harmony and, for a few minutes, they succeeded in dismissing all thought of fleeting time. It was Peter who unwillingly reverted to it.

"I've been here rather a long time. I'm afraid I have to take a look at that watch of yours now," he said. "It's quarter past five. It doesn't seem possible, does it, that the whole world could have changed in an hour? But, as you said, it has. And there's daylight coming in at the porthole. I'm afraid I should go back to my cabin."

"We couldn't be together again—just for a few minutes?"

"Darling, if you feel that way, there's got to be time."

There was more than one reason why he had not dared to ask her. He had been afraid, not in the same way as before, but that a second act of love might seem an anticlimax to the first. But he was wrong. There was less sense of conquest this time, of course. On the other hand, there was a greater sense of ecstasy. His beloved was now completely his own. He kissed her knees before he parted them and she lay relaxed and responsive, as if there were no limit to the rapture she wanted to share with him. At last she sighed, ever so softly, as if in supreme contentment and kissed him as a drowsy child might have done. The next instant he realized that she had gone peacefully to sleep.

He wanted to tell her again how much he loved her and insist that they must get married at once; but he could not bear to wake her. He fought off the delicious somnolence which threatened to engulf him, too, and after one last caress reluctantly freed himself. Then he returned to his cabin, where he lay down on his berth, intending to be instantly alert when the boat docked. He must have dozed, for a slight rustling sound roused him and, as he sprang up rubbing his eyes, he saw that a scrap of paper had been slipped under his door. He snatched it up and unfolded it.

It was heaven, but it was stolen heaven. We mustn't ever see each other again. I don't know your name and you don't know mine. It's better that way, so please don't try to find me.

4

Cursing himself for the worst kind of a fool, he dressed swiftly, thrust the note into his breast pocket and stepped into the corridor. Early risers were already hurrying back and forth; the door of the next cabin was open and it was empty. He could not question the purser, as that would betray the fact that, far from being a relative or close friend of "her ladyship," he and she were strangers to each other. He charged through the boat, searching the lounge, the dining saloon, the corridors and the decks, finally coming to a stop at the gangplank, where his steward, whom he had neglected to tip, came up to him and spoke to him politely.

"Shall I have your luggage put on board the train for you, sir? It'll be leaving soon now. I can attend to everything for you."

"Thank you very much. I'd be grateful if you would," Peter said, forcing himself to speak pleasantly, in order to make up for his over-sight, both about the tip and the amount of his hand baggage, which the fishing tackle and golf bag had more than doubled. He pressed a pound note, which he knew was far too much, into the steward's hand, left the gangplank and made a thorough search of the pier. At last he concluded that the girl must already be on the train for Dublin, though this did not leave for an hour after the ship had docked, in order to allow the passengers time to take it at their leisure. However, to be sure he had overlooked no possible hiding place, he got on so be-latedly that, as in the case of the Irish Mail, it was already in motion when he boarded it. But this time his tardiness was not rewarded.

The trip from Kingstown to Dublin took half an hour and every moment seemed to separate him further and further from the object of his search. When the train reached Westland Row Station, a porter promptly seized his multitudinous baggage and tore through the crowd toward a cabstand as if he were laden with nothing heavier than a candy box. Peter had known that he would have to change stations when he reached Dublin, but now he halted at the curb with another question for which he could find no answer: he knew his train for Londonderry left from Amiens Street Station, wherever that might be in relation to Westland Row; but was the Londonderry train the one the girl he had lost would be taking? He thought he remembered his grandmother saying that if he had been headed direct for Cloneen he would have taken a train from Kingsbridge Station and that he must be sure not to get mixed up, because there was still another one called Broadstone from which trains for the west left. Apparently, no matter in what direction you wanted to go in Ireland, you must leave from a different Dublin station. In view of this complicated, not to say clumsy, arrangement, his lost love might have left from any one of these. The only thing to do was to search them all. Unfortunately, the stations were so far apart and the trains left at so nearly the same time that this was physically impossible; despite his determined efforts, he eventually let the train he had meant to take leave without him, paid off the porter, reassembled his baggage, took another cab and reached Kingsbridge Station in time to search the train for Cork, Waterford and Limerick. By that time, the train for Londonderry had left.

He went to the post office and sent a wire to Dermot McKeever:

UNEXPECTEDLY BUT UNAVOIDABLY DETAINED IN DUBLIN STOP WILL WIRE AGAIN WHEN I SHALL BE COMING BUT PLEASE DON'T BOTHER TO MEET ME STOP APOLOGIES AND REGRETS STOP PETER

By now he was beginning to feel as if his baggage were hanging around his neck, though it had been capably and pleasantly handled by a succession of porters. Before he did anything else, he proposed to have it located more stably. After all, since he had no idea of leaving Dublin until he thought he had exhausted its possibilities, he might as well go to a hotel, especially as it was raining hard. He was sure he had heard his grandmother say there were several in the vicinity of St. Stephen's Green. The clerk at the reception desk of the first one he tried looked at Peter severely when the latter admitted he had no reservation; they were, of course, very fully booked straight through the next three months, the clerk informed Peter in a manner that suggested he should have been aware of this. The baggage was again reassembled and Peter tried two more hotels with similar results. At the third, he happened to glance in a mirror that hung opposite the reception desk and was forced to admit to himself that he did not look

33

as if he would be much of a credit to an exclusive hotel's clientele. He was unshaven and tieless; his shirt was the same one in which he had traveled from London; the rest of his clothes had been so hastily thrown on that they might be almost any shape, and the drenching to which they had been subjected as the rain increased in violence, while he was taking one cab after another, had not helped, either. So far as he was concerned, there was very little humor in the situation. But perhaps the receptionist, being Irish and not English, might be tempted into visualizing some.

"I'm not really quite as much of a roughneck as I look," Peter said. "It's just that I've spent all my time since I got off the night boat going from station to station, trying to catch the right train and missing them all. I don't seem to have mastered your system of transportation, which seems rather complicated to a simple-minded American. Are you quite sure someone hasn't canceled a reservation—say, to a three-room suite, so there'd be room enough for this baggage? Well, all right, a two-room suite. And what's all this I've heard about hearty breakfasts in Ireland? So far, I haven't had anything to eat, either. I could do with a man-sized meal in my private parlor."

As a gambit, it lacked elegance, but it worked. The suite into which Peter was shown without further delay was very comfortable, as soon as he had persuaded the astonished valet to light fires in it, and the hearty breakfast was very good. He sent the suit he had been wearing and another which he hastily unpacked to be pressed with the request that one, at least, should be returned to him promptly; then he took a hot bath in a hip tub that was brought to his bedroom, shaved and put on clean underclothes and a clean shirt; by the time he was knotting his tie, one of the suits was back. He went downstairs, accepted the loan of an umbrella from the understanding receptionist and went to a nearby store, where he purchased a mackintosh. Then he plodded on and on through the rain amidst crowds of people who seemed to be taking the weather very much in their stride—as well they might, he said to himself, judging from all the precautions they had taken to protect themselves against it. Never in Boston, during mid-winter, had he seen anyone so muffled and booted—and this was June!

It was not until he was literally overcome with fatigue that he faced a grim realization: what he was doing was not only futile, but ridiculous. If his lost love were in Dublin, she would not be out walking through rainswept streets; she would either be riding in some elegant closed carriage with a plush rug over her knees and a coachman and footman on the box or she would be sitting before the fire in a beautiful Georgian drawing room drinking tea—doubtless with some congenial companion. But the chances were ten to one—one hundred to one—that she was not in Dublin at all. She did not live in a city, but on a great estate. And that might be no more than twenty miles from where he was standing that moment or it might be as far north as Rosapenna or as far south as Killarney. And if he had only acted with as much sense as any human being not actually confined to an institution for the mentally deranged might be supposed to possess, the girl would not only be identified to him by this time, but he might well have been an accepted part of her life.

He returned to the hotel, shed his mackintosh and restored the umbrella to its rightful owner, drank more and ate less than was good for him and went early to bed. There he slept soundly but fitfully and dreamed so much and so vividly that he was not sure what was reality and what was fantasy. And then he was on the train for Londonderry, desperate and bereft, going to visit the cousins whom he did not want to see because the only person in the whole world whom he did want to see was the girl he had lost, except in his dreams.

PART TWO

Late June, 1882

The American
Nephew

"Ireland, oh, Ireland! centre of my longings,
    Country of my fathers, home of my heart,
Overseas you call me, *'Why an exile from me?*
    Wherefore sea-severed, long leagues apart?'

As the shining salmon, homeless in the sea-depths,
    Hears the river call him, scents out the land,
Leaps and rejoices in the meeting of the waters,
    Breasts weir and torrent, nests him in the sand;

Lives there and loves; yet with the year's returning,
    Rusting in his river, pines for the sea;
Sweeps down again to the ripple of the tideway,
    Roamer of the ocean, vagabond and free."

        —quoted in *Highways and Byways*
        in Donegal and Antrim
        by Stephen Gwynn.

5

It would be difficult to conceive a frame of mind less propitious for meeting strange relatives than that of Peter Bradford as he boarded the Great Northern train for Londonderry twenty-four hours after his arrival in Kingstown.

This train left Dublin at nine in the morning and reached its destination a little before three in the afternoon and Peter again had reason to be thankful that Irish breakfasts were hearty, for no luncheon baskets appeared, providentially, as they had at Chester. The countryside through which the train passed did not prove particularly appealing, but under the circumstances that would almost inevitably have been the case, even if it had offered scenery unique in the world. Instead, it bore a close resemblance to that with which Peter was familiar in New England; blue lakes alternating with green hills and fields where cattle and sheep were grazing. If anything, Vermont and New Hampshire seemed to him the more attractive, especially since at this time of year the landscape was usually bathed in sunshine. Ireland, he had decided, must have escaped submersion by some miracle. The rain, which had come down in sheets the day before, was now coming down in torrents. He had still not succeeded in persuading himself that an umbrella should be permanently added to his already-multitudinous gear, but he turned up the collar of his new mackintosh and buttoned it closely around him as he alighted from the train at the Foyle Road Station and went to look for a jaunting car, which he had been told should be his next mode of transportation. Partly because of unsatisfied curiosity to see one and partly because of his grandmother's description, he had visualized this type of open, two-wheeled vehicle with seats on each side, set back to back, and a perch in front for the driver, as having elements of romance; he found these entirely lacking when he confronted the actuality. However, the welcoming grin of a burly driver did much to mitigate the drabness of the drenched car. Doing his best to match this cheeriness with his own expression, Peter asked to be driven to the Lough Swilly ferry.

"You'd be meaning the Middle Quay Station, wouldn't you, sir? You'd hardly be wanting to drive all the way to the ferry in this weather, when it's that easy to go by train. But it's for you to say. I can take you, if that's what you want."

"Well, how far is it from here to the ferry?"

"Something better than ten miles. But it's less than one to the Middle Quay Station—just a bit of a way up Foyle Street."

"My God! Do all the cities in Ireland have stations located as far apart as possible? And trains running to no two places where you might want to go from any one of them?"

"As to that, I couldn't say, sir. We've got four stations in Londonderry and they are quite well separated, as you might say. But I'd be very pleased to drive you in any direction you like and make special rates for you by the day or week."

Despite the dreariness of his mood, Peter laughed and was disappointed to find this was not what he was supposed to do; the driver was far from joking. Salesmen very often did exactly that, he went on to explain; it saved them all the bother about changing trains and catching ferries. If the gentleman were a traveling man. . . .

"I seem to be, but not quite in the sense you mean. I haven't anything for sale and I don't want to buy anything—or, rather, the things I want can't be bought. So I think I'd just better settle for the drive up Foyle Street, as you suggested in the first place—that is, unless the last train I can get to wherever I ought to take the ferry has gone by that time."

"No, sir. The one you want to take is the four-twenty mail train. We can make it all right. But if, sometime, you should feel like taking me up on my weekly proposition. . . ."

"I'll be sure to let you know."

The driver guided Peter to his high and precarious seat, helped a porter arrange the baggage and then, climbing to his own perch, flicked his long whip and shouted, "Giddap, Beauty!" His horse, who seemed to Peter rather inappropriately named, started off at a smart clip over the cobblestones and the driver immediately burst into song:

> "There's a railway in Derry, the Swilly, you know,
> That is famed for going exceedingly slow.

It leaves Londonderry about ten minutes late
And if they don't watch it may run through the gate.
In five minutes more a whistle is heard
And old Lizzie Harkin is getting prepared.
Proceeding along and turning a bend
The train shortly reaches the station Bridge End.
At the next stop a man in a suit navy-cut
Calls out that the train has arrived at Burnfoot."

"Please go on," Peter, who was actually beginning to enjoy himself, called to the driver when the latter came to a stop.

"Sure and that's all there is to the song. Lizzie was the agent at Gallagh Road, the first station you come to and, though she kept track of what happened at Bridge End and Burnfoot, she didn't know much about what was going on beyond there. She wasn't like James Bond, the agent at Fahan, who knows everything that's going on everywhere and has a hand in it, too—runs a pub and a chemical plant and built a generator which furnishes electricity for the station, the only one in these parts that has it. . . . Of course, I could start the song over again and sing the same verse if that would please you, sir."

"It would, very much—especially as it's a relief to my mind to know that the train I'm about to take generally leaves about ten minutes late. Perhaps I'll manage to catch this one with a little more time to spare than I've been having lately."

After a few more admonitions to Beauty, the driver resumed his song. The ride to the station, which would have been extremely pleasant in fair weather, was interrupted by frequent stops to retrieve pieces of baggage that kept tumbling from the car. The necessary pauses caused Peter some anxiety about loss of time. The afternoon train of the Londonderry and Lough Swilly Railway, headed for Buncrana and intervening points on the Inishowen Peninsula, was already drawn up at Foyle Street Station, which, despite its name, proved to be simply a large shed. However, when the genial driver shouted, "Whoa!" to Beauty, there were no indications of the train's immediate departure. Peter approached the shed and asked for a ticket.

"And what kind would you be wanting, sir?" inquired the agent pleasantly.

"I don't know. I'm going to take the ferry at Fahan for Rathmullan. Is there more than one kind of ticket I can have?"

"Sure there is. You can have first, second or third—it's likely you'd have known that and I'd have guessed first from the look of you, sir.

41

But there's special railway and steamboat tickets over to Rathmullan, via the Fahan-Rathmullan steamboat service, and if it so happens Rathmullan's where you're headed, it'd be worthwhile for you to take that; and, unless you're settling there for good, it ought not to be a single; it ought to be a return. Then there's excursions for sea bathing and golf and from the look of what you've got with you that might be what you'd be wanting. Too bad you haven't got a dog or a perambulator or a cycle, because there's special tickets for them, too, not to mention those for harvestmen and fish-workers, to which you wouldn't be eligible, seeing as how you're going first class."

Peter had sincerely believed that morning he would never laugh again; now he did so for the second time that day.

"I'm going to Rathmullan," he said. "So I guess a special rail and steamboat ticket is what I want and you might make it return because, in spite of what you've gathered from my baggage, I'm going there just for a brief visit."

"You wouldn't be going to The Lodge, would you now, sir?"

"I am if that's where the McKeevers live. I'm a cousin of theirs."

"Are you now, sir? I knew they were expecting a visitor, but he was supposed to come yesterday. They'll be relieved you finally got here all right. But then, it's quite a trip from Boston and no mistake. I've got relatives there myself; Grady, the name is, and they're doing right well now with a kind of pub."

"A saloon?"

"That's it, sir. Do you know it? It's near a place called Scollay Square."

"I'm sorry to say I don't, but I'll look it up when I go back if you'll give me the name of the saloon and its address. Now, about my ticket. I don't seem to be very good at catching trains lately and I think maybe I'd better be getting on this one."

"Just a minute more, sir. It was a return rail and steamboat ticket you decided on, wasn't it, sir? I've got to be sure, because first class single one way is pink, just for rail, but white if it's rail and steamboat. I wouldn't want you held up, sir, at the ferry just because you didn't understand and got a ticket that was the wrong color."

"Very thoughtful of you. White it is then."

Finally pocketing the proper ticket, Peter said good-by to the agent and left the shed to find that the friendly driver was still waiting for him, in order to make sure that he got into a compartment all right or be ready to drive him all the way to the ferry in case he did not. The train was on a narrow-gauge track and its engine appeared to Peter surprisingly large in comparison to the rest of its equipment: one "composite" carriage with space for both first and second-class passengers and two third-class carriages.

It seemed to Peter, comfortably settled in solitary occupancy of the first-class compartment, that the train had gone less than a mile when it began to lose speed and then finally drew to a stop. Smiling at the thought of Lizzie "getting prepared," he hailed the conductor and asked if they had already reached Gallagh Road.

"Oh, no, sir. This is Pennyburn."

"But I thought Gallagh Road was the first station after we left the city."

"It's the first *station,* sir, but here at Pennyburn the track crosses the Strand—Londonderry's main road to the north—and the law is very strict. In the early days, trains could go no faster than six miles an hour between Middle Quay and here, sir. Then in fifty-nine, the authorities announced that steam locomotives couldn't even cross over the highway any more or 'propel or draw any Carriage across the said Road by means of a fixed Engine and Ropes, or otherwise by the use of Steam Power, but the Traffic across the said Road and along the Railway from thence to the Londonderry Terminus shall be worked by Horses or other Animals,'" he concluded a bit breathlessly, but triumphantly.

"Do you mean to tell me—" Peter began.

"Yes, sir. They've already detached the locomotive and are hitching up the horse to the carriage. It won't be a minute in this direction, sir. It's when you're coming the other way and have to go from Pennyburn to Middle Quay that it takes a long time. Here we go now, sir. Once across the Strand, we'll be at Gallagh Road before you know it."

As soon as the horse was unhitched, a locomotive was quickly substituted for it and when the train was once more in motion, Peter found he was actually beginning to enjoy the landscape. It had stopped raining; the afternoon light was clear and mellow. But he was getting hungry and thirsty and looked forward to refreshment at James Bond's pub. He hoped there would be time for this before he took the ferry.

This hope was fulfilled, but a new complication, about which he had not been warned, now arose. As soon as he stepped from his train, at what really was a station this time and quite a tidy little one at that, he headed toward a door marked REFRESHMENT ROOM, only to notice that an adjacent door was marked in the same way. While he was hesitating as to which he should enter, the second door was flung open and he found himself confronted by a respectable-looking, middle-aged woman who seemed to be in a violent rage.

"Don't you dare go into that pub of James Bond's!" she shouted. "Ruining legitimate trade, he is, and taking the bread right out of my mouth besides. As if he weren't stirring up enough trouble with his tower and his dynamo and all the rest of his nonsense! And asking the company to provide a uniform, so he can give himself more airs than he's got already! Kelly's my name, Miss from choice, and I'm the proprietress of the Fahan station Refreshment Room, so I'll thank you to walk in through this door and leave the other for the ragtag and bobtail, of which there's plenty coming along, as you'll see for yourself."

Peter had really looked forward to meeting the versatile James Bond, but the situation offered still another source of welcome amusement and he followed the irate Miss Kelly into her establishment with apparent meekness and asked her what she would recommend to a weary traveler, who was both hungry and thirsty.

And rich, Miss Kelly said to herself, apprizing Peter swiftly and accurately, as she rattled off an extensive list of drinks and added, "You can also have a ham or cheese sandwich."

Taking a seat near the window, while he ate his sandwiches and drank his beer, he looked out with interest at the varied activities within his range of vision. The station with its complement of several railway houses and a stone shed was about two hundred yards from the pier, to which a curved siding ran; Peter could see cattle and sheep being unloaded from a boat and driven into pens near the shore. Barrels from the same boat were placed in horse-drawn wagons and transported from the station. Peter turned from the window and asked Miss Kelly what these barrels contained.

"Some of them stout and some of them blubber," was the surprising answer.

"Blubber? Surely that isn't one of your local products!"

"Our trade isn't confined to *local* products," Miss Kelly retorted with scornful pride. "A whaler came in just yesterday from Spitzbergen and unloaded part of its cargo before going on to Galway. And tomorrow, as like as not, a freighter will come in from Newcastle with coal. It's that way all the time."

Duly impressed, Peter apologized for having underestimated the status of the port and mendaciously complimented Miss Kelly on the excellence of her fare, by way of *amende honorable.* Then he paid his bill and strolled down the pier, where he joined the other passengers who were boarding the *Menai*, a converted yacht now serving as a ferry. Peter's hopes for more solid sustenance had risen when he heard the word yacht; but the conversion had been so complete and the passage across the lough theoretically so brief that no provision was made for refreshments; and, as the Swilly was actually an inlet of the North Atlantic, the boat was obliged to make a five-mile detour if the tide happened to be low. *Of course, this would be one of the times when it was*, Peter said savagely to himself, for, despite Miss Kelly's contribution, he was by now ravenous and somewhat anxiously began to wonder at what time and in what dimensions the McKeevers ate at night. If their one evening meal was a late and hearty tea, he had probably already missed it; if, on the other hand, they had a light and early tea, which was hardly a meal at all, a substantial dinner would still be in prospect; and certainly they would have made special provision, in any case, for a belated guest. While he was trying to comfort himself with this reassurance, he remembered that he had never sent them a second telegram, as he had promised, telling them when he would arrive. His agitated thoughts, except when briefly diverted by the exigencies of actual travel, had centered on the girl he had met and lost. It was not until the *Menai* began to edge its way up the long pier that he realized there would be no one there to meet him.

There was, however, the usual supply of husky porters and, when Peter mentioned that The Lodge was his destination, the man who had begun to pile the traveler's baggage onto a handcart assured him that there was no need of going to the expense of hiring a trap; a five-minute walk would take them there. It was raining hard again, but Peter felt it would be a mistake not to show his appreciation for such consideration of his budget. So he turned up the collar of his coat and strode along beside his new-found friend, who advanced rapidly, pushing the cart with such ease as to suggest that its load weighed no more than a cream puff; and presently, on an attractive elevation beyond a luxuriant growth of trees and a long expanse of green lawn, Peter caught a glimpse of a spacious white house, gleaming with lighted windows.

"That's The Lodge right before us, sir," the porter volunteered, without slackening his pace. "We can go round by the avenue, if you like, or we can take a short cut through this gate near by. There's a slight rise in the ground just ahead, but nothing to slow us up."

"All right. Then let's take the short cut by all means," Peter responded, hoping the porter did not notice that he was already panting.

He had abandoned all such hope by the time they surmounted the slight rise, but he managed to get his breath while they waited, dripping, at the front door for an answer to his ring. Obviously, no one had been expected, for there was a prolonged delay before the door was opened, in a rather gingerly way, by an elderly maid wearing a very correct uniform, who regarded them with much the same expression of disapproval as the receptionist at the hotel, where Peter finally gained admittance, had regarded him the morning of his arrival in Dublin.

"I'm the American relative," Peter said apologetically. "I promised to send word when I'd be arriving and I forgot. But I think if you'll just tell the family that I'm standing outside the front door, half drowned and half famished, they'll suggest that you let me in." The words were not out of his mouth when he heard a welcoming shout and Alec came rushing forward, followed at a slightly more leisurely pace by a pleasant-faced, middle-aged couple, all three beaming with friendliness.

"Let you in! I should think we would!" Alec cried. "We'd just about given you up for lost."

"Come in and tell us everything that's happened while you have a drink before dinner," his father chimed in. Then Mrs. McKeever added thoughtfully, "Unless you'd rather read the very important-looking letter that's waiting for you and get dry first. Desperate weather we're having—so close." Peering past Peter, who was by now under shelter, toward the porter and his cart, she continued, "I see you fell into good hands even if they weren't ours. Thanks for looking after our relative, Barney. Go around to the kitchen and Sadie will look after *you*. She's always glad to see you. And let Con give you a hand with the unloading."

6

The evening could not have been pleasanter.

Alec shepherded Peter to a large light room with a bay window overlooking the lake and, after asking him which bag he needed most, went to ensure its immediate arrival, together with a hot whiskey. ("Mother calls this weather close, but I'd know you were just about frozen even if I didn't see you shivering and hear your teeth chattering," he said cheerfully as he lighted the fire.) The hot Irish whiskey, which tasted smoky and was faintly flavored with cloves, and a pitcher—which he was promptly told he must call a jug—of hot water for washing arrived together and Peter sipped the welcome drink as he stripped off his wet clothes and got into dry ones. Then, feeling very much better and reassured as to the imminence of dinner, he decided he could stave off hunger long enough to break the seal of the crested envelope that had so impressed Mrs. McKeever and see what sort of a message it contained.

CLONEEN

CLONCOOLE, IRELAND

25 June, 1882

My dear nephew—he read—

Your letter of 23d June, written from London, gave me great pleasure and seemed to promise even more. I was delighted to learn that you were planning to visit me and fully expect to find enjoyment in your company.

I am sure the McKeevers will make you very welcome and that they will naturally resent the effort of any other relative to shorten your visit to them. However, I hope that, within a fortnight or so, you will be able to tear yourself away from Rathmullan and come to Cloneen. I shall eagerly await another letter, telling me when to expect you.

Affectionately, your uncle,

James Arthur Frederick O'Toole

Certainly nothing could sound more cordial than that, Peter said to himself as he went down the stairs, and the McKeevers, to whom he showed the letter on the way to the dining room, quickly agreed with him. "Of course, you must write the first thing in the morning and tell the Earl we expect you to stay at least a fortnight," Mrs. McKeever told him, as she ladled steaming soup from a huge tureen; and her husband and son hastened to say the same.

"Perhaps you'd like to leave tomorrow free to look around Rathmullan and see what sights we have to offer," Mr. McKeever suggested. "But the next day, if the weather's favorable, we must strike out for the pool near Ramelton. The salmon have never been running better than they are right now and we don't want to miss as good a chance as that to show you the finest sport in Ireland."

"I'm afraid I'm going to disappoint you," Peter said, between grateful spoonfuls of soup. "As I told a girl I met on the Irish Mail, I never did know how to cope with fishing tackle and, before this, I've never much wanted to learn. Now I'd like to. But you'll have to be patient with me. And I think I would enjoy having tomorrow free, to answer my uncle's letter and some others I've rather neglected and get my bearings a little. You know I've never been to Ireland before and that was quite a trip I took yesterday—at least, I believe it's actually less than two hundred miles, but it seemed about a thousand. And coming right on top of the trip from London to Dublin—"

"Of course, you want time to get your bearings," Mrs. McKeever said soothingly. "And first, you need to get rested. These men don't seem to realize you must be tired to death. And then you got upset about something, didn't you? Your telegram said you'd been unavoidably delayed and you forgot to send another. What you want, as soon as you've had a good hearty dinner, is a good long sleep. I won't send you any early-morning tea. When you wake up of your own accord, just go out in the corridor and call—someone's sure to hear you. Now I hope you like roast beef because that's what we're having tonight. I expect you do, because Alec's told us the Bradfords always have it in Boston for Sunday dinner."

Peter assured her, with much more sincerity than he had praised Miss Kelly's sandwiches, that there was nothing on earth he liked better than roast beef, for dinner on Sunday or any other day. He might have added, with equal sincerity, that, in his opinion, Mrs. McKeever was an ideal hostess, kindly, understanding and undemanding; but he hesitated to do so on such short acquaintance and was thankful that

48

she did not invite or seem to await any comment on the vegetables that accompanied the beef—boiled cabbage, boiled turnips and boiled potatoes. He had heard his father say that the main reason he never came to Ireland was because these three vegetables, prepared in just that way, were even more unescapable than early-morning tea and had put it down to the elder Bradford's chronically caustic attitude toward everything Irish—an attitude which lacked complete consistency, for he had remained faithful and attentive to his Irish wife, claiming that she had been so young when he married her and so willing to be transformed into a Bostonian, that he had succeeded in forgetting where she came from. As a matter of fact, Peter had moments of believing that his mother had almost forgotten, too, and he knew that Lady Susannah grieved over this. But he himself had never taken it to heart, because there had never before been any real reason for him to do so. Now, after only a few hours in the hospitable home of the McKeevers, to which his mother never came, he was beginning to wonder if she had not sacrificed something of her birthright. . . .

But he was both too tired and too comfortable for real concern and, anyway, it was ridiculous that a few boiled vegetables should have started him on such a sober train of thought. He sopped them up in the gravy from the succulent beef, ate them without distaste, washed them down with sound red wine and attacked a fruit tart, drenched in rich cream, with appreciation, but without the same avidity which had marked his progress through the first part of the meal. He was getting drowsy and he began to wonder how long he would be able to keep the McKeevers from guessing this. But, as they rose from the table, Mrs. McKeever put her hand on his arm and gave him a gentle push.

"Did you hear what I said about a good long sleep?" she asked. "As the Chinese say, it's later than you think. If you don't get started on it right away, morning will be here almost before you know it. I'm going to treat you just as I would Alec if he'd been through what you have in the last few days and order you to bed."

And at that, she really has no idea what I've been through, Peter said to himself, as he tumbled into bed. *She knows I'm all in for some reason and lets it go at that. Maybe she does think in terms of travel. If she does, so much the better. But if I were going to confide my troubles to anyone, which of course I'm not, I wouldn't need to look any further.* He pulled the bed coverings up closer to his chin and, as he stretched out luxuriously between the linen sheets under the soft blankets, his feet felt the comforting solidity of a hot stoneware bottle and he was grateful for the additional warmth that it gave. It was the last sensation of which he was conscious for many hours. . . .

With returning consciousness came confusion. He was lying, safe and warm, in the same wonderful bed into which he had tumbled the night before and the room was flooded with bright and benignant sunshine. But something, somewhere—he could not guess just what or how near—was very wrong. He heard a sharp crackling noise, uncannily like a pistol shot; it tore through the quiet air, shattering its tranquility and, as Peter swung out of bed, feeling for his slippers, reaching for his dressing gown, he heard two others like it, which lasted longer and seemed to quiver before they died away. Still confused and increasingly appalled, he stumbled to the door of his room and, as he flung it open, came face to face with Alec, who was fully dressed and hurrying from his.

"What is it? What's happening?" Peter asked thickly.

"I can't imagine. I'll find out as quickly as I can and let you know."

"But weren't those shots?"

"Yes, I think so. But they could have been quite close or at least half a mile away—sounds carry a long distance in this atmosphere. Please, Peter, go back to your room and get dressed. There's nothing you can do right now, whatever has happened."

Reluctantly aware that this was probably true, Peter retreated and began pulling on his clothes. He had just reached the point known as "decent" in theatrical circles when there was a gentle tap on his door and, this time, when he opened it, it was to find Mrs. McKeever standing outside and smiling with the same kindliness and composure as the night before.

"You overslept, exactly as I hoped you would," she said placidly. "It's nearly ten o'clock. Would you like some tea brought to you now or will you come downstairs as soon as you've finished dressing and have a proper breakfast?"

"Please forget about the tea, if you don't mind, not just today, but every day I'm here." Then, realizing how very abrupt this must have sounded, Peter added, "I don't mean to be rude or unappreciative, but honestly I hate early-morning tea. And I don't believe I could swallow anything until I know what's happened."

"Of course, you did quite right to tell me how you feel about the tea. And everything in this house is all right, my dear boy. Beyond that, I can't tell you, though I think that if anything untoward had happened in the village, we'd know it by this time. The trouble, whatever it is, must be further off. My husband, who's the local magistrate, started out when he heard the first shot and Alec wasn't much later. One or the other will bring us news as soon as he possibly can. And it won't help any for you to hear it on an empty stomach. I'll send you up some hot water for shaving and tell Molly you'll be coming down for your breakfast by the time she has it ready."

It was unreasonable, Peter knew, to find the composure which had so attracted him the night before so aggravating now. But he could not seem to help it. In his impatience, he cut himself while shaving and yanked a button off a clean shirt while putting it on. Further delayed by the necessity of mopping up his wound and unpacking another shirt, he went downstairs in a black mood which did not improve when he found Mrs. McKeever quietly knitting beside a laden breakfast table. He made an honest effort to respond courteously when she talked to him and to do justice to his breakfast; but he could think of nothing to say on his own initiative and he was repelled, rather than tempted, by the excellent fare that had been provided for him. At last he pushed back his plate and rose.

"Would you mind very much if I went to see what I could find out myself?" he asked.

"Not at all. But if you did that, you might go in the wrong direction and miss Alec, who, by this time, must have found out which is the right one and be on his way back to tell us. If you feel restless, why not take a little turn around the garden and grounds? You couldn't see anything last night in that pouring rain and the roses are at their loveliest right now. I'll come with you, if you like, but it would be quite natural if you felt more like being alone, so I think I will go into the library; though I will call you immediately if I hear anything before you do."

"I'll accept your suggestion of a little turn outdoors. And I do rather feel like being alone. It's wonderful of you to be so understanding. I wanted to tell you that last night and I didn't quite dare. Now I can't help doing so."

His black mood was lightening under her imperturbable serenity and, as he wandered around the garden in the sunshine, the world again began to seem to him a happier place. When, a few minutes later, Alec came to find him, he had almost convinced himself that he had made a great deal of fuss about nothing. Why should his peace of mind have been shattered by three distant pistol shots? Probably they represented nothing more serious than some sort of a signal. . . . Then, as soon as

Alec was near enough for Peter to see his face, the latter knew that his first premonition had been the right one.

"Our neighbor, the Earl of Hartley, has been murdered on the open road between Hartley Castle and Rathmullan. His clerk and his driver have been killed, too. The assassins have escaped."

7

For a moment Peter stared at Alec, speechless with horrified amazement. To him, the report seemed not only dreadful, but fantastic. His voice shook as he answered.

"Three men killed? On a highway? In broad daylight? And the murderers got away?"

"I'm sorry to say it's true. The woods come very close to the road on one side, at the point where this happened, and the killers must have been waiting in ambush for the Earl to pass by. On the other side, the road skirts the lake, where a boat was in readiness for them. They were probably halfway across Lough Swilly before help came."

"But why should anybody have wanted to murder three men so much that they'd lie in ambush for them? And how would anybody know when they'd be passing a point where it would be so easy to commit a murder?"

"I don't think anybody was out to kill *three* men. Somebody did want to kill the Earl and knew he'd pass that point on his way to Rathmullan to take the ferry. The other two killings were just incidental."

"*Just incidental!*"

"I mean, the other two wouldn't have been killed if they hadn't been with the Earl. I told you one of them was his clerk and the other his driver. Evidently, the first shots killed them instead of the Earl. His valet, Dan Mullen, was following in another vehicle with the luggage, but he'd fallen behind, because his horse was lame. By the time he got to the place where the shots had been fired, Eddie Breen, the driver, was lying dead in the middle of the road, and Jack Barry, the clerk, was badly wounded and half drowned in a ditch beside it. He was brought to town on a stretcher, but he didn't live long enough to tell his story. So there's really no one to tell it accurately, for the Earl was dead, too, by the time Mullen got to the scene of the murder. He says he saw two

53

men struggling with his master, whom he was trying to reach, and he saw one of them raise a weapon of some sort and strike the Earl a terrific blow with it, which would probably have killed him, even if the third shot hadn't. Then those two made their getaway."

"But I still don't understand. In the first place, why should anybody have plotted to kill the Earl? And, in the second place, why should they have been so determined to do it that they wouldn't mind committing wholesale murder if they could succeed?"

Alec hesitated. "I'd rather not tell you," he said haltingly. "I hate to think this assassination is going to be the first event to mark your stay in Ireland and that you'll never be able to forget it. But I suppose if I don't tell you what I'm afraid is back of it, someone else will. You must have heard plenty of lurid stories about landlords who evicted their helpless tenants, who were wantonly cruel to them for little or no reason or who just trumped up some excuse. Well, the most lurid tales you've ever heard couldn't begin to tell the whole story of what the Earl of Hartley has done; and there have been attempts on his life before, not as well organized as this one, so they failed. But a little while ago, a girl whose whole family had been evicted and who was—employed— in the castle drowned herself. Since then, it's been only a question of time before the man who expected to marry her would try to avenge her."

Without even trying to answer this time, Peter sat down on the nearest bench and turned away, hoping he was not going to be sick.

"I said I hated to tell you," Alec muttered miserably. "I know just how you feel: that things like this don't happen in a civilized country, that you're beginning to understand why your father and mother never come to Ireland. But you've got to be fair. Some dreadful things have happened in the United States, too. Why, when the Bradfords get started talking about slavery—"

"They're very opinionated on that subject, you know that. They exaggerate."

"I hope so. But it doesn't seem to me the Indians have been very well treated, either. And, after all, it was their country your Bradford ancestors you're so proud of took away from them."

"I'm not so proud of them. Father is, but I've always had some doubts. At this moment, I'm wondering what connection I should be proud of —except the Glovers. How do I know that the Earls of Cloneen have treated their people any better than the Earl of Hartley treated his?

They've been landlords, too, haven't they, ever since the Dark Ages? What kind of a heritage is it, I've come to claim?"

"It's a very fine one and you wouldn't doubt it for a minute, if this dreadful thing hadn't happened, just when it did. Hartley wasn't a typical landlord; if he had been, he wouldn't have been nicknamed 'The Bad Earl,' as if he were a great exception to the rule. According to everything I've heard, his heir's a very fine man, who'll introduce an entirely new order of things at Hartley Castle and that's just what I'd expect. After you've met your great-uncle, after you've had a chance to talk with him and stay with him, you'll realize what a mistake you're making now. Please try to buck up, Peter. Father'll be coming along pretty soon now and he'll blame me for not keeping some of the sordid details to myself."

"You couldn't very well, could you, when I kept asking you questions? As a matter of fact, he'll probably have a few gaps to fill in himself. Incidentally, you didn't tell me what finally happened to Mullen, who was so slow in catching up with the others. Was the lame horse part of the plotted picture?"

"I'm afraid so. Of course, Mullen has been taken into custody for further questioning. The other horse—the one Breen was driving—bolted and went galloping into town, still hitched to the empty carriage. This was the first indication of the accident. . . . Well, as you say, Father'll have a few gaps to fill in and I'll try to keep him so busy with his story that he won't have time to find fault with mine. But it would be a help if you'd buck up."

They were very close to bickering when Dermot McKeever joined them in the garden, his kindly countenance worn and worried. He was seemingly little disposed to discuss the tragedy, with the aftermath of which he was gruesomely occupied. The body of the Earl had now been brought to Rathmullan for an autopsy and, after this had been performed, it would be placed in the estate office while awaiting the arrival of the eldest son, to whom a telegram had immediately been sent. The Earl, who for many years had been a widower, was on bad terms with most members of his family and none of them had been visiting him at the castle lately; McKeever had no idea where they would wish the burial to take place. Search parties had, of course, started out after the assassins, but there was no trace of them as yet and it was quite possible they would be able to make their way north through the wooded area of the Inishowen Peninsula and, still undiscovered, escape to Scotland on a fishing vessel. McKeever would have to stand by, not only to learn the results of the autopsy and to keep in touch with the police, but to meet the heir on his arrival and to be as generally helpful as he could in every possible way.

"Which means the end of my plans for taking you around Rathmullan today," he said, putting his hand on Peter's shoulder. "But I want you and Alec to go fishing just the same. Neither of you has any responsibility and there's nothing either of you can do to assist in a very ugly and sordid situation. The sooner you get away from it, the better." And, when Peter tried to protest, McKeever said more firmly, "A picnic lunch is already packed for you and a trap is at the door. Go get your waders and your rod and reel. Everything else you need is in the trap and Con's in the driver's seat. You'll pick up Eddie, my best ghillie, at his house as you go along. When I see you next, I'll expect you to be bringing in at least one fine salmon as your catch. Now be off with you!"

Inevitably, the murder was the chief topic of conversation as they drove along, for Con and Eddie both had their contributions to make. Evictions on the Hartley estate had nearly reached the hundred mark, according to Con; one victim had sought shelter for himself and his family overnight with his brother; the next night, the brother was also homeless because of this meager hospitality. And as for that poor girl who drowned herself, chimed in Eddie, she wasn't the first, by any means, who had been taken to the castle against her will. When you came right down to it, there was many a child, among those left homeless, whose likeness to the Earl was the topic of much smothered talk. His own flesh and blood, these children were, and still The Bad Earl turned them out into the world to freeze and starve. . . .

Alec saw that Peter was looking sick again and gave each of the scandalmongers a vigorous nudge, hoping to silence him. But the talk went on and on. What about weapons? Had any been found? And could their owners be traced and thus discovered as the murderers? The trap had covered six or eight miles along a highway bordered with bright yellow gorse and passed through the town of Ramelton, where numerous anglers were fishing along the banks of the Leannan, before there was a break in the gossip. Then they turned into a quiet side road, skirting the same stream, which suddenly seemed clearer and swifter as it slipped along over smooth stones, and Con turned to Alec.

"Shall I pull up here, sir? Or on the other side of the bridge?"

"This is all right. It's easier to get down to the pool on this side.

Mr. Bradford and I will walk across and eat our lunch beside the waterfall. That'll give him a chance to enjoy more of the scenery before his first lesson begins. . . . Would that suit you, Peter? We think the view from Drummonaghan Bridge is one of the loveliest in the country."

"Then I'd certainly like to see it."

He quickly decided that Alec had not overestimated the scene's attractions. The river came sparkling over the falls above the bridge and then raced on over the stones, brown and frothy, through a shaded gorge where the trees almost met above it. If it were not the loveliest sight in the country, it was certainly the loveliest he had so far seen in Ireland and his response to it was immediate. By the time he had finished his share of the excellent lunch that had been provided, not a trace of his black mood remained.

Leaving Con to mind the trap, the others now pulled on their boots and, clutching their gear, scrambled down to the river, with Peter bringing up the rear. Alec moved slowly downstream until he located a stone that offered secure footing. Then he began to cast while Eddie showed Peter the proper way to tie the flies on his line.

"Now, sir, if you'll watch me, you'll see what to do. First you let out a few yards of line and then cast slightly upstream. That's right. Just let the fly float down with the current. Wait a minute or two and then cast again. And that's all there is to it—to begin with."

Maybe that's the way it seems to you, Peter said rather ruefully to himself, as one attempt after another to cast as far and as easily as Eddie was unsuccessful. Eddie kept trying to reassure him by telling him he was doing very well for the first time out and that he should not be discouraged; but when they had been at the pool nearly an hour, Alec, who had already caught two brown trout, called out jeeringly, "What has happened to that beginner's luck we hear so much about?"

"I thought you were supposed to keep quiet when you were fishing," Peter said to Eddie, ignoring his cousin.

"Oh no, sir, the salmon don't mind talking a bit."

Suddenly Peter felt a slight tug on his line and turned excitedly and expectantly to Eddie. The latter merely shook his head and reached for Peter's rod.

"I'm afraid, sir, your hook's caught on a rock. I'll work it free for you."

Somewhat sheepishly, Peter took his freed rod from the ghillie and cast again. "Just in case you *should* get a rise, sir, be sure to hold the bit of line that's under your thumb tight for a second or two, so the hook will catch in his mouth, but then let go, so he can run, or you'll lose him for sure." As Eddie spoke, a silvery fish leaped high into the air and then, with a loud splash, dove under again.

"Would it do any good to cast where we saw him?" Peter asked eagerly.

"No harm in trying. But I'm afraid he's moved on by now."

"And was that silvery fish really a salmon, Eddie?"

"It was, indeed, sir, and a beauty."

"But I thought salmon were pink! Or is that just American salmon? We always have it for our Fourth of July dinner, with the first green peas from our garden."

A hoot of derision from Alec followed this observation, and Eddie seemed to be having some difficulty in keeping his face straight as he answered respectfully, "It's the same with Irish salmon, sir—on the inside."

"Well, thank you for enlightening me so pleasantly," Peter said, with a withering glance in Alec's direction, which was entirely lost on its intended recipient. "Let's go on from here, Eddie. You started to tell me what to do if I were lucky enough to get a rise, but I'm not sure I know what you mean by letting him run."

"I mean you should let him have all the line he'll take and not try to hold him back. He'll slow down when he gets tired and then comes the interesting part. You must have heard people talk about 'playing' a fish."

"I suppose I have, but I never really paid much attention."

"When you realize your reel's stopped spinning, that's your signal to go to work. Very, very slowly, you begin to reel in Mr. Salmon. If he begins to pull, you ease off for a bit and then begin all over again. And so it goes, first your way and then his. Eventually, if you've really hooked him, you'll end up with him practically at your feet. Then it's quick with the net and salmon for supper."

"You certainly make it sound simple, but—" Peter broke off, as his rod bent suddenly, and then added, "I've caught another rock, I'm afraid."

"Not this time, sir. Remember now, easy does it. Give him his head and all the line he wants."

Peter tried to control his excitement and remember all Eddie's instructions, as he listened to the line zip out from the reel, but found it impossible to remain calm and was sure he would forget some vital point.

"There, sir, he's beginning to tire a bit, but let him have a little more line before you begin to reel in."

Under Eddie's quiet encouragement, Peter patiently began to "play" the fish and for a time found an unexpected exhilaration in the tug-of-war between himself and the salmon. Then he, too, began to tire. Only grim determination on his part prolonged the struggle and he had almost decided to give it up when he heard Eddie cry, "You've done it, sir! By God, you've done it! And he's at least a twelve-pounder! Let me net him now and he'll be all yours."

8

The long sleep of Peter's second night at The Lodge ended as peacefully as it had begun. His first waking thoughts were not of the murder, but of the pool and waterfall by Drummonaghan Bridge, of the clear stream's loveliness in its frame of luxuriant green and the startling beauty of the silvery salmon as they leaped above the surface of the Leannan. He had thrilled with pride when he held up not one, but two fine salmon for Dermot and Sandra McKeever to admire; and it seemed to him that no supper had ever tasted so good as the one that night for which he furnished the main course. He could not believe that twenty-four hours earlier he had actually disliked the idea of fishing; now it seemed as if he could not wait to spend another day as he had the last. Nothing had been said the night before about further excursions; but he dressed hurriedly, eager to find out at the earliest possible moment whether or not there were any in prospect.

The family was already seated in the pleasant dining room when he entered it and he did ample, if tardy, justice to the "proper" breakfast so bountifully provided. Still more tardily, he realized that, instead of impatiently awaiting a disclosure of plans for his pleasure, he should show his concern for Dermot McKeever's gruesome preoccupations. But, again, the older man seemed averse to talking about them. No, there was not any trace of the assassins and, without doubt, they had escaped to Scotland. The autopsy had established the fact that the terrific blow was unquestionably the direct cause of the Earl's death—the wound made by gunshot he might have survived. The heir had taken the nine o'clock train from Dublin to Londonderry and, following the same schedule as Peter, would be at Rathmullan late in the afternoon. Dermot McKeever would meet him at the ferry and, meanwhile, would begin following such instructions as had come in by wire.

"And I must be up and at it without wasting any more time," he said, rising almost abruptly. "If you've finished your breakfast, Peter, come out on the steps with me for a minute. I want you to have a look at the view." Then, as they passed through the entrance and stood facing the blue lake and the green land beyond, he again put his arm around Peter's shoulder in the same affectionate way that he had the day before.

"Look carefully!" he said. "If you do, I don't think you'll have any trouble seeing a medieval merchant ship materialize down there at the pier. There's been a brisk sale in the wines it brought here and now Red Hugh, the heir of the O'Donnells, is supping as the guest of the captain in his cabin. In a few minutes the anchor will be weighed and the ship will sail for Dublin with Red Hugh still on board. He won't realize what's happened until it's too late to save himself and he'll be a prisoner for years in Dublin Castle. But he'll make his escape and come back to be the greatest power in Donegal. Doesn't that ship seem very real to you as you look out there?"

"Yes, it does, the way you talk about it."

"All right. Now look again and you'll see another ship, perhaps a survivor of the Spanish Armada, a small one of only eighty tons or so. But it carried a cargo that ended one era and began another. The Earls of Tyrone and Tyrconnell fled in it, with a goodly number of their relatives and attendants, and after a perilous voyage of three weeks they reached France and safety. Then they went on to Rome, where they were the Pope's guests and where they finally died. Didn't Lady Susannah ever take you to see their tombs at San Pietro in Montorio? It's been a place of Irish pilgrimage for years! . . . Well, to get back to the ship: this 'Flight of the Earls' freed them from bondage, but it left the way clear for the confiscation of their vast estates and the Plantation of Ulster. So it was a deliverance for them, but the beginning of harsh rule by English and Scottish colonists. Can you see that ship, too—and understand what it meant?"

"I think so."

"Then you're beginning to learn Irish history in a place where it ought to come alive to you, because this is where a great deal of it was made. And that's the way I want you to feel about Rathmullan. Not that it is a place connected with murder, but as a place that marked two great turning points in Irish history. Now I must get on with my work and you must be off for another day at the Ramelton pool and after that we'll talk about plans for a trip to Gweedore, so you can see where your grandfather, who was also my uncle, made history of another kind when he laid the foundations for a great industry based on cottage weaving."

"So I'm going fishing again today?"

"Isn't that what you'd like to do?"

"More than anything else I can think of."

"Then be on your way. It's what I'd like to do, too—and with you. But there'll still be plenty of chances for that before you start south. Now my hands are full right here. And that looks like the messenger boy from the post office coming across the lawn with another telegram for me."

"Beg pardon, sir. This one isn't for you. It's for Mr. Peter Bradford. And they told me at the office I must put it straight into his own hands."

The boy spoke breathlessly. It was obvious he had come at top speed up the slight rise of ground which Peter knew from experience was not easy going. He felt in his pocket for a shilling before he stretched out his hand to take the telegram.

"Oh thank you, sir! But that's too much! Thruppence, they generally give me for delivering, if they give me anything."

"Nevertheless, a shilling's quite all right, in this case."

"God bless!" the boy exclaimed joyfully and started off again. Peter tore open the envelope, gave one quick glance at its contents and called him back.

"Wait a minute! You'll have to take an answer to this."

"Yes, sir."

Peter let the envelope drop to the ground and handed the message to McKeever.

"PETER BRADFORD, ET CETERA"—he read—"YOUR UNCLE IS ILL AND WANTS VERY MUCH TO SEE YOU STOP PLEASE WIRE ME EARLIEST POSSIBLE TIME YOUR ARRIVAL. MAC AULIFFE, SOLICITOR."

In a matter of minutes, the whole tenor of the day had changed. McKeever dashed off a return message, saying that Peter would leave Rathmullan immediately and that a second telegram would advise what train connections he had been able to make and when he would arrive at Cloncoole. Meanwhile, Peter hurried to his room and threw his most requisite gear into a bag; the rest of his equipment would have to follow somehow—or perhaps most of it could stay where it was, he told himself hopefully; perhaps he could come back to this pleasant place before too long. When he went downstairs, he learned there would not be another ferry until nearly noon, but since the tide would not be against him this time, he should reach Fahan in time to catch the twelve-twenty train for Londonderry. He could go on to Dublin that same day on a slow train, but when he reached there, the last train for the south would have gone; it probably would be better to spend the night in Londonderry and make the trip on connecting trains the next day.

"Well, just as you think best," Peter said dejectedly. "Since I've got time maybe I'd better go back to my room and pack a second bag, so you won't have to send so much after me." He had just begun to recover his normally cheerful outlook on life, which the shock of his lost love had upset, to tell himself that, of course, he would find her in due time and that, in the meantime, life with his newfound relatives was very well worth living. Now he was to be wrested from them, to go to the bedside of an ailing old man whom he had never seen; inevitably, the prospect was depressing.

"It won't be any trouble to send whatever you need after you," McKeever assured him. "But I do think you'd be wise to take more than the barest necessities with you—no telling exactly what you'll need in the way of clothes at a place like Cloneen. The fishing tackle might as well stay here, for we hope the Earl will make a quick recovery and that you'll be able to come back for the good long visit we planned. As far as the golf clubs are concerned, I doubt if you'll need those anywhere—golf is only just beginning to come into its own in Ireland. It's too bad you bothered with them at all. . . . Alec will go over to Londonderry with you and stay with you until you take your train for Dublin, whichever it is. My sister'll be delighted to have you spend the night at her house if you decide to delay your departure until morning and that would give more of my family a chance to get acquainted with you, as they've been hoping to do."

"You're wonderfully kind and thoughtful. But I'm afraid I'm a good deal of a nuisance. First I forget to tell you when I'm coming and then I turn around and leave almost as soon as I get here."

"You'd never be a nuisance to us, Peter, whatever you did. Your cousin Sandra and I've always wished we had more than one son and we're counting on you to help make up for the lack. Now get to work on that second bag and when you come down we'll have a bite of lunch ready for you and Alec. I'm not going to leave you to the tender mercies of Miss Kelly at Fahan again."

Peter did his best to show his appreciation of the McKeevers' continued thoughtfulness and hospitality and was glad the train schedule was such that he could conscientiously stay the night in Londonderry without unduly delaying his arrival at Cloneen. Dermot's sister Eleanor, whose husband, Alexander Conway, was associated with McKeever in the distribution of tweed, bore a close resemblance to her brother and presided over a house on the River Foyle as spacious and pleasant as The Lodge. The afternoon was devoted to a walk around the ancient walls, which Peter found extremely interesting, and the evening to a spirited game of whist. But the next day's train trip was a hard one. The newspapers were full of Lord Hartley's murder and Peter could find nothing else to read. Parliament had now taken up the cry of condemnation: in the House of Lords, Oranmore and Browne declared, "Until the Legislature affords protection to the tenants, landlords will from time to time be consigned to a bloody doom, like that which overtook Lord Hartley." In the Commons, where the killing was also raised, one of the speakers was Mr. Parnell, who warned the House that the manner in which Irish tenants were abandoned to the worst caprices tended to destroy all hope in Constitutional agitation amongst the Irish people. Mr. Frank O'Donnell brought a motion before the House to the effect: "That the action of the Government, following the killing, was unsuited to promote the ends of justice and calculated to foster disbelief in the impartiality of the law." He asked members what the reaction would be if, say, the people of Cumberland had been for years at the mercy of one of iron will and ruthless passion. "The relations between the landlord and the tenants have never been stained by one excess of an agrarian character on the side of the unfortunate tenantry," he said, "and the only case in which the landlord has been exposed to outrage was his attempted assassination by the uncle of the humble girl he had dishonored." When he was interrupted by shouts of "Shame!" Mr. O'Donnell explained that he had presented an imaginary case, from which the House might be able to ascertain if there were a parallel "capable of application elsewhere." He added: "If it is found that this man, known as 'The Bad Earl,' had carried on this practice of debauchery, only by means of his authority and power of eviction, what would the reaction be?" When Mr. O'Donnell attempted to speak of the fate of the peasant girls on the estate, Mr. King Harmon moved that further discussion be in secret session and no more charges were made openly, but the implied comparison between English and Irish landlords had not lost its effect.

The waves of sickness which had almost overpowered Peter when Alec came to bring him the news of the murder in the garden, and when he listened to the ghillie and the coachman on the way to Ramelton, swept over him again and he could not shake them off. The train went on and on, through the pouring rain and the gathering dusk; when it finally came to a stop at Cloncoole Station, Peter saw a ruddy, thickset man, wearing a long black frieze coat, who was waiting on the platform and looking so searchingly at the passengers, as they left the train, that it was evident he was watching for someone. With hardly a minute's hesitation, he came up to Peter, touching the brim of a tall hat banded with crepe.

"It's Mr. Peter Bradford and no mistake, isn't it, sir?" he asked; and, as Peter confirmed his identity, the man reached for the traveler's luggage and added, "I'm that sorry for your trouble, sir. It's a long hard trip you've had and then to find the Master gone and all."

"Gone! You don't mean he's dead?"

"That's right, sir. Just last night and very peaceful, in his sleep. But a terrible shock, suddenlike, to her ladyship and to all of us. Och, you mustn't be standing out here in the rain. You'll be hearing all about it at the house. I'm Ryan, the coachman, and I've the carriage waiting for you, sir, just beyond the platform."

Peter nodded, followed the man and entered the closed carriage in a dazed state. Since the time he had received the cordial letter from his uncle, the old Earl had ceased to be merely a name to him and had become a personality. The solicitor's telegram had not unduly worried him. Like most young persons, he did not connect illness intimately with death, only as an unwelcome interruption of normal occupations. Reluctant as he had been to leave Rathmullan, he had pictured himself as doing his best to beguile a convalescent's dragging hours to the satisfaction of both concerned. It would be quite another matter to attempt the consolation of a grieving widow, a task for which he felt woefully inadequate. The prospect was appalling.

The carriage came to a stop before iron gates which were parted, at its approach, to their enormous width by a man who stood silently beside them. At first, only the creaking noise of the gates themselves, opening and shutting, broke the oppressive stillness. Then Peter heard a weird sound that seemed to come from the gatehouse a few yards further on. The upper part of its door, which was divided in the middle, stood open, revealing an interior lighted by rush candles and a large fireplace; and on either side of the hearth sat a woman with folded arms and a bent head, who rocked to and fro as she wailed. This, then, must be the keening for the dead. Peter shivered and he knew this was not only with the cold.

The carriage started again and wound its way slowly along a drive bordered with tall trees which formed an archway overhead. Beyond, on either side, the woods looked impenetrable and the outside world seemed a dim and distant place. At one point the density of this forest was less engulfing and Peter thought he glimpsed some lofty ruins and the sheen of water; but the carriage lamps gave so little light that he could not be sure and he soon felt he must be mistaken, for the tall trees closed in around them again. They went on and on until, at last, the drive widened abruptly into a graveled area and the carriage crossed this to stop before steps, glistening in the rain, which led to a wide portal, flanked with lanterns, their light obscured by the downpour on their glass. The coachman threw open the door of the carriage, offering the protection of an umbrella, at the same moment that the door at the top of the steps was opened by another servant in mourning livery, who bowed deeply as he ushered the traveler into the portico and said in a somber voice, "A grievous homecoming for you, my lord."

Again Peter was so taken aback that he found it hard to answer. He knew, of course, that he was his uncle's heir—his grandmother had reminded him of this often enough; but somehow he had not connected his legacy with an inherited title. If the butler observed the startled expression with which Peter looked at him, or found anything unusual in the choked response, nothing in his impassive manner betrayed this.

"Permit me to relieve your lordship of his cloak," he went on, opening the door into a small square hall. "Would your lordship care to take any refreshment before I show him to his room or will he be served there? Her ladyship would wish him to follow his preference."

"I think I'd like to go straight to my room if I may, to get cleaned up a little," Peter managed to say, choking a little less. "And a drink would be very welcome and. . . . Is it too late for me to pay my respects to the Countess? I mean, to offer her my expressions of condolence?"

"Her ladyship is expecting your lordship. She is still at prayer by my late master's side, but she has instructed me to conduct your lordship there as soon as he is ready. She thought it would be more fitting for your lordship to see the late Earl there, laid out on his own bed, before he is taken to the library for the lying-in-state."

"Perhaps she's right. Anyway, of course I will be guided by her wishes."

66

"Naturally, my lord. My name, your lordship, is Wade. I have had the honor of serving my late master for more than thirty years. If your lordship will come this way."

This colloquy had taken place just inside the small square hall and Peter had been too disconcerted to take much notice of his surroundings. Now he saw that the hall he had entered led into one that was very much longer, and that at the end of it was the tallest flight of stairs he had ever seen. This, apparently, ended beneath a stained-glass window and it was not until he had gone past protracted lines of ancestral portraits, hanging on either side of the hall, that he realized the stained-glass window did not mark the end of the staircase, only a landing; and that, from this, shorter flights branched out on either side. Having finally mounted one of these to a gallery, he discovered he was still nowhere near the end of his journey; the butler now led the way to the last room in a corridor which stretched on and on. There the door was opened to disclose massive furniture, brightened by chintz hangings and upholstery and, best of all, as far as Peter was concerned, by a glowing log fire. An easy chair was drawn up near the hearth and a small table, set with decanters, a carafe and a plate of sandwiches, stood in front of it. At the further end of the room still a third servant in black livery, a younger one this time, whom Peter had not seen before, was setting down the valises which, obviously, had been spirited up some rear staircase.

"If your lordship will hand me his keys, I will unpack for him immediately," the newcomer said obsequiously.

"Good grief!" Peter exclaimed, before he could stop himself. "I mean," he added, conscious of the bewildered look on the boy's face, "I'd rather unpack myself. You see, I never in my life had anyone do it for me."

"Tim, his lordship does not require you at present," Wade said, turning quietly to the younger man. "Later, if he should need you, he will ring for you." And, as Tim, still looking bewildered and rather grieved, hastily left the room, the butler added, addressing Peter, "Shall I return for your lordship in, say, half an hour or would he prefer to ring?"

"No, half an hour would be fine."

He nodded a dismissal and, when he was sure he was alone, muttered to himself, "That boy would get an awful shock if I had to confess I didn't have any keys—lost them long ago—and a worse one when he saw all the dirty clothes jumbled in my bags, hit or miss. Darn it, I didn't mean to hurt his feelings. But I didn't have time to get any laundry done or even to pack properly after the telegram came. And, of course, in spite of Cousin Dermot's thoughtfulness, I haven't the right clothes to wear. I didn't know the poor old man was dead until I got here. I've got to make sure all these faithful retainers understand this, that I'm not willfully going against their customs." He fixed a stiff drink of whiskey and, as soon as he had swallowed it, poured a second and bit into one of the excellent sandwiches on the plate beside the decanters. Then he shook his head and, recognizing with regret the flight of time, opened one of the valises, took out a suit which was badly in need of pressing, but which at least was a black one, and rummaged for a clean shirt, flinging aside soiled ones as he did so. A metal container, which he had learned at Rathmullan to call a jug and not a pitcher, carefully covered with a neat towel, stood on the washstand among the flowered crockery and he knew that the water in it would be piping hot. He decided to risk a quick shave, as well as a quick wash, and was just shrugging into his coat when Wade tapped at the door.

"I hope I didn't hurry your lordship, but it is getting so late—"

"No, it was an almost perfect connection."

"Thank you, my lord. This way, my lord."

Again the corridor leading from the gallery was a long one and Peter was ashamed to feel glad of it this time. With all his heart he wished that he had never come to this place, that there had been no reason for him to come. He could feel no personal grief for the loss of a man he had never seen, and the burdens represented by the legacy of this unknown relative, far from satisfying some long-felt desire or ambition, appalled him as a menace to a carefree life, quite aside from aversion to the principle of Irish landlordism, intensified by the dreadful impressions he had received at Rathmullan. He dreaded the entry into the death chamber, the sight of the man who had so suddenly died and the meeting with his widow. Postponement would have been a relief. And yet, perhaps it was better to have the ordeal behind him than ahead of him.

Wade paused before a double door which stood open and silently withdrew. The room was lighted only by candles at either end and the great four-poster, where the dead man lay, was at the further end of it, on the side. Shadows lay between it and the entrance and, at first, Peter felt engulfed with these, rather than guided by the faint gleam of the candles. He shrank from passing through these shadows;

it took grim determination to put one foot in front of the other and, when he was only halfway across the room, he stopped short.

A girl dressed in black was kneeling by the bed. Considering her flowing dress and her position, he might have mistaken her figure in the dim light, though he did not believe this possible. But there was no mistaking her hair. It glowed like burnished gold in the somber room and something of its radiance seemed reflected on the still form in the bed.

His uncle's widow was the girl he had met on the train, the girl he had possessed on the boat, the girl whose image had dominated his thoughts since he parted from her.

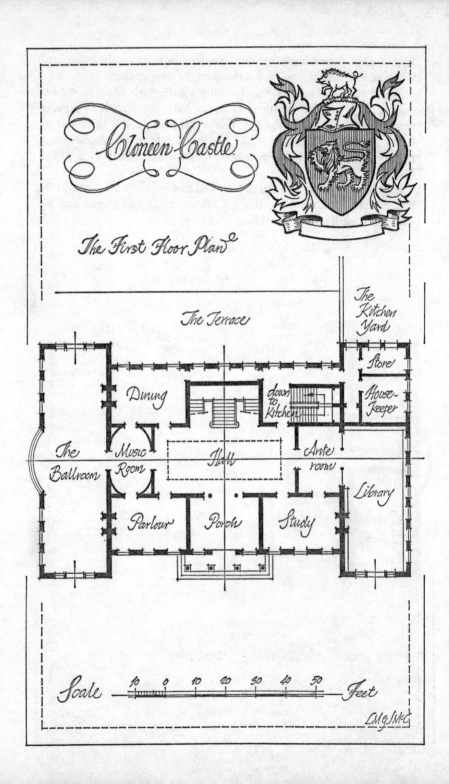

Cloneen Castle

The First Floor Plan

The Terrace

The Kitchen Yard

Store

House-keeper

Dining

down to Kitchen

The Ballroom

Music Room

Hall

Ante room

Library

Parlour

Porch

Study

Scale   10 0 10 20 30 40 50   Feet

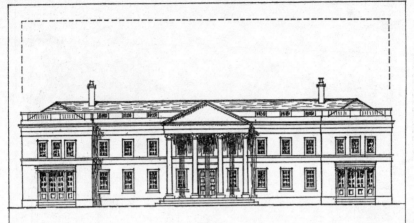

Front Elevation

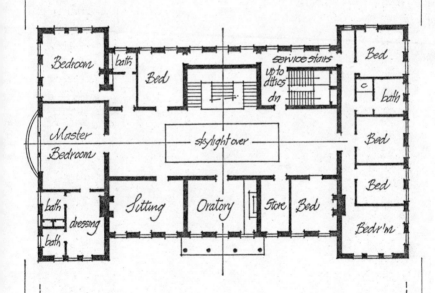

The Second Floor Plan

PART THREE

Early July
to late August, 1882

The Heir Apparent

A great lady is as simple as a good poet. Neither possesses anything that is not ancient and their own. . . .

—*Autobiographies* by W. B. Yeats

9

He was seized by a desperate impulse to rush from the room before she saw him. But he did not act on it quickly enough. She crossed herself, rose from her knees and looked him full in the face.

For a minute they stared at each other, speechless and unbelieving. Then the girl gasped and her incredulous gaze changed to one of horror. "My God! Are you really—" Peter began brokenly, but before he could finish the sentence she turned and fled.

He started after her, but she had left by a side door, closing it behind her; he heard a bolt sliding home and the sobs which she was no longer trying to restrain now that she had shut him away from her. His own impulse to flee was increasingly urgent. Nevertheless, something stronger still impelled him not to leave the death chamber until he had walked over to the bed and looked down at the still figure which was lying there, perfectly at peace.

It was clad in the habit of St. Francis, with a crucifix clasped in the hands on the breast. The calm face was strong and austere. But its nobility seemed less that of lofty lineage than that of a man who, all his life, had been upright and humane and who was carrying the stamp of these qualities with him to his grave. He might have been a severe judge, but never one who was unjust.

It was proper, Peter knew, to offer some sort of a prayer in a death chamber, though he had no idea what was suitable, especially in such an awe-inspiring presence; he had never been devout, but that he should pray before he left seemed suddenly inescapable.

"Our Father, who art in heaven, hallowed be Thy name," he began, because he could think of nothing else. "Thy kingdom come; Thy will be done on earth as it is in heaven. Give us this day our daily bread; and forgive us our trespasses. . . ."

He stopped abruptly. It was all too true that he should be asking forgiveness, but he was not sure whether this should be part of his prayer to God or a petition to the dead man. For some mysterious reason, it did not seem to Peter that this kinsman of his was irrevocably separated from him by a gulf between living and dead which could never be bridged. "You'd have understood, wouldn't you?" he found himself whispering, as if his uncle were still within the range of his voice. "I wasn't consciously doing you a wrong. I didn't know she belonged to you. I believed she belonged to me. I love her; I'll always love her." The longer he spoke, the stronger became the feeling of a mystical bond. "And she didn't mean to betray you, either," he went on passionately, "but she felt, God knows why, that she belonged to me. Perhaps you already understand that. But please believe that neither of us will ever do anything again that's disloyal to you and that I'll never let her suffer for what's happened already. I'll atone for it, somehow. Please believe me. I swear it. I swear it."

He never knew how long he knelt there. But when he left the room, the urge for flight was gone and he was ready to face whatever was before him.

Wade was standing at a respectful distance in the gallery, patiently waiting for him. Peter realized that he must have been there a long time.

"I'll have to depend on you these next few days, Wade, to tell me what I ought to do, and when," he said quietly. "I think her ladyship wants to be alone and that's very natural. Is there anyone else I ought to see this evening?"

"Mr. MacAuliffe will be calling later on, your lordship, in the hope that it will be convenient for you to receive him. Of course, he has charge of all arrangements for the funeral and he'll be needing to talk them over with you. But he wouldn't be coming until after dinner."

"I've had a drink and some hearty sandwiches, you know. That's all I need for tonight."

"My lord, her ladyship would be greatly distressed if she knew you went without dinner. And so, begging your pardon, would Cook. She's tried hard to think what might be tasty, with you so tired and all. Everything's in readiness for your lordship. If you'll follow me. . . ."

After telling the old butler that he would accept advice and guidance for the next few days, Peter could hardly decline to do so, reluctant as he was to face a solid and solitary meal. He descended the staircase, which seemed to him still loftier than it had before, and was ushered into a vast dining room where a small table seemed almost lost in its surroundings. To Peter's surprise, he saw that it was set for two, but before he could ask the reason, Wade enlightened him.

"Her ladyship is very tired and begs to be excused. She hopes you will understand."

Peter understood only too well. It had not occurred to him that she would dine with him—indeed, it had not occurred to him that a formal dinner would be served that evening. However, it was now obvious that this was part of the protocol, that she had intended to preside at this table—until she discovered his identity. Then she had known that she could not act the part of the gracious hostess to her husband's heir, that such a role would be a mockery of what had happened between them and, though in time she might learn the hard lesson of playing such a part, she was still too distraught to do so.

"Yes, of course," Peter answered belatedly. "Of course, she must be very tired. Of course, she shouldn't make any such effort."

Wade bowed gravely and drew out a chair. There was no fire in the room and Peter tried to tell himself this was the reason he felt so cold. He did his best to ignore his discomfort and overcome his lack of appetite, as one course after another, each with its appropriate wine, was served him with as much ceremony as if a distinguished company had been present. He had done what justice he could to the consommé, the salmon, the lamb, the trifle and the cheese and, with less difficulty, to the sherry, the Chablis, the claret and the port, when Wade paused beside him after putting down fruit and a finger bowl.

"Her ladyship has rested a little and asked me to say she hoped you might take coffee with her. She thought it would be helpful if you and she could have a few words in private before the arrival of Mr. Mac-Auliffe."

So something had made it necessary for her to see him, after all! The momentary panic which Peter thought he had entirely conquered overwhelmed him again. But he managed to answer without betraying it.

"No doubt she's right. Where shall I find her?"

"In her private sitting room. I will conduct your lordship."

Again those seemingly interminable stairs, again that long gallery. Except for the entrance to the death chamber, the doors had all been closed when Peter passed along this before. Now two stood open—one leading into a small chapel, where candles were burning on an altar, and another, next in line, leading into a small parlor, exquisitely furnished in Louis Quinze style. As Peter entered this room, his uncle's widow rose from a *bergère*.

"I know that you have had a long journey and that you must be very tired," she said calmly, reseating herself. "But since Mr. MacAuliffe feels he must see us together this evening, I thought it best that you and I should have a little talk beforehand."

"Yes. So Wade told me. And I said I was sure you were right."

"I think Mr. MacAuliffe will be here soon, but I believe there's time for coffee first. May I pour it for you? How do you take it? Won't you sit down?"

A silver service stood on the table in front of the *bergère* and Peter, after telling her that he took after-dinner coffee clear, sat down opposite her and accepted the cup Wade passed to him. He had noticed the girl's fingers again—not, this time, because of the great rings, for those were gone, leaving nothing except the narrow band, which one of them had completely concealed, but because he was amazed to see that her hands did not tremble as she poured the coffee. The lovely color had gone from her cheeks, which were now as white as her brow and her throat, but there was no sign of agitation in her face. She had completely recovered her self-control. If she could do so, surely he ought to be able to do this, too.

"I hope Wade has seen to it that you are comfortable," she went on evenly. "Tomorrow morning, Mrs. Brennan, our housekeeper, will come to consult you about your personal tastes and requirements, but I thought you really would rather not be bothered tonight."

"You were right about that, too. Besides, I couldn't possibly be more comfortably and pleasantly fixed. And I'll have to confess that the fire felt awfully good to me."

She turned to the butler. "Wade, did you have a fire for his lordship in the dining room?"

"I'm sorry about that, my lady."

"I'm sure you'll remember from now on—every evening and morning, too, if his lordship breakfasts downstairs. . . . Do you like our hearty Irish breakfasts?"

"Very much, thank you."

"A good Irish breakfast for his lordship, Wade, at—?"

"Is eight all right?"

"Eight is just right, for breakfast. And what about early-morning tea?"

"I think you've guessed that the answer to that would be no."

"No early-morning tea, Wade. And you may remove the coffee. That will be all until Mr. MacAuliffe arrives. Then you may serve port, as usual." She was silent until the butler had cleared the table and left with the tray. Then, speaking with equal detachment, she went on, "Perhaps now that Wade has left us, I ought to give you a few autobiographical details, to avoid some possible awkwardness. Of course, he takes it for granted that you know all about me—he and the rest of the staff. Naturally, I want them to and you might unconsciously betray the fact that you don't, though probably you have guessed that I am French."

"I knew you weren't Irish—except by adoption, as you yourself put it. But I couldn't quite place the accent."

"Norman. Home is an *haras*—a stud farm, near Lisieux. My maiden name was Anne de Briare. I never lived in Ireland until I married and I still go back and forth between Cloneen and home, partly because my parents miss me so much and partly because of the horses. I take them back and forth, too—or, rather, I arrange to have them taken. We were getting two new ones for Cloneen when—when you saw me on the train—Guillaume le Conquérant and Reine Mathilde. I intended to ride them at the Dublin Horse Show in August and I had all their papers in my bottle bag. That's why I'd promised never to let it out of my sight. Not because of the jewelry. There isn't much danger that ancestral jewelry will be stolen—it would be too easy to trace. But studbooks are something else again."

For a moment, while she had been thinking about nothing but her beloved horses, she had been able to dismiss from her mind the horror she had felt when she had been confronted by Peter in her husband's room, the horror which still lay close beneath the calmness of her voice and manner. But only for a moment. Speaking more formally again, she said, "I think now you have enough autobiographical details to avoid awkward breaks."

"But I haven't!" Peter burst out. "You haven't told me how you happened to marry a foreigner, a man old enough to be your grandfather. You must know I'm deeply puzzled about that. You might at least tell me—"

"I've told you all I think it is necessary to tell you at the moment. There isn't time for a longer conversation just now and, even if there were, this isn't the proper occasion for it. Of course, you and I met for the first time in my husband's room, a few hours ago—not only as far as the staff and our families and friends are concerned, but as far as you and I are concerned. *Please don't forget this.* I shall go to the dower house as soon as I can properly leave this one, which is now yours, after the funeral and the reading of the will. In the meantime, we will see each other only in the presence of others. As I told you, I spend a great deal of time in Normandy. We shall never need to meet very often and I shall count on you to help me limit the number of these meetings."

"Anne, don't send me away like this—" Peter began desperately, but she interrupted him.

"I think Mr. MacAuliffe will expect you to address me as Lady O'Toole," she said, "and here is Wade come to announce him."

10

Mr. MacAuliffe, whom Wade had already served with port, was awaiting them in the library, which Peter now entered for the first time. It was a room of great splendor, more than fifty feet long and half again as wide, with a ceiling of rococo plasterwork, chandeliers of Waterford glass and Persian rugs. On two sides it was lined from floor to ceiling with beautifully bound books and a gallery, reached by a small circular staircase, gave access to the upper shelves; at either end was a marble fireplace, set into oak paneling and surmounted by Lely portraits of the first Earl and his wife Susannah. Despite its majesty, it was not as overpowering to Peter as the gloomy hall, the lofty staircase and the cold dining room had been. The Bradfords belonged to that breed of New Englanders to whom books came next to bread in the necessities of life and, in any case, there had been plenty of money for both in this particular family throughout many generations. The library in the house on Beacon Hill, where Peter, like his father, his grandfather and several other forebears had been born and raised, was not quite as large as this one; nevertheless, it was a room of noble proportions and contained almost as many books, equally valuable rugs and two early family portraits by Copley which bore favorable comparison with the Lelys. Had it not been for his state of emotional turmoil, Peter would have admired and enjoyed this room from the moment he set foot in it and would soon have felt at home; even under the most depressing circumstances of his introduction to it, he could appreciate it.

Anne had gone rapidly down the stairs ahead of him, as soon as she had spoken her words of warning; hence, there had been no possibility of a chance to plead with her—a contingency which she had obviously foreseen. She was already greeting the solicitor when Peter joined them, and her presentation of the heir was as brief as was consistent with courtesy. But MacAuliffe, a portly, balding man, was constitutionally so genial that nothing could entirely obscure this quality, and so shrewd that his first glance told him something more shattering than the death of an elderly relative he had never seen was afflicting this good-looking young man, to whom he took an immediate liking.

"It's good to know you're at Cloneen, sir," he said, with a hearty handshake. "Your uncle was looking forward to your visit more than I've known him to do toward anything in a long time. Ah well, while it's too late for him to enjoy it, as much as I'm sure he would have, it's a relief for me to know there's a kinsman of his here with whom I can share my responsibilities. They've been weighing on me heavily and I don't mind admitting it. I can tell that, from now on, they won't be more than half as burdensome, if they are that."

Gratitude, such as he had seldom felt for anyone before, welled up in Peter's heart. "You may depend on me to do anything I can to be helpful," he said feelingly. "But of course you know all this is completely new to me, as well as—very sad. Will you tell me where and how to begin?"

"I think you should begin by getting a good night's sleep, as soon as Father Carroll has left. He'll be here in a short time now, to lead the rosary and we'll join with him in that; but he can wait until morning to discuss arrangements at the church and so can Mr. O'Grady, who'll take charge of preparing the late Earl for his lying-in-state—here in this room." Peter's gratitude increased as he observed how skillfully the solicitor was avoiding such grim words as "funeral" and "undertaker." "The lying-in-state will last all day tomorrow and day after tomorrow," Mr. MacAuliffe went on. "And I'm afraid it's necessary for you to face the fact that a good many persons, all strangers to you, will be coming to the house for it. But if you feel you can stand by and receive them, it wouldn't be necessary for the Countess to see most of these people— only a few high-ranking officials and a few intimate friends, and those could be brought to her in her sitting room, if she'd prefer."

"Naturally, you may count on me to stand by."

"Thank you, sir. . . . Is the schedule I've outlined so far agreeable to you, Lady O'Toole?"

"Entirely so. Wade will know who my special friends are. And you can indicate to him which official callers you feel I can't escape receiving."

"Exactly. But there's one potential visitor I think I should ask you about." He drew a telegram from his briefcase and read it aloud: "'Please present expressions of condolence to Lady O'Toole from me and advise by wire whether or not funeral is to be private or if I might properly attend.' The signature is Lawrence Donovan. . . . I know Mr. Donovan has occasionally been a guest here," Mr. MacAuliffe continued, "and that he has frequently ridden your horses at the Curragh Races and elsewhere. In fact, I understood he was to ride with you at the Dublin Horse Show this coming summer. But, somehow, I thought it best to consult you before replying."

"I'm glad you did," Anne answered, in a changed voice. "I don't see how we can decline to let him come to the church—or to the lying-in-state, for that matter," she said. "But if you mean, is he one of the friends I would wish to have admitted to my private sitting room, he certainly is not."

She spoke not only quickly, but vehemently and Peter observed with surprise that color had suddenly come into her pale cheeks. "Would it be in order for me to ask for a little more information about this Mr. Donovan?" he inquired. "That is, I've never heard of him before and, apparently, he's someone I'll be running into."

"Yes, certainly you should be informed," Mr. MacAuliffe agreed immediately. "He's an attractive young gentleman and he's a good deal in evidence these days. I mean, he's become quite prominent politically as a staunch supporter of Mr. Charles Stewart Parnell. The late Earl was in sympathy with his triumphant efforts which led to the passage of the Land Act last year, but at the same time—"

"At the same time," Anne interposed, speaking quickly again, "you know my husband had grave doubts about Mr. Parnell's infallibility as a leader."

"Perhaps I'd better know why," Peter said eagerly. "Because he's a very distinguished man, isn't he? I know he's considered so in Boston. His grandmother, Delia Tudor, who married Admiral Stewart, belonged to one of our most important families and their daughter, Delia, married John Henry Parnell. The Tudors have a Delia in every generation, just as the O'Tooles have a Susannah. Perhaps that's been a sort of bond between the Tudors and my family. Anyway, Mrs. John Henry Parnell, who, of course, is an American, is a great friend of my grandmother's."

"You mean your Grandmother Bradford or Lady Susannah?" Anne asked, still quickly.

"I mean Lady Susannah, who is Granny Glover to me. Is there any reason why they shouldn't be friends?"

"I suppose not. But, under all the circumstances, I'm glad Lady Susannah is in Boston and not in Ireland."

Mr. MacAuliffe coughed slightly and, for the first time in the course of the conversation, seemed upset. Until then, his expression had been one of gravity, suitable for the occasion, but also one of composure. "When the mention of Mr. Donovan's name led, logically but somewhat unexpectedly, to a discussion of the Parnells," he said, "I was planning to refer next to another wire I had received. I could not report on it before this evening, since it reached me only as I was leaving my house to come here and I gather that its contents will be quite surprising." He reached for his briefcase again and drew out a second telegram. "This one comes from Queenstown, dated today, and it reads: 'Arrived after last train for Cloncoole had left Stop Spending night in Cork Stop Letitia with me Stop Please meet one fifteen tomorrow Stop Glover.'"

"Granny Glover!" exclaimed Peter in accents of unmistakable joy. "That's just like her, to pack up and come, without any warning to anyone. Perhaps she wrote Uncle James as soon as she'd suggested I should get in touch with him from London and received a cordial reply even before I did; or perhaps she thought it would be all right for her to come, anyway, taking a chance on her welcome and mine. At all events, it doesn't make much difference now, does it? Of course, it will be a dreadful blow to her that she couldn't get here before he died, but she'll bear up under it and she'll help everyone else to bear up under it, too. Oh, Anne—I mean, Lady O'Toole, you'll like her. You may not think so, but you won't be able to help it."

"But who is Letitia?" inquired Anne and Mr. MacAuliffe simultaneously.

"Granny Glover's colored maid. She always goes everywhere with Granny."

"By colored, do you mean a Negress?"

"Why yes. Before our Civil War, the Bradfords were very anti-slavery and helped any number of slaves to escape through the Underground Railway. Practically all our servants are descendants of those early runaways. The Bradfords belong to that group which puts up signs, 'No Irish need apply.' Of course, this didn't bother Granny Glover at all and I don't think it bothered Mother much, either—after all, they weren't applying for anything. They were there."

Anne had risen before he finished speaking and the bright color was still flooding her cheeks. "Since we are to have another guest so soon,

I must see Mrs. Brennan at once, in order that proper preparations may be made for Lady Susannah and her maid," she said. "As you say, Mr. MacAuliffe, this is a very great surprise. My father, from whom I have already received a cable, is paralyzed and unable to travel; my mother and my elder sister, Cécile, never leave him. Normally, my cousin, Maurice, would of course have represented the family, but, as he is on his way back to France, with the horses he is taking in exchange for Guillaume le Conquérant and Reine Mathilde, he has not yet heard of my bereavement. Obviously, Lady Susannah thinks nothing of crossing the Atlantic. I cannot help wondering, since this is the case, why she did not come to visit us long ago, unless, as her grandson has intimated, she may be doing it on his account." Anne paused for a moment, with her hand on the back of her chair. "We seem to have strayed a long way from what we meant to discuss," she said and now her voice was very hard. "I am afraid I am not equal to returning to that sad subject tonight. Most of the details, as you said, Mr. MacAuliffe, can wait until tomorrow morning, in any event. As far as the others are concerned, I am perfectly willing that you should make decisions without me. I appreciate what I know is your desire to defer to me in everything, but I shall be glad to have you take all responsibility for me. When Father Carroll arrives, I will rejoin you for the rosary. Meanwhile, I should be grateful if you would excuse me."

She swept from the room, her black draperies trailing after her. Mr. MacAuliffe coughed again and replaced the two telegrams in his briefcase. There was a short silence which Peter did not feel qualified to break. Then the solicitor spoke with great kindliness.

"The Countess is exhausted," he said. "I wish she could go to bed and stay there these next two days, but of course she won't. She'll do everything that's expected of her. I think maybe I'll have a word with Dr. Carey. I know him well and he's a very able physician, there's no doubt of that, but naturally it's the Earl who's been chiefly on his mind, not the Countess; and it was the Earl she always thought of, taking as much of the management of the estate into her own hands as she could. He depended on her and he had reason to. But this is a big place and it's been a strain for her. I don't know much about these French parents of hers, who don't feel equal to coming to her in her hour of need, but I'd have been inclined to think more highly of them if they'd made the effort. On the other hand, I'd think better of Lawrence Donovan if he'd stayed in the background just now. But he's young, he can't be expected to use good judgment always. . . . Well, as I said, the Countess has been under considerable strain for a long time and now she's had a bad shock, losing the Earl so suddenly. It's a great way to die—in your sleep. That is, for the one who's doing the dying. But it's a cruel thing for the one who's watched a man go to sleep and left him, thinking all was well, that they'd be chatting together again the next morning—and then to find that, after all, they'll never be speaking to each other again. And, in a few days, that first silence begins to seem a great deal deeper."

He sighed and looked at Peter, with great kindliness but with increased attention. "Perhaps I've talked too much," he said, helping himself to another glass of port. "But this family has meant a great deal to me all my life, as my father was their legal adviser before I succeeded him. And I was pleased when you asked me to tell you what you could do to help. Though, since everything is strange to you, I feel you've got to see the general picture a little more clearly than the Countess would show it to you, for fear of disloyalty in one direction or another, and than Wade would think it proper for a servant to do. . . . Incidentally, I think I hear Wade speaking to Father Carroll now. Shall we go out and meet him? He's another friend on whom you can depend."

They had just reached the threshold when they met Wade and the priest coming toward it from the opposite direction. Father Carroll was a tall, spare man, who carried himself with dignity and whose manner, at first glance, seemed austere rather than tolerant. However, his abundant white hair and his clear healthy color served to mitigate a general impression of asceticism; and Peter was both relieved and surprised to find that his handclasp was warm and firm and his voice cultured and compassionate.

"This is a sad homecoming for you, my son," he said gently. "We will do what we can to help you through the ordeal of the next few days. But, from the very nature of things, the heaviest burden must rest on your shoulders. May I say I am confident that they will be strong enough to carry you through triumphantly?"

"Thank you, Father. I'll do my best."

"I am sure you will. Shall we sit down and talk quietly for a few moments before we begin the rosary? I have an idea that much you will need to know and do will be completely strange to you and that, in order to meet the situation adequately, you should begin by understanding it better. Am I right?"

"Yes, Father. And I'll be very grateful for anything and everything you will tell me."

The priest seated himself beside the solicitor and motioned toward another comfortable nearby chair as a good one for Peter to choose. "I doubt if there has been time for anyone to explain to you why the funeral services will be in the parish church of the village and the burial in the old cemetery on the hill," he said in the same quiet way he had spoken before. "Am I right again?"

"Yes, Father."

"Well, that is quite as I should have expected. I am sure your Irish grandparents would have tried to teach you some Irish history, but you would have had no special incentive, until now, to consider how it affected you personally. That is, you certainly know that, during the Cromwellian invasion, churches and castles were mercilessly attacked and often wantonly destroyed; but I am not sure whether or not it has been brought home to you that the chapel of the O'Tooles was one that suffered so severely it could not be restored. Their castle, though badly damaged, remained more or less habitable, largely thanks to the good offices of kindly neighboring peers who were Protestants and gave it the protection of their name; and when the baronetcy became an earldom, a vault was constructed close to the ruined chapel to serve as a tomb for the descendants of those who had been buried there. The vault has been so used ever since. Is that clear to you now?"

"Yes—at least, I think so."

"Therefore, the burial, three days hence, will be in the vault on the hill. But the Funeral Mass will be at the church in the village, which did not, in fact, could not, come into existence until after the passage of the Catholic Emancipation Act in 1829. Perhaps some day, in some way, it will be possible for the O'Tooles to redeem and restore the chapel. But that day has not yet come. And that is why you must prepare yourself for three different ceremonials in the funeral proceedings."

Father Carroll rose, stretching out his hand to Peter, who, of course, had also risen.

"Possibly this did not seem to you a very appropriate moment for a history lesson," the priest said and, for the first time, Peter saw that he was smiling slightly and that his smile was very pleasant. "But I believe tomorrow and the next day you may be glad we had it."

"I'm glad now," Peter said quite sincerely. MacAuliffe had been right. Here was another friend on whom he could depend.

11

"Granny, you've no idea how glad I am to see you!"

Lady Susannah, an imposing sable figure in a plumed bonnet and a beaded dolman, preceded by Letitia, wearing a neat black uniform and a cap with long streamers, had hardly descended, with the assistance of the porter, from the last step of the railway carriage to the station platform when her grandson flung his arms around her, enveloping her in a hearty hug. She kissed him fondly in return, but disengaged herself with gentle dignity from his embrace.

"Has it been awful? I was afraid it might be. Well, you'll tell me about it as we drive along. I see the pony trap is waiting for us and take it that Letitia and the luggage will follow in another conveyance with Ryan." She greeted the latter pleasantly and added, "I'm relieved to see you still at your post. I rather expected there'd be a new French coachman."

"Indeed no, your ladyship. The Mistress has never made any changes, except to bring over a maid for herself and, occasionally, a French groom as an extra. And it's thankful we all are to have your ladyship with us again at last, in this sad hour."

He eyed Letitia a little doubtfully, but without audible objection, and handed Lady Susannah into the trap. Peter climbed in after her and picked up the reins. As soon as they were beyond earshot of the others, she repeated her earlier question.

"Is it so awful?"

"Well, I know I ought to be facing up to it much better. But of course I didn't expect it to be like this. I mean, I'd looked forward to a very pleasant visit with the old gentleman; and even after I knew he was ill, I didn't think about keening and crepe and all that sort of thing. I'd never seen anyone dead before or had anything to do with a funeral, either. It wasn't so bad while he was still upstairs, in his own bed—in fact, I felt very close to him somehow. And I'll always be glad I saw him, even if it had to be like that—he must have been a wonderful man. However, I knew nothing whatsoever about a lying-in-state, much less about the customary 'suite' of three coffins—satin, lead and oak. Naturally, I've had to be the one to deal with the undertaker, to supervise the transfer of the body from the bedroom to the library. And since then I've stood there, by the open coffin, watching hundreds of people I never saw before filing past. Most of them are tenants on the place, I guess, some so old they can hardly totter along, some just little babies, in their mothers' arms. If the babies weren't asleep, they were crying; and lots of others cried, too. Some of these people stopped and spoke to me and I didn't know what to say to them, even when I understood them—the brogue's still very difficult for me to follow. And every time someone calls me 'my lord,' I get a fresh shock, especially when it's said by someone who's weeping because I'm not my uncle."

Lady Susannah nodded. "It's always hard for the young to make friends with death," she said. "Even when it's part of normal home life, when everyone in the family shares the experience and the older members can shield the younger ones from most of its horrors. I think it's to your credit, rather than otherwise, that you've taken it so hard. I'd have thought you very callous if you hadn't. I wish I could have arrived sooner. Of course, if I'd foreseen all this, I might have prepared you, at least a little. But I never did hear, you see, that James was ill and it wasn't until I got to Queenstown that I knew he was dead. If I'd only started when I first began to dream about the foxes!"

"Dream about the foxes! What foxes?"

"Hasn't anyone told you? Didn't you hear anything strange last night?"

"I've heard all sorts of strange sounds, but I didn't connect any of them with foxes."

"Well, I'll show them to you tonight—that is, I believe I'll be able to. And I'll take over in the library this afternoon, if that's agreeable to my sister-in-law. By the way, how do you like her?"

"Your sister-in-law?" It seemed to Peter that he was continually repeating something that made no sense to him, that he must be slower and even more stupid than he had suspected, although he had always been prone to belittle his own mental powers.

"Didn't you realize that the Dowager Countess O'Toole is my sister-in-law?" Lady Susannah asked rather drily. "Well, it's hard for me to visualize her in that light, so I'm not surprised that you didn't, either.

But she must have made some kind of impression on you and you haven't even mentioned her. There's hardly time to give me a detailed description of her now—I see we've passed the ruins of the old castle, so we must be almost to the house. But give me at least a thumbnail sketch."

"Anne's the most beautiful person I ever saw in my life," Peter said fervently. Then, conscious of his grandmother's searching glance, he added hastily, "I understand from Mr. MacAuliffe, who's looking forward to seeing you, that she's more than fulfilled her every obligation as chatelaine here—in fact, he admires her very much and so, obviously, do all the servants. I gather that Uncle James had unbounded confidence in her, that she relieved him, in a good many ways, of matters that would have been burdensome to him. And, of course, he must have loved her very much."

"I see," said Lady Susannah, still drily. "But what do *you* think of her? I mean, besides appreciating these extraordinary good looks of hers?"

"Granny, I've been here less than twenty-four hours. You wouldn't expect me to learn much about her in that length of time, would you? Naturally, she must be very heavy hearted just now, and Mr. MacAuliffe thinks she's been under a long strain and that she's completely exhausted. Even so, she's more than equal to the requirements of the situation. I'm sure you'll think so yourself. . . . And, incidentally," he added, more boldly than he had ever done in speaking to his grandmother before, "if there was a little antagonism in your estimate of her, as I rather gathered from the way you asked about French servants and referred to her as your sister-in-law, I'd appreciate it very much if you didn't show it when you're talking to anyone but me about her and when you're speaking directly to her. I realize there must have been something about the marriage of which you and Mother didn't approve or there wouldn't have been this long estrangement."

"It was primarily your father who didn't approve. Your uncle wrote us briefly from Paris, saying he was about to marry a young French girl, whose name he didn't mention, and your father exploded. He said that if James had become engaged to an aging Irish or English lady of rank, no one could have said a word of objection—it was natural enough that he should want companionship in his old age; but, according to your father, a cheap little hussy, who was grasping at his title and money, was the only kind of a girl who would marry a man old enough to be her grandfather. He convinced your mother that he was right and by the time they found out that he wasn't, that James was marrying into a proud old Norman family, the damage was done. No prompt and cordial reply had been sent to his letter and that seemed to James unforgivable."

"But did Father convince you?"

"Not wholly. So what I did was unforgivable, too. Instead of writing independently, I let the matter slide. The prospect of the marriage was disappointing to me, but I couldn't believe it was disgraceful. Your uncle never did anything disgraceful in his life, or anything stupid, either. I felt sure he wouldn't marry a hussy, because he'd have known that she would not only be a source of embarrassment to him, but a nuisance. However, he might understandably marry a well-born young girl, and if we'd only received one of the usual elaborate engraved invitations that the French send out in the names of both contracting parties, complete with all kinds of titles and decorations, we'd have known that was exactly what he did do. Instead, we received only a brief announcement, mailed after the marriage, according to custom if the ceremony has been private: *Le Comte de Briare, Chevalier de la Légion d'honneur, et la Comtesse de Briare ont l'honneur de vous faire part du mariage de Mademoiselle Marianne de Briare, leur fille, avec le Comte de Cloneen. La messe de mariage a été célébrée dans la plus stricte intimité*, et cetera. I forget the name of the chapel and the officiating *abbé*. I suppose the wedding had to be as quiet as possible—the age of the groom certainly didn't lend itself very well to a big showy ceremony! And though I don't know much about the De Briares' circumstances, many of those old Norman families are rather hard up, which might well be one of the reasons Anne's parents sanctioned the marriage. James not only would have taken her without a dowry, but he would have given her a handsome settlement, and if the De Briares have a stock farm, as they probably do—Normandy is dotted with them —that would account for the original association with the family. They would have been assured of a steady income from their horses he bought every year. Many a young girl has been importuned to marry an old man who could offer less and could also be a horrible old roué into the bargain, instead of the soul of rectitude like James."

In two or three shrewd sentences Lady Susannah had cleared up the mystery to which Peter had found no previous solution. In her "autobiographical details," Anne had evaded his impassioned exclamation, "You haven't told me how you happened to marry a man old enough to be your grandfather!" and he had never dared ask her a second time. Now that he understood, he was sick at heart.

"Even when we got this announcement, the bride's Christian name was given as Marianne," Lady Susannah went on calmly, "and 'le Comte' didn't immediately ring a bell for 'the Earl,' either. Besides, this announcement was sent to Beacon Street when none of us was in Boston. We were all in Italy for the summer and it was weeks before the information caught up with us. Though I did write then, it wasn't much of a letter and your uncle didn't answer it. Not that I blame him. He had a reason for doing what he did."

"Do you know what the reason was?"

"Of course, I do. He desperately wanted an heir. It wasn't just a personal yearning, either. He found it hard to face the fact that, if he didn't have one, the direct line of his branch of the O'Tooles would end with him. An aging lady of rank wasn't the answer to his need—aging ladies, noble or otherwise, don't conceive children. But young girls generally do, granted the opportunity. Anne must have known she was expected to produce an heir, preferably nine months after marriage, so that there'd be no doubt of her fertility, but certainly within a year. Her mother would have talked all that over with her beforehand, in the practical French way, making her see this to be her duty to her husband, just as the marriage itself was her duty to her parents. No doubt she's disappointed because she didn't fulfill the second obligation—not as disappointed as my poor brother, naturally, but perhaps as disappointed as I was over the marriage."

"But why should you—"

"Because I wanted the title for you. You know very well you've always been my white-headed boy. And now you've got it. I'm very happy about that. But I'm not happy because I didn't defy your father and welcome Anne into the family or at least give her the benefit of the doubt. I realize now how much lost ground has got to be retrieved and what's more, I'm very much ashamed because I didn't take a firm stand, supporting my brother, but I'll try to make up for it now."

They were already turning into the graveled area that marked the end of the drive and, glad as he still was to see his grandmother, Peter was thankful that there was no more time for conversation just then. It had been something of a shock to learn that Lady Susannah, for whom his admiration and affection had always been unbounded, had been remiss in anything and he did not feel that her partiality for him justified her in countenancing the estrangement. However, as the day wore on, his first relief in her presence increased. He could dimly remember that, when he was a little boy, she had been very merry and her hair had been bright red and irrepressibly curly, which somehow seemed to give it special harmony with her merriment. It had become snow white, but it was still curly and now that the plumed bonnet had been discarded, the ringlets were freed to form a frame for her face, which was less joyous than when she was younger, but still very pleasing. Her skin was smooth and fresh, her eyes bright and her teeth, generously revealed when she smiled, white and even. The removal of the dolman disclosed a majestic figure, but her portliness was actually an asset rather than a liability. Unquestionably, her dressmaker, on whom she never economized, deserved some of the credit for this, since everything Lady Susannah wore was made of the best possible material, cut and fitted with care. But all this would not have helped if she had not herself possessed a sense of style and great *joie de vivre*. Peter, to whom her looks had always represented everything that a grandmother's could and should be, now became equally proud of her self-possession. She did not even suggest that she would like to go to her own room to rest a little before a late luncheon, much less that she would prefer to have this in privacy; she accepted without question the fact that she was expected to lunch with Peter and Anne in the dining room, directly after her "sister-in-law" had received her in the small formal parlor, hung with handmade Chinese wallpaper and furnished with Chinese Chippendale, at the left of the square entrance hall. Her response to Anne's correct but guarded greeting left nothing to be desired; it was tinged with just enough cordiality to show that though they had long been strangers to each other, the causes for this estrangement would be tactfully left unmentioned and, in any case, it was now at an end. Through lunch she talked easily about her voyage and expressed her pleased recognition of Wade, of the crested china and of the view from the windows; she hoped Letitia would fit into the servants' hall without making trouble for anyone—personally, she had always found this particular maid most adaptable. When coffee was served in the drawing room afterward, Lady Susannah commented on the Georgian silver and the family portraits with the same nostalgic appreciation she had shown in the dining room and complimented Anne on the replacement of the dark old upholstery by some that was, at one and the same time, brighter and more elegant—that faded old velvet had already been shabby when she was a girl! Then, as if it were perfectly natural to shift from one such subject to quite another, she said she would like to go to the library. She understood that there had been a break in visiting hours during the family luncheon and, before the doors were open to the public again, she wanted to be alone with her brother. No, she would prefer that neither Peter nor Anne should come with her; she would signal to Wade when her private vigil was over and then she would remain where she was until the doors were closed for the night. At that time she hoped Peter would join her briefly on the terrace. It would do them both good to have a breath of air and she would enjoy the gloaming, which she had missed so much throughout her years of exile.

It was nearly dark before Peter was free, for a number of matters arose to which it seemed he should give his attention. There was, for instance, the question of immediate disbursements: in the form of gratuities for the women who had tended the body immediately after death, the undertaker's men who performed the coffining, the sexton at the church and later the men who would assist at the vault; each of these functionaries would expect a gold sovereign for his services as soon as these had been completed. Furthermore, Mr. O'Grady wished Peter to approve the lid for the coffin, on which an earl's coronet and a gilt shield formed part of the mounting and the gilded brass bore the inscription:

JAMES ARTHUR FREDERICK O'TOOLE

SEVENTH EARL OF CLONEEN

BORN MAY 2, 1808—DIED JULY 1, 1882

Mr. O'Grady felt it would also be well to discuss the details of the procession from the house to the church in order that there might be no confusion later. Because of the treble coffin's enormous weight, it would be necessary that this should be conveyed in a hearse, even though the distance was short. Peter would follow alone in the first coach, the Dowager Countess and Lady Susannah together in the second. At the gates, the family and estate servants would be joined by the local people, thus swelling the size of the procession. The shutters and blinds of all the houses along the way would be closed and, though there would be no singing or keening, Peter must be prepared for a low murmur of conversation about his uncle and himself as the coaches passed by.

When Peter had signfied his understanding and acceptance of all this, he found that Father Carroll also wanted to talk to him about arrangements at the church. Matins and Lauds from the Office of the Dead would be chanted before the Solemn Requiem. The Bishop had expressed a wish to preside at this and would also personally impart the

Solemn Absolution before the funeral procession left the church for the cemetery. There would be a choir of priests from the surrounding parishes. Lastly, Father Carroll was afraid no one had told Peter that he must be the one to enter the family vault with certain retainers: first, to make sure it was in order to receive the new coffin, next to supervise the placement of this and lastly, to lock the door after the obsequies were over.

Peter had gone very white before Father Carroll had finished talking to him and hoped that his expression did not betray his involuntary shuddering. It probably would escape the attention of the undertaker and the priest who, though properly grave, did not seem to shrink from the discussion of these subjects which were, after all, quite natural, as far as they were concerned. But Lady Susannah would notice at once that he was upset; and though she had been kind enough to say— and Peter believed had truly meant—that she felt his sensitivity did him credit, he could not help being ashamed of it as an evidence of unmanly weakness. However, it would cheer him to be with her again and to find out what she had meant, when she talked about dreaming of the foxes and hoping to show them to him. He was not sure just where he should look for her, so he went to ask Wade and the butler, instead of instantly directing him to her, told him that one of the callers that afternoon, whom the Mistress had not felt she could receive privately, was waiting in the Chinese parlor with the hope that his lordship would do so.

"Who is this insistent caller?" Peter inquired a trifle brusquely.

"It's Mr. Lawrence Donovan, your lordship. He's a family friend."

"But I gathered from what Mr. MacAuliffe said and from the fact that the Countess did not receive him today herself that he isn't an intimate friend."

Wade appeared to hesitate. "Perhaps not, my lord. But if your lordship would consent to see him, I believe it would be much appreciated, both by the Mistress and by Mr. MacAuliffe."

"In that case, of course I'll see him. Please find Lady Susannah and explain to her that I've been unavoidably detained, but that I'll be with her as soon as possible."

Mr. Donovan, dressed in deep black, was standing by the west window when Peter entered the Chinese parlor. *I'd like to know where on earth,* he said to himself for the twentieth time, *all these people manage to get mourning garments at practically a moment's notice. They must keep a supply on hand all the time or begin preparing for the worst whenever anyone has a bad cold or a digestive upset.* As the caller turned to greet his host, Peter saw that he was strikingly handsome in what the newcomer considered "the typical Irish way." He had thick wavy black hair, worn longer than an American would have done; blue eyes brighter and at the same time darker than an Englishman's or a German's; a strong chin, full red lips and a straight nose; the fresh color that seemed the natural result of excellent health and a great deal of outdoor life in a cool, rainy climate; and the good build that bespoke both a great deal of exercise and corresponding moderation of eating and drinking. Taken all in all, he was such an arresting and attractive figure that Peter could not understand why he did not find him more appealing.

"It's very good of you to see me, sir," he said with evident sincerity. "I wouldn't have imposed on you today, if I hadn't felt it was really necessary. Perhaps you know that Anne brought over two new horses from Normandy a short time ago; she'd already entered them for the Dublin Horse Show. The plan was that I was to ride one and she was to ride the other. Now, of course, she won't be able to participate, and the schedule's made up so far ahead it's necessary for me to know what she wants done."

"You mean it's necessary to know immediately—even before the funeral?"

"Well, it would be a great help. You see, there are several alternatives. She might withdraw them altogether, which would be a terrific disappointment to the Committee, because they're almost sure to be prize winners. Or she might choose a substitute rider for herself. Or she might let me ride both of them, which naturally I'd be very proud to do."

"Under the circumstances, I can understand that you are eager to know her decision." It was not hard for Peter to gather that Donovan had hoped and, perhaps, had expected to hear this direct from her and that the fact she had not received him privately was rankling a little. This might also well have something to do with his insistence. And, as far as rankling was concerned—why, Donovan had referred to "Anne" as if it were natural for him to do so! "But surely the Committee doesn't expect the Countess to make her decision just now. She isn't thinking of her horses," Peter continued, slightly stressing the word "Countess."

Donovan shook his head. "I wouldn't be so sure of that," he said with emphasis. And, as he spoke, Peter had a feeling that the Irishman could be right. After all, she had spoken about them to him, Peter, just the day before and he had been struck by the change in her voice and manner when she did so. It had been as if she were able to dismiss everything else from her mind. "I take it you haven't been out to the stables yet," Donovan went on.

"Hardly." The word had an implication of discourtesy, but Peter could not help it. "After all, I've been here only twenty-four hours and there's been a good deal else to do."

"I appreciate that. If you like, I'd be very glad to act as your deputy —until you've more leisure. Farrell and I have seen a good bit of each other and we're on excellent terms."

"Farrell?"

"Andy Farrell, the head groom." If there had been an implication of discourtesy in Peter's "Hardly," there was an implication of tried patience in Donovan's "the head groom." "Ned Flynn and Art Nolan are the stableboys for the pleasure horses," he added. "Of course, the stud has its own stables and its own staff and a very competent studmaster, Bart Riordan. Hasn't he reported to you yet?"

"No, not yet, but I think that shows consideration, rather than discourtesy, don't you? He must realize there were a good many other people I needed to see first."

Again Peter realized that he himself was guilty of discourtesy, but his annoyance with Donovan was increased by his puzzlement, for which the visitor was not to blame. Presumably, "pleasure horses" was the Irish term for saddle and carriage horses and, obviously, the stables for these and the stables for the stud were two entirely separate establishments —a fact of which he had not been aware before. He had an appalling number of things to learn all at once and was reluctant to let his visitor guess how many.

"It was very kind of you to suggest taking over in the stables, but I think I can manage to get out to them tomorrow. I suppose the sooner I learn the ropes myself, the better. Now that my grandmother's come, she's relieving me part of the time in the library . . . and, incidentally, she's waiting for me now and has been for some time. So, if you'll excuse me—"

It was true that Lady Susannah had been waiting for him some time, but he knew he shouldn't have mentioned it in that way. After all, Donovan was, apparently, a favored friend, even if Anne had not been willing to receive him that afternoon. Hastily, Peter strove to make amends. "I understand you're an associate of Mr. Parnell's. My family and his—I mean on the American side in both cases—have been friends for generations. I'd like very much to meet him."

"You mean personally or politically?"

"I meant personally. I'm still very confused about the political situation in Ireland. I couldn't commit myself to anything until I understand it better."

"That's natural. But we'd be very glad to help you do that. Socially, Mr. Parnell leads a rather secluded life. However, if the Bradfords are friends of the Tudors, I'll see about arranging a meeting. Meanwhile, let me know if you change your mind about having me act as your deputy. I'll be coming to the funeral, of course, and I'll probably drop in for a few minutes tomorrow, too. Anne may feel equal to seeing me by then and, if she should, I can learn her decision about the horses from her. Do forgive me for detaining you so long. My respects to Lady Susannah."

Lady Susannah was on the terrace overlooking the flower garden when Peter finally went to find her, and the sound which he had not been able to distinguish from other sounds the night before was easy enough to identify now: a strange, muffled whine, curiously akin to keening, though it did not seem like the lament of a human being, but rather the cry of some stricken animal.

"Look!" Lady Susannah said, linking one arm in Peter's and raising the other to point into the distance. "Over by the border of the woods. Can't you see them?"

At first, he could see nothing. Then, as he succeeded in focusing his gaze on the place toward which she had pointed, he was aware of golden eyes glowing through the gathering darkness and next of vague, furry forms, some still, some gliding through the bracken. Mostly these creatures stood and moved in pairs, but in one place four or five were crouching together and in another there was a lone watcher. Except for their chorus, the place was very still; except for their presence, it was deserted.

"What has happened? Why aren't they afraid to come here?" Peter asked, increasingly conscious of something eerie in the atmosphere.

"This has been going on for centuries. James Michael Patrick O'Toole, the first Earl of Cloneen, spared a cornered fox when he saw it was a vixen, trying to protect her cubs. He ordered the hounds called off. Ever since then, the Cloneen foxes have come to keep watch as the current Earl lies dying. They gather under the windows of his death

98

chamber and whine all night. Then, when morning comes, they walk among the poultry without touching it and cause no fear as they do so. They do that all day and the next night they come to keep watch again. They do not go back to their dens until after the funeral. So you can see them again tomorrow, if you want to. You do, don't you? It's such a lovely sight. If you dwell on it, it will help you to forget some of the other things you'd rather not remember."

They sat together for some time, watching the foxes. Then, arm in arm, they walked slowly across the terrace. Neither was inclined to break in on the wail of the foxes which followed them as they went. But, when they were almost to the door, Peter spoke without preamble about something that had no connection with what they had seen.

"Lawrence Donovan is in love with Anne!" he said vehemently. "For God's sake, help me to keep him away from here!"

12

It was all over at last.

The pilgrimage to the old cemetery on the hill beyond the village, when Peter was accompanied by some of the estate workers, to open the family vault and make it ready to receive the Earl's coffin the next day, at which time it would be placed amid not only those of the heir's immediate forebears, but many of his remote ancestors.

The enclosure of the satin coffin in the coffins of lead and oak and the lowering of the lid, mounted by an earl's coronet and a shield, at the end of the lying-in-state.

The transfer of the coffin to the parish church that same evening, when the mourners' coaches and the workers on the estate escorted the coffin to the gates, where the rest of the villagers joined the procession.

The reception of the coffin by Father Carroll, dressed in a black cope and stole, and the recitation of the appropriate prayers.

The night-long vigil by the heir in the church, shadowy despite its candlelight, and shrouded in velvet draperies as black as the pall on the coffin. The consciousness of the cloistered nuns behind the grille which separated the apse from the rest of the church and therefore made them invisible, but who were keeping their vigil, too.

The full Office of the Dead, chanted by most of the priests of the diocese, followed by the Solemn Requiem Mass, with the Bishop presiding and, afterward, the Solemn Absolution pronounced by His Excellency.

The touching assemblage of tenants and villagers on the green during the ceremonies in the church, since this was barely large enough to accommodate the clergy, the mourners and the invited guests, whose coaches and mounts surrounded the green: the First Secretary of the Viceroy; several peers, among them Lord Slattery of Shanapark; four

Members of Parliament, including Charles Stewart Parnell and A. M. Sullivan; Major Laird-Holmes, the Commanding Officer of the military barracks at Cloncoole, whose uniform stood out amid the encircling black; the District Commissioners of the Constabulary; the Justices of the Peace from the district; Sir Jonathan Dwyer, the Master of the local hunt, and other prominent personages of the vicinity.

The second procession, headed at first by Father Carroll, who led the pallbearers with their burden from the church and then left, accompanied by some of the villagers and tenants, to take the old lane, which provided a short cut to the graveyard on the hill, in order to be at the gate to meet the coffin.

The two-minute pause of the main cortege at the gates of the estate in respect to the memory of the dead; the progress of this cortege along the old road to the graveyard, with the villagers reciting the rosary as they advanced.

The solemn reception at the gate of the graveyard and the final stage of the procession past the ruins of the old church to the vault while Father Carroll intoned the *Dies Irae*.

The final absolution and solemn ritual as Peter came out of the vault and locked it after him and then the recital of the rosary by the entire assembly before it dispersed and Peter found himself again helping his grandmother and Anne into the coach which they were to share on the return to the house.

Anne could not have seemed more remote to him if they had been continents apart, even when they had been sitting side by side in the family pew. Throughout all the services and processions which had taken place in the last eighteen hours, she had been dressed so heavily in black that he could not see even the outline of her face and figure. In front, a crepe veil, attached to her bonnet, fell in folds to her waist; at the back, a second crepe veil fell almost to her feet and its amplitude permitted her to wrap it around her like a cloak. Thus shrouded, she did not speak at all and moved only as she was directed. When they reached the house, she went up the steps into the square hall and acknowledged Wade's respectful greeting with a murmured word of thanks. Then, still silent, still intangible, she went down the long hall and up the long flight of stairs to her own room.

Lady Susannah, who had stopped at the open door of the Chinese parlor, now entered it and sat down, removing her wraps and also her veil which, to Peter's relief, had been nowhere nearly as heavy and all-enveloping as those which Anne was still wearing when she left them.

"Come in," his grandmother called to Peter, who stood hesitating on the threshold, uncertain what to do next. Then, as if guessing how deeply he had been affected by Anne's self-immurement, she added, "Don't let all this crepe depress you too much; it's part of the proper picture at times like this, as far as both Celts and Latins are concerned. Anne would be criticized for not showing proper respect to the dead unless she swathed herself like that. So you might as well get used to it. It's to be hoped she'll wear white in her own rooms and get a little air and exercise on her own terrace and grounds, bareheaded; but she won't appear downstairs except in a black dress or go off the estate without her veils for at least a year."

"It's all very well for you to tell me not to let all this crepe depress me, but I think it's barbarous. And as for dressing like that a whole year—"

"Peter, you're not a carefree young American any longer. You're an Irish earl. Try to act like one, even if you don't feel like one. 'Assume a virtue if you have it not.'"

"You don't call all these hideous practices a virtue, do you?"

"I was quoting Shakespeare, my dear boy. Your generation's ignorance of the classics appalls me. I hoped you'd find the quotation applicable, even if not strictly suitable."

"I recognized the quotation all right. You may have forgotten that Father would have seen to it that I knew enough about the classics to do that, even if Harvard hadn't. But I'm not in the mood for similes— or much of anything else. It isn't just the crepe that got me down, though that's bad enough. It's that grim procession past a wonderful old church that's been allowed to go to rack and ruin instead of being beautifully preserved. It's the words of that dreadful *Dies Irae*—'Day of wrath, day of wrath! Heaven and earth in ashes burning.' What sort of promise for resurrection is there in that? And then, to make matters worse, there's nothing to give you a feeling of immortality in that gruesome vault! All those coffins piled on top of each other, row after row! It wouldn't be so bad if you didn't have to *see* them in their various stages of disintegration. When you go into a vault with names inscribed on the smooth stone walls, you know that coffins are behind those slabs. But you also know that every one of them has been neatly placed in an indestructible receptacle, built on purpose to hold it and nothing else, not shoved hit or miss over another! What is the use of a mounting with an earl's coronet and a gilt shield and a brass inscription if it's going to be covered by another coffin in a few years' time, unless it slides off into space? It won't be so long before my uncle's is covered by mine and then by my son's, if I have one and, if not, by some distant relative's and, presently, the ones on top will begin to topple over and—"

"Peter, I can understand that all this has been a shock to you. But—"

"A shock! It's been worse than that. It's made me feel that I can't take it, that I've got to get away from here. You know those men Father is always talking about, who've gone right on living in Philadelphia or Chicago or wherever it is, being good average American citizens? Well, that's what I'd better do, if I'm ever to have a good night's sleep again. I keep dreaming about that murder at Rathmullan and all it represents. Now I'll probably dream about the vault and all that represents, too."

"I know you've had a series of shocks, but you'll be strong enough and sensible enough to see them in their proper perspective to life in general as soon as you get your bearings. There's not the slightest resemblance between the standards of the Hartleys and the standards of the O'Tooles; and when you think what that gruesome vault, as you call it, represents, you'll find it the reminder of a great tradition you're carrying on."

"I don't know what you mean."

"I mean you have succeeded a very wonderful man and many other wonderful men who are entombed there. None of them were absentee landlords and none of their tenants ever went hungry, even in famine years. The O'Tooles have always managed to take care of their own. What's more, they have always been faithful to their church and their king, even when nearly everything they owned was confiscated and their very lives were in danger because of their loyalty. There were mighty few Irish Catholic peers who managed to stand up against Cromwell and his murderous hordes, but James Michael Patrick O'Toole was one of them. Every one of his descendants has shown the same kind of spirit that made a grateful king raise his rank from a barony to an earldom after the restoration of the monarchy. Your great-great-grandfather and your great-grandfather both worked with Daniel O'Connell when he founded the Catholic Association that led the agitation for Catholic emancipation, and your great-grandfather and my brother James—young as he was—helped Grattan to bring about the Emancipation Act. In my small way, I've carried on the tradition myself. I've battled Boston Brahmins for years, so that your mother and you and your sisters shouldn't be excluded from their narrow bigoted circles as 'Irish Catholics.' The poor ignorant creatures that wanted to keep you out of their social circles imagined that was a term of contempt. It's one of the proudest titles and one of the rarest that you can give a peer of the realm."

"Granny, when you talk to me like this, I do realize I've a lot to live up to. But in that vault—"

"Lawrence O'Toole was Archbishop of Dublin in the twelfth century and he's been acknowledged as Ireland's greatest churchman and hailed as a saint," Lady Susannah rushed on, bypassing the vault. "I believe that your great-great-grandfather, Carew O'Toole, would have gone just as high in the Church if he hadn't been obliged to leave the seminary when his twin, Cullen, was killed in a hunting accident, and take over his brother's duties as heir. He was a dedicated soul if there ever was one and was sadly torn between his sympathy for Robert Emmet, the brilliant leader of United Irishmen, and his horror over the murder of the Viceroy Kilwarden by Emmet's men. I am sure he spent many hours on his knees, praying for the souls of both; and when Emmet's sweetheart, Sarah Curran, was bereft, because he paid with his life for his last visit to her, Carew was one of the first who sought to comfort her and to recognize Emmet publicly as the great hero of Irish patriots."

"I'd like very much to hear more about that love story, Granny."

"And so you shall, but not now, for there isn't time to do it justice before you're needed elsewhere. But at least I hope I've made you understand that the O'Tooles are an integral part of Ireland—a big part. And it's not just as landowners and Catholics they've been a great force. They've served in the Irish Parliament and, after the Union, in the London Parliament. They haven't confined their efforts to seeing that their own tenants were humanely treated; they've sponsored and furthered the Land Acts that are designed to make the Irish people, as a whole, better off. The second Earl, Burke Andrew, was one of the 'Wild Geese' that made up the Irish Brigade and fought under the Earl of Lucan at the Battle of the Boyne; and the spirit of all these men has survived. It's only their bodies that lie in that vault. I'm counting on you to ensure the survival of that spirit still further, in every possible way." She turned and glanced out of the window. "At this moment, all you have to do is to receive the Bishop. I can see him getting out of his coach, so he'll be here almost immediately. But he won't stay long. He'll probably take advantage of his presence in the village to discuss parochial matters with Father Carroll."

"He won't be staying for luncheon?"

"No. He'll offer the proper condolences and you'll respond to them. Then he'll be off to the parochial house. Of course, it would be gracious of you to say that you're sorry he can't remain and that you hope some other time . . . but it looks very much as if you and I would have luncheon by ourselves."

"Nothing would suit me better."

"You didn't hope that Anne would be with us?"

"She seems to want to be alone as much as she can. I'd be the last to insist that she shouldn't follow her own inclination as far as all this dismal protocol will allow."

In his turn, he glanced out of the window. The Bishop had just reached the bottom step. Peter hastened to the hall and when Wade opened the door for his lordship his host was waiting for him.

Mr. MacAuliffe had timed his return to the house tactfully. Lady Susannah and Peter had eaten their luncheon with no sense of intrusion or haste when his arrival was announced, coupled with the statement that he would be at their disposition and that of the Countess in the library when they were ready to see him. Somewhat to their surprise, they found that Anne had preceded them and was already ensconced in a large chair beside Mr. MacAuliffe, facing the ones which Peter and Lady Susannah would normally take. His first sensation in looking at her was one of relief in seeing her unveiled at last and seemingly less remote, but his relief was short-lived. Her pallor was alarming and, though her expression was still one of self-control, he instinctively felt that she was very near the breaking point. However, if Mr. MacAuliffe had the same impression, nothing in his manner suggested it.

"Since it is not necessary that anyone else should be present while I read the will," he said cheerfully, picking up the document which lay before him on the desk, "I'll begin at once. In the name of God, Amen," Mr. MacAuliffe began and paused to cross himself. Instantly, all his hearers did the same.

"I, JAMES ARTHUR FREDERICK O'TOOLE, *Earl of Cloneen, of Cloncoole,*" the solicitor continued, "*being of sound mind, memory and understanding, do hereby make this my last Will and Testament and I hereby revoke all previous Wills and Testamentary dispositions at any time heretofore made by me. I APPOINT my family Solicitor George MacAuliffe and my family physician Dr. Daniel Carey Executors and*

Trustees for this my Will. I DIRECT *that my funeral be without scarves or hat bands."*

Peter opened his mouth to ask a question and closed it again, deciding this was not the time for queries. He would find out about scarves and hat bands later.

*"*I DIRECT *my said Executors to pay all my just debts, funeral and testamentary expenses,"* Mr. MacAuliffe went on, *"and after payment thereof* I DIRECT *as follows:*

*"*I GIVE, DEVISE AND BEQUEATH *to my beloved wife, née Anne de Briare, all funds of which I may die possessed and leave to her discretion the sums which shall be given out of these funds to the faithful retainers, both in the house itself and on the lands at large, as I have complete confidence in her generosity, judgment and discretion."*

Anne looked across at Peter, meeting his gaze directly, and he saw that, for the first time, there were tears in her eyes. It was as if she were saying to him, "My husband had complete confidence in me and I betrayed it when I welcomed you to my bed. I shall never forgive myself, never, never, never!"

"I further give, devise and bequeath to my wife all jewellery and household equipment, including silver, crystal, porcelain, paintings and furniture purchased by me during my lifetime and which were not acquired by me as part of my inheritance," Mr. MacAuliffe droned on placidly. He had not raised his head from the script and was unaware of Anne's tears, which had now overflowed from her eyes and were running down her cheeks, as she continued her mute accusation of Peter. "He trusted me and he loved me. He left me everything it was in his power to give me. It was only the part of his inheritance which he couldn't control that he left to you!"

"In the event of my dying without issue, I give, devise and bequeath estates which would pass by inheritance to such issue to my great-nephew Peter Glover Bradford, son of Susannah and Edward Bradford of Boston, Mass., U.S.A., and grandson of my sister Susannah, the widow of the late Sir Michael Glover, absolutely," the solicitor read on. *"It is my wish that my wife shall be permitted to use the dower house for her life or for so long as she shall remain unmarried and that the said Peter Glover Bradford shall maintain this establishment for*

her at his expense. It is also my wish that a carriage and pair be kept at her disposal without cost to her and that she be permitted to choose among the saddle horses any two she may prefer for her own use, in addition to those she has imported or may import from her family haras in Normandy. Since she is fully capable of advising and directing the operation of the stables and since it gives her pleasure to do so, it is my wish that she shall continue and that any one employed in whatever capacity, whether as studmaster, trainer, head groom or stable-boy, be directly responsible to her or her personal representative. All monies received from the sale of horses, service of stallions or prizes at races in excess of expenses are to be added to the income she receives from other sources I have provided."

Anne had taken a black-bordered handkerchief from her pocket and dried her eyes and cheeks. "I don't suppose you'll begrudge me the dower house and my horses," her look said now. It was no longer sorrowful; it was scornful. Peter wished that she would speak, so that he could answer her. But it was, he knew, just as well that she should not; there would have been anger, coupled with his remorse, if he had replied.

"All the rest, residue and remainder of my property I give, devise and bequeath to my beloved wife absolutely," Mr. MacAuliffe was saying.

"In the witness whereof I, the said James Arthur Frederick O'Toole, Earl of Cloneen, have hereunto set my title of honour and affixed my seal the day and year first herein written.

1st May, 1882

"Signed, published and declared by the said Testator as and for his last Will and Testament in the presence of us both present at the same time who in his presence at his request and in the presence of each other have hereunto signed our names as witnesses.

JAMES ARTHUR FREDERICK O'TOOLE,
EARL OF CLONEEN"

"NEAL CARROLL"
"LIAM WADE"

As he spoke the butler's name, Mr. MacAuliffe raised his head, indicating the completion of his task. At the same moment, Lady Susannah rose and, crossing the narrow space which divided her from Anne, put her arm around the girl's shoulder.

"A wonderful will," she said. "Very few widows are privileged to listen to such an eloquent testimonial of their husbands' high regard. You must be very proud, Anne."

13

The next morning Anne began her preparations to leave for the dower house.

It had never been completely closed, as an elderly couple, Maggie and Rory Dunn, past the stage for active service at the mansion, had been retained as caretakers and they had felt great pride in keeping it well aired and well cleaned and were even more proud because the Mistress had said she was sure, with the help of her personal maid, Solange, they would be able to do everything for her that she required; she intended to live very simply and, in any case, there would of course be no entertaining until after her period of mourning was over. Thus reassured, the Dunns were zealous in anticipating her every wish and, if it had not been for her decision to take with her the French furniture which had made her private sitting room so attractive and similar equipment in the guest rooms and drawing room, she could have moved immediately; the porcelain, crystal and silver which had been part of her dowry and the corresponding items left her by the Earl's will could have been packed and transferred gradually. As it was, a little time was needed for the removal and rearrangement of the furnishings, ornaments and paintings destined for the dower house and the removal of such paraphernalia to the attic. Moreover, Anne was scrupulous about finding replacements in kind for everything she took away. When Lady Susannah and Peter sat down to dinner, the night of Anne's final transfer, they did not face a bare sideboard or bare walls. Georgian silver, in chastely classic designs, gleamed as brightly as its more elaborate French counterparts had done, and O'Toole ancestors, long forgotten, were hung in the place of some very beautiful Fragonards. Nevertheless, Peter's first remark after taking his seat was to the effect that the room seemed terribly bare and empty.

"Why, I think Anne's done a remarkably good job," Lady Susannah said, quickly rising to her sister-in-law's defense.

"A very conscientious one—almost too conscientious, isn't it? Almost as if she were determined we'd never be able to say we had a single teaspoon less than before."

"You're very unfair to her, Peter."

"I don't mean to be. As a matter of fact, when I spoke of emptiness, I wasn't thinking just of portraits and silver and things like that. I was thinking of Anne herself. She has a very pronounced personality, even if it is obscured by all those dreadful black clothes."

"Yes, she has. We'll miss her. But she had a right to leave and to take her own belongings with her and that was what she wanted to do."

"Obviously, and as rapidly as possible. Now that she's done it, I suppose you and I can start planning what we'd like to do. Personally, I'd like to leave as soon as you do. As you know, I wasn't particularly enthusiastic about coming to Ireland in the first place, but—"

"But, my dear boy, I haven't the slightest intention of leaving until autumn! After all, Sue's very suitably settled now and Elizabeth and Janet won't be back in Boston before October. That'll be time enough for me to start worrying about them again. I'm very happy in my old home."

It was on the tip of Peter's tongue to say he did not feel so sure there was nothing to worry about, as far as Janet was concerned, but decided there was no use in dragging a Polish prince into the picture at the moment. It was sufficiently involved without him.

"Well, as I started to say, I wasn't particularly enthusiastic about coming to Ireland in the first place, except that I have always thought I'd like to see the place where Grandfather began to develop home weaving into a big industry. You know that, and now that I'm here with no plans for going anywhere else, I might as well see more of the country. What I'd really like would be to travel around in one of those gaudy painted wagons the tinkers use and camp out by the roadside at night the way they do. Perhaps I could join up with one of those roving families. That really would be a new experience. But I suppose—"

"My dear boy! The heir to an earldom traveling around like a tinker, even joining up with them!"

"Granny, you taught me it is very rude to interrupt, but that's what you've done twice within the last few minutes. I started to say, I supposed that wouldn't be considered quite the thing for me to do."

"The thing for you to do is to take a groom, who could double as a valet, and travel in a nice trap, planning your itinerary so that you could visit our friends at their country places along the way."

"You know as well as I do that I wouldn't know what to do with a groom who could double as a valet! I nearly fell through the floor the first night I was here because a nice, red-haired boy named Tim wanted to unpack for me. And if, by country places, you mean a series of Irish castles, I think we'd better forget about that, too. Since regretfully dismissing the tinkers from my mind, I had thought of asking Alec McKeever to go with me. He ought to be interested in the background of the weaving industry, too, since he's going to be the one to carry it on. And I don't see how I could have a better guide to Donegal. My idea was to put up at country inns wherever we happened to be at nightfall. Some of the places I haven't seen have lovely-sounding names and it might be fun to find out if they live up to them: Glencolumbkille, Rosapenna, Kilmacrennan, Arranmore, Cardonagh. And, of course, I want to get acquainted with 'Dublin's fair city, Where the girls are so pretty.' But naturally I won't desert you if you want to stay here," Peter went on. His grandmother again interrupted him.

"It isn't a case of deserting me," Lady Susannah said rather sharply. "It's a case of taking up your responsibilities here. You've been reminded of those already, but apparently you need more than one reminder. You've strolled out to the stables only to make casual visits—stables where such horses as Invincible, who won the Grand National, were bred and Forge Ahead, who won the Conyngham Cup at Punchestown. You look surprised. You don't mean to tell me you didn't know that!"

"No, I didn't. You've dwelt on the ecclesiastical and military glories of the O'Tooles and extolled their patriotism, but this is the first you've said, since I got here, about their triumphs on the turf, and if you told me long ago in Boston, I'd forgotten. Of course, I'm aware that there are almost as many paintings of horses as there are of ancestors in this house, but I haven't had time to look at them carefully or to notice their names—people or horses, either. Was Uncle James much of a horseman himself?"

Lady Susannah groaned. "Your uncle was one of the best amateur steeplechase jockeys in Ireland and rode any number of winners, most of them bred right here. You ought to be riding every morning and preparing to follow in his footsteps."

"You mean in his stirrups, don't you? Well, I'm perfectly willing to ride every morning, in fact I'd like to, but that isn't saying I'll be good at steeplechasing. I'd better try for point-to-point first, hadn't I? I believe Anne enjoys that and, perhaps, later on I could persuade her to give me lessons."

"Certainly you can, but it isn't only the stables you're neglecting. You've hardly looked at the accounts and those are very complicated. You haven't once been over the property with Danahy, the land agent, and you have more than fifty tenant families."

Peter groaned in his turn. "I know, it's appalling. But I wanted to wait until Anne could go over the accounts and the property with me. After all, her husband left the responsibility for those and everything else in her hands, didn't he? That includes the stables and the grounds. I suppose that, when she feels like talking about such things or doing anything in connection with them, she'll let me know. Provided she does want to consult me. Personally, I believe she'd rather take complete charge herself, now she's got her moving off her mind. If she invites me to tea—or anything else—I'll ask her whether I'm right or not. And if she doesn't invite me to anything within a reasonable length of time, I'll broach the subject to her."

"What do you consider a reasonable length of time?"

"Well, another week at least. Maybe two. But I think that should be a maximum. I realize we can't rush our fences. Perhaps I'll meet her on the grounds somewhere and have a chance to bring up the subject of responsibilities casually. I believe she does take a little walk now and then and so do I, even if I haven't done it accompanied by the land agent. I've just gone thrashing around in the wooded areas by myself. I don't pretend to know much about forestation, but I'm under the impression that some of that so-called parkland could stand thinning out to advantage. Later on, I want to get expert advice on the subject, but meanwhile, I enjoy my solitary tramps, and in the course of one I came face to face with a big husky fellow, who was carrying a very purposeful-looking gun and was accompanied by two terribly handsome dogs which sniffed at me suspiciously. I thought for a moment it must be one of the poachers I'd heard so much about. Then I discovered it was exactly the opposite. After he'd sized *me* up, in one very swift, very discerning glance, the man took off his cap and said respectfully, 'Good evening, my lord. I'm Mark Fagan, the gamekeeper.'"

"Why were you surprised?" Lady Susannah inquired. "You must have known that, of course, there'd be a gamekeeper at Cloneen and that if you went wandering around in the woods you'd be bound to meet him sooner or later. Besides, you saw him at the funeral."

"Good Lord, Granny, you can't expect me to remember, much less identify, everyone I saw at the funeral! I suppose I should have known there'd be a gamekeeper on a place like this and that he'd go wandering around in the woods, well armed, but he wasn't one of the retinue that had immediately been called to my attention, like the butler and the coachman and the head groom and the studmaster. There are probably half a dozen more I ought to be aware of and that will come to light eventually. Anyway, I found this Fagan a very pleasant fellow, in spite of his ferocious looks and, presently, the dogs stopped acting suspicious and became friendly. We walked along for a while together, passing the time of day; it seems he isn't very busy at this season, but in September his troubles begin with grouse, partridge, pheasant and wild duck all coming into season and all representing an equal amount of temptation and an equal reason for watchfulness. Finally we came in sight of a nice-looking little Georgian house which it turned out was his home and, incidentally, is one of the lodges of the estate—how many has it got, for heaven's sake? One for the mansion, one for the dower house, now this one beyond the parkland, and perhaps there are half a dozen more of those, too. By the time we reached the cottage, it had begun to rain, so Fagan asked me if I wouldn't come in until the shower passed, which I was very glad to do, because it was one of that sudden intense kind in which I might easily have drowned. He has a very nice wife and two well-behaved children. I was offered tea and willingly accepted that, too. None of them would take it with me and I was sorry for that, but somehow I feel I would be welcome to go to the Fagans' cottage again whenever I wanted to."

"I'm sure you would, though I doubt if they'll ever feel it's fitting to sit down and take tea with you. However, I'm glad you found something to stimulate your interest in the grounds."

"Oh, I've been interested in them all right from the beginning, but I haven't felt I was really making much headway in them and grasping their importance until today. I'm also very interested in the old castle. That doesn't take so long to get acquainted with and, strangely enough, it doesn't seem to have any kind of a keeper. I've prowled all over it."

"You shouldn't do that. It's past the stage where a keeper would do any good. There's nothing left to protect or preserve. In fact, it's in a dreadful state of disrepair, so bad that it's dangerous."

"Then don't you think it might be a good idea to repair it?"

"*Repair* it! Have you any idea what that would cost?"

"Not the slightest. But I've gathered lack of funds isn't our chief trouble."

Lady Susannah rose and Peter immediately went around the table and drew back her chair.

"If you're serious, we'd better continue this conversation over our coffee," she said, sweeping ahead of him toward the drawing room.

"I'm completely serious. And I'd be very glad to continue this conversation over coffee," he said, still with somewhat exaggerated courtesy. "Where would you like to sit? . . . Yes, I think perhaps that is the best place for a nice long quiet chat. . . . Wade, will you look in on us again after an hour or so and bring us some fresh coffee if we're still here? Thank you. . . . Do you mean to tell me I'm the first member of the family to suggest we ought to restore that castle? You told me that nice Lord Slattery who called yesterday lived in one that had been built in eleven hundred and something. If that's still habitable, I don't see why ours couldn't be."

"Slattery's castle never got *out* of repair; the family has lived in it *continuously*. The O'Tooles had to give up living in theirs because it was partially destroyed by fire during Cromwell's 'punitive expedition'; and though they made shift to live in it somehow, until the restoration of the monarchy, when the barony became an earldom, it seemed more sensible to build a new house than to go on trying to patch up a ruin. After that, they managed to keep going and put up a good front; but your uncle and I were very happy when the Glover money made the upkeep easier. I thought that had all been explained to you."

"Yes, that has; but now that we are not so hard up any more, I thought we might consider some salvage, beginning with the tower, which would be ideal for a bachelor's establishment. I've always had a secret yen to live in a tower. Now I hope you'll encourage me to realize my ambition."

Though she did not actually encourage him, she listened to him and finally she remarked, rather drily, that as far as expenses went there was probably no sound reason why he should not fix up a decrepit old tower, since he had money of his own, if that was what he was crazy enough to want to do, when he had a beautiful Georgian mansion in perfect condition already at his disposal. The subject was not raised again for several days and, meanwhile, they had several more callers: the Tyrells, who lived in the oldest fortified house in Ireland, the first known to have been built for private occupancy; the Singletons and the Dwyers, who, like the Slatterys, lived in old castles. After that, feeling that the cards were stacked against her, Lady Susannah decided to mention the controversial question herself: since the weather was actually fine, for a change, she thought she had better improve the chance to get a little exercise, before it started to rain in torrents again. She would be glad to walk over to the ruins with him and let him explain this crazy scheme of his to her, if he could.

They set out before she had time to change her mind and walked down the main drive, past the rockery and across the river, while she listened attentively as he outlined his plan of action. She even went into the tower with him and admitted that the foundations were sound, though she declined to go off the ground floor. Yes, he was right, she further admitted; such towers had been built with just one main room to a floor and winding stairs enclosed in the wall not only because, otherwise, the rooms would have been very small, but by making their upper regions difficult of access, they offered special vantage points of observation and defense. She had known all this herself, of course, but she had not credited her grandson with so much information about medieval architecture or so much interest in it. Yes, she could see what he meant: a ground-floor kitchen with a turf fire in the big wide hearth, a living room with a view over the river, a bedroom with the same charming outlook and, perhaps, an observatory to top them all off. Several O'Tooles had been deeply interested in astronomy and he could carry on the studies already made. His idea of restoring the tower wasn't so bad, after all.

"Of course, you've a right to go ahead and do anything you like with the old ruin because that's part of your heritage," she said as they walked away. "And, as a matter of fact, the more I think of it, the more I believe it will make a very good impression on the old county families. I've been very pleased that so many have called and so promptly. I realize these were just visits of condolence, but all the same I have the feeling that the groundwork's already been laid for an entente cordiale if you return the calls as soon as you properly can and make it evident that you intend to identify yourself with local interests and diversions. In a way it's rather a pity you don't want to hunt, because so much of the social life centers around that; but you'll be following Anne's policy in this regard, so it won't be held against you—in fact, you'll be respected for it. . . . Incidentally, as a matter of courtesy, I hope you will consult Anne about the restoration of the tower."

"Yes, if I get a chance to speak to her alone. I haven't, even yet, though, to my great relief, she has begun coming out to the stables. That self-important friend of hers, Lawrence Donovan, who's just a shade too good looking for anyone but a matinee idol, very promptly offered to take over their supervision—not only promptly but prematurely. He did it at the same time he came, dressed in the deepest mourning, to make his *visite de condoléance.* Talk about not waiting until the deceased is cold in his grave! Donovan didn't wait until the gilded lid covered the coffin! I told him I thought I could manage, that I already knew what a horse looked like, or words to that effect, though I didn't confess I'd never heard the term 'pleasure horses' before or known they had stables separate from the stud. Donovan's come back, anyway, more than once. He was there yesterday, when Anne came out for the first time herself, and wasn't in the least embarrassed because she'd found him there. I wouldn't put it past him to come back again, in spite of the way she told him she was almost ready to take hold again herself and that, anyhow, Farrell and Ned and Art had done just fine without her and she was sure they could keep on doing so if necessary. And, of course, as far as the stud is concerned, Bart Riordan is supposed to be the best studmaster in Ireland. Anne didn't mention me at all, so apparently she didn't think I'd done just fine; but Farrell said a few words of encouragement to me after Donovan had been persuaded to leave and Riordan has been very civil to me every time I've ventured out to the stud, so I'm hoping no harm will come to the stables without Mr. Donovan's watchful care."

"I'm afraid you're prejudiced against Lawrence Donovan," Lady Susannah remarked. "You said the other evening that you thought he was in love with Anne and asked for my help in keeping him off the premises. I'm not sure I understand why it should annoy you so much that an attractive young man should find her attractive, just because you and she rub each other the wrong way. It seems to me quite natural. Anyhow, I think Anne's shown she's quite capable of handling the situation herself."

"Of course it's quite natural, and maybe she is. But it doesn't annoy me any the less on that account."

"Why? Anne will probably marry again. In fact, I think she should, after a proper period of mourning."

"I agree with you. But not Lawrence Donovan. . . . Well, I'm glad I won you over to my idea about the tower, anyway. I'll try my luck with Anne on the subject the first chance I get. And I'll watch for a chance."

It came sooner than he expected. He walked back to the mansion with his grandmother and from there went on to the stables, which fascinated him. He had never seen any built as these were, of stone, in the form of open rectangles leading into each other. The one nearest the house, which was also the oldest and largest, had provided enough space for both pleasure horses and stud, until the association with the De Briare *haras* indicated their separation, and was now devoted exclusively to the pleasure horses, their grooms and equipment. It had an entrance gate almost as imposing as the one to the estate and directly opposite this, dominated by a huge clock, cozy living quarters with adjacent offices for the head groom. There was no separate carriage house and the rest of the square comprised sections to take the place of this, as well as the rooms where harness and saddles were kept, box stalls and quarters for the assistant grooms. A wide door at the rear led to the next enclosure, where the farm horses and farm machinery were kept, under the supervision of two resident farm workers, and which was also equipped with bins and lofts for fodder and hay. When the need for a separate stud arose, this second quadrangle had been left unaltered and a third created beyond it, by taking over part of the immense garden and allotting the charming little stone house, originally intended for the head gardener, who had been provided for elsewhere, to the studmaster. Peter could feel a kinship between the first rectangle and the neat stables with coachman's quarters above on Lime Street at the foot of Beacon Hill, which were maintained by most of the families who lived on Chestnut and Mt. Vernon Streets and Louisburg Square; the second had its counterpart in the neat farms of Vermont and New Hampshire where he often visited relatives. Though, to his own annoyance, he still felt out of his element in the stud and with the studmaster, he was completely at his ease elsewhere in the stables and, as he entered them after discussing Donovan with his grandmother, he was glad to see Andy emerging from his tidy front door, wiping his mouth with a gusto that suggested he had just finished a hearty tea.

"The Mistress has been here, but she left half an hour ago," he said. "We talked over this and that and everything seemed to be to her satisfaction, as I hope it is to your lordship's. She's going to cancel all the entries for the Dublin show and right glad I am that's her decision. She's the one who should ride those two beauties she's just brought over from France and no one else. The boys and I can keep them exercised for her until she feels like taking a canter around the place and St. Patrick himself wouldn't think she was showing disrespect for the dead if she did that any day now. Doesn't your lordship agree?"

"I do, most decidedly—both about hoping she'll ride around the grounds herself pretty soon and about not letting anyone else represent her at the show this year. I'd like to ride every morning myself if that's agreeable all around and it might help with the problem of exercise. . . . Has the Mistress said anything to you yet about choosing her carriage horses? Lady Susannah wants to be sure she doesn't inadvertently suggest that she'd like to use the ones the Countess prefers, so be sure to let me know the answer as soon as you have it."

"That I will, your lordship. But I know the Mistress wants her ladyship to have anything that's available, to make her visit pleasant, so there's no hurry, and the Mistress didn't stay long today—just to tell me about the Dublin show. Such a fine day it is, she said maybe she'd take a little walk by the lake. It's glad we all are to see her out and around again, so I hope she does, and maybe your lordship could find her and pass the time of day with her by the lakeside."

"That's another good idea, Andy. I'll act on it. See you tomorrow."

They parted with a sense of mutual good will and Peter took what he believed to be a short cut to the lake, through the rose garden. But he did not instantly catch sight of her, as she was partially hidden by the branches of the trees which bordered the lake near its inlet. Parting these as he went along, he saw she was sitting on a slight rise of ground, apparently completely at ease. Her back was toward him so he could not see her expression, but from her attitude he gathered that she was gazing intently at something on or very near the lake. The lace mantilla which she had been wearing had slipped to her shoulders and her masses of golden hair, uncovered and slightly disarranged, were shining in the sun; her simple black dress looked less lugubrious now that it seemed more casually worn than anything in which he had seen her since her husband's death. Peter had come up to her as quietly as he could, but he had not been able to do so noiselessly and, just before he reached her, she turned, as if to identify the sound she had heard. When she caught sight of him, she instantly pointed toward the lake and then put a warning finger to her lips, showing that she wanted him to be as still as possible and that she did not want him to come any closer. He stopped short and looked in the direction she had indicated; at first, he could see nothing, though he thought he heard a faint rustling sound. Then, seemingly from a nearby clump of blackthorn, two swans sailed out toward the lake, the cob leading, the pen following, both very white and stately; between them, in single file, swam three gray cygnets. With great dignity they passed on, not breaking their line before they were out of sight in the wider water, behind a clump of reeds. Anne, who had been watching them with the same intentness that he had, turned toward him again. Her eyes were overflowing with tears and, for the first time since their meeting in her husband's death chamber, there was no antipathy in her manner.

"Wasn't that a lovely sight?" she asked in a hushed voice. "I've lived here four years and this is the first time I've known a swan to build a nest here, though I've known swans to nest on many Irish lakes. When that happens it's supposed to be a good omen."

"Then can't you accept it that way?"

Peter, too, had found the sight extremely moving. He longed to sit down beside Anne, to take her hand and beg her to be his friend, even though she could not be his love. But he did not dare to try to say anything more or even to take another step forward. To his great relief, Anne spoke again, still without showing animosity, though she made no direct answer to his question.

"I've been hoping and hoping that would happen," she said, still speaking in a hushed voice. "Because of something else that did happen a long time ago."

"Would you feel like telling me what it was?"

"Yes. I was sitting here, in this very place, at twilight, not long after I came here to live. It's always been a favorite spot of mine. And suddenly I heard a great clamor of wings and then I saw the snowy plumage of many swans, rushing down the lake and striving to rise from its surface. At last their wings caught the air and, after circling over the lake, they disappeared above the grove where we are now sitting. It was like a vision of fairyland."

"You never saw them again?"

"No, never. I've watched and watched for them and they never came."

"And that was how long ago?"

"I thought I told you—nearly four years."

It was not that she had told him; she had said she had lived at Cloneen nearly four years and had never known a swan to nest there before. But he did not contradict her. He realized that in some mysterious, perhaps tragic, way she connected the swans which had disappeared with the five that had nested at their very feet and that, though she was now confused, she was comforted. Her next words confirmed this impression.

"One of the loveliest Irish legends is about swans. Don't you know it?"

"No. I haven't had time to go in much for legends. I've been too busy with actualities."

"Would you like to hear it now?"

"Very much. May I sit down beside you while you tell it to me?"

"Of course. It's the age-old story of the wicked stepmother, in its Gaelic version. Lir, Lord of Sidhe Fionna, was happily married to Niamh, the foster daughter of Bodbh Dearg, and she bore her husband two fine healthy children, twins, a boy and a girl, who were named Aedh and Finola. Then, a year later, Niamh again gave birth to twins, both boys, who were called Fiachra and Conn. But, this time, she died and Lir was left with no wife to love and to return his love. He was so lonely that, eventually, he married Niamh's sister, Aoife, and for awhile he was happy again. But Aoife had no children of her own and though, at first, she was kind to the twins, she became bitter and jealous and resolved to rid herself of them. So one evening she led them to the shore of a lake and suggested they should go for a swim while supper was being prepared. They dashed joyfully into the water, but, one by one, as they passed her, Aoife struck them with a golden druidical wand and transformed them into four beautiful snow-white swans."

"And is that the end of the sad story?"

"Oh no! It's a very long story, so long I shan't try to tell all of it to you now. But I will tell you this much: the swans retained the same power of speech they had possessed as children, so they could talk to each other and comfort each other; and Finola, the only girl, became the leader and counselor of her brothers and guided them safely through all their trials and tribulations and their journeys through the strange cold waters of Moyle's wild sea before they finally came home again. To this day, songs and poems are written about them. One of my favorites is Thomas Moore's, which begins:

> 'Silent, O Moyle, be the roar of thy water,
> Break not, ye breezes, your chain of repose,
> While, murmuring mournfully, Lir's lonely daughter
> Tells to the night-star her tale of woes.' "

"You don't remember the rest of it?"

"Not well enough to quote it."

"But you could refresh your memory, couldn't you, and quote it some other time—when you tell me the rest of the story?"

"I might. But now I think it's time I went home."

She reached for her mantilla, which had fallen to the ground, and draped it over her hair. Though she did not do this hastily, it was clear that in a moment she would rise, and Peter realized that any attempt to detain her would be a mistake, reluctant as he was to have the idyllic interlude come to an end. He held out his hand, hoping she would accept the help she did not need and was inordinately pleased when she did so.

"Let's come here again and watch the swans while you tell me the rest of the story," he said. "I have a feeling that they're going to stay with us and that their coming *is* a good omen; but I'm afraid they've gone for today. So perhaps you're right, we should, too. . . . By the way, I'm thinking of moving now that you have. The mansion seems awfully empty without you and it will seem emptier still when Granny's gone. Would you feel like coming with me to see what I hope is going to be my new abode?"

14

Though the meeting by the swans' nesting place did not constitute a lasting cessation of strain between Peter and Anne, it at least marked a truce. She did not invite him to take tea with her at the dower house, as he kept hoping she would; but she made no objection to his plans for renovating the tower, when he outlined these to her, carefully explaining that this was to be an independent project, undertaken at his own expense; and she told him she would be glad to have him assume the supervision of accounts and the disbursement of monies, aside from her personal expenditures for dress, travel, charities and so on, which her marriage settlement covered and which she would continue to handle privately, as she had always done. She added that she would come to the office from time to time to see how he was getting on and that, meanwhile, he was to regard himself as her "chosen representative," in accordance with the terms of the will.

He set to work at once with great gusto, mingled with the rueful recognition that he had much to learn about the administration of a twelve-hundred-acre estate, comprising a mountain, a lake, grazing lands and forests, enclosed by a ten-mile wall. Even so, the task was much more complicated than he had imagined. He was appalled to find that there were five separate sets of statements with which to deal: one for the household, one for the farm, one each for the pleasure stables and stud and one for rents. The books dealing with household accounts were the only ones kept in the study, which also served as a personal office. Those for the pleasure stables and the farm were kept in the offices that adjoined Andy's quarters, those for the stud in the charming little stone house where Bart Riordan lived and where Peter still felt so ill at ease, and those for the rents at Danahy's house in the village. Furthermore, Mr. MacAuliffe was called upon to approve all of these. The books were, of course, available for Peter's inspection whenever he elected to go to these separate locations or to have the statements brought to him; but he felt that a great deal of time was wasted in this manner and that some way to centralize such material would make for more efficiency, as far as he was concerned. However, he realized that he must not be too hasty in trying to change an established pattern, especially since he was not yet sure how to improve it. So he continued to struggle along as best he could, happy because Anne came more and more frequently to the study and both thankful and surprised to find her a lucid teacher. Up to that time, he had made no suggestions for changes in the arrangement of furniture or the equipment in any of the rooms; but he had finally decided that he would be justified in saying that he thought conferences could be carried on and routine work done much more effectively if a double desk were installed in the personal office.

"You know, one with kneeholes, flanked with drawers on both sides," he explained, as Anne looked slightly puzzled, though not antagonistic. "Then the conferrers or co-workers could face each other in comfort and have all the space they needed for their papers and reference material. Perhaps there's an old desk on the place somewhere that's been stored away because no one has needed it lately. I saw a magnificent specimen of the type I'm trying to describe at a *Herrenhaus* in Prussia once. It was enormous and still it had graceful lines. If you don't mind, I'll hunt around and see if anything of the sort is concealed at Cloneen. If not, I'd like to buy such a desk—with my own money, naturally."

"Why don't you get Wade to unlock one of those rooms on the third floor that are never occupied? A lot of disused equipment is stored in them. I confess I've never been through them thoroughly, because I wanted to make room for my own French furniture, not to find more Irish furniture, when I was already crowding a good deal out. But I can't believe that the O'Tooles didn't have something just as good or better than what you saw in a Prussian *Herrenhaus.*"

"Would you come with me and look? Then we'd be sure I didn't choose something you wouldn't like."

"Well—I might. Let me think it over a little."

Evidently, he had chosen exactly the right example of what he wanted, without consciously selecting it: as a Frenchwoman, Anne could not endure the thought that only Prussia could provide the right model for an ideal working desk. The next day she appeared shortly after luncheon, saying casually that, before they settled down to the afternoon's work, they might as well see what was available. The unoccupied rooms proved a treasure trove of rare antiques; and among them was a massive but elegant desk which the O'Toole twins, Cullen and Carew, had used together more than a hundred years earlier and which Carew had never wanted to see again after his brother's tragic death. It more than met Peter's requirements and was equally satisfactory to Anne; so it was promptly removed from seclusion, carefully brought down the endless stairs by four strong and willing men and, after being painstakingly polished, set up in the study, displacing the smaller desk that had been there and, also, a sofa and a large armchair.

"Couldn't we make room for these in the Chinese parlor, without having it look too crowded?" Peter asked, surveying the three pieces as they stood in the hall. "I think if we can make the tone of the study more and more businesslike, that'll be all to the good. But then, perhaps we ought to make the parlor increasingly serviceable and comfortable, so that, if we have to ask someone to wait, before seeing us in the office, it would seem a logical part of our setup. Probably you'd want different upholstery on the sofa and chair and a different desk set; but that's the sort of revision you have a genius for."

Apparently, he had again succeeded in saying the right thing. All the suggested changes were made without friction, the Chinese parlor ceased to look stiff and superfluous, and Anne came more and more frequently to the transformed study. Occasionally, MacAuliffe or Danahy or Riordan or Farrell was called into consultation with them both; but for the most part Anne and Peter worked by themselves when she joined him and there were no differences of opinion about expenditures other than those for wages, which seemed to Peter abnormally low, and rents, which seemed to him abnormally high.

"Bridie gets sixteen pounds a year!"

"Sixteen pounds and three shillings."

"But that's only about eighty dollars! And Art Nolan gets only eight pounds!"

"Eight pounds, ten shillings."

"But that's only forty dollars!"

"Peter, you must stop translating these wages into dollars."

"I have to, as a starter. I've never learned to figure quickly in pounds, shillings and pence."

"You will pretty soon, if you try. But that's not what I meant. You must stop thinking what it would be fair to pay a servant in *Bos-*

ton. That's what I mean by thinking in dollars. The servants at Cloneen are very well paid by Irish standards."

"But I thought there was beginning to be a feeling that these standards weren't high enough. I mean, in human values."

"That feeling hasn't extended to domestic servants. They're fed and clothed and they're perfectly satisfied. And just think how many we have at the mansion—nine, now that I've taken Solange over to the dower house and three there. The total annual pay is pretty formidable. I don't see how we could afford to increase it." She turned to the solicitor, who had arrived to signify his approval of their latest reports submitted to him, and asked, "Do you, Mr. MacAuliffe?"

"No, I'm afraid not. Besides, it's a different kind of labor that's causing trouble."

Peter turned over the sheets that he was holding and studied them with a troubled face.

"Art isn't a house servant," he said.

"The grooms are provided with quarters, but sometimes stableboys prefer to live with their families on outlying farms. He's one that happened to and so do a few of the herdsmen. But they're all fed."

"And what about the temporary annual staff—the turf cutters and harvesters and shearers?"

"Oh, if you're going to start worrying about them!"

"I don't want to, Anne. But I can't help it. I have a feeling that, somewhere along the line, trouble's brewing."

"Neither Mr. MacAuliffe nor Mr. Danahy feels that way about it. Surely they understand the situation better than you do. It's kind of you to take so much interest in these employees, to want to better their lot, but you know you haven't had much experience with labor problems in Ireland."

"I haven't had any. But that doesn't prevent me from reading the handwriting on the wall. However—"

Anne did not convince him, even though she had the support of MacAuliffe and Danahy; but he had the good sense to realize that this was not the best time for an argument. Anything that precipitated one might easily lead to a resumption of open hostility.

His moderation was rewarded; Anne recognized that he had made a concession which, to him, was a very considerable one and that he should be given credit for it—just as she was forced to give him credit for the fact that never once, while they were working at the same desk, had he introduced any subject alien to accounts, much less tried to touch her in any way which he could have pleaded was accidental, when he handed her a pen or straightened a paper she had displaced. As the days lengthened into weeks and there had been no change in his circumspect behavior, she decided that something should be done to show her appreciation of this, if only to encourage its continuance: she told him, as they were closing their books for the day, that she had decided to start riding again and asked if he would like to accompany her.

"Certainly," he said quietly. "Did you mean now? It's a beautiful evening."

"Well, I had in mind tomorrow. I thought of asking Danahy to go with us. We haven't talked with him very much and it's about time we discussed the haymaking."

"Just as you say. You'll let Farrell know which horses you want and what time."

They had both risen and now she followed his glance toward the window. It was, indeed, a beautiful evening.

"I don't suppose there's any reason why we shouldn't go now," she said, a little hesitantly. "I'll run along to the dower house and get into a habit. You can give the orders to Farrell. I'll ride Reine Mathilde. You can ride whatever you choose."

"What about sending for Danahy?"

"It's a little late for that now, isn't it? We can talk to him tomorrow. Can you meet me at the dower house in twenty minutes?"

"If you can make it that fast, I ought to be able to. I've been riding every morning, as you probably know, but not always dressed with much formality. If you're getting into full regalia, I ought to do the same, oughtn't I?"

He was the more convinced that he had made no mistake in the impeccability of his outfit when he saw hers. Coat and skirt were of the finest material, beautifully cut, the tall boots and the top hat sleek and shining. It did not seem to matter that these were all black, because this was a different kind of black; even the light face veil which did not conceal her features bore no relation to the heavy crepe in which she had so long been shrouded; and the snowy edge of her fine collar— the first touch of white she had permitted herself—was visible above her closely buttoned jacket. After the horses had been brought around, she stood for a few moments stroking Reine Mathilde's nose and murmuring to her; then she leaped so quickly and lightly into the saddle that Peter did not have time to help her. In fact, she was already moving along the driveway ahead of him, sitting easily and erect in her seat, when she called back to him.

"We didn't decide where we wanted to go, did we?"

"No, but I had thought of the swans' nesting place."

"So had I."

"We might go through the woodland beside the lake. I think some thinning out needs to be done in the eastern grove, but I'd like your verdict."

"You don't ever go out, even for a pleasure ride, without thinking of things that need to be done, do you?"

"Not any more. I'm beginning to realize how much is involved in the management of an estate like this."

They rode along at a leisurely pace, for the most part in pleasant silence, except for Peter's suggestions and Anne's agreement with them, until they reached the inlet where they must ford the stream. Recent rains had swollen this and its banks were slippery. Peter reined in his horse.

"You're sure it's all right to cross here?"

"Oh, yes. I've done it dozens of times when it was much worse than this."

Again, she moved on ahead of him and her confidence in the feasibility of the passage seemed fully justified, for both animals went easily splashing through the water. However, as they climbed the further bank, Reine Mathilde stumbled slightly and, though she instantly recovered her footing, Anne stopped her.

"Sorry, I feel faint," she murmured and pitched forward in her saddle.

Peter dismounted so quickly that he was able to reach her before she had actually fallen, but she did not answer him when he spoke to her and, thoroughly alarmed, he lifted her from her horse and carried her toward the house, calling to one of the men who was working nearby to look after the horses. As they approached the terrace, Lady Susannah, who had been strolling in the rose garden, caught sight of them and called out anxiously.

"What on earth has happened?"

"I don't know. We were riding quietly along and had just crossed the ford when Anne fainted."

"Good heavens! Did she fall?"

"No. Luckily, I was able to reach her before she tumbled from the saddle, but apparently she's still unconscious."

"I'll ring for Letitia and we'll get her right to bed in her old room. Meanwhile, you'd better send Ryan for Dr. Carey."

"Then you think it's serious?"

"It probably isn't. Don't worry. But it's better to be on the safe side."

As Wade had insisted that Peter must be moved into the master bedroom immediately after the funeral, he was of course familiar with the location of the secondary room which opened into this on one side and into Anne's private sitting room on the other. But he had instructed that the connecting doors were to be kept closed and had never entered Anne's former chamber. Its emptiness gave it the bare cheerless atmosphere common to all living quarters deprived of their normal inhabitants, even when they are not stripped of every ornament and small personal belonging as this one had been; and, as soon as Peter had laid Anne down on the smooth silk counterpane of the unused bed, he hastily drew back the window curtains to admit the pale sunshine and bent over to light the neatly laid fire.

"Do get rid of that hard bolster and make her comfortable, won't you?" he asked his grandmother, who had managed to join him very quickly.

"Of course. First, we must get her out of her tight habit and her corsets. Then we'll see to soft pillows and a hot-water bottle and everything of the sort," Lady Susannah answered soothingly. "As you know, Letitia is a born nurse, like many of her race. Anne's taken away all her own things, so I'll have to put her into one of my nightgowns, which will be pretty large for her. But I'll send over to the dower house right away for Solange, with a message telling her to bring some of her mistress's clothes."

"You mean you think she'll have to stay here?"

Lady Susannah glanced at the bed, where Anne lay still completely immovable. "She's a long time coming to. I wouldn't know. But Dr. Carey will. Do stop fussing around and get hold of Ryan."

Ryan, as usual, proved to be readily available when needed and Dr. Carey was fortunately at home and came along at once. It seemed to Peter that endless hours passed between the time the family physician went upstairs and rejoined him in the office. He tried, without success, to busy himself with accounts while he waited, but the figures simply danced without meaning before his eyes. He was in that desperate state of feeling that he would have to storm upstairs and find out for himself exactly what was happening when Dr. Carey, a tall, thickset man with a big bushy beard, appeared in the doorway, looking quite calm and collected.

"I don't think there's the slightest reason for alarm," he said quietly as Peter sprang forward to meet him. "You did quite right to bring the Countess here and see that she was promptly put to bed. You are fortunate in having Lady Susannah and her remarkable maid with you at this time. Lady O'Toole should keep very quiet, at least until tomorrow, when I'll come to see her again. Then, if there are no new developments, there's no reason why she shouldn't go back to the dower house, if she's determined to do so. She's conscious again, clearheaded and in no pain. Her fainting fit was so sudden that it caught her unawares. Nothing of the sort has ever happened to her before. Her only concern—aside from the fact that she's very anxious to return to the dower house—is that you must have thought it was a very silly thing for her to do."

"I didn't think anything of the sort, but I confess that it frightened me pretty badly. You say nothing like this has ever happened to her before. Is anything of the sort likely to happen again?"

"Quite possibly."

"Then something must be the matter that you haven't told me about. Why should she start having fainting fits, right out of a clear sky?"

"I'm trying to tell you, sir. The Countess admits that, though she hasn't fainted before, she hasn't felt quite as usual this last week or so."

"Then why didn't she send for you at once?"

"Because she thought the symptoms were inconsequential. She had slight headaches, a disinclination for food, especially in the morning, drowsiness even after a good night's sleep. Of course, she's worked hard, because of her insistence on getting to the dower house in record time, and it's been a radical change for her to live there entirely alone, except for the servants, to eat solitary meals, to do without her usual horseback riding; and then there's the natural depression of a newly made widow. So, as I said, she thought her slight malaise would pass, that she really didn't need to send for me. No harm has been done because she didn't. But I'm glad I've been sent for now."

"Because the malaise, as you call it, is serious after all?"

"No, sir. It isn't serious. But it may persist for a few weeks, perhaps for a few months, though the latter's unlikely. Lady O'Toole is a very healthy young woman. I think she'll be feeling quite herself again fairly soon, able to lead a normal life—except, of course, that she shouldn't ride horseback."

"But that's what she loves to do best of all! And she's waited to do it until now because she was so afraid of showing disrespect to the dead."

"Yes. And she can resume her favorite occupation next spring." The doctor looked at Peter with an expression which was kindly but somewhat quizzical. "I am afraid we have been slightly premature in addressing you as Lord O'Toole, sir," he said. "If Lady O'Toole should have a daughter, that would still be correct. But if she should have a son, he, of course, would be the heir to the title, as direct issue of the late Earl. Mr. MacAuliffe must be advised of the situation immediately. But I am afraid we cannot deal with it, in a legal way, except incompletely, before March. Unless I am greatly mistaken, the Countess is about two months pregnant."

PART FOUR

*Late August, 1882,
to late March, 1883*

*The Heir
Presumptive*

"Though riders be thrown in black
    disgrace,
Yet I mount the race of my life
    with pride,
May I keep on the track, may I
    not fall back,
And judge me, O Christ, as I
    ride my ride."

—Douglas Hyde

15

Inevitably, Peter was deeply troubled, but his distress lay largely in an even greater realization of disloyalty to a kinsman than had previously harassed him. The fact that, through his brief possession of a beloved woman, he had begotten a child, filled him with a sense of triumphant virility that no pangs of guilt could subdue. Moreover, paternity almost automatically involved responsibility which no illicit intimacy, if unfruitful, could claim. Anne would not, in fact, could not, long be blind to this. But since she persisted in seeing him only as a partner in a sin, for which she was determined to atone, and required him to pursue the same course of action, she might conceivably do him the injustice of believing that he would add to his wrongdoing by taking unfair advantage of her predicament. As soon as possible, he must disabuse her mind of any such idea and at the same time leave her in no doubt as to the course he did mean to take.

The difficulty lay in a means of approach. A note would remain unanswered, and there was always an element of danger in the written word, even in a household as well regulated as this one. A request for a personal visit, made through a third person, would certainly be denied and, in any case, who should this third person be? So far, he had scrupulously avoided any action which interfered with Anne's obvious disinclination to see him. How could he suddenly reverse this policy without rousing curiosity? He was sure that, from the beginning, his grandmother had divined that there was some obscure reason for Anne's antagonism and his courteous and unprotesting acceptance of it. But the reason had remained obscure and he had no mind to risk clarifying it. Mr. MacAuliffe was not a member of the household; for that reason alone, though there were plenty of others, a message sent through him would certainly seem contrived. Dr. Carey seemed equally disadvantageous, though for different reasons. He had said that Anne should be kept very quiet until she was radically better; he would almost certainly look upon visiting as a source of disturbance and, of all persons, he was probably the one against whom it was necessary to be on guard, lest, inadvertently, a disastrous slip might be made. When Anne had arranged for the latest importation of horses, she had been in France for at least two weeks, possibly more. Peter had never been told exactly how long—there was no reason why he should have been—but he was sure it was that long. Her husband, a man of seventy-four, had already been ailing on her return and had become seriously ill shortly thereafter. Nothing in Dr. Carey's manner had indicated surprise over Anne's pregnancy; but just as Peter was sure his grandmother had been suspicious about their relationship on some other score, he could not help believing that the physician might have found it hard to suppress reservations on this one, though it would not have been the American who aroused them. Someone in France, unknown to the doctor? Someone in Ireland, whom he did know? Lawrence Donovan, for instance? Suddenly, a savage desire to proclaim his paternity swept over Peter. If even a whisper were murmured against Anne's character, there must be no possibility of linking her name with anyone in either country. He could have taken his Bible oath that the hours spent with him on the boat were the only ones in which she had permitted the desecration of her bed. If there were to be the slightest danger that the child would not be accepted as the late Earl's, nothing should prevent its true father from stepping forward to claim it.

Fortunately, Peter was not so lost to reason that he did not quickly realize that this was not a moment for yielding to wild impulses; it was a moment for pondering the best ways of safeguarding his beloved, by his own sane and tender conduct, from the very calumnies that he visualized. He reverted to his consideration of the best means by which to approach her and, somehow, possessed his soul in patience until Dr. Carey had made his morning call and reported a definite improvement. There was no reason why Lady O'Toole should not return to the dower house that evening if she continued to feel better, as that was what she wanted to do. Meanwhile, since it was her own preference to remain in bed through the morning and then put on a dressing gown and recline on the chaise longue in the sitting room while she ate a light lunch, he was in accord with that program. Perhaps, after that, the hours might begin to drag a little. If this proved to be the case, there was no reason why she should not have a family visitor.

"Do you mean me or my grandmother?"

"Why, either, or both. But perhaps it would be just as well if you didn't go together. A three-cornered conversation is always a little more of a strain than a tête-à-tête."

So it was the doctor, after all, who had provided him with his contrivance! "You're right, of course. I know Granny's been eagerly waiting to look in, but she didn't dare risk disturbing Anne until you'd given the word. Maybe you'd report to her yourself and suggest that she make her visit right after luncheon. When I think she's stayed long enough, I'll join them—having warned Granny beforehand that'll be her cue for departure."

It sounded foolproof, but Peter was still unable to believe this until he was actually in Anne's sitting room and his grandmother rose to leave it. "Doctor's orders!" Lady Susannah said, shaking a finger at Anne as the latter urged her to remain. "No three-cornered conversations! It's Peter's turn here now and I'll see him later, at tea time." She leaned over the chaise longue and, for the first time, spontaneously kissed her young sister-in-law. "This room has lost its cachet since you took your beautiful French furniture to the dower house," she added. "My sister-in-law Iris was a very worthy woman, but she didn't begin to have your taste. I've already told you how much I think you've improved the drawing room and I'm sorry to see Iris's solid, serviceable things in here again. But let me say how pleased I am that you took the hint when I reminded you that French queens always wore white mourning. I believe the Chinese still do, don't they? Anyhow, that negligee is a dream and the little white bows that fasten your long braids add a finishing touch to the ensemble. . . . I wish we could persuade you to stay here, my dear," she continued affectionately. "Of course, we want you to live where you'll be happiest. But can't help feeling this is where you really belong—especially under the circumstances."

"It certainly is," Peter agreed lightly. "As you say, it's my turn now and I'll see what I can do to convince Anne of that." He wished he might echo his grandmother's remarks about the furniture, the dressing gown and the little white bows on the long golden plaits, which lay over Anne's breast, but wisely decided it would be better not to do so. He walked to the door with Lady Susannah, kissed her and closed it after her. Then he came back to the chaise longue and sat down quietly beside it.

"Aren't you taking an unfair advantage of a situation I'm powerless to prevent?" Anne asked coldly.

"I was afraid you'd ask that. But, as Granny observed, I'm following doctor's orders. And I confess I'm very grateful for them. I realize that, without them, it would have been very much harder for me to find a means of talking with you privately, unless I actually forced my way into your room. And I didn't want to do that."

"But you would have?"

"Not willingly, as I've just remarked. Only as a last resort. But if I'd been driven to it, I'd have taken whatever means were necessary to convince you that, though I had no right to see you in private because we were briefly lovers, I have a right to do so as the father of our child. We can't decide separately what we're going to do next. We've got to have an understanding about it."

Anne turned her head away without answering, but he could sense her rigidity and her anger. "Haven't we?" he asked, speaking as gently as he could. "It shouldn't take more than a few minutes. Then I won't intrude on you again against your wishes, unless and until it seems absolutely necessary." And, when she still did not answer, even though he repeated the question, he asked another. "You don't deny, do you, that it is my child?"

"No. I wish to God I could!"

"Because it was conceived in sin or because you hate me?"

"Both."

"I don't believe it."

"It's true."

"It's only half true. You sinned when you had never sinned before, in any way that counts, when you had led a singularly blameless life. You can't forget it. You can't forgive yourself for it. And you hate my share in that sin. But you don't hate me as a man. You try to pretend you do, but once in a while you forget—like the time you found the swans' nest. Actually, you love me."

"How dare you say such a thing?"

"Because that *is* true. We love each other. I didn't seduce you. I asked you if you were sorry I had come to your room and when you said no, I asked if you might not be sorry afterward and you taunted me with being afraid. You wanted me as much as I wanted you. If you hadn't, you'd have stopped me long before I got so far that you couldn't. I'll always be thankful that you didn't, partly because I never would have got over it if I felt I'd forced myself on you, but mainly because your free offering of yourself gave me the most glorious experience of my life. And you *weren't* sorry afterward. You were just as glad as I was that I had taken you. You said that at last you knew what it meant to be a woman! You even *thanked* me. It was as if you had been waiting for me a long time and were so happy that I had finally come you must prove to me that you were really mine. Isn't that what happened?"

"How can you talk about it in that way? We committed a mortal sin. It's true that I didn't think of it that way at first, but I realized it as soon as you left me. That is why I ran away and didn't give you a chance to find me."

"I know. You were unfaithful to your husband and I took another man's wife. It was a double act of disloyalty, and disloyalty is an un-forgivable sin if it's conscious or deliberate. This wasn't. I didn't know you belonged to anyone else and I didn't think of you, for one moment, as a light-o'-love. I thought of you as the one woman in the world for me, then and always. I've never stopped thinking of you in that way. And you forgot, for a few hours, that you belonged, legally, to some-one else, because you instinctively recognized me as the lover you'd never had and for whom you'd been waiting and longing."

"You talk as if that made what we did justifiable!"

"No, I'm not saying that it was justifiable, but I am saying that it was understandable. We fell in love the minute we looked into each other's eyes and by the time we reached the boat we were so deeply in love that nothing seemed to matter except fulfillment. It was so sudden and so urgent that it was overpowering. It was what you'd call a *coup de foudre* in your own language. Given all these circumstances, I believe it was not only understandable, but forgivable. Don't you have a saying, '*Tout comprendre, c'est tout pardonner*'? I believe your hus-band would have understood why it happened. I believe he would have forgiven you. I'm not sure that he didn't."

"But he never knew!"

"How do you know that? You mean you never told him. But I tried to tell him, when I went to see him in his death chamber, and it didn't seem as if he were so far away that I couldn't reach him. When I left him, it was—well, it was almost as if I'd confessed and received absolu-tion. Don't you know that the soul doesn't always leave the body as soon as there's been a pronouncement of death? There's an ecclesias-tical provision for that contingency, a form of Extreme Unction that begins, '*Si capax*—If it is possible,'" he quoted and then continued, "'*ego te absolvo a peccatis tuis, in nomine Patris, et Filii, et Spiritus Sancti. Amen*—I absolve you from your sins in the name of the Father, and of the Son, and of the Holy Ghost. Amen.' In other words, the priest still has authority to grant absolution as long as there's a living soul, and if there's even the chance of it he proceeds accordingly. I'd heard of this provision and, just to be sure I wasn't misinformed, I asked Father Carroll about it. I told him there was something I'd wanted very much to say to my uncle and that I had a strong feeling I hadn't been too late. Father Carroll said that was quite possible and quoted the same words I've just repeated to you. He didn't seem at all surprised at my statement about hoping for communication—after all, he knew I'd made a great effort to get here." Peter stopped, struck by a sudden thought. "Since you feel so strongly about having committed a mortal sin, did you confess it?"

"Yes, immediately."

"Then Father Carroll knows!"

"No, I confessed to a priest to whom I was a complete stranger— in a church where I'd never been before—that same morning in Kingstown."

"And did he refuse to give you absolution?"

"No."

"Then why should you believe that what we did was unforgivable?"

"I can't discuss that with you. He said I must repent and atone."

"Is it going to help us to repent and atone if we don't act like normal human beings?"

Again, she did not reply, but Peter knew it was less because she was bent on repulsing him than because she did not have a ready answer. He pressed his advantage.

"Listen, Anne," he said. "And, by the way, that's what I'm going to call you from now on. If you want to go back to the dower house, I'm not going to try to stop you, though I shouldn't be at all surprised if Mr. MacAuliffe told you this is where your baby should be born. But I think it would be better for everyone concerned if you just acted as though you didn't like me much, instead of acting as though you were afraid of catching leprosy or something when you are in the same room with me. People will begin to say to themselves, 'There must be some reason why she avoids that inoffensive young man'—for, believe me, most people do regard me as quite inoffensive. Not important or anything like that, but at least inoffensive. And then they'll begin to wonder what the reason is. So please try to act as if I were a passably acceptable nephew or something of the kind. Incidentally, now that I think of it, I *am* legally your nephew."

"You sound as if you thought there were something amusing in the situation."

"No, I don't think there's anything amusing in it. But I refuse to regard it as one of deep and perpetual gloom. I'll go away tomorrow if you like. But I really think next week or the week after would be better from the viewpoint of disarming curiosity. My visit to the Mc-Keevers was cut short. It would be perfectly natural for me to go back and complete it. Granny wants to visit them, too, before she starts back to Boston and she thinks she ought to be doing that pretty soon, so she can keep her eagle eye on my sisters, who'll be home again in September. After she leaves, I'd like to travel around and see something of Ireland. I suggested it once before to her, but she thought I ought to stay here and assume responsibilities. So I gave up the plan for the time being. But I never really abandoned anything, except the idea of a tinker's wagon, which would have been my first choice for a vehicle. I consented to a trap, instead, and she compromised on Alec McKeever for a companion, instead of the groom she first proposed. While I'm gone, you could run everything to suit yourself—until March. Then, if our baby's a girl, I guess I'll have to come back and make a stab at being the eighth Earl of Cloneen. If it's a boy, that lets me out, as far as the title and all its perquisites are concerned, so I hope, with all my heart, that it *is* a boy. I never wanted that title or those perquisites. I only wanted you. I still do, I always shall. I would have asked you to marry me that morning in Kingstown, if you hadn't eluded me by going to church. Of course, you'd have had to say no then, but . . . I *will* ask you, when your proper period of mourning is over. And I hope you'll accept. Partly because you do love me, whatever you may say or even think just now. And partly because you shouldn't be so unfair as to ask me to stand aside and let some strange man become the step-father of my child."

16

As Peter expected, he found his grandmother waiting for him in the library when he went downstairs. The previous evening, she had remained late in Anne's sitting room, in order to be readily on call; when she finally left it, she was tired and quite ready to go to bed herself. The next morning, when she was rested and reassured, she asked for Peter and was told that he had already gone out to the stables. At the luncheon table, where they eventually met, Wade was in alert attendance so that did not provide a favorable opportunity for intimate conversation. Now the propitious moment had come.

"Well," she said, as he drew up a chair and lighted a cigarette, "I was brought up to expect the unexpected and I thought I always had. But I must admit I didn't expect this."

"Neither did anyone else, I take it."

"I can't pretend that I'm pleased. I thought I'd come here to celebrate your accession to the peerage. Instead, you've been relegated to a very ambiguous position which you won't be able to escape for about seven months and, at the end of that time, your elevation or demotion will depend on the sex of this *enfant de miracle*. You'd be excusable if you were very much irritated."

"I'm not in the least irritated. As you know, I never cared about the title, and my present ambiguous position worries you and Dr. Carey a lot more than it worries me. Perhaps it worries Mr. MacAuliffe, too, but I haven't found out about that yet. Remember, I've been planning to take a jaunt around Ireland as soon as you left, but I've just had another idea. Instead of going back to Boston next month, why don't you stay on here until after the baby's born? Then you could mitigate the hardships of my ambiguous position by your tact and companionship, not to mention being right on hand, with Letitia, if Anne required

140

special attention. I think she needs you more than the other girls do just now."

"I'd thought of that myself. But problems, like troubles, never seem to come singly. Janet has just presented me with one. I had a very agitated letter from her this morning. She doesn't want to go back to school in Boston. She wants to finish her education in Paris. And she says she's sure her father and mother would be willing, if I would stay on there with her."

Peter laughed. "Is that what she said, 'finish her education'?"

"Why, not those words exactly. But that must be what she meant. She has only one more year of school, you know, before she makes her debut."

"She didn't say anything about a Polish prince, did she?"

"What on earth are you talking about, Peter?"

"Since Janet was considered too young to go to grown-up parties in London, she had a good deal of free time on her hands."

"She *was* too young," Lady Susannah said rather sharply. "She's only sixteen."

"You're not keeping the close track of birthdays that you used to, Granny. Janet was seventeen last week. How old were you when you defied the family by insisting that you were going to marry Michael Glover, who was just a plain mister then?"

"He wasn't plain at all. He was strikingly handsome."

"I wasn't referring to his looks, but to his rank. Anyhow, as I started to say, I was supposed to be looking after Janet in London on account of her tender age, but I had other interests, too. And at some garden party, which she *was* allowed to attend, one of her fellow guests was a Polish prince. After that, he was very much in evidence, so Father and Mother took fright—that's why they cut their stay in London short and dragged Janet off to Florence to look at pictures. Evidently, they haven't connected her sudden yearning for a French finishing school with the June menace to their peace of mind and, if I were you, I wouldn't call the matter to their attention. But, personally, I'd be very interested in finding out whether Stefan Walewski hasn't been transferred to Paris."

"Transferred? Was he in London officially?"

"Yes, despite the partition of Poland, Galicia still has some sort of supervised representation. A very pleasant fellow, too."

Lady Susannah appeared to be doing some serious thinking. "Walewski is a fine old Polish name," she said slowly, "and the Walewski estates are among the few that still unencumbered. Obviously, your father doesn't know all that, though he certainly ought to. If you really think Janet has a chance of contracting such an alliance, of course, I ought to do everything I can to help her. Why, marrying into the Cushing family, which was considered such a triumph for Sue, is a completely insignificant achievement compared to what that would be! And Janet doesn't begin to be as pretty as her sisters!"

"That might be a matter of opinion. According to this high-born Pole, she's probably a paragon. I'm afraid I've done myself a disservice by telling you about him. You immediately see him as a most desirable *parti*, not only in himself, but as a means of putting the Bradfords and the Cushings in what you consider their place. Well, I'll miss you very much, but I won't interfere with the course of true love. I wouldn't want anyone to interfere with me under similar circumstances and I'm glad you have something so exciting to divert your mind from my ambiguous position. If you'll tell me what you want to say, I'll send Ryan to the post office with a message announcing that you'll be on your way to Paris within a week and that you'll cable again as soon as you know exactly when that will be. . . . Ah, here comes Wade with our tea. I could do with a big one, couldn't you, in the face of all these problems?"

"I beg your pardon, my lord, but Mr. MacAuliffe is waiting in the office to see you as soon as that's convenient for you. He told me that you were on no account to hurry your tea, but that he wanted to let you know he was here, in accordance with Dr. Carey's request that he should come as soon as possible. I was to tell you he'd had his tea before he came."

"That means this is strictly business," Peter observed to Lady Susannah, as Wade took his departure, "and it means he *is* worried, so I mustn't linger with you, pleasant as that always is. Don't forget about that cable. You can compose it while I'm gone." Hastily, he gulped down a cup of tea, picked up a scone and went out of the room with it in his hand. "Don't look so anxious," he said, glancing back, "I won't go into the office still chewing, as if I had gum in my mouth. But, as I told you, I do feel the need of nourishment. I can't help wishing the good man of law could have waited another half hour before his worries drove him to my side."

Actually, he was facing the solicitor in better spirits than he had dared to hope; he was greatly relieved by his grandmother's preoccupation with Janet's romance and, as a matter of fact, this had furnished a welcome diversion for him. Ever since hearing Dr. Carey's announcement the day before, Peter had been in a state of extreme tensity; now he began to relax. Devoted as he was to Lady Susannah and sincere as he had been in saying he would be glad to have her spend the winter with him, he knew that many questions, which it would have been hard to avoid answering in her presence, would now take care of themselves: by the time his position was no longer ambiguous, some of them would have answered themselves and some would not require an answer. He greeted Mr. MacAuliffe cheerfully and cordially.

"I'm afraid that, unintentionally, I've made you a great deal of trouble," he said, shaking hands. "Sit down and tell me what you think I can do to make amends."

"There's not the slightest question of making amends, my lord." Mr. MacAuliffe's distress at Peter's choice of words was obvious. "You're not an outsider, much less an interloper. Don't think for a minute that anyone feels you are."

"It will help me not to feel so if you will stop calling me 'my lord.'"

"Very well, sir," the solicitor went on hurriedly. "As I started to say, you are the late Earl's nephew, his next of kin in the male line. He was looking forward immensely to having you here. Because, unfortunately, he didn't have a chance to tell you so himself, that shouldn't change your feeling that you are more than welcome at Cloneen. Quite aside from this relationship, if I may say so, you have made yourself greatly liked for your own sake in the short time you have been here. Everyone feels the same way—Father Carroll, Dr. Carey and myself; Danahy, Farrell and all the household staff. I assure you, I'm not exaggerating."

"Then please go a step further and call me Peter. And do sit down."

Mr. MacAuliffe drew a deep breath which ended in a murmured expression of hesitation about doing both, but he belatedly accepted the proffered chair. "We're only sorry for your possible embarrassment and eager to find a way of avoiding it as much as we can," he said when he had collected himself somewhat. Peter, who was greatly touched by his visitor's kindness and determination to make this unmistakable, felt a slight huskiness in his throat as he attempted to answer and hoped that it was only the smoke from the turf fire that made his eyes smart.

"I appreciate all you've said more than I can tell you, but I wonder if it wouldn't help the rather complicated situation if I went off and didn't return until March. I've been thinking of taking a trip around Ireland with my cousin, Alec McKeever, as soon as my grandmother left and she's just had some family news that will probably advance the date of her departure. I could leave next week or the week after."

"I very much hope you won't resort to any such extreme measure, Peter, and I know Dr. Carey would agree with me in this. He's anxious that Lady O'Toole's strength should be spared in every possible way. If you left, there'd be no one to share the responsibilities which you, as her kinsman, can take over and for which you've already shown great aptitude, if you'll permit another personal remark."

"But perhaps Lady O'Toole would rather resume these responsibilities herself. Shouldn't you consult her, as well as Dr. Carey?"

"I don't think so. Not when her health is involved."

"Her husband's will indicated that he expected her to assume responsibilities. He had the greatest confidence in her judgment."

"Yes. But he didn't expect her to be in her delicate condition. He had given up all hope of an heir when he wrote that will."

"Well, suppose we say that I'll go away, as I'd planned, after Lady Susannah leaves, but if you or Dr. Carey feel, for any reason, that I ought to return, I will."

"I'd much rather you didn't leave at all. There are a good many aspects of the situation—more than I feel qualified to discuss tonight— that make me feel it would be better if you stayed. I am especially sorry to have you absent during harvest, particularly as so far you haven't given anywhere nearly as much time to the farm as you have to the stables."

"I'm afraid that's true. I'm much more interested in horses than I am in cows and, besides, I thought they were of a good deal more importance to Cloneen. Then, too, though the farmhouse and barns are only on the further side of the vegetable garden, the farmer's family seems a separate entity; I don't inevitably come into daily contact with them, as I do with the grooms in the normal course of my own daily life. And, to tell you the truth, I'm appalled by the number of children who come rushing out every time I try to talk to Healey. When I begin a statement or question, there are only two or three, but before I've finished, there are at least half a dozen. And, finally, Mrs. Healey appears in the doorway with another at her skirts and still another in her arms and, unless I'm very much mistaken, she's expecting a further addition to the family at almost any moment. I don't want to arrive in the middle of a confinement."

Mr. MacAuliffe laughed. "I realize just how you feel," he said good-naturedly. "And it's quite true that the horses are of more importance to

144

the estate than the cows, though the late Earl was very proud of his blue-black Kerry cattle and the high standard of cleanliness—for Ireland, anyway—in the barns. But if we didn't raise good crops, the horses wouldn't have the kind of feed they get now; and though I don't think any of the farm laborers actually shirk, you don't need to be told that the Irish aren't usually as energetic as Americans and sometimes are inclined to drag their feet a little. There's an old saying that there's no spur more effective than the supervision of the Master and I believe it's true. You didn't go out in the fields at all during haymaking and you missed a beautiful sight: the line of spalpeens swinging their scythes in unison the whole length of the field and the grass laid after their blades as even as a string."

"I know. I've seen the same thing in New England and it's a very stirring spectacle. I'm sorry to have missed it, not only because it was worth seeing, but because I take it the spalpeens are among those seasonal workers whose wages are worrying me."

"Well, they're the hired scythemen, if those are included in your worries."

"They are, indeed. I'll try not to be guilty of another such oversight and I'll risk a visit to the Healeys today. But I'm afraid I have to stick to my plan of returning to Donegal, as soon as Lady Susannah leaves. I think Lady O'Toole would prefer it that way. However, as I said a few minutes ago, I'll return if either you or Dr. Carey feels that I should."

"I still feel it would be better if you didn't go away at all, but I'll accept your compromise if you insist."

"Thank you. And don't forget it wouldn't take me long to get here if you did need me. Let's have a drink to seal the bargain." Peter went to the cabinet which he had adapted to serve as a small bar, as he did not like to ring for Wade, to make a ceremony of serving him, every time he felt in need of liquid refreshment during his long working hours. "Would you feel like trying some of our American whiskey for a change? If you don't like it, please tell me so." He poured out the bourbon judiciously, mixed it sparingly with soda from a siphon and watched Mr. MacAuliffe's expression while the latter tasted it. It was one of unquestionable approval. "Good. Let me know when you're ready for a refill. And now, I want to ask you something else. You know I'm restoring the old tower. The work on it's going ahead fairly fast now. It ought to be habitable before too long and I've really looked forward to having bachelor quarters in it. If I could manage to do that, couldn't you persuade Lady O'Toole to come back here? Isn't this the place where her baby should be born—not the dower house?"

Mr. MacAuliffe coughed, a little uneasily. "Theoretically, you are right, but, as you know, Lady O'Toole was determined to move to the dower house at the earliest possible moment and she took all her personal possessions with her. It would be quite an undertaking to move them back here again and Dr. Carey feels she shouldn't, on any account, attempt it. He pointed out that we'd never forgive ourselves if she overtaxed herself and brought on a miscarriage. She is under no actual obligation, legally, to have her baby here; it's just a matter of tradition that the heir should be born at the mansion and Dr. Carey feels that this case might be the exception."

"So, whatever I do, Lady O'Toole will remain at the dower house?"

"Yes. And it'll be very helpful to all of us if you'll consent to remain here at the mansion. Let the work on the tower continue, by all means, if it interests you. You might enjoy picnicking there in pleasant weather."

It was clear to Peter that Mr. MacAuliffe regarded the tower in the same light that he did the summerhouse, which had been built at the end of the formal garden as a so-called "folly," to provide work for hapless tenants during hard times; but this did not seem the moment to plead its purpose as a residence, much more congenial than a mansion to a young man living all alone.

"I know it will be a very lonely winter for you," he went on. "You're not accustomed to our short, chill days and our long, dark nights. You'll get so you actually listen to the silences. You'll be without companions of your own age. Until the year of mourning is up, there can't be any entertaining here and you can't accept invitations to entertainments elsewhere, except perhaps for a few quiet neighborly visits on both sides. It will be very different from the life you've led so far. But if you can see your way to staying until everything is settled for the best, whatever way that may be, that would prove you're a real O'Toole, whatever else you may be called, and that this is where you belong."

17

The response to Lady Susannah's cable came in the form of a long one from Mr. Bradford, saying that he would be taking his wife and daughters to Paris the following week, so that they could have their final fittings for that season at Worth's and that, if his mother-in-law cared to join them at the Meurice, he would be glad to talk things over. . . . "That means he's already practically decided to let Janet stay," Lady Susannah told Peter. "He must have been making inquiries at this late date about Stefan Walewski and found how surprisingly satisfactory the answers are. Well, I'll be on my way as soon as Letitia can do the packing and you can get reservations for me at the Royal Hibernian in Dublin and on the Irish Mail. Now that it's settled, I'm really sorry to go. Anne still isn't feeling like herself and she probably won't for another fortnight at least. She appeared surprised and disappointed when I told her I was leaving. It seems she'd taken it for granted I was going to stay indefinitely and, apparently, she's become rather attached to me. She was also rather impressed with Letitia's aptitude in a sickroom. Evidently, there's no one in Anne's own family available to stay with her. I tried to tell her I was sure you'd be glad to keep her company, any time she'd like to have you."

"And so I would. Any time she'd like to have me. But not until then."

There was a certain finality in his expression that made Lady Susannah realize it would be unprofitable to pursue the subject much further. However, she made one last attempt.

"Anne likes to play chess. Also bezique and cribbage. She told me so herself. That is, she said she'd played a great deal, long winter evenings."

"Which probably means she doesn't want to play those games any more. No doubt she's sick to death of them."

"Well, you could read aloud to her."

"How do you know she likes to have anyone read aloud to her? You don't."

"Peter, if you're determined to leave her alone—"

"Until she feels like seeing me, I am. I hope she will some day. I'll even go as far as to say I believe she will. Be patient, Granny."

He smiled, putting his arm around her. Then he said he was needed in the stables and left her. It was at last clear to her that nothing would induce him to talk about Anne and that he had no present plans for keeping her company. She would be alone at the dower house and he would be alone at the mansion and, for all her successful maneuvering with the Bradford girls, there was nothing that she, Susannah Glover, could do in this case. She did not even have the satisfaction of knowing, as she went to supervise the rest of her packing, that Peter wrote Anne a note before his departure with his grandmother and, though Anne did not answer it, she not only read it, but reread it more than once.

September 1, 1882

Dear Anne—

Since I'm going up to Dublin with Granny, to see her safely on the mailboat, I think I'll continue on to Donegal to round out my visit at Rathmullan and ask Alec if he would like to go on a driving trip with me. If he agrees, we can take a trap from there or come back here for one, just as he prefers. In any case, I will keep in touch with you and Mr. MacAuliffe, so either or both of you can get hold of me if you want or need to, which I realize is doubtful, so it may be some time before I see you again.

Do you know how to knit? If not, I'm sure you ought to learn. Then you could while away many tedious hours making little jackets, bonnets and blankets. Perhaps even bootees. (I believe that's what they're called.) The next time I pass a window full of yarn—I saw dozens when I was in Donegal before—I'll send you a supply, pink and blue, just on the chance.

For reading material, I recommend Romeo and Juliet. *I think you need to refresh your memory about them. It took just one glance in their case, too, and no one has ever blamed them, except their stupid parents, for making up their minds so quickly. They were luckier than we were in that the good old friar was handy and that it was all right for them to go to him at once. But, after that, Romeo didn't show much sense or he never would have had to say, "Well, Juliet, I will lie with thee tonight," when he headed toward the vault with a vial of poison in his hand. There are a few other famous love stories I'd like to call to your attention, but this will do for a starter. I've always heard that it was very important for a lady in an interesting condition to read just the right things.*

My own reading has included some poetry by a young man named Yeats, who is beginning to be known, and I find two more lovely lines about swans. They go like this:

"I know of the sleepy country, where swans fly round
  Coupled with golden chains, and sing as they fly."

I believe they'll mean as much to you as they do to me.

As ever,
Peter

Although the statement, "I'll keep in touch with you and Mr. MacAuliffe," was the only reference to future correspondence in this letter, Anne had fully expected that she would hear from Peter again the next day. When she did not, she began to fidget and, when still another day passed without a letter, she began to worry and to imagine all sorts of improbable accidents as being responsible for his silence. Nothing would have induced her to take the initiative in communicating with him, no matter how concerned she became; but she had begun to cast around for some pretext for wiring Lady Susannah when the long-awaited letter finally arrived in the morning mail, along with numerous bills, pleas and notices. Pushing aside the breakfast tray which, though daintily set, had failed of appeal, she tore the letter open and read it with an avidity which quickly overcame her morning lassitude and queasiness.

September 5, 1882

Dear Anne:

I hadn't expected to be in Dublin as long as I was or to find my time so variously and agreeably employed. It was quite a pleasant surprise.

When we got in Monday, Granny decided it wasn't too late in the afternoon to inscribe our names in the Visitors' Book at the Viceregal Lodge and that, as far as our mourning was concerned, it was perfectly proper to do so. To be quite honest, I don't think she was too sure of this, but I believe she did secretly hope that it might result in an invitation to lunch the next day, which is exactly what did happen, and she obviously enjoyed it so much that I'm very glad everything turned out approximately as she wanted it to, though I think she would have been still more gratified if the Spencers had gone back to Dublin Castle for the winter and the party had taken place there. I liked them both and very quickly understood why he is nicknamed "The Red Earl" and she is Spencer's "Faerie Queene"; for, certainly, he has the biggest, bushiest red beard I ever saw in my life—even bigger and bushier than Dr. Carey's—and she is a dainty little creature and a charming hostess. They spoke about Uncle with great admiration and with equal admiration about you. Personally, I thought, as a function, the luncheon, served entirely on gold plates in a dining room with two hideous black marble mantelpieces, was a good deal like those at our legations, except that there were more footmen in livery standing around and more ceremony about presentations. (To host and hostess—very few, of course, to fellow guests. I had a feeling, perhaps unjustified, that they were a little doubtful about me and were afraid I might begin murmuring, "Pleased to meetcha," but maybe I do them an unfairness.) The entrance to the Lodge was very heavily guarded, so I gather there's still some uneasiness about a possible sequel to the "troubles" last spring. (Such a genteel way of referring to murders!) I was glad to see Phoenix Park and assume that the spaciousness of this is what you're supposed to admire, as it doesn't have statues or fountains or even flower beds to attract your attention, but it is big and it is nice and green and has lovely slopes and hollows.

As I didn't do anything the last (which was also the first) time I was in Dublin, except make futile attempts to find out what trains went where and when from which stations and walk around in the rain, hoping against hope that I might find you, I decided that, this time, I would try to do a little sightseeing and went to St. Patrick's Cathedral. I think the chances are ten to one that you've never been there. It provides various noteworthy features, among them the most massive monument I ever saw—three stories high, no less—ornamented not only with the figures of the entombed Earl and Countess of Cork, but with the kneeling figures of their ten children, four sons and six daughters. (My idea of about the size family you and I should have.) This tomb is polychrome, but most of the others are rather glaring white marble, interspersed with bright brass tablets, some very old, some very new, but you can't tell the difference, unless you look at the dates with great care, because those that are pre-reformation are just as spotless and shiny as those that were set in last year. I didn't spend too much time on them because, like ninety-nine of every hundred persons who go to St. Patrick's as sightseers, what really interested me was its associations with Swift and his Stella. Now that really is something to note: a man who was dean of a cathedral for more than thirty years and who, for a large part of that time, had his "pupil" Esther Johnson as a lady friend and official hostess. (I believe Héloïse was Abélard's pupil, too, wasn't she? Certainly they sinned but she became a great abbess and he a great teacher and the letters they exchanged are among the foremost literary treasures of all time; and those are the things the people who go to put flowers on their graves still remember—also that they loved each other very much and that each was the other's only love.) I suppose you can't say without benefit of clergy, as far as Swift and Stella are concerned, for, of course, he was a clergyman, but anyway, without any proven marriage ceremony. As if this weren't enough for him to get away with, there was his other lady friend, Esther Van Homrigh—Vanessa—pleasantly situated nearby where he could visit her whenever he felt like it. And now Swift and the first Esther—Stella—are buried side by side in his cathedral, with bright brass plates to mark the spot. I suppose Swift wasn't actually a bigamist, because he wasn't married to either of these ladies, but just what would my paternal ancestors, who were all Puritans, have called him, instead? (I think I know the word, but I won't write it out.) I somehow can't imagine a church in Boston, Protestant or Catholic, having this kind of mementos. I heard someone say a little while ago you should never try to understand the Irish, you should just enjoy them; and I guess that's so. But what I'm getting at is: why should they be shocked at any other love affairs they happen to hear about or even suspect when they readily accept Swift and both Esthers? I don't think they should be. And later, after the meeting I attended, I was a good deal disturbed at hearing some very snide mutterings about a very great man. I hope they can be disproven. If they can't, I'm afraid Ireland will suffer for it and heaven knows she needs every friend she can get and keep.

My sightseeing began and ended with St. Patrick's as Granny and I left for Kingstown early enough to have dinner there. Then I saw her safely installed in her cabin which, believe it or not, proved to be Number 25 and, as you can imagine, that gave me something of a shock. I think, however, that she's perfectly safe from intrusion. Letitia's in Number 27.

When I got back to the Royal Hibernian, I thought maybe a drink would taste good, so I went to the bar and the first person I ran into was your friend Lawrence Donovan. Of course, he's very disappointed because you withdrew your horses from the Dublin Show and I gather doubly so because he didn't get to ride one of them, though he didn't actually say that. He's still resentful because you haven't invited him to come and see you since your return from France and I believe he's inclined to blame me for your continued seclusion, though he didn't actually say that, either. I told him you weren't very well, but I didn't enlarge on that, because I didn't feel at all sure you'd want him to know the cause of your indisposition, at least for the present; in fact, I felt quite sure you wouldn't. Without much enthusiasm, he accepted my invitation to have a drink and, after he had consumed two or three, he seemed in better spirits and asked me how I'd like to go to a political meeting with him at the Mansion House in behalf of the Evicted Tenants' Fund.

Naturally, I said I'd like very much to do so and, as the hotel is diagonally across the street from the Mansion House, it didn't take us long to get there and, though the meeting was already in full swing, we didn't miss much of any real importance. The Round Room, where it was held, was admirably adapted for such a gathering, as it is huge. (Donovan says it was especially built for the purpose of entertaining King George IV.) The Lord Mayor, Mr. Charles Dawson, who is a member of Parliament, was in the chair and any number of political celebrities were present, nearly all of them Members of Parliament, young for official positions of such importance—that is, in their early thirties. Among them were Mr. Parnell, Mr. Thomas Sexton—formerly a journalist connected with The Nation—Mr. Arthur O'Connor, who holds very radical views, and Mr. Timothy Healy, who has more ambition and ability than background and who seems to have attached himself to Mr. Parnell as a sort of Man Friday. (I hope he's trustworthy.)

I was very much interested to meet all these celebrities, especially Mr. Parnell. He is definitely not the sort that we would call a typical politician in the United States and, without really knowing anything about it, I shouldn't think he would be in Ireland. He doesn't seem like the maligned squire of song and story, either—hard drinking, hard riding, loudmouthed, overfed and overbearing. If I'd met him somewhere without having the slightest clue to his identity, I'd have put him down mentally as a very distinguished scholar, possibly a clergyman, but more likely the head of some department, like Greek, at a major university. I still can't visualize him as having spent six months in Kilmainham Jail, because of his agitation on the Irish Land Question or of being accused, however mistakenly, of being even remotely connected with the Phoenix Park murders. (Of course, it's been proven now that all the letters attributed to him were forged.) He's very pale and I couldn't tell whether this was the result of his long imprisonment or whether it's his natural coloring, but I think partly both; and his full beard helps to conceal his expression, but I believe it's one of great self-control. At first, he gives the impression of being very cold, but when he smiles, his face is completely transformed and you know there has been kindly feeling underneath all the while. I can't imagine him being what we call a rabble-rouser, who stirs up crowds into whatever violent action he favors by a very impassioned type of oratory; on the other hand, he does pretty quickly give you the feeling that there's grim determination underlying his very calm and courteous manner and that he could wear down a lot of opposition simply because he could and would hold out longer than his antagonists. This is only a snap judgment after seeing him just once and I may have a different report to make later on. When I mentioned the long friendship among the Bradfords and the Stewarts and Tudors in Boston, he responded very cordially (that's where the smile came in!) and said he'd often heard his mother speak of my father's family and thought he'd met some of them himself, on one of his fund-raising trips to the United States. I also plucked up courage to tell him how much I admired his remarks in the House of Commons about the underlying causes of the Hartley murder and he smiled again and said, "Oh, are you already taking an interest in Irish politics? I'm very glad." Lots of other people were clamoring for his attention, so there wasn't time for anything more just then. But later, when Donovan and I went to bid him good-by, he said he hoped we'd come to the reaping at Avondale the next day and, if we did, he'd be very pleased to have us lunch with him.

I had no idea what this reaping was, but Donovan explained, as we walked back to the Royal Hibernian, that a fifty-acre field of oats, which was part of the Parnell property, was to be harvested, as a gesture of good will, by the farmers and country people in the vicinity of Avondale and that some hundreds had been mustered for that purpose. (The field in question had been sown for Mr. Parnell with Tartary oats by the same people who were now coming to reap the crop for him.) We succeeded in hiring a trap and set out bright and early—or, rather, just early, for the first part of the morning was dark and threatening; but gradually the clouds cleared and, eventually, the sun

153

really was *bright. Avondale is about twenty-five miles from Dublin, near a town called Rathdrum and, long before we got that far, we were in the midst of crowds: people on foot and people in all sorts of vehicles and most of them wearing green emblems of one sort or another. A group from the Labour League marched together, accompanied by the Rathdrum-Parnell band and later in the day another band, The Cryhelp Brass—honestly, that was its name!—came along, too. The actual work began around eleven with twenty-two machines in operation, all but one of them loaned for the occasion; the one that belonged to Mr. Parnell was worked by members of the Labour League. The process of reaping and binding into stocks went on simultaneously and, large as the crop was, by half-past six the field was completely transformed. Besides all the reapers and harvesters, there were a large number of visitors who came just to look on, a good many of them ladies, both young and old. Donovan apparently knows almost everyone and saw to it that I met a number of very interesting and attractive people, besides those who were our fellow guests at luncheon. The grounds are beautiful, especially the trees, and the mansion is a very pleasant one, about the same size as the McKeevers' at Rathmullan, perhaps a little larger, and has some fine paneling, an impressive staircase, a big library, et cetera. I really enjoyed my luncheon there more than I did the one at the Viceregal Lodge, though perhaps it's lese majesty to say so and you'd better not quote me on that. And I couldn't help feeling a little guilty at having been absent from the reaping at Cloneen and present at Avondale.*

It was so late when we got back to Dublin that I tumbled into bed, as soon as I had bolted my dinner, and slept so late that I barely caught my train for Londonderry. (You'll begin to think that allowing plenty of time to catch trains is not one of my strong points and you would be right.) Now that I know the ropes, the trip didn't seem quite as bad as it did the first time and I took the precaution of having some sandwiches made at the hotel to take with me. I had a warm welcome from all the McKeevers and now, between tea and dinner, have shut myself up in my pleasant (though rather chilly) room overlooking Lough Swilly to write you before I do anything else. I haven't even broached the subject of a driving trip to Alec yet, but I will, either after dinner or the first thing in the morning, and report the results.

As ever,
Peter

Peter received no letters from Anne during his brief stay at Rathmullan, but, as he had not expected any, this was not a source of sufficient disappointment to mar the pleasure he took in his trip through northwestern Donegal, in the course of which, however, he did receive a communication from Lady Susannah, which furnished him with considerable food for thought.

September 10, 1882

Dearest Peter—

Everything marches satisfactorily. Janet is entered as a day pupil at the Sacré Coeur, which means she'll have evenings, Thursdays and Sundays at home with me. I found exactly what I want for a house: it's just off the Quai St. Bernard and the front entrance, with very impressive grilled gates, is actually on the Rue Linné. However, there is another entry from the Rue Cuvier, with two-story lodges flanking it, and I'm sure we'll use this more often than the main one with its long winding drive. As you face the hôtel from the former, you get the impression that, though very elegant 17th century, it isn't large. But, when you get around to the front, you find the house stretches on and on and has a terrace at the far end, in addition to being completely surrounded with beautiful gardens. It's a little more important than I had in mind, but now that I have seen it and it is available, I wouldn't dream of changing; and Janet couldn't have a more distinguished background—which is all to the good, considering the qualifications of her suitor.

Stefan Walewski has been to call—on the assembled family—and has made a good impression. He has also invited the assembled family to lunch at his "modest bachelor establishment" on Sunday and the invitation has been accepted by all except myself. Since it is quite likely there will be similar opportunities later on, I decided to profit by your parents' continued presence in Paris to take a little trip to Normandy. Of course, after they go I won't be able to leave Janet, though I'm on the lookout for a suitable governess—perferably a French lady of exalted lineage and high title, in reduced circumstances—to live in and relieve me of a certain amount of responsibility. But, as you know, I have been very curious, ever since meeting Anne, to learn more about her family and, though she doesn't actually avoid talking about them, she doesn't offer much information, either. It's a little late in the season for Trouville, but I believed that would seem to the De Briares the most logical place for me to be visiting; so I decided to make my headquarters at the Hotel des Roches Noires and write from there to the Countess, saying that, as I was in the vicinity of their haras and we were now connected by marriage, I should like very much to have the pleasure of making her acquaintance, et cetera.

The results were just about what I expected. The Countess replied promptly and not very warmly, saying that they were much complimented by my delicate attention, that, unfortunately, the state of her husband's health made it impossible for them to receive formally, but that, if I would be good enough to excuse a very simple repast, they would be glad to have me lunch with them the following Thursday. That was the day I really meant to go back to Paris, but the tone of the letter made me realize it was then or never, as far as the De Briares were concerned, so I put off my departure, hired a carriage and set out.

I'll say one thing for the French: they're much more generous about giving glimpses of their estates, and especially their châteaux, than we Irish are with our corresponding properties. I don't know of a single important place in Ireland where the main house, whether or not it is really a castle, isn't approached by a very long, very winding drive, thickly wooded on both sides, so that you don't have the slightest chance of seeing the mansion, or whatever, until you're almost to the front door. In France, on the other hand, in nine cases out of ten, the château is located at the end of a comparatively short, completely straight avenue, and you get your first impression of the principal buildings before you are actually inside the gates. Generally, these impressions are very favorable; they certainly were in this instance. The château is made of rose-colored brick, with cream-colored stone trim, and has a tile roof with ornamental dormer windows and chimneys. On either side of the avenue, as you approach the château, are the pavillons des communs in the same style; these, placed as they are at right angles to the château, form a most distinguished ensemble. The stables are all in the rear and, as no one suggested I should visit them, I didn't like to make a point of it. However, I did see, from the dining room windows, an immense pigeonnier, as old as the château itself, which means the period of Henri IV. There are the well-tended grounds usual in such places.

Four persons were waiting in the drawing room to receive me: first, the Count, who is partially paralyzed and confined to a wheelchair. He must have been very good looking once, but seems rather apathetic, quite aside from (or, perhaps, because of) his crippled condition. Second, the Countess, who is quite obviously the dominating force of the family. She is still extremely handsome in a rather severe way, has a figure that most thirty-year-olds could envy, a very grande-dame manner and is much better dressed than her Irish counterpart would be. (No economy there, unless she has one of those "little dress-makers" that I am always hearing about, but have never found myself.) Her English is surprisingly good, the result of a "Miss" (governess) in her early years. Third, the unmarried daughter, Cécile, who looks old enough to be Anne's mother, resembles the Count more than the Countess and, though equally well dressed, doesn't do justice to her clothes, which, as you know, is rare in a Frenchwoman. She also needs some helpful suggestions about what to do with her hair. She has as much as Anne and perhaps it was once the same glorious shade, but now it's that drab color which golden so often turns to. As far as age goes, she would have been a much more suitable match for James than Anne and, no doubt, this was called to his attention, but you can't blame him for choosing the younger sister, considering the contrast be-tween the two in Anne's favor. There's a picture of her taken when she was sixteen which is about the loveliest portrayal of a young girl I ever saw in my life, and no man between the ages of eighteen and eighty could be blamed for wanting to marry her if he could get her. Mlle. Cécile didn't have a "Miss" for her early education and seemed almost pathetically grateful to find that I could speak French.

The last member of the group was a very attractive young man whom I couldn't place at first, for I knew my host and hostess had no sons. (It seems they had two, between Cécile and Anne; both were killed in a hunting accident. I somehow gathered that it was this lack of a direct heir, rather than pedigreed horses, that established the first bond of sympathy between James and the De Briares.) Eventually, he was ex-plained as a cousin who either lives with my hosts or very near them, I couldn't at first make out which, and manages the haras for them. His first name is Maurice and I think the last is De Briare, too, though of that I'm not sure.

Luncheon was announced promptly and the butler wheeled the Count into the dining room—family portraits all around, better painted and going further back than ours do, table silver massive, but little racks to put the fork on between courses, so it could be used again. Food delicious. I was a little afraid, in view of the locality, that I might be treated to tripes à la mode de Caen, which I can't even swallow without gagging, but I needn't have worried. There was poulet à la vallée d'Auge, followed by pré salé, both superbly seasoned. The sweet *was* baba au rhum, *the best I ever ate, for the simple reason that the Count, emerging from his lethargy after one taste, said it lacked strength and ordered a bottle of rum brought to him, with which he proceeded to drench the baba! After doing this good deed, he relapsed into the comparative silence which he and Cécile had maintained throughout most of the meal, but the Countess and Maurice more than made up for this. She said all the right things and he a number of entertaining ones. When we went back to the drawing room for coffee, I noticed that the Count was drooping even more visibly than before the baba, so I suggested that perhaps he generally took a little rest in the afternoon and was immediately assured that he did; if I would excuse the Countess just a few minutes, Cécile would entertain me while the Countess saw him settled; then she would return for a little talk with me. I can't say that I found Cécile very entertaining, but she faded away as soon as her mother came back and Maurice disappeared without saying anything to me about a visit to the stables—I gather both acting on the Countess's instructions, so that she and I wouldn't be disturbed during the course of our little talk. This, of course, related largely to Anne's condition and I couldn't help gathering that the Countess was very annoyed because her daughter hadn't become pregnant immediately after marriage; certainly, she (the Countess) had impressed on her (Anne) that this was expected of her. In that case, if the first child hadn't been a boy, there still would have been time for others before her husband's death. I said I was very sure that Anne would always do her best to live up to expectations, but there were some things that couldn't be done to order and this, definitely, was one of them. Instead of regretting that she hadn't had prospects earlier, shouldn't we be glad that she had them now? I managed, though not without maneuvering, to guide the conversation to other channels and I feel sure that, if Anne has a boy, her dereliction, if such it may be called, will be speedily forgiven and forgotten; but, if you inherit the title, I'm afraid the De Briares will be very much displeased. Anyway, now that I've seen the family, I understand that the Countess really can't leave her crippled husband and that it's quite out of the question for him to travel; that Cécile would only be one more burden to everyone at Cloneen; and that Maurice could well be much more of a menace to your peace of mind than Lawrence Donovan.*

As I was saying good-by and thanking the Count and Countess for their hospitality, their cousin reappeared and asked me if I wouldn't give him the pleasure of coming to take tea at his modest bachelor

establishment before I went back to Trouville. As it was too late for me
to return to Paris that evening, anyway, I decided I might as well,
though, having gleaned that he was in rather straitened circumstances,
I thought his bachelor establishment really might be very modest,
whereas I knew perfectly well that Stefan's would not. Well, we
branched off into one of those narrow side roads, with high hedgerows,
and presently we came to a white gate, labeled Haras du Lieu Plaisant,
with wonderful half-timbered buildings just beyond it—stables, commons, manor—all grouped around lovely green lawns with flowered
borders. Maurice insists this is only a farm, not an estate, but that he
prefers to live here by himself, rather than with his relatives, because
in this way he can be completely independent; and that he has a very
good housekeeper who looks after all his material wants. I can't be glad
enough that I went there because, though everything about the De
Briare château is completely and classically and traditionally correct,
this place has something about it that the other lacks—something that
goes deeper than charm or antiquity or individuality or any word I can
think of to describe it. I can only say that, if I were a young woman,
just starting my married life and very deeply in love with my husband,
this is the sort of place I'd want to go to as a bride and then live there
happily ever after.

I told Maurice this and he replied that I couldn't possibly have said
anything which would have pleased him more, that his father and
mother had been ideally happy there and that he hoped, when he had
a wife, he and she would follow in their footsteps. I left there feeling
rather thoughtful and, perhaps, you will be, too, when you read this
letter.

Much love always,
Granny Glover

Although this letter did provide Peter with considerable food for
thought, he did not refer to it when he next wrote Anne.

Gweedore House
September 15, 1882

Dear Anne,

When I last wrote, I still didn't know how Alec was going to feel
about taking a trip with me. I found that he would not only be glad
to do so, but that he was perfectly willing to leave the itinerary to
me, though it hadn't previously occurred to him that it was the rather

rugged territory where my grandfather Glover laid the foundation for his fortune and earned his title which had the most appeal for me. But then, he didn't realize how much I loved that grandfather. Perhaps you didn't either, though you do know how much I love Lady Susannah, for I'm sure I never told you about him. But now I do feel like it, so you'll understand where I've been, what I've been doing and why. (If you're not interested in "why," just skip the next five paragraphs.)

When I was a little boy, Sir Michael and Lady Susannah used to come regularly to visit us in Boston and I looked forward to these visits because Grandfather always told me such wonderful stories: fairy stories when I was very small and then, as I grew older, stories that still had a lot of magic in them, as far as I am concerned. It was an easy step from the one about the little people who secretly finished the tired weaver's work for him every night until he spied on them, to the one about the rescue of hundreds of famished people by a man who was the first to realize that the cottage weaving, which provided them with nothing more than a scant supply of the material for their own crude clothing, could be developed into a great industry.

This man was Lord George Hill. He was Grandfather Glover's great hero and no wonder, for he was one of the most humane, as well as the most resourceful and far-sighted, men of his era. He disproved the old theory that the younger sons of noblemen don't usually amount to much, for he was the fifth son of the Marquis of Downshire. Grandfather was the son of a captain in the army and, despite the difference in their backgrounds, they had known each other in Londonderry, where both the Hill and the Glover families had bases. So, when Lord George bought 23,000 acres around Gweedore, where the countryside was very poor and the people in desperate need of succor, Grandfather went to him and asked for a chance to help with the work of reclamation. Lord George already had an agent, but he said he could use a manager who was willing to learn Irish, live in the area and start with a very small salary; and that was how the professional association began.

I think we should really give Granny Glover credit for part of its success. She'd been in love with Michael ever since they met at a military ball when she was sixteen (a fact of which I recently reminded her when she said Janet was too young to know her own mind). But her parents had opposed her marriage because of the difference in rank and religion and had persuaded her to wait until she was twenty-one before she married. (They knew, too, after that she could do so without their consent and they didn't want to risk an elopement.) So my mother was a brand-new baby when the Gweedore project began. It couldn't have been easy, brought up as she was, for Granny to join in the pioneering, but apparently she never hesitated a second between sharing her husband's hardships, whatever they were, and remaining in comfort with his parents at The Lodge in Rathmullan, the ancestral home of Michael's mother. Some day I hope I can get Granny's version of exactly what Gweedore seemed like to her. I don't blame her for enjoying luxuries increasingly as she grew older.

Lord George built a church, a shop and a grain store at Bunbeg, the little port of Gweedore, and gradually he built good roads, too. The grain store provided an alternative market for the corn that had previously been sold to poteen makers, and during the Famine it was turned into a food depot and helped ward off starvation. He built the hotel where Alec and I are staying now and for a long while it was the only one for miles around where a stranger could get a decent lodging, so outsiders began to come here; besides, it furnished needed employment and a market for local produce. But his most important work lay in his direct contact with his tenants. I think he's likely to be my great hero, too, for I honestly believe no one man has done as much to redeem the reproach that rests on Irish landlordism. If I can feel, when I die, that I've done half as much as he did, I'll believe my life has been worth while. There were no more evictions on the Gweedore property after Lord George took over and, when he had reformed the land holdings, he offered prizes for the best crops, the best-kept cottages and so on. He could speak Irish, which he'd learned as a child from his nurse, so there was no language barrier between him and the many tenants who couldn't speak English; and he regularly visited every one of the cottages himself. So did my grandfather. Naturally, he didn't have the capital that would permit him to build a grain store or a hotel; but he learned to speak Irish, too, and he was just as quick as Lord George to see that more could be done about marketing the local weaving than had been tried so far. He encouraged the people around Gweedore and Bunbeg to take their woollen goods to Ardara, where fairs were held every spring, and compete with the craftsmen who lived nearer that center, some of whom had been the victims of eviction to make room for the large-scale grazing of imported Scottish black-faced sheep. A lot of these sheep were killed and there were many acts of violent retaliation. But the weaving went right on, because the weavers couldn't move their looms and they became the only settled tradesmen, so to speak. And every farmer grew a little flax, thus the people had homemade linen for sheets, towels, shirts and the like, as well as warm cloth for their other clothes. Grandfather told me that on Fair Days the whole street at Ardara would be lined with hogsheads of flax. The cottagers brought their flannels there to sell and then these were bought by small dealers and hawked around the country towns—Strabane, Castlederg, Castlefin, Letterkenny—and even as far away as Londonderry. And so Grandfather Glover founded the family fortune because, of course, he had a finger in all these pies (or should I say a finger on all these goods?). He and Lord George both dressed in homespun and for a while it looked as if there'd be only the white and gray and black they wore, since, though he'd experimented in selling dyes at Bunbeg, that hadn't worked very well; then the people themselves began to use vegetable matters, briar roots, heather, lichens, crotal—even soot from their chimneys. They drew their own designs, too. They made blankets, petticoats, dresses, trousers, drawers, wrappers—almost everything you can think of—and succeeded in getting a beautiful shade of blue that was used principally for men's clothes and that required the services of a special craftsman called a dyester. Then there were other craftsmen called clothiers who had small mills known as "tuck" mills and run by water power. One of these, on a tributary of the Ardara River, is still in use and has a mill dam to catch the water in dry weather, a mill wheel, et cetera.

After supplying the hawkers and small dealers with products he could control or at least supervise, Grandfather Glover's next step was to begin collecting Donegal tweed and selling it to institutions. By the time this had been going on with great success for about twenty years, he was considered almost as important a public figure as Lord George Hill—really a civic benefactor—and he was knighted. But it still didn't occur to anyone that this homespun product could become a fashionable, as well as a practical, material. We have to give Grandfather's nephew, Dermot McKeever, who went into business with him, credit for that and for having it exhibited at the Dublin Arts and Crafts Show last spring. Actually, it's too soon to know whether or not it's going to catch on, but I'm taking the liberty of sending you two lengths that I bought in Dunlewy. I should think they'd make up very well for winter wear at Cloneen. But let me know what you think, both about the materials and about the colors. Naturally, I know you wouldn't wear the blue until you're out of mourning, but you could put it away and keep it until then and meantime wear the white. The blue would be wonderful with your hair.

Well, two days after I arrived at Rathmullan, Alec and I set out on horseback, having decided this was the most practical as well as the pleasantest, way to travel, after we found it would be possible to send by mail car all the gear we could not conveniently carry in our saddlebags. The McKeevers have an ample supply of pleasure horses, though no stud, so two could easily be spared. Meanwhile, we had been back to Ramelton, which was something I had wanted to do ever since I was there before. I still think that the view from Drummonaghan Bridge is one of the most beautiful I have seen in Ireland and, besides, I had discovered that I enjoyed fishing a great deal more than I expected. The place is even lovelier now than it was in June, but the salmon are no longer gliding quietly around in the pool, very skillfully eluding anglers. They are leaping up the waterfall, so many that the place seems alive with them, and it's the easiest thing in the world to catch them. But though the closed season doesn't start for another fortnight and I did land one, I didn't feel it was sporting to try for more than that, for the reason these fish are rushing upstream is because they are simply wild to reach the fresh water and their spawning grounds. They do not seem like real fish to me, these sparkling, silver creatures that return year after year to the same spot to lay their eggs, just as a swallow returns year after year to its nest. Alec told me that he once fastened a copper ring around a salmon's tail and that, for three successive seasons, it returned to the same place. He also told me that gold and silver rings had been attached by Eastern princes to salmon, to prove that a link existed between the Persian Gulf and the Caspian and Northern Seas. I'm quite ready to believe it and I'm only surprised there aren't more Irish legends about salmon or, perhaps, it's that I haven't run across them yet. Certainly, they're not only like birds in some respects; they're almost like human beings. If swans can form a part of folklore, why shouldn't salmon, too?

Well, here I am rambling on again, without telling you anything definite about my trip with Alec. The first day out, we reached Doe Castle, once the stronghold of the MacSweeneys, in time for tea, and Ards House for dinner and the night. Dermot McKeever had sent a wire to Mr. Alexander Stewart, who owns both places and has members of his family living in both, asking if it would be convenient to have us stay and had received a most cordial reply. The castle still has a dungeon, drawbridge, et cetera and, like every place connected with Red Hugh O'Donnell, who lived there for a time with his foster father, Owen MacSweeney, still retains the stamp of his vitality, undimmed by the centuries that have passed since he was there. Ards has an equally beautiful location on still another peninsula of Sheep Haven Bay, an avenue five miles long, splendid grounds and every amenity in the thoroughly modernized house where we were so hospitably entertained.

Mr. Stewart urged us to prolong our visit for at least a day or two, but as we were due the next night at Ballyconnell, the Olferts' house near Falcarragh, and Gweedore was still my main objective, we left at a comfortable hour and jogged along all day with the sea on one side of us and the mountains on the other, with long stretches of peat bogs and fields dotted with bog cotton and wreathed with purple heather and wild fuchsia along the roadside, besides the usual pastures densely populated by sheep and cows. And, every now and then, we saw a lone swan in a cove and, once, almost a flotilla of them surprisingly close to the highway. Ballyconnell is another fine estate and is set in a natural garden. Like most gardens, this one seems a peaceful place; though the white Stone of Cloghaneely, which is elsewhere on the grounds, has anything but a peaceful story. (I'll have to save that for some other time.)

Much as I appreciated and enjoyed the hospitality of the Stewarts and the Olferts, I was glad we didn't have to make Gweedore for dinner on any given night, because, after leaving Ballyconnell, we chanced upon a spinning party. It seems that, half a century ago, these were fairly frequent: a group of girls, who all had spinning wheels in their own houses, brought their wheels to one house and worked together until the men came in from the fields in the evening. Then they'd all dance. We were lucky enough to run into just such a party, though they're rather rare now, and while the farmers didn't give us a very warm welcome, we pointed out that we were no more de trop than the male weavers who hadn't been in the fields and who, by this time, had joined the party, too. Naturally, the type of dancing was all new to me and the Haymaker's Jig was beyond me, but I didn't do too badly with the Turnpike Reel. We ended up spending what was left of the night—which wasn't much—at a neighboring cottage and then going on to a housewarming the next day.

Now that we are finally settled at Gweedore, Alec thinks we ought to climb Errigal if we are going to get everything we can of the local color out of this neighborhood, and probably he's right. It's one of the most astonishing mountains I ever saw for, instead of being a gentle blue slope, like most Irish mountains I've seen, it's a whitish crystal cone, fantastically like Fujiyama! Personally, I'd be just as well satisfied to see all I can of the buildings Lord George put up in Bunbeg and of the home weaving that's going strong all around us. I'd also like to put in some more time fishing, as there are two rivers and three lakes near by available for that purpose. I don't believe I'll ever recapture the thrill of my first sight of the leaping salmon at the waterfall by Drummonaghan Bridge; but in the Gweedore River there's a salmon leap about half a mile from here and below that a series of rapids and holes, in any one of which a fish may lie, so that there is always broken water to fish in, and I suppose I ought to give it a trial.

We have no definite plans for leaving, nor do I want to make any, unless something arises at Cloneen which you feel needs my attention and I realize that isn't likely. After all, lightning never strikes twice in the same place, so I'm not looking for another urgent telegram.

As ever,
Peter

Peter put too much reliance in the old proverb. While he and Alec were still at Gweedore, he received the following telegram:

CRISIS IN STUD STOP LADY O'TOOLE SERIOUSLY ILL STOP IMMEDIATE RETURN IMPERATIVE STOP   MACAULIFFE

18

This time, when the train stopped at Cloncoole station in the gathering dusk and Peter went down the steps to the platform, after a long tedious trip with equally long and tedious waits between connections, he knew that a ruddy, thickset man, wearing a long black frieze coat, would be waiting for him and he also knew that the news this man brought him would be bad. But at least there was no band of crepe around the tall hat.

"Well, Ryan," he said, going forward rapidly, "I hope it isn't always going to be something sad that brings me to Cloneen. Of course, you know the first question to which I want an answer: how is her ladyship?"

"Confined to her room, sir, with Dr. Carey in attendance."

"Yes, I gathered that. But is she any worse than when Mr. Mac-Auliffe wired me that she was seriously ill? And do you know what this illness is?"

"I understand she's no worse, God be thanked. I took the liberty of bringing the trap, sir, instead of the carriage, because I knew you'd want to hear everything I could tell you right away and that would be easier than if you were sitting behind me."

"You did quite right," Peter said, climbing in, thankful that Ryan did not feel called upon to delay his news by waiting for assurance that he had not taken a liberty. "Please go on."

"As to the nature of her ladyship's illness," Ryan continued, gathering up the reins, "we'd been given to understand, from Mrs. Brennan, that the Mistress was in a delicate condition. Of course, that was news we'd all been hoping for this long time and everyone on the place was more than pleased to learn of her ladyship's expectations and anxious that nothing should happen to upset her or worry her."

"But something evidently did happen to upset her. Please get on with the story, Ryan."

"It was the Moonlighters, sir."

"The *Moonlighters!* What on earth are those?"

"It's some sort of a secret assassination club with revengeful purposes, sir, successors to the Ribboners and kin to the Invincibles, who committed the Phoenix Park murders; only the Moonlighters do their evil work in the country, instead of the cities."

"Are you trying to tell me that there was an attempt on her ladyship's life?"

"No, sir, not on her ladyship's own life, thank God. But what comes close to it." Ryan stopped, choking over the words. "Her horses."

"Her horses! Have the Moonlighters killed her horses?" Peter asked, choking, too.

"Not all of them, sir. The hooligans didn't get beyond the stud before they were discovered and stopped."

"But how did they get that far? I understood the grooms in both stables and stud took turns as watchmen and that Farrell and Riordan were on call besides."

"Right you are, sir, and we thought they could all be trusted, but the watchman that night was an out-and-out traitor. He let the Moonlighters in. Since he was Monarch's own groom, the stallion was used to having him come into the stall and sometimes to bring another man with him; so, beforehand, it seemed to them it would be easy enough to cut Monarch's throat with a slasher and finish him off then and there. But he plunged and burst out into the yard, kicking them both, and the other Moonlighters attacked with pitchforks and billhooks and cut him down. By this time, the racket had roused Riordan and the other grooms and there was a free-for-all with injuries on both sides; but some of the Moonlighters managed to get to the paddock and rip open four of the brood mares, two of them in foal for the first time, before they made their escape. Riordan had no choice but to put the mares out of their misery. It was the shots that woke the Mistress and she leaped from her bed and rushed over to the stud. No wonder she fainted at what she saw there. She was carried back to the dower house and Dr. Carey came at once and gave her something to put her to sleep. But the shock was such a great one, loving her horses as she does—"

Ryan stopped, unable to go on. But Peter had to know the worst and he phrased his next question bluntly and cogently.

"You mean she has lost her baby?"

"No, sir, not as yet. We're all praying and the last we heard Dr. Carey was still hopeful that she wouldn't, but that it was still touch and go. Would you wish me to take you straight to the dower house, sir?"

"I think you'd better. If the Mistress is under sedation—I mean, if Dr. Carey is trying to keep her half asleep—he won't want her disturbed. But if he's there perhaps I can get the whole story from him and understand it better than I can, getting it piecemeal. So far, I don't understand why the Moonlighters wanted to slaughter her ladyship's defenseless horses. In fact, I don't understand anything, except that the Mistress is seriously ill and that, unless and until she's out of danger, nothing else matters much."

"And you're right, sir. Except that, until you do understand everything, don't think too harshly of Riordan and the stud grooms, even if there was one traitor among them, without whose help the Moonlighters couldn't have got in or killed Monarch; and he's already punished, for he was kicked so hard that he's gone astray in the head, besides being crippled. There's two of the young boys bad hurt, sir, from trying to defend the mares and Riordan's got a wicked head wound. Dr. Carey is at the dower house, waiting to see you and, after he's relieved your mind, you'll be wanting to see the Chief Constable, who's waiting for you at the mansion with Mr. MacAuliffe."

"All right. But before I see anyone else, I've got to hear what Dr. Carey has to tell me."

The doctor was awaiting Peter in the library at the dower house and, without preamble, told him what he most wanted and needed to learn.

"If we can get her by one more night without disturbance, I think we can say the danger of miscarriage is averted," he said. "Of course, the obstacle to success lies in the fact that the disturbance may come from her troubled thoughts and not from anything that's happening or that she fears is happening around her. There's a limit to the amount of sedation I can give her, without affecting the child, as well as herself, but we haven't reached that limit yet and I don't think we'll have to go too close to it. She understands how important it is that she should bring a healthy baby into the world—not merely important to her personally, but in many other ways. And now that she's getting her second wind, so to speak, she'll begin to dwell on that and not on the shambles she saw. I believe tomorrow she might see you for a few minutes. A short sensible talk with you might do a great deal toward bringing her back to her usual sane viewpoint."

"Unfortunately, I don't feel sure that she wants to have a talk with me, either short and sensible or long and visionary," Peter said, sitting down. "But if she asks for me or if you want me to try, even if she doesn't, naturally I will. Now I think I'll ask Solange to bring me a drink, in which perhaps you'll join me, while you explain some of this disaster's background, unless you feel you need to go immediately to Riordan, who's in a bad way, if I understood Ryan correctly."

"He is in a bad way, but I think he'll recover and I don't need to go to him immediately. His trouble's partly mental, too. He feels sure you'll blame him for what happened on account of his background, though you haven't a more loyal employee on the place and that's saying a good deal. And he's just about heartbroken over the slaughter—he loved those horses almost as much as Lady O'Toole did."

"I don't know anything about his background, so I can't put the blame for what happened on that, anyway."

"You didn't know that his grandfather—maybe his father, too—was a tinker? There are no people that know more about horses, instinctively, than they do and, when they rise in the world enough to get beyond a hedge school, they tend to learning all they can about veterinary practices and to breeding better and better strains. Unfortunately, the term 'tinker' has a pretty close association with stealing, poaching, trespassing—what have you; also association with other lawless groups, like Moonlighters, for instance. I expect Riordan thought he'd lived all such associations down. Now he knows he's open to suspicion. But the man you ought to blame for this disaster isn't Riordan. It's Danahy."

"Danahy!"

"Yes. I hope you won't be too hard on him, either."

"I'm beginning to think you don't want me to be hard on anyone. Meanwhile, the fact remains that Lady O'Toole is seriously ill, that several men are badly injured and that the stud is a shambles."

"Yes, I know. It's a tragic situation for anyone to face and especially for a young man who hasn't lived with battle, murder and sudden death all his life the way we Irish do and doesn't know how far the spirit of revenge can go. It's in our blood, just the way the passion to conquer and rule is in the Prussians' blood. When I said I hoped you wouldn't be too hard on Danahy, it was because he's devoted to you. He really thought he was serving your best interests when he decided that those bare acres, which the shiftless, lazy Sullivans won't take the trouble to cultivate, had better be planted with trees. He knows how interested you are in forestation."

"So was the Earl of Hartley, if I haven't been misinformed."

"That's true. But you can't compare what happened to the Sullivans with what happened to Hartley's unfortunate tenants."

Well, what *did* happen to the Sullivans and what connection has that with what happened in the stud?"

"They hadn't paid their rent for more than a year or anything on account. They wouldn't try to raise anything, though they'd been warned again and again that they must. And they had relatives to whom they could go and who weren't penalized for taking them in."

"Won't you put what you're saying into plain English? Do you mean they were evicted?"

"I'm afraid so. But there wasn't any force used. No one was hurt or injured."

"Weren't my uncle's orders that no one should be evicted, unless the case were first brought before him? Isn't Lady O'Toole trying her best to continue all his policies? Aren't I doing the best I know how to help her? And yet, when she's ill and I'm away. . . . Those people must be put back in their home!"

"Mr. Bradford, there isn't any home for them to go back to. It's torn down and the ground where it stood is planted with trees. And Angie Sullivan's brother, Dan Foley, is a Moonlighter. And her brother-in-law, Frank O'Leary, was one of the grooms in the stud. One traitor among all the faithful made it easy for the Moonlighters to get in. There's your story in plain English."

After dawn the next day, Peter was still at his desk writing letters. Not that any of them was long. But all had required a great deal of thought before he put pen to paper. And he did not try to decide what he should say until he had talked with every man on the place and sat for some time at Riordan's bedside, finding at last that he and the studmaster were not strangers to each other, but friends and allies. ("Here what I've been longing to do ever since I reached Ireland has been to make friends with some tinkers and, if possible, travel with them for at least a little while and I never knew that right at my doorstep was the very man to make this easy for me.") He had also seen Danahy and promised to reserve judgment until he could give the situation more thought. ("Of course, you know that my first reaction was to tell you that you were through, that you'd deliberately disregarded orders that had been given you by the dead, whom you were in duty bound to obey faithfully, and that once was too often to have that happen. But my sober second thought is that you acted according to your lights and your tradition and that if we put our heads together maybe we can think of a way to salvage something constructive out of the wreckage.") He had talked with MacAuliffe and the Constable about the criminal aspects of the outrage and now he was as nearly ready to write the letters as he ever would be and might as well begin.

The first one was to Donovan.

Dear Larry—he wrote—

I'm sure you have read in the papers of the terrible catastrophe that has befallen the Cloneen Stud, but I think perhaps you do not know how seriously this affected Anne when she saw the shambles. I realize you feel that she has not been as cordial to you lately as you would have liked and, under normal circumstance, would have felt justified in expecting, considering your long friendship. But I do not think you know why she has led a more retired life than usual, quite aside from her mourning: she is hoping for a baby in March and she has had some of the discomforts which I understand are usual in early pregnancy, including sudden attacks of faintness. One of these overcame her the first time she went out riding after the Earl had died and was also the first indication of her condition, which she had not suspected. Naturally, after that she had to be very careful. She meant to tell you about her happy prospects, as soon as she was well enough to receive visitors again; but now that she has had such a terrible shock in the slaughter of her horses, Dr. Carey is keeping her quieter than ever. So I am giving you her news, as the time has come when I think you should have it and, unfortunately, there is no telling when she can do so herself.

Of course, when she does come out again, she ought not to see any empty stalls and I am hoping you will be willing to help me take care that she doesn't. I don't think I should leave here again, even for overnight, until after the baby is born, because so much went wrong in the short time I was in Donegal; and, supposing that I could and did, I wouldn't know what to buy or where to look for it. But I can go anywhere you would advise if I can make the trip between daylight and dark. Poor Riordan will do all he can to help me, but he won't be up and around for quite awhile and you can realize there's no time to lose in getting started. If you could tell me where to locate a stallion and six brood mares worthy of the Cloneen Stud or, if not that many, at least two or three and maybe go with me to see them, if the trips could be short, or go by yourself if they had to be longer, I would be everlastingly your debtor and I believe that, for Anne's sake, you might be willing to undertake the commission. I know she would have confidence in your judgment and so would I. I also know you are very busy with public affairs which require a great deal of your attention, so I hope you will not feel my request is presumptuous.

With kind regards, I am

Sincerely yours,
Peter Bradford

He hesitated a minute, still holding his pen. Then he wrote a postscript:

I realize that what I've suggested would cost a great deal. I think I can take care of that part all right.

His second letter was to Lady Susannah. It came easily now to write about Anne and his determination to rebuild the stud. It was not quite so easy to confess that he had put his pride in his pocket and disregarded his fears of personal rivalry to the extent of asking Larry Donovan to help him. And the last part of his letter was still harder going.

Of course, I can't ask Father to do anything toward financing this and while I haven't any idea how much it is going to cost, I do have a pretty good idea that it will be more than I can meet out of my income or even by using a certain amount of capital—which, obviously, would mean less income in the future, perhaps less than will be required to keep this place going or I wouldn't hesitate a minute. So I am wondering whether you would be willing to lend me what I need, in a completely businesslike way—I mean, charging interest and so on. I wouldn't want to borrow it with any other arrangement. If this would be offensive to you, would you be willing to give me, outright, as much as I need and deduct that sum from whatever you meant to leave me in your will? I wouldn't suggest this if you hadn't told me yourself that you had made me your heir, with just token gifts to my sisters, and *that you knew this was what Grandfather wanted you to do. But, under all the circumstances, I hope and believe you won't feel I'm grasping or anything else objectionable, because I love you very much and wouldn't for the world consciously do anything that would make you think less of me.*

Naturally, I'm calling an immediate halt to work on the tower. That can await a more propitious time to spend money just for fun. The present crisis is anything but that.

> *Devotedly, your grandson,*
> *Peter*

The third letter was the shortest and the hardest to write.

Dear Anne,

Dr. Carey tells me that you should keep as quiet as possible, so I shall not try to see you, though I should feel much better if I could have your assurance that everything I am doing, as your "chosen representative," meets with your approval. As you know, I left here a fortnight ago, partly because I wanted to see something of Ireland, but mostly because I felt you'd be happier if I were gone. Before I went, I told you I'd let you run everything to suit yourself until March and then modified that, in a letter, to say unless I were sent for. As you also know, I was sent for and I shan't leave again until after the baby is born. I won't ask you to see me, unless I feel, for some reason, that it's absolutely necessary, but you know you have only to send for me at any time that you think it is necessary or advisable. But, perhaps, when you feel better, you'll send me a message from time to time, just to let me know that you think things are going all right.

Let me say that, for the present, there will be three men on watch, day and night, one in the tower, one on the grounds and one at the stud and that the gates will be kept locked. Wade, Tim and Luke will take turns sitting up at night in the house; Andy, Ryan and Ned in the stables; and I am planning to stay at the stud cottage until Riordan is better and will take turns in keeping watch with the stud grooms that seem to me most reliable after I have had a chance to talk with them. As to the best means of dealing directly with the Moonlighters, I'm still undecided in my own mind and haven't had time to seek expert advice. My instinct is to go after them hot and heavy and bring them all to trial and, if possible, to execution. But I'm not sure that's the best policy. I'm inclined to think vengeance has played too large a part already in Irish history and that maybe it's time to try something else. Anyway, I'll give the matter prayerful thought and I'm not joking when I say that.

All my love,
Peter

19

By the time the letters were finished, broad daylight had come and it seemed hardly worth while to go to bed. However, Peter had gone practically without sleep for two nights, he had eaten little and irregularly, he had neither bathed nor changed his clothes and he had been in a constant state of emotional turmoil. As he sealed the last envelope, he decided he could deal with the whole harrowing situation, and especially the interview with Danahy, more competently if he were not so exhausted, both mentally and physically. Taking the letters with him, so that, as soon as he rang, they could be handed over to Tim for delivery and posting, he toiled up to his room, to find that the boy was already there and that, as usual, a cheerful fire was burning on the hearth and a tray, invitingly set with food and drink, was on a nearby table.

"I thought there might be something you would require, sir, before you retired and, seeing as you're always so thoughtful, you might not ring, thinking I'd be abed at this hour," Tim said, almost apologetically. "So I took the liberty of coming without waiting to hear from you. I hope that was in order, sir."

"It was tremendously kind and considerate. I'd like you to take the letter addressed to the Mistress over to the dower house and tell Solange to give it to her as soon as she wakes, unless Dr. Carey has issued orders which would forbid this. Get the other letters to the post office in time to catch the first mail. I don't want or need anything here—you seem to have provided for my requirements already. The study must have been colder than I realized for the fire feels extra good and, while this isn't my usual hour for whiskey, I believe I'll have some, along with a sandwich or two. I'm afraid I shan't do much washing until I've had some sleep, but I know I'm safe in assuming that there's a jug of hot water wrapped in a towel on the washstand, so that's taken care of, too, if I should change my mind."

"I'm sorry about the study being cold, sir, but we thought you wouldn't want to be disturbed. I'll take care of the letters right away. And you're sure there's nothing else just now?"

"Very sure. And you were right not to disturb me in the study. Good night, Tim. I mean, good day to you. And thank you for everything."

Peter slept until nearly noon and, when Tim reappeared, it was to bring the best of news: the Mistress had had a very good night and Dr. Carey, who would be in to see the Master later on, had not forbidden her to have the note; in fact, he had given it to her himself and remained beside her while she read it; he would be bringing a message from her when he came along later on. Riordan was so much improved that he was bound and determined to get up, and Dr. Carey thought it probably would do him no harm to stir around a little in his own house. As to the injured grooms, they were holding their own and that was all that could be expected at present. Dr. Carey thought it might be best to send them to hospital, but he would talk that over with the Master. Mr. Danahy was waiting in the office at the stables, to learn at what time the Master would wish to see him.

"As soon as I've had my breakfast, which will also be my lunch, so tell Cook to make it one of her biggest and best. And then get a tub and lots of hot water here as quickly as you can."

"That I will, sir."

The breakfast was, indeed, one of Cook's biggest and best and Peter ate it with healthy appetite. Dr. Carey had said, in referring to Anne, that now she had her second wind things would go better with her, as they had; and Peter felt the same might be true of him. As soon as he had finished his copious meal, he went to the study and sent for Danahy. When the agent came in and stood, awkward and tongue-tied, near the door, Peter quietly asked him to be seated on the opposite side of the double desk.

"As you see, I'm beginning to make this room into an out-and-out office," he said. "And I'd like very much to borrow something of yours that I've coveted ever since I first saw it."

"What's that, sir?"

"Your fan-shaped rent table. I realize it's valuable as an antique, besides being very serviceable as a piece of office equipment. Perhaps you can find me another like yours, so we'd each have one; but meanwhile I'd like that one here, so that I could examine its contents at any time, without waiting to go to your house. I've got a pretty heavy schedule and such an arrangement would save me a lot of time."

"You don't mean that, if I'd lend you the rent table—which, of course, I would—you'd let me keep on with you?"

The man's voice was heavy with incredulity. He looked across the desk at Peter, a gleam of hope in his eyes.

"Well, that's one of the easier conditions. You may not agree to the others, which are a little stiffer."

"Mr. Bradford, I'd been the late Earl's agent for nearly thirty years when he died and my father was his father's agent before that. I wouldn't know where to go if I had to leave Cloncoole and I couldn't stay there and stand the shame, if you discharged me. I can't think of any condition you'd make—"

"The Sullivans must go back."

"Go back! But that's impossible! Their house, such as it was, is torn down and the land's all planted with trees!"

"The house, such as it was, happened to be their home—their only home. I believe the Irish have a very strong feeling about their homes, which isn't hard for me to understand, not only because I'm half Irish, but because New Englanders have it, too, and the other half of me is a New Englander. Where I come from, we cling to our homes from generation to generation, even when they're just little old farmhouses that a Midwesterner, with a pseudo-Gothic monstrosity, wouldn't look at twice. . . . The trees at the Sullivans' haven't been planted long enough to take root. After all, I was gone only about a fortnight and I don't suppose the eviction took place the minute my back was turned. It should be easy enough to dig them up and plant them someplace else, where they wouldn't be in the way of anyone's house—with twelve hundred acres available, it ought not to be too hard to find one. Perhaps we could persuade the Sullivans to help with the replanting. I know they seem rather averse to doing any kind of work, but forestation might just happen to interest them. They might even be willing to help build themselves a new house, perhaps a little better than the old one, and have a housewarming. I went to one in Gweedore and everyone seemed to be having a very good time. There was a fiddler and a flute player and even an old harper, to furnish music, and all kinds of dances I'd never so much as heard of before. Not just Haymakers' Jigs and Turnpike Reels, but square dances with queer names like 'The Walls of Limerick' and 'The Siege of Ennis.'"

Peter stopped, conscious that Danahy's first look of mingled hope and incredulity had now changed to one of utter bewilderment. If the agent had understood correctly, his employer was proposing to re-establish a completely unreliable and unremunerative tenant who, moreover, was indirectly responsible for the most serious agrarian crime the Moonlighters had perpetrated since Danahy could remember. The very idea was so fantastic that he simply could not grasp it.

"Of course," Peter went on, "I don't know just how the preliminaries should be handled. It's very important that you should save face, as the Chinese say—not just on account of your own feelings in the matter, but on account of your future authority. For you must have authority —only you'll share it with me. We'll settle everything between us, right here in this room, with that rent table fanning out beside this desk and every one of its drawers properly docketed. You will have duplicate records, because the tenants will continue to report to you and pay their rents at your house, and you'll continue to take charge of the actual monies. Then you'll come to me by yourself, barring some exceptional cases where you feel the tenant has got to be brought into the discussion. If you and I disagree, it will naturally have to be my decision that prevails and, if you misunderstand my decision, as you certainly seem to have done in the case of the Sullivans, you would have to leave my employ without any further notice. This time, I think I'd better go to see the Sullivans myself. I was planning to do so, any-way—I mean, I was planning to visit all my tenants, so I could talk to them, and I'm also planning to study Irish, to make that more prac-tical. My grandfather Glover used to visit all the tenants, when he was Lord George Hill's manager, and he studied Irish, not to be outdone by Lord George, who had complete mastery of it. There were no ten-ant problems in Gweedore after they took charge. Did you know about that?"

"I can't say I did, sir. It's the O'Toole history that I'm better ac-quainted with."

"All these people were men of a great tradition. Now to get back to the Sullivans: I'll tell them I had given instructions before I went away to plant more trees, wherever this was feasible, which is true enough; and that, unfortunately, it hadn't occurred to me to specify exactly what places I considered feasible, which is also true; and that then you misinterpreted my instructions. If there's what Lady Susannah calls a lavender lie wrapped up in this, I think we'll get absolution for it. I don't need to tell the Sullivans that I know Angie's brother is a Moonlighter and that her brother-in-law was a groom on this place.

That is, I don't need to *say* I know it. If they don't catch on to that pretty quickly, they haven't as much intuition as is normal in the Irish."

"And do you mean to say, sir, you'd tell this lavender lie, as you call it, to save my face and let the Sullivans live in this fine new house you'd give them and crow over the fools they's made of us and brag that it's easy enough to get away with murder if you only know how?"

"I'll answer part of that by telling you a little story, Danahy, about something that was once said by one of our most prominent politicians —the only one I know of, by the way, who was never defeated for any office. Some little upstart journalist wrote a rather impudent piece about him and sent him a copy, before publication, offering to revise it if there were anything in it that would embarrass him. The politician replied in just one sentence, 'Nothing that you could say could possibly embarrass me.'"

"So you think—"

"I think the Sullivans couldn't convince many people that you and I are fools, because we're not and this is very generally recognized—or if it isn't yet, it will be. In other words, nothing they can say is going to embarrass me and I hope it won't embarrass you. Naturally, this new house will be theirs to keep only on the condition that, henceforth, they raise something on their land and pay something on account as soon as they do so. If the land is so barren that it's hard to find anything that will grow on it, except trees, then it's up to us to get expert advice on what will. This is September—harvest time. I think they ought to have a year, that is until the next harvest time, to see what they can produce. They may not come up with much, but I believe they'll come up with something."

Danahy moved uneasily in his chair and again looked across the desk at Peter, this time without speaking.

"As to what you said about murder being easy, if you know how," Peter went on, "I know it does look that way sometimes. I was rather close to one that did in July and it made a pretty deep impression on 'me. However, there's no cause for comparison between what happened then in Donegal and what's happened here and why. So far as I know, there's never been a murder involving a human being at Cloneen, which isn't a bad record for a place in Ireland or any other oppressed country; and there never will be one for the same reason that murder occurred near Rathmullan. Perhaps you're right, perhaps some people may call me a fool, but I doubt if anyone will nickname me 'The Bad Earl.' On the other hand, though I hate to say it, I know the murderers of Hartley had many sound reasons for feeling that vengeance was justified. There's no possible justification for the wanton destruction of harmless, innocent animals, in order to wreak vengeance on their owner, especially when their owner is a lady of infinite goodness, with expectations of a long-awaited child. The Sullivans must have their home back or, rather, one to take the place of the one they lost; but no one even remotely connected with them can ever have a job at Cloneen again. The risk is too great. There's no question of discharging Frank O'Leary, because he's so badly hurt, through his own wicked folly, that he'll never be able to do a strong man's work again. And I believe that will be a bitter pill for him to swallow when we get the new stud going."

"You're going to have a new stud, sir? After what happened in the old one?"

"Certainly. I hope to get it started within a month. It will depend a little on the answers to three letters I sent out this morning. But it won't be much longer than that. Meanwhile, do we have everything settled about the Sullivans?"

Danahy rose slowly and pushed back his chair.

"It looks that way," he said slowly. "And it isn't for me to complain that you're going too far in being fair to them, seeing that you've also been more than fair to me. The O'Tooles have always had the name of being just men. But you're more than just, sir. You're generous to the point of being free-hearted. Perhaps it's because you're half American and that half gets the better of your nature when, otherwise, you'd be vengeful like a true Irishman."

Peter rose and held out his hand. "I'd like to think I really deserved that analysis, but I think I ought to admit that, if the news from the dower house had been bad, instead of good, this morning, the vengeful half might have won out."

Anne's answer was the first to reach Peter. Dr. Carey gave it, verbally, when he called that evening.

"Lady O'Toole, who is very much better, desires me to tell you that she saw very clearly she had made a wise decision in choosing her representative."

Peter flushed and turned aside, so that the doctor should not see his telltale expression of exultation. Then they went on to talk of other things. Frank O'Leary had been sent to the county infirmary, as he was too badly hurt to be treated at home; he probably would become a charge on the public purse, able to do nothing more active than basket making. The other grooms—those who had tried to defend the mares—were making satisfactory recoveries and could continue to be cared for at home, while Riordan was improving by leaps and bounds. "Perhaps I should add," Dr. Carey concluded, "that I have been called upon to set several fractures and treat a surprising number of bruises for men who are not normally my patients. But, unless you insist, I shan't mention my suspicions about them to anyone but the Constable until I have more proof. All Moonlighters operate masked and wearing their coats turned inside out, and it's pretty hard to determine their identity past any shadow of a doubt. For the moment, I think it's best they should remain anonymous, as far as you're concerned."

Lady Susannah's answer came next, by cable:

> Go out and buy whatever you want and dont talk nonsense about business arrangements Stop Janet comma Walewski and I would like to spend Christmas holidays with you Stop Please let me know if agreeable Stop Much love Granny

Lawrence Donovan's answer came last and was delivered in person. He arrived unheralded, ran up the steps and pounded on the front door, instead of ringing the bell. Peter, who, as usual, was in the erstwhile study, now completely transformed into a private office, heard the racket and, without summoning Wade, went himself to see who the importunate visitor might be. Larry fairly flung himself across the threshold.

"I got your letter and ran for a train on the chance of catching one right away, which I did," he announced, all in one breath. "I didn't stop to pack—I expect you can lend me a clean shirt. There wasn't any kind of a trap at the Cloncoole station, so I ran all the way out here. Then they stopped me at the lodge. First time I've ever known the gates to be locked in the daytime. But, fortunately, they recognized me and let me through. Tell me quickly, how's Anne?"

"Very much better."

"Well, praise be for that! Can I see her? Have you?"

"Ask Dr. Carey for an answer to the first. No is the answer to the second. Come on in. Which do you want first, a clean shirt or a drink?"

"You ought to know the answer to that one. I say—you have been making changes here, haven't you?"

"Yankee efficiency or, at least an attempt at it. How do you like the results? . . . Say when."

They sat down opposite each other, glasses in hand, all previous stiffness and strain between them forgotten; they were friends and allies already, though nothing had been said to bring about a change.

"You can't have any idea how much feeling against the Moonlighters this act of sudden violence has stirred up," Donovan said. "Anne's very highly regarded and, of course, her delicate condition makes her an object of special sympathy, quite aside from general anxiety about the possible loss of a direct heir to an old and honorable title, for which hope had at last been revived. Naturally, that item isn't in the papers, along with all the lurid details that have been given full play; but from the moment Anne fainted away, there have been whispers and rumors—a horsewoman of her caliber doesn't tumble out of her saddle because a mount stumbles going up a slippery bank, unless there's some contributing reason. You've been discretion itself every time you've mentioned her, but I guessed right away; and after her collapse in the paddock, anyone could guess. However, even if the news of Anne's expectations hadn't got around, which, as I said, it has, the fact that, though recently widowed, she is courageously carrying on has balanced the scales in her favor. . . . I don't say the fact that she's young and beautiful, as well as courageous, has nothing to do with the case," Larry added with a grin, "but, be that as it may, I do say any man who was caught inflicting further injuries on Cloneen, at least until this excitement has died down, might just as well recognize that he's signed his own death warrant; and there's no faction more concerned about criminal lawlessness than the Parnellites, as some people are beginning to call us—the group that's trying to bring about reform by orderly means. Parnell himself is simply sick over it. He's talked about it with me quite frankly: 'How can I go on if I'm stabbed in the back this way?' he wanted to know. I had a chance to speak with him last night at a meeting—we're trying to organize a National League—and, after discussing with me in a general way finding some means of counteracting the harm the Moonlighters have done, he asked me to give you his personal regards the next time I saw you and convey his regrets for what had happened at Cloneen. Naturally, he had no idea then I was to see you so soon or he probably would have sent you a note. As it is, I wouldn't be surprised if he wrote you a letter. He's very thoughtful and painstaking about things like that."

"He's got so much on his mind, I shouldn't think he could take time to write personal letters."

"You'd be surprised. Now, to get down to business. You've run into tough luck, but after all it isn't as if you had to start from scratch," Larry said sensibly, plunging into the subject of the stud. "You've got the stables, which the Moonlighters didn't dare take time to damage —it isn't as if you had a wreck or a burnt offering on your hands. And you've got the men you need—well, you'll require at least two for replacements and perhaps two more if you start expanding. But Riordan's one in a million and he's always had top quality in his grooms, with this one tragic exception. If you can't find the stallion you want right away, it won't matter much, for all the foals that are to be dropped next spring are bred already; so take your time about making that purchase. But get started looking for the promising fillies you want to breed next year. That'll probably be easier than finding any brood mares—no one wants to part with one, when he's got her that far along. And I know that's what you need most, to make up to Anne for what she's lost. I'd be delighted to give her one of mine, but she wouldn't accept it as a gift and I wouldn't take money from her. Well, we'll find something somewhere."

He went on to say they must go together and have a talk with Riordan, stopping first for a word with Andy, and then they had better ride over to see Dwyer, the M.F.H., and a very sound man when it came to advice about building up a stud and where to look for immediate *matériel*. Then, the next morning, they would make an early start and comb the countryside. That is, if it were really all right for him to stay on.

"Don't be an ass," Peter said cordially.

20

Encouraged by Peter's expression of hospitality, Larry seemed more than content to prolong his visit and, once he had dispatched a few telegrams, revealing his whereabouts, quite untroubled by any unsatisfied demands upon him from the outside world. He maintained an establishment on Clare Street, with accommodations in the basement for the Creedons, the capable couple who looked after him, law offices on the first two floors and bachelor quarters, with strikingly beautiful ceilings, above. In addition to this, he had a small but superior stud farm and a small but superior country house, both well staffed, within easy driving distance of Dublin. None of his properties seemed to cause him much concern. His law practice was one of inheritance and both his father and his grandfather had been such brilliant practitioners that the family fortunes were already secure when Larry came along; it suited him very well to leave most of the actual work in the famous firm of Donovan and Donovan to his juniors and devote his time to politics and sports, for both of which he showed great aptitude; and, while he was considered something of a lightweight, he was trustworthy, he was popular and he knew how to get good service from his subordinates. A wire to the Creedons quickly supplied him with the essentials of a suitable wardrobe; a wire to Parnell's headquarters assured his availability if he were needed to further the formation of the National League; and a wire to Malone, his studmaster, resulted in the arrival of a beautiful mare, Lucy Locket, which he said he might want for a mount, nonchalantly dismissing the superfluity of riding horses already at hand and supervising the installation of Lucy in one of the empty stalls of the stud with very vague references to this as a temporary arrangement.

Larry was already on much more familiar terms than Peter, not only with the Slatterys, but also with the Tyrrells, the Dwyers and the

Singletons and he insisted on dashing off to see them all, either with or without his host. He had been right about the predisposition in the newcomer's favor. Peter had made a good impression on the county from the beginning and his neighbors rallied around to assure him of their sympathy and support. Inside of a fortnight, he had two promising yearlings in his stud and leads toward several other possible additions. Though complete replacement was still far in the future, at least he was on his way to it.

Anne had received the news of Larry's visit with comparatively little comment, but that little had not been ungracious. Within a few days of his arrival, she sent him a note, saying that Dr. Carey was now willing she should have visitors and that, possibly, he and his host would like to take tea with her. This, of course, was the message they had been eagerly awaiting; both of them because this would mean she was better; Larry because, after all, though he had really been glad to help Peter and complimented because asked to do so, the hope of seeing Anne was his principal reason for coming to Cloneen and staying on there; and Peter because he realized that common courtesy would require her to invite Larry to the dower house, as soon as she was able to see him and that she could not do so without including his host in her invitation. She received them in her upstairs sitting room, wearing a black *robe d'intérieur,* which was less suggestive of the bedroom than a negligee and still one step removed from a fitted dress; greeted them both with adequate but objective amiability; and made inconsequential small talk, avoiding, with equal adroitness, the subject of her health and that of the stud, while seemingly much occupied with the service of a copious and lavish tea. At the end of half an hour, Solange came to her with a whispered reminder that she was not supposed to stay up very long. Neither of her guests doubted in the least that this summons was one of prearrangement between mistress and maid.

Peter could not help remembering how skillfully Anne had avoided identification on the Irish Mail and mentally made some half-nostalgic, half-rueful comparisons between her handling of the basket lunch that had been brought to the train at Chester and the elegant silver and Sèvres tea service in her Louis XV boudoir. He was thankful that the ice was broken at last, that his long exile from the dower house was over, even though that, apparently, was not much of an advantage. Larry, on the other hand, was baffled and annoyed; he was very close to sulking the rest of the evening. Although certainly there had been nothing in Anne's manner to indicate partiality for Peter or even special interest in him, Larry visualized him, rather tardily, as a possible rival and began to scrutinize him in this light. He had not noticed before that Peter was so good looking. He was over six feet tall, but he was extremely well built and he carried his height with ease and grace. Larry knew that he had excelled in several collegiate sports and had not failed to observe that he rode, not only with the nonchalance of long accomplishment, but with the rare effect of complete harmony between himself and his mount. This was the more remarkable because he was not riding the same horse all the time or any to which he was especially attached or with which he had long been familiar; he was simply trying to do his share in seeing that all the horses got sufficient exercise. Probably he would give the same effect of harmony with his partner when he danced, and Larry could not help being pleased because mourning would preclude that diversion for the present. Peter's sense of humor, though suppressed just now, might well be fairly close to the surface and another source of annoyance; there was something very contagious about his smile, which a flash of fine teeth and a twinkle in fine eyes did not wholly explain. Charm entered into it, the charm that had nothing to do with urbanity, but was congenital, like his firm chin, his regular features and his fresh coloring, and doubly dangerous on that account. He was so tanned that his skin, his hair and his eyes were much the same shade; and he had that just-shaven, just-scrubbed look in which a certain type of American seemed to excel, without effort. Obviously, he was quite free from vanity about his appearance, or not even much concerned about it, when he was doing accustomed things and wearing accustomed clothes. The deep black of the mourning attire he had worn at the funeral and in Dublin was unfamiliar and unbecoming and he was clearly uncomfortable in it; that was why Donovan had been misled. In riding habit and in dinner jacket, Peter cut quite a different figure. His manner, too, had undergone a change; that also had been formal and Larry had set it down to lack of general savoir faire; now he realized that only the suddenness with which Peter had been catapulted into totally unfamiliar and very somber surroundings had been responsible. Actually, he had a generous supply of the social graces and he was taking hold of his new responsibility in a way that had won him the respect of everyone in the county and the unquestioning deference of everyone on the estate. Besides, he was immensely rich and the chances were still even that he would be the next Earl of Cloneen. Decidedly, the more Anne's attention could be diverted from him, the better; and this was easier said than done, considering that Peter not only had an opportunity, but an obligation to remain at the mansion.

After waiting several days for Anne to suggest a second appointment at tea time, Larry decided to risk a casual call, in the course of a stroll around the grounds at a time when Peter was deep in conference with Danahy. Again, she received him pleasantly and, this time, she came downstairs dressed to go out. She was just on the point of taking her first walk since her illness, she said, and perhaps Larry would like to go with her. She took the path along the lake, skirting the woodlands and showing no inclination to head toward the mansion or the stables; and though she chatted pleasantly and inconsequentially as they went along, presently she said that she thought she had walked far enough for that day and turned back toward the dower house. When they reached it, she thanked him for keeping her company and shook hands; but she did not suggest that he should come in with her.

Decidedly, he was not making very rapid progress, Larry told himself as he went back to the mansion, to find a telegram, saying that he was needed in Dublin for another meeting in further preparation for the foundation of the National League. He felt justified in delaying his departure until the next day and in allowing time, on his way to the station, to stop and say good-by to Anne. She had already gone out for a walk, without mentioning the direction she meant to take, Solange told him; she was nowhere in sight and there was not enough leeway before train time to look for her. Larry scribbled a farewell message on a card and left rather out of humor, which did not improve when he reached the station so early that he realized he might have risked a delay. Ryan, when addressed in reproachful tones, seemed quite unmoved; the Master had lost several trains and barely caught several others because he did not allow enough time, unless he were cautioned, and so he had asked that the coachman should take the responsibility of seeing that this did not happen to him any more and, above all, that it should not happen to his guests. Ryan expressed himself as being very sorry if he had inconvenienced Mr. Donovan, but Larry did not believe he was sorry. He thought the old servant was secretly delighted at having prevented another meeting between the guest and the Mistress. Ryan, like all the others, was eating out of Peter's hand and, indubitably, matchmaking plans were already being hatched in the stables and the servants' hall, premature as these might be.

Peter was genuinely sorry to have Donovan leave; he was deeply grateful for the help, both direct and indirect, that Larry had given him; and nothing had happened to make him feel that his guest was furthering his suit by his presence at Cloneen. On the contrary, Peter gathered, quite correctly, that Anne was so determined no advantage should be taken of it that she was ready to lean over backward in seeing that this did not happen. The mansion seemed actually cavernous for sole occupancy and he began to understand, all too well, what Mac-Auliffe had meant in saying it would be an endurance test to spend a long cold winter there alone. Peter had begun his systematic visiting of his tenants, looking in on two or three every day and stopping long enough to size up the condition of the property, without seeming inquisitive or intrusive; he tried to talk with every member of the family whom he could persuade to engage in conversation; and he had induced the young teacher at Cloncoole to give him lessons in Irish. Peter had been surprised to learn that this was not part of the curriculum, since it was the language most in use among the illiterate and semi-literate, and it seemed to him logical that they should be taught to read and write it correctly; but that, it appeared, was not the viewpoint of the English authorities. However, Mr. Quinn not only spoke, read and wrote it with facility himself; he was proud of his ability to do so and glad of a chance to teach it to so distinguished a pupil. Peter insisted that he would rather come to the school, at the end of the day's session, than to have Mr. Quinn come to the mansion; it would give him another chance for getting away from the office and into the fresh air and it would also give him a chance to see the children as they came out and, gradually, to get acquainted with them; perhaps he and Mr. Quinn could plan for some special prizes, in memory of his uncle, and for some kind of a party, say, at Christmastime; but they would all feel easier if they were not total strangers to each other. He had not yet hit upon a means of making his visits to his tenants free from strain on both sides, but he was beginning to feel the strain slackening and was full of hope. He could not help being appalled by the prevalent dirt and disorder, but it did not surprise him in view of the conditions under which most of these people existed. Some of the cottages contained only one room and though the majority had two—a living room-kitchen and a bedroom—sizeable families were often raised without more space than this. Privacy was impossible, decency commendable. He took what comfort he could from the fact that the turf fires, where the cooking was done in iron pots and pans, were usually large and glowing and that the pots and pans seemed, on the whole, to be fairly well filled. But what happened when there was a birth or a death; a long serious illness, either mental or physical; a crippled condition at any age; a squandering of scarce pennies on drink? He gave long hours of thought to these questions, he talked them over with Father Carroll, Dr. Carey and Mr. MacAuliffe and still it did not seem to him that he was finding the right answers; he knew he would have no rest until he did.

One of the cottages where he had gone at Gweedore had been painstakingly prepared for a spinning party, the other for a housewarming; and he had comfortably assumed that their cleanliness and attractiveness were typical, instead of exceptional. Now that he realized his mistake, he blamed himself for stupidity; what was worse, he was haunted by the consciousness that it was largely rent from these wretched hovels that made it possible for a landlord to live in the luxury of an estate like Cloneen. How could he become part of a system which was abhorrent to him, unless he could discover some way of changing conditions, as George Hill and Michael Glover had done? Yet, how could he do that without seeming to cast discredit on a humane man like his uncle, or dispensing charity, with its implication of obligation, instead of merely administering justice?

Greatly as he wished he might also talk these questions over with Anne, he recognized that the time was not yet ripe for this. However, as soon as Larry had gone, he wrote her a note which he hoped would be a first step taken in that direction.

Dear Anne,

Of course, I greatly enjoyed having tea with you and was delighted to see you looking so well. Since then, I have learned that you have begun to get out a little and I am wondering, as this is the case, if you would not soon be going to church again and if we could not go at the same time, as we did when Granny Glover was here? This would not only mean a lot to me personally, but I am sure it would mean a lot to Father Carroll and—though, perhaps, through inexperience, I am mistaken in this—I believe it would be regarded by the people in the village and by our tenants as the proper thing for us to do, given all the circumstances. As you know, I am eager to get into closer touch with them and this might be one of the ways that would help. Unless I hear that it would not be agreeable to you, I will call for you, in the coach, next Sunday at a quarter before ten and consider that the beginning of a regular practice.

As ever,
Peter

There was no answer and, since he had written so plainly that silence would mean consent, the coach, with Ryan on the box and Peter installed on the red velvet cushions, drew up before the dower house at the time specified. Anne was awaiting their arrival and promptly came down the steps; she spoke very little and she was, of course, enveloped in veils; but her greeting and few remarks she did make were amicable, and the veils did not trouble Peter as much as they had when he first saw her wearing them. They no longer seemed to sever her from him completely, the way they had then. After all, she was there beside him, of her own free will, and he could rejoice in her presence, instead of grieving over her absence; and, unbidden, the realization that she was carrying his child, that this, in itself, prevented her complete detachment, swept through him in a wave of triumph that no sense of guilt could dim. He did not try to detain her when they reached the dower house on their return from church or say anything that could be construed as a hint that he hoped she would ask him to come in. Instead, as he left her, he said only, "Thank you for going with me. I trust it hasn't tired you too much. Next Sunday at the same time, unless you send me word to the contrary?"

October had almost passed before there was any change in this set schedule. They met occasionally on the grounds and walked a little way together and, when they did, they talked briefly about the state of the woodlands or the garden or wherever they happened to meet; then they parted again to go in different directions. But the days were getting short now and there were high winds and a great deal of rain, often coming on suddenly out of a clear sky, which meant that Anne's outings were limited. It was not until a violent storm arose, in true Irish fashion, out of a bright and unmenacing sky, and it was obvious that she must take shelter as rapidly as possible, or get drenched and chilled, that Anne ran from the lawn to the portico of the mansion and recognized the absurdity of not going in. Peter, who had failed to catch sight of her until she was on the steps, rushed out to meet her and install her in the Chinese parlor, where she willingly shed her wet coat and was induced to take off her wet shoes. But when he tried to persuade her that she needed to discard more than these and asked her to let him see what Mrs. Brennan or Bridie could offer, she shook her head and made light of her predicament.

"I'll sit close to this nice fire you've lighted and dry off in no time."

"You won't, either. Your stockings are soaking, your skirts are wet all around the bottom and your hair is dripping."

"I'll turn up my skirts a little and take off my stockings and unpin my hair. I'll be perfectly all right before you know it."

The picture she conjured up was very alluring, but almost instantly she spoiled it by adding, "I meant, of course, after you left me to send a message to Solange, telling her to bring me dry things."

"Oh! I'll get it off right away. And, meanwhile, I'll send you some hot tea by Bridie. She'd be terribly disappointed if she didn't see you, now that you're here, and so would Mrs. Brennan. I'll tell Ryan to have the carriage ready to take you back to the dower house whenever you want to go."

He knew that she had been quite right to dismiss him and he could and did take comfort in the fact that she had done it pleasantly, almost casually, and that he could still visualize just how she looked, with those voluminous black skirts and white petticoats turned back from her slender ankles and bare white feet and her hair spread out like a golden cloud over her shoulders. When he was readmitted to the Chinese parlor by Solange, the wet clothes had all been gathered up and neatly packed and Anne, fully dressed in warm dry wool, was finishing her tea before the fire. It had, however, not been possible to dry her hair enough to do it up properly. This, as Peter had rightly observed, had been dripping and it was still damp. Solange stood behind her mistress, alternately rubbing it with a towel and combing it out to full length, and Anne, without apparent self-consciousness, occasionally ran a hand through it to hasten the drying process, which Peter hoped would take a long time.

"I think I'll be able to do something with this in a few minutes," Anne said disappointingly. "But, as long as I'm here, I'd rather like to have a look at the office and see how you have it arranged now. The double desk was there before you went away to Donegal, remember? But I haven't seen the rent table in place."

As Peter had never mentioned the rent table to her, he concluded that Larry must have done so without consulting him, but decided not to raise the issue.

"I'd be delighted to have you come and see the rent table," he said. "It meant the elimination of another armchair, which has been sent to one of those convenient attic storerooms until you could tell me what you'd like done with it. Personally, I think it would look very well in here, if you fixed it up to match the others you recovered."

Anne nodded, ran her hand through her hair again and rose. Peter opened the door for her and they went on into the office together, leaving Solange to remove the remnants of Anne's tea. No one had done this with Peter's and, as he apologized and hastened to make up for the omission, she cut him short.

"It's I who should apologize," she said quite sincerely. "Of course, when you offered me tea, I should have asked you if you wouldn't take yours with me. But I wasn't thinking of anything except how nearly drowned I felt. I'm sorry." She paused and glanced around her with obvious approval. "It's all very efficient looking," she said, "and I know how hard you're working here. It's about time I came back to work, too, isn't it?"

"If you really feel strong enough. You'd better consult Dr. Carey first. And if he approves, I hope you'll feel like coming not only to the office, but to the stables. You can't fully grasp what I've been trying to accomplish here unless you do. I realize it'll be hard for you the first time, but perhaps after that . . . and there's never any use putting off something just because it's hard. It simply gets harder and harder."

"I'm afraid you're right. If Dr. Carey raises no objections, I'll be over tomorrow right after lunch. We'll go to the stables together and then we'll come back here and work the rest of the afternoon. And have tea."

Dr. Carey raised no objections. On the contrary, as long as she did not overtire herself, either physically or mentally, he thought a normal amount of activity would be good for Lady O'Toole. She and Peter went to the stables by themselves, and she was silent when she went through the stalls that were still empty, and full of praise for the promising yearlings. But when she came to Donovan's mare, she halted abruptly.

"Where did this come from?" she inquired.

"From The Pocket. At least, I believe that's the name of the place. This is Lucy Locket. Perhaps you don't know the old nursery rhyme." He recited it:

> "Lucy Locket lost her pocket,
>   Kitty Fisher found it.
>   Not a penny was there in it,
>   Only ribbon round it."

The blank look which had come to Anne's normally expressive face did not leave it.

"But why should Larry send her here?"

"He said, to ride. But then he never rode her. She went right into the stud, where a brood mare belongs."

"This brood mare doesn't belong in my stud, unless you've bought her. Did you?"

"Certainly not. I wouldn't have made a purchase as important as that without consulting you. And, anyway, Larry said he wouldn't take money from you."

"Then you'd better write him to come and get Lucy Locket. No, not that. My cousin Maurice is the only man from whom I'd accept a horse as a gift, but I don't want a scene with Larry over this one. Riordan had better just take her back."

"Anne, Larry would be terribly hurt if anything like that happened. He said he was afraid you wouldn't accept a gift from him for your stud, when he first talked to me about it, but apparently he decided to risk it. And now that Lucy's been here this long, why not let her stay? It isn't as if he couldn't well afford to give her to you or as if you and he weren't very old friends. He doesn't mean to be presumptuous."

"Whether he means to be or not, he is, and I rather think he does. His motto has always been, 'Audace, audace, toujours l'audace,' and, to tell you the truth, I'm rather surprised to hear you pleading Lawrence Donovan's cause."

"Are you? Well I've never consciously adopted *Audace*, et cetera, or any other as my motto. As you very well know, the O'Tooles don't have a motto on their coat-of-arms—they've evidently never felt the need of one, either to give them more courage or to impress their inferiors and, in this case, I'm all for following tradition. But I did *act* on the principle of *Audace* once, when I had no right to, and to atone for that I think I ought to be charitable to those who confess it openly and don't do anything worse than give an unconventional present to a woman they love and want to marry. I never could see much sense in this rule about candy, flowers, music and books, as an approach to diamonds. The change-over is rather abrupt, it seems to me."

"And you wouldn't mind if Larry Donovan offered me diamonds?"

"I'd mind very much if you accepted them, as you know without being told. But I think he has a right to choose his own way of trying to lead up to them. And it doesn't look to me as if he's made much headway so far. The best he could do, while he was right here on the place, was to get one invitation to tea and, in addition to that, the satisfaction of not being turned away when he came to call or cause you to flee when he met you on the grounds. And now that he isn't here any more and you discover that he's loaned or maybe given you a horse, you're furious and want to send it back. It will be easy enough to say, after Lucy drops her foal in the spring, that you understand she was sent here in order to provide her with better winter quarters than she could have at The Pocket—something like that. But that you've taken a great fancy to Lucy, junior, as an addition to the stud you're restocking and would Larry consider, et cetera, et cetera. And about that same time you might mention that you're thinking of marrying again and have practically decided whom and that, although Larry will always be welcome at Cloneen as a friend, you can't encourage him to suppose, et cetera, et cetera. Meanwhile, I think I can afford to be tolerant of him as a suitor. And I think you can afford to be courteous to him, without thinking he'll assume that you mean to marry him."

Peter was never sure just what Anne's expression was meant to convey, as she looked at him steadily while he was making this speech; but he could not help feeling that, while she knew him to be in deadly earnest at the beginning of it, she was inclined to believe that he was making fun, both of her and of his rival, before he finished. He decided that, in any case, the moment had come to change the subject and he did so with total disregard for a suitable approach.

"We've got a Holy Day of Obligation coming up, haven't we? All Saints'? That means an extra drive to church, because it isn't a Sunday. Possibly two extra drives. Do you want to go to the cemetery that day or the next—All Souls'—or both? I'm perfectly willing to do whatever is most 'meet, right and our bounden duty,' to borrow a phrase from the Book of Common Prayer, which has lots of them that are not to be despised, either by way of sentiment or expression. I owe my knowledge of them to the Bradford family and am glad to give credit where credit is due."

"I am sure the Reverend Mr. Cavendish, the rector of the Church of Ireland in Cloncoole, would be much gratified at such an acknowledgment coming from you," Anne said demurely. "You should make it in his hearing sometime. . . . Were you always so scrupulous about observing Holy Days of Obligation when you were at Harvard?"

It was the first time she had spoken to him archly and teasingly. He shook his head and smiled.

"No. But I'm not a student and I'm not at Harvard any more. I'm a member of the county gentry, living on an Irish estate. It's up to me to assume the obligations these indicate and, at the same time, to make up for my former sins of omission and commission. Surely you want to help me do both."

21

As the carriage drew near the village on All Saints' Day, Peter and Anne saw that Ryan would have hard work getting them to the church. The green was crowded with cattle and so were all the approaches to it, while the owners or would-be owners of all this livestock were engaged in such tumultuous bargaining that they paid no attention to the oncoming vehicle; an attempt to drive straight ahead, regardless of the consequences, seemed a perilous undertaking, with some injuries to man or beast, possibly both, its inevitable sequel. The arguments which accompanied the trading were carried on in voices raised to a pitch that rendered normal tones inaudible and, after several attempts to make himself heard, Peter asked Anne if she would not prefer to turn back, rather than risk running someone down. To his surprise, she laughed good-naturedly.

"Oh no! It's always like this on All Saints' Day—in fact, on most Holy Days of Obligation. I understand that, when the Protestants came into power, they made rather a point of getting the people to hold cattle fairs at such times, to divert them from their churchgoing. As things turned out, it didn't work quite the way it was intended to. More men from scattered farms managed to get to the village than ever had before and then it occurred to them that, as long as they were here to go to the cattle fair, they might as well go to Mass, too."

"Good Irish reasoning," Peter said rather drily.

"Yes, if you want to look at it that way. On Christmas Eve, all these same men will be going to the pub. It's an unwritten law, if you are that kind of a man, that you must spend Christmas Eve at a pub. But, since you're out anyway, of course you'll go to Midnight Mass before you go home. I think you'll get quite a surprise—I mean, you personally—when you see the turnout then. All we have to do now is to wait patiently for a few minutes. Actually, all that shouting is perfectly good-natured. I know it sounds as if these men were getting ready for what I believe you call a knockdown and drag-out fight, but nothing is further from their thoughts. Presently someone will stop arguing and look around long enough to recognize the carriage and then the crowd will part very respectfully to let us through. And when we come out after Mass everything will be very quiet and orderly."

Anne proved to be right and the Mass on All Saints' Day was a landmark for several reasons.

For the first time, as he came out of church, Peter not only nodded or spoke briefly to the fellow worshipers he knew by sight; he was now sure enough that he had begun to identify several so that he could call them by name and make some friendly reference to their interests and occupations: he had gone himself with Farrell to the smithy when Reine Mathilde needed shoeing, because he was concerned about her sensitivity; he wanted to be reassured regarding the way her hooves were pared and Gannon, the blacksmith, had been able to do this to Peter's complete satisfaction; it was a pleasure to report that there had been no more signs of trouble. . . . Peter had found several old saddles in the tack room, which apparently had been discarded, but, as far as he could see, there was no reason why minor repairs would not make them usable again; Meagher, the saddler, had confirmed Peter's judgment and congratulations were in order. . . . Duffy, the publican, was also a pillar of the church. He took up the collections and—Peter was informed—knew to the last penny just how much every one of Father Carroll's parishioners could contribute and was contributing; those who were not living up to their obligations could not get credit at the pub. The imminence of All Souls' Day had necessitated an extra passing of the basket, both today and the previous Sunday, to collect the envelopes containing the lists of "Dearly Departed;" but this was as it should be and Duffy was beaming with satisfaction at the congregation's generous response, no doubt the result of the example set by those from the mansion and the dower house.

As Peter and Anne left the porch, a subdued murmur of gratified voices followed them and two or three of the school children, who were now used to seeing him almost daily and recognized his friendliness, spoke to him shyly of their own accord. Then two little girls, who stood somewhat apart, whispered to each other in voices which carried further than they were meant to do and thus were overheard. "You told me her ladyship was uncommonly pretty," one of them blurted to her companion. "How can you tell, with all those veils?" . . . "She didn't used to wear them. Perhaps she won't always," the other replied hopefully.

Peter made no comment on these confidences and was not even sure that Anne, who was already getting into the coach when they were made, had heard them. But the next day, when they started to the Mass for the Commemoration of the Faithful Departed, he saw that a great and very welcome change had been made: the long crepe veil, which hung almost to her heels behind, was still there; but the shorter one, equally heavy and lugubrious, which had hung as far as her waist in front, had been displaced; its substitute, though black bordered, was otherwise almost as transparent as what she would have worn with a riding habit and came no further down than her chin. When Peter paused to speak to his new acquaintants after church, she stood close by, smiling and adding a few words to the exchange of greetings; and, before she got into the coach, she stopped and waved her hand to the abashed little girls, who had retreated, putting them at their ease again.

After Mass, they went to the old cemetery to place a wreath at the vault and, when this was done, Peter showed a disposition to linger. "That ruined church over there disturbs me more and more all the time," he said, looking toward it. "I wouldn't feel so badly if it had a roof on it and glass—any kind of glass—in the windows. But those slabs in the floor must cover the tombs of the earlier O'Tooles—the ones before the barons became earls and burial began in the vault. The early abbots or priors or whoever presided over the Community in the beginning must lie there, too. The inscriptions on the stones are almost illegible already, but it's still possible to decipher them, with a little care and patience; if they get any worse, it won't be. Granny Glover keeps urging me to remember that the vault, which still gives me the creeps, is part of Irish history. Isn't this church part of Irish history, too?"

"Unquestionably."

"Then don't you think it ought to be restored and preserved?"

"I know that your uncle wished it might be. He felt just the same way about it. But he didn't see how it could be. It was so far gone before there was any money to spare that it seemed hopeless. And he was old and tired; he didn't feel equal to any new undertaking."

"Well, I do. I keep hearing how hard it is for the seasonal workers to get jobs in the winter—that many of them take to the roads, along with their families, just hoping something will turn up. Almost anyone, under proper direction and supervision, can work on a roof. For a starter, it might be worth while experimenting with some of the unemployed seasonal workers. Don't you think so?"

"It's a generous impulse, anyway."

"My generous impulses, if that's what you want to call them, usually have a very practical basis. Come on over with me and take a look at some of those tombs. The arches and the towers, too. I think you'll feel just as I do about wanting to save them. It's a beautiful day. Why don't we stay here and look over the possibilities—and talk them over? We can send Ryan back for something to eat if you think you'd get hungry."

"That's a very good idea. I'd like to stay."

Acting upon instructions which puzzled him, but which he followed faithfully, Ryan brought a well-filled tea basket, which Peter recognized as the one Anne had had on the train, but which she had not stocked because the five-shilling luncheon, provided at Chester, was so satisfactory; the coachman also brought a stiff broom and two stiff brushes. Until his return, Anne and Peter wandered about in the church while he pointed out the arches and towers which had so strongly appealed to him and whose ruin he so deeply deplored. When Ryan arrived with his heterogeneous equipment, he was dismissed with orders to return before sunset and Peter swept the area around one of the tombs and began to rub it briskly with a brush, suggesting to Anne that, if she felt like it, she might help him. Presently, the dirt encrusted in its inscription was sufficiently dislodged so they could decipher this and the crest above it; with growing excitement they recognized the wild boar of the O'Tooles and the epitaph of the first Earl's father, Baron James Edward Peter O'Toole, who had been killed in 1646 at Benburg on the Blackwater, fighting with the Confederate Catholics under the leadership of Colonel Owen Roe O'Neill.

"And this is only one of half a dozen," Peter exclaimed. "We must have a look at some of the others before we leave, but I'm getting hungry. What about you?"

"Oh, I'm hungry all the time nowadays. I'm more than making up for all the meals I missed."

"I'm delighted to hear it. What about a nice big ham sandwich to start with or do you want some tea first?"

"No. That means waiting until the kettle comes to a boil. I'll start it going right away and it won't take long, but meanwhile I'll have a glass of wine and eat that nice big ham sandwich."

The basket contained a tea cloth and they spread it over the tomb they had cleaned and set the dishes out on it. Despite the complete difference of *mise-en-scène*, there were many aspects of the pleasant picnic that reminded Peter of their midnight lunch on the train: Anne's housewifely care to make it attractive; the informality and intimacy of sharing the ample but excellent fare provided; the detachment from everyone in the outside world. He wondered if Anne felt the same way about it and, somehow, felt that she must; but he did not dare to ask her, because he knew her sense of disloyalty to her husband still outweighed her other recollections of that night; he wanted to do nothing which would bring that to the forefront of her consciousness when she seemed content in the quiet companionship of the moment; and eventually, of her own accord, she referred to an experience which for her had been meaningful and precious before they knew each other.

"I'm so glad we've had this pleasant day together," she said, "because usually All Souls' is a rather dismal one for me—not so much in itself, but because it is just before the Feast of St. Hubert on November third and I begin to be homesick for that. We make a great deal of its celebration because St. Hubert seems so essentially Norman that we claim him, though actually he belongs to the Ardennes."

"Tell me about him—and about the way you celebrate. I'm afraid I never even heard of him before. I'm sure he isn't in my Missal."

"I'll have to give you one that's more complete. He was the eldest son of the Duke of Aquitaine and he's the patron saint of hunters. Like many other saints, his early life was joyous and carefree rather than sanctified. He was a worldling with charming manners and his chief passion was the chase, to which he devoted a great deal of time. He paid very little attention to holy days and actually went hunting on Good Friday. He was pursuing a magnificent stag when suddenly the animal turned and Hubert saw there was a shining crucifix between its antlers. Then Hubert heard a warning voice."

"What kind of a voice?"

"I don't know exactly. But the words Hubert heard were something like this, 'Unless thou turnest to the Lord and leadest a holy life, thou shalt quickly go down to hell.' Hubert dismounted and prostrated himself, asking, 'Lord, what wouldst Thou have me do?' So he must have been convinced at once that the voice was divine. He was then told by the same voice to go and seek Lambert, the saintly Bishop of Maastricht, and receive instructions. He renounced his wealth and title and became an eloquent preacher. Eventually he was appointed Bishop of Liège and worked many miracles. His saint's day is celebrated in many places by a very special Mass. In the Cathedral at Lisieux there's always a chorus of ten, dressed in hunters' pink, stationed in the choir. They play the *Obyre-Tindare* music on hunters' horns. Maurice and I always used to go to this Mass together. He has great devotion to St. Hubert. I believe that somehow there is a definite link between them."

"What makes you think so?"

"I can't explain exactly. But when you meet Maurice, I believe you'll understand—a sort of rare capacity for saintliness concealed by a very charming, almost insouciant exterior. I've always been sorry he wasn't called Hubert instead of Maurice. It *was* one of the names given him in Baptism, but for some reason his parents didn't like it well enough to use it. Sometimes I do, when we're alone. He likes to have me."

She continued for some time to talk about her cousin and, though Peter could think of other subjects that he would have preferred, she seemed so happy in doing it that he entered into her mood without undue effort.

They lingered over their picnic so long that there was time to scrub only one more tomb before Ryan appeared again, but that proved even more exciting than the first one—it was that of an adventurous younger son who had joined the revolt of "Silken Thomas" Fitzgerald in 1534 and had received "the pardon of Maynooth"—that is, execution—when Sir William Skeffington had reduced Fitzgerald's stronghold with artillery.

When they parted at the dower house, nothing had been said to disturb the serenity of Anne's mood, but when she came to the office the following afternoon, Peter almost immediately guessed that awakened memories had disquieted her, for her manner was more formal than it had been in some time. However, his own awakened memories had brought with them only happiness and he was still in the best of spirits. He had two pieces of good news for her: the owner of an exceptionally desirable filly, which was in foal for the first time, had agreed to accept Peter's offer for her, after holding out a long while; and Riordan's younger brother Matt, who, according to all reports, showed signs of developing the same genius in dealing with horses as Bart himself, had agreed to start work at the stud the following Monday.

"There's just one hitch to it," Peter told her. "Matt's still very young and this will be his first job. Incidentally, he's an expert fisherman as well as a natural horseman, and when he came to see me about the job, he brought me some fine trout he had just caught—with his hands!"

"Many Gypsies can do that. I'm surprised you hadn't heard of it before."

"I've told you that I learn slowly, but steadily. . . . Well, when I spoke about wages and mentioned what the other grooms, who've been here a long time, were getting, Matt looked very disappointed. He didn't refuse to come for what I suggested, but it was clear that he wanted more. And he's probably worth more. I'd hate to lose him to another stud, after he'd proven his value to us, just for the sake of a few shillings."

"If you gave him more, wouldn't you have to raise all the other wages correspondingly?"

"Yes, I'm afraid so."

"We can't do it, with all the expense of restocking the stud."

"I told you I'd take care of that and—"

"And I told you, when we were discussing Larry, that the only man from whom I'd accept a horse as a gift was my cousin Maurice," Anne said, almost sharply. "I'm grateful because you've gone ahead and got everything so well reorganized while I've been incapacitated and taken care of expenses until we could balance the books at the end of the year and see just how we stood. But it never occurred to me that you'd consider these costs a gift."

"And it never occurred to me to consider them anything else," Peter said, trying not to speak sharply in his turn.

"Then I must ask you to let the decision be mine. If there isn't enough surplus from previous years to take care of this year's deficit, I'll agree to accept a loan from you until the new stud begins to pay. But it's my stud and my ultimate responsibility. And until it shows solvency, if not gains, I'm not going to raise wages."

"I realize this is the second time you've mentioned your cousin Maurice in connection with the stud." It was now impossible for him to subdue his rising anger. "Since you don't mind being indebted to him for gifts you won't accept from Lawrence Donovan and myself, why don't you ask him to come and take charge of the restocking?"

"I have, but he replied that it didn't seem best for him to come to Cloneen at present. I meant to go home for Christmas, but to my great disappointment Dr. Carey has forbidden it. If I had gone, I would have found what I wanted for the stud myself and Maurice could have taken charge of the shipment as usual. However, as things have turned out, he won't come until next summer."

Peter was speechless with rage. Comments in Lady Susannah's letter about the De Briares, which he had almost forgotten, suddenly sprang to the forefront of his consciousness: "The last member of the group was a *very* attractive young man whose first name is Maurice and who could well be much more of a menace to your peace of mind than Lawrence Donovan." So it was this cousin to whom Anne turned instinctively; to whom she did not mind being under obligations; whom she had counted on seeing at Christmastime; but who preferred to wait until summer—that is, until her year of strict mourning was up—before he came to Cloneen! It was he, all the time, of whom Peter should have been jealous and not of poor Larry, who obviously did not have what it took, despite his good looks, to be a formidable rival! And this was only part of the affront: not long before, Anne had accepted him, Peter, as the "chosen representative" which her husband's will empowered her to select—she had even sent him a cordial message that she saw she had chosen wisely; and now she was declining to accept his advice about a decent wage, she was talking in italics about *my* stud and *my* responsibilities! Most of all, from the way she spoke about her disappointment over her physician's verdict, it was easy to guess that she had considered disregarding it, that she had toyed, perhaps was still toying, with the idea of taking a long hard trip in midwinter, when her recent serious illness had made it all too evident that hers was not the sort of pregnancy in which caution did not need to play a prominent part. He wanted to take her by the shoulders and shake her, not hard enough to hurt her, but still hard enough to make her realize that he had heard enough nonsense for one day and did not propose to listen to any more; that, if she even dared take so long a walk that she paid for it by exhaustion, he would himself lock her in her room and see that she stayed there until after the baby was born; and that, if she ever again referred to her cousin Maurice in the way she had done twice too often, he would eliminate that Frenchman from the picture in his own way and it would not be a gentle way, either.

As he stood glaring at her, with the unspoken words dangerously close to angry utterance, Anne laid down her pencil and closed the account book in which she had just entered the purchase of the filly and the wages she was willing to give the new groom. "I believe we have worked together long enough for today," she said evenly, and he knew that she had guessed everything or almost everything that had passed through his mind. She had been in the office less than half an hour, instead of the whole afternoon, and when she left it Peter knew it would be worse than useless to urge that she should remain and, also, that she would not be back the next day or the day after. The future, which had begun to look so bright only the day before, when she came to church wearing the short transparent veil that revealed the lovely, long-hidden face, was suddenly dark again.

It had been Peter's intention to speak to Anne about the approach of Thanksgiving, the celebration of which was doubtless quite unknown to her, and to ask if they might not make it something of an occasion. The McKeevers, of course, were familiar with this through Alec, since he had spent it with the Bradfords every year that he was at Harvard. Peter thought it quite likely that they would be willing to make the trip from Donegal, in order to give him a sense of family feeling on the festival which, above all others in New England, was one of reunion among relatives, both close and distant. But of course it would not be feasible to ask them to stay at the mansion, unless Anne would preside at dinner, for her absence on such an occasion would betray their strained relations and arouse curiosity as to the underlying causes for these; and he was both too hurt and too angry to ask her, unless she returned to the office in a chastened mood, which she showed no signs of doing. Even if he humbled himself to make such a request, he knew that in her present frame of mind, she might refuse to grant it and then matters would go from bad to worse. However, as November dragged its cold and gloomy way to a close, he decided that he could not pretend the last Thursday was just like any other day, or sit down in solitary state to a dinner that would puzzle Cook both by its dimensions and the nature of its ingredients. On a sudden impulse, he decided to speak to Father Carroll.

"Have you ever heard of Thanksgiving?" he inquired, surprising the priest at home one evening when the latter had just settled down to reading his Office before retiring for the night.

"Why certainly," Father Carroll replied, with increasing surprise. "Surely you know that the giving of thanks is a Christian obligation."

Peter shook his head. "I don't *mean* that kind. I mean Thanksgiving with a capital T. A special day. It was originated by a group of Pilgrims who wanted to give thanks because they'd escaped religious persecution in England; because they'd crossed the Atlantic in a dirty little ship called the *Mayflower*; because enough of them had survived starvation and massacre by the Indians for nearly a year; because they'd somehow succeeded in raising crops beyond their expectations and harvesting them. They were facing their second New England winter and they certainly hadn't much security to look forward to. But, when the *May-*

flower sailed back to England, not a single one of those half-starved, half-frozen Pilgrims took advantage of the chance to go with her. They had got what they came for—freedom. Not just freedom to worship according to their faith. Every kind of freedom. So they wanted to give thanks for that, too. I should think an Irishman would be the very first to understand how they felt."

Father Carroll laid aside his breviary. "Sit down, Peter," he said. "I do understand how they felt and so will every true Irishman to whom you tell that story. It's a pity it isn't better known here."

"I'd be very pleased to make it better known. Perhaps Mr. Quinn would let me tell it to the children. But what I really came here for wasn't just to tell you a story. It was to ask if you wouldn't have Thanksgiving dinner with me. I thought if you said yes, I'd ask Mr. MacAuliffe and Dr. Carey. Possibly we could play whist afterward, while we're getting over the dinner. You see, Americans have come to make the occasion more of a feast than the Pilgrims were able to, though we got the idea of the main dish from the wild turkeys they caught. We have a huge dinner and relatives come from near and far so they can eat it together. In a way, it's even more of a family feast than Christmas, because that centers around grandparents and parents and children. But Thanksgiving takes in maiden aunts and widowed uncles and distant cousins that we don't see much at any other time, but that we wouldn't think of allowing to eat their Thanksgiving dinner alone. Somehow, I just can't bear the thought of doing it, either. This is the first time I've been away from home on that day and I thought that maybe—"

Father Carroll did not ask him why he had not told this story and made this appeal to Anne, as Peter knew would have seemed more natural on the face of things. If the priest guessed or knew that there was some strain between the mansion and the dower house, he gave no sign of it. He only said that he would be very pleased to dine with Peter on the last Thursday in November and he was sure Dr. Carey and Mr. MacAuliffe would be equally pleased. He hoped Peter would tell them the story about the Pilgrims, just as he had told it at the presbytery, and yes, it might not be a bad idea at all to tell it at school. As for the game of whist, he would enjoy that very much. He was afraid he was rather out of practice and it would be a good thing to get his hand in again. Perhaps it would be possible to have a foursome once a fortnight or even once a week, not always at the mansion, either. The players should take turns in providing refreshments.

Cook proved most cooperative when Peter broached the subject of Thanksgiving to her. A large roasted turkey—why, that was no problem at all. Oysters for the first course; celery and olives could easily be added. Chestnut dressing she had not heard of, but it sounded easy. Perhaps the Master would try it once beforehand at some other meal and see if she got it right. Cranberries did not grow in Ireland, as far as she knew, but if the Master would tell her what that jelly ought to taste like, she would experiment with a combination of others and see how she came out. It was only at the mention of squash and sweet potatoes that she shook her head and seemed discouraged; but when Peter told her it would be all right to have regular Irish potatoes mashed —what she called creamed—and onions and vegetable marrow, she brightened again. As for plum pudding, she was really in her element; she would make him the finest one he ever saw and send it in flaming like a bonfire; and, of course, he could have apple tart, too, if he wanted it. They had *how* many kinds of pie in New England?

"I didn't mean to startle you, Cook," Peter said, laughing. "We do begin the day with chicken pie for breakfast, but I don't want to tackle that alone and I'd really like an extra hour of sleep. So I'll treat myself to that, instead, since this is going to be my holiday. And, naturally, no one person eats all the different kinds of pie for dinner—people take their choice. It's quite a sight when mince, pumpkin, apple, squash, lemon, custard and cranberry are all set forth together to choose among. There are some more, though I forget the rest. I believe fourteen make up a completely furnished feast."

Cook said that just hearing about that many pies took her appetite away, but she chuckled when she said it and Peter knew the dinner she sent in would do them both credit. After his conversation with her and one with Wade about wines and the best china and silver, he dismissed the preparations for his party from his mind. But he paid one more call on Father Carroll to mention a matter he had forgotten the first time in his misery over his feud with Anne and his increasing loneliness.

"There's something else I should have told you about Thanksgiving, Father. Something very important."

"Yes, Peter."

"We don't just have a big family dinner and invite all our relatives. We—I mean those who can afford to do that—try to see that lots of other people have those Thanksgiving dinners, too—people who couldn't otherwise afford it. The best grocery stores make a specialty of preparing baskets, which they charge to their regular customers, as directed; but often, in order to give a more personal touch, the baskets are prepared right in the family kitchens of the people who are providing them. That gives the lady of the house a chance to add special things, like extra candy if there are a lot of children, or calves'-foot jelly if there's an invalid, for example."

"I see. So you thought—"

"I wondered if I couldn't do something like that here, without giving offense. I don't mean turkeys, necessarily, for a lot of people, but something that would make a meal taste extra good and look attractive. I'd like to share my Thanksgiving with those you know are in want, just as the Bradfords will be doing that day in Boston. You could set it down to a queer American custom if you had to explain it to the county people; if I'm not here next year then there wouldn't be any surprise that the bounty wasn't repeated."

"What do you mean, Peter, if you're not here next year?"

"Why, if Lady O'Toole has a son, I won't be the heir any more. And probably there won't be any reason why I shouldn't go home. Anyhow, it rather looks that way to me now."

There was a long silence. It was the priest who broke it.

"You would be very much missed if you went away and you're very much needed here, no matter how it looks to you just now," he said. "I hope and believe that, in time, you may feel differently. As to sharing your Thanksgiving, it's a very generous thought. I'm not sure just what form it ought to take, but I'll try to find one. And then we'll have another talk. Don't worry, I'll think of something."

When Peter returned to the office after his next conference with Father Carroll, he felt he had made considerable progress in the right direction, as far as sharing his Thanksgiving was concerned; and there was no question that his speech at the school had been very well received; but he still had heard nothing from Anne and his sense of personal loneliness remained unassuaged; with this was coupled unaccustomed weariness, from which he was not released by sleep. The bad dreams about the Hartley murder, which he could not disassociate from the whole troublesome question of landlordism, still bothered him intermittently; and he had not yet been able to visualize the vault only as it was regarded by Lady Susannah. He knew now that he would be welcome at half a dozen pleasant houses in the neighborhood whenever he chose to go to them, but he was in no mood for society; and though he faithfully went to the stud, the stables and the farm, these visits represented an obligation and not a search for congenial companionship. The gamekeeper seemed to him less indicated for regular conferences than the rest of the staff; and when he was told that Fagan was waiting to see him, he was tempted to send word it would not be convenient for him to do so that evening, unless the matter were very urgent; he was afraid the keeper felt it his duty to report some additional instances of poaching and that, this time, he would not be able to plead convincingly for leniency. However, he genuinely liked the man and there was no use in putting off an interview which, sooner or later, would be inevitable; and, when Fagan came into the office and set a covered basket carefully down on the floor beside him, Peter was thankful that he had not done so.

"My boy Mark told me about the speech you made at the school, sir," Fagan said. "Very taken with it, he was, too, and all his classmates, according to what he tells me. Now there's a rumor going around that you're planning to send out some baskets with things in them that people might like—different things, according to what the families need, because, in your country, Thanksgiving is a time people like to share with others."

"That's true, Fagan. I hope the idea isn't distasteful to you. I consulted Father Carroll and he thought—"

"Excuse me, sir. The idea isn't distasteful to me. I don't see how it could be to anyone, but it set me to wondering whether anyone had thought that maybe you'd like to have something brought to you in a basket, something you might especially like."

"Why, no. But there isn't any reason why anyone should."

"Maybe not. But I thought there wasn't any reason why a person shouldn't. Is there?"

"No, certainly not. If there were something special that person wanted to share," Peter replied, wondering if it were his imagination that muffled sounds seemed to be coming from the basket.

"Well, sir, maybe I'm mistaken, but every time I've seen you looking at my dogs, I thought there was something in your face . . . and the mansion's a big house for a man, a young man, to be living in all by himself, if I may say so. I can't help thinking that maybe you were a mite lonely here and that a dog might make a difference. And it happens that my bitch Tessie had a fine litter about six weeks ago. You didn't see it when you came to the house, because my wife makes me keep Tessie in the shed when her family's young. But the pups are old enough to leave her now and more or less housebroken and they're purebred Irish setters. So I thought that, maybe. . . ."

Fagan uncovered the basket, where the sounds had become a little louder. He reached down into it and brought out a beautiful red-coated puppy which looked first at him and then at Peter with trustful eyes and made no protest as it was passed from one to the other. Then, settling itself comfortably, it licked Peter's hand and snuggled closer. Through his clothes he could feel the warmth of its little furry body.

"I don't know how to thank you," he said a bit huskily. "I've kept thinking what a difference a dog would make here, but I didn't like to suggest buying one for fear it would bring up a subject that was better dropped. You see, her ladyship told me that, after his eldest dog had died, my uncle didn't want another in its place. He was old himself and he seemed to dread the thought that, when he died, his dog, if he had one, might be inconsolable and refuse to be separated from him and that this would create one more difficulty for her ladyship to deal with. It very well might have, too. And now you've solved the problem for me in the perfect way. Has this little fellow a name already? And what about his food?"

"We've been calling him Rufus, but he isn't registered yet, so you can change it if you want to . . . milk mostly, but some meat chopped up very fine. You needn't worry that he won't thrive; he's a good healthy puppy."

Fagan leaned over and petted the dog's head. Peter spoke with some concern.

"Look here, this is a very valuable present you've given me and, what's more, perhaps you're attached to him already. If it would be a wrench for you to part from him—"

"It's no wrench. It's glad enough I am to be able to do something that'll give you pleasure, sir. Lots of the men on the place have been saying they wished they could, but they didn't know exactly what would serve. I thought I did. And it looks as if I'd guessed right."

Fagan rose to leave, beaming with satisfaction, as Peter continued to stroke the nestling puppy. At the door, the gamekeeper paused. "I hope you won't take it amiss, if I say it's time to put an end to poaching, sir," he said. "You've got a kind heart and you can't help feeling you'll never miss the game that disappears; but pheasants and partridges and grouse are property, just the same as horses, and it's my duty to preserve it for you, just as it is Farrell's and Riordan's to look after the stables and the stud. Besides, poaching is only stealing by another name and, if we're going to call a spade a spade, why shouldn't we call poaching by its real name, too? I suppose maybe you'll be telling me you're afraid the poachers might be hungry, sir. Well, if they're hungry, they can snare rabbits and I might close my eyes to that, once and again, though, likely as not, they'd spend what they'd saved on poteen. You don't hunt, so I understand, but surely you'll do some shooting and, even if you don't yourself, you'll be having guests staying with you who'll want to. Besides, with all the good harvests we've had and all these Thanksgiving baskets that are going around, there's not many a one that will be really hungry, and if there is I'll know it and see he doesn't have to stay that way. Him or his family, either. We have plenty at the lodge to share a little ourselves."

Except for Sundays, when they continued to go to church together and Anne continued to wear her light veil, Peter did not see her until the day after Thanksgiving. Then she came to the office just as he was getting ready to close it for the day and sat down on her side of the desk, as if there had been no interruption in their work together.

"What are all these rumors I'm hearing?" she inquired, without appearing to notice the puppy curled up at his feet.

"About what?"

"About a speech you've made to the school children. About a lavish dinner party you gave yesterday, with whist afterward. About wholesale largesse to heaven knows how many families."

"Do you object? Do you feel I've exceeded my prerogatives, as you did when I said I'd be responsible for the expenses of the new stud?"

She flushed. "Of course not. But I wish you'd told me about these plans."

"I didn't think you'd be interested. Besides, I really haven't had much of a chance. You haven't come to the office and you haven't suggested that I should come to the dower house. The drive to and from church doesn't give time for much discussion."

"Will you tell me now?"

As briefly as possible, he outlined what he had done and why. She did not seem to be satisfied.

"You made a great impression with some story you told about the Pilgrims. I keep getting echoes of it, without hearing the whole thing."

"I couldn't begin to do justice to the whole thing. But I'll repeat what I've told elsewhere as nearly as I can remember it." He did so and then waited a long time for her to speak again.

"I'm sorry you didn't tell me this story before, but I know it's my own fault that you haven't," she said, "and I know it's too late for me to have any share in your Thanksgiving now. But I would like to have one in your preparations for Christmas. I understand that Lady Susannah and your sister Janet and Janet's fiancé will be spending it with you—perhaps the McKeevers, too? You'll want to do a great deal of decorating, won't you, so that everything will look beautiful when they arrive? Will you let me help you?"

"I'd like very much to have you help me with the decorations, but first I need help with the accounts. You may remember that the last time you came to the office, you left before we finished the day's work. Would you feel like doing it now?"

He knew that he was taking a long chance in making such an answer, instead of accepting, without question or condition, the olive branch she was extending. But he also knew that, if he did, he might as well abandon for good and all the hope of improving living conditions among wage earners by increasing their pay; and he also knew that, if the means and the manner of restocking the stud farm became a bone of contention between him and Anne, the situation would be even more tense than it was at the moment. Moreover, though she had not retracted the desperate statement that she hated him, made when she first discovered her pregnancy, he had never ceased to believe that she loved him and wanted him as much as he loved and wanted her and that, when her sense of guilt had ceased to overpower her sense of fulfillment, and when she was no longer restricted by the exigencies of official mourning, she would confess this. Besides, she certainly would love him and want him less, rather than more, if she found he would submit to unjust dictation rather than lose her. Since there was only one kind of a man whom she would have accepted as a lover—and he could not doubt that she had been telling the truth when she said that—it was equally true that there was only one kind she would accept as a husband and it was the same kind.

The pause before she answered was even longer than it had been when he finished telling her the story of the Pilgrims, and he began to think he had overplayed his hand. Still, he knew he could not have done otherwise and, eventually, without speaking, she pulled from its drawer the account book in which she made the first informal entries and opened it at the unfinished page.

"We were discussing gifts versus loans, if you remember," he said pleasantly, sitting down opposite her and pulling his correlative account book from its drawer. "I had got as far as saying that I would take care of restocking the stud and was on the point of telling you how when you interrupted by talking about Lawrence Donovan and Maurice de Briare, neither of whom I had intended to mention. While you were too ill for me to consult, I wrote to Granny Glover and told her I didn't know whether or not I had money enough to buy everything that I considered necessary for the stud out of my income, but, as she had told me I was her heir, I would like to feel I could draw on her if I needed to—on a business basis. I said that, of course, for the time being I had stopped work at the tower. Her reply, which came by cable, was indignant. She told me to go out and buy whatever I wanted and not to talk nonsense about business arrangements. This was followed by a letter in which she made it still clearer that she wanted the new stud to be her financial responsibility. It will be all right to pay her back if you want to, but I don't suppose you put taking a gift from your sister-in-law in the same category as taking one from your suitors and I hope you will be careful not to hurt her feelings. Anyway, the new mare has already been paid for by her and it isn't necessary to make any entry in your book about that, because no bill has come here and none will be coming. Is that clear?"

"Yes," said Anne, rather unsteadily.

"All right. Now as to Matt's wages. He was put down, as I told you, for the same that the other grooms are getting and he was disappointed, but he didn't refuse to come and, so far, none of the others has complained. But it's no news to you that I've never felt eight pounds, ten shillings a year decent payment for an able-bodied man who works long hours six days in the week or seven if he's needed. Should the moment come when he tells me he's had a better offer somewhere else, I want to meet that better offer and keep him if I can; that may well mean raising wages all around. And, thanks to Granny Glover's generosity, we can afford to do it. However, we'll cross that bridge when we get to it. Meanwhile, I'll give Christmas bonuses all around. Their size will be based on length of service, as well as a percentage of wages, so Matt won't get much money this year; but he'll grasp the basic idea and so will everyone else and I think it will be considered fair. I don't know whether or not it's the custom in Ireland to give Christmas bonuses and I don't greatly care. So you can just put it down to another queer American habit, like largesse at Thanksgiving, if any question comes up after I've gone."

"What do you mean, after you're gone?"

"That was the arrangement, wasn't it? That if the baby were a girl, I'd stay on and do my best to be an Irish earl. If it were a boy, I'd leave immediately if you wanted me to."

"I haven't said I wanted you to."

"No. But sometimes you've made me feel that I couldn't stay on your terms. For instance, when you don't have confidence in my reliability after you've told me to use my own judgment. That means right now. And if you don't love me enough to tell me you'll marry me, as soon as it's proper for you to do so. That means next spring. . . . Please write down Matt Riordan, eight pounds, ten shillings, plus Christmas bonus in your little book and we'll call it a day."

Anne hesitated. "If you give all those bonuses, will it mean you'll have to stop work on the tower?"

Peter sensed that the question had been prompted by a realization that the work on the tower meant a great deal to him, rather than a desire to argue further about a wage schedule, and was correspondingly pleased. "No," he said, "you know that I've felt I'd like to live there, at least for awhile. I first thought of it as a good place for a lonely bachelor and since then I've had a different idea—but we can talk about that later, if you'd rather. Anyway, I'd still like to finish what I've begun; even if I'm not here to see the end of the work, I'd like to feel I'd left everything in the best condition I could."

"I'd like very much to hear about your second plan now," Anne said, disregarding the latter part of his speech.

"I thought possibly you and I might use the tower as a sort of hideaway when we were first married, if you made up your mind to marry me. I have an idea that more than one of the early O'Tooles found it a convenient bower for a lady love and that, perhaps, I might, if my lady love decided to marry me. How would that strike you?"

"If we should marry, it might not be a bad idea. I'd dreaded going back to my old rooms here because—well, for certain reasons I won't go into now."

"You don't need to. I never intended that you should. If the baby's a boy, remember he'll be born an earl, so he ought to have the Earl's apartments right away. You and I should have entirely different ones, newly equipped and furnished for us on the sunny side of the house."

"And what if the baby's a girl?"

"Oh well, she'd be born Lady Susannah, the fourth or the fifth, wouldn't she? I think she'd deserve to be treated with just as much deference as a boy."

The conference, which had been shot through with danger signals when it began, had developed into an amicable conversation charged with pleasant prospects. However, Anne asked one more question.

"What about the old church?"

"Oh, that will be all right, too. I didn't intend to do any more there at present than roof it over and get glass in the windows. A project of that sort takes time to think about, as well as to carry out. I wouldn't want to hurry it, even if I could afford to. I've suggested a stained-glass window in the new church as a memorial to my uncle, and Father Carroll is thinking it over—I mean, whether to do that now or to wait until it could go in the old church as a memorial to all the O'Tooles of Cloneen. I'm going to let him decide. Meanwhile, Riordan is going to superintend the roofing and glazing job and he's already got some tinkers lined up to help with it." And when Anne failed to suppress a gasp of surprise, Peter laughed. "Surely, they ought to be very good at that sort of work. And there isn't anything in the cemetery to which they'd want to help themselves. Besides, Riordan is vouching for them. Now I'll repeat my request in case you've forgotten it in the course of all this pleasant discussion about future plans."

Without answering, Anne wrote the item and closed the book. Then she looked across the desk at Peter, who had already risen and was smiling.

"Now can we talk about the decorations?" she asked.

"By all means. Do we begin with wreaths or candles or what? I'll leave that to you."

22

Mrs. Brennan said that never, in her day, had there been such superb Christmas decorations at Cloneen. Wade, whose day at the mansion went even further back, agreed with her.

"The first Lady O'Toole—of course, I mean the late Earl's first wife, may she rest in peace—wasn't one to spend much time on such fussy things," he said, pausing to get the effect of the wreath he was hanging and making sure it was placed neither too high nor too low on the window. "And, after her death, there was a long while when there wasn't a mistress to brighten the place at Christmas or any other time. Our present Mistress, may God bless her, has tried to do that; but no doubt she felt, coming here young and strange as she did, that she must follow the customs of her husband's country and not try to change or improve them, even when she knew what they were. The new Master likes changes, if he thinks they're an improvement. And I'll be the first to say they are."

"But not the last," observed Mrs. Brennan, steadying the ladder that Wade was descending. "Who isn't saying it?"

There was not the slightest question that Peter's lavish idea of Christmas decorations met with widespread favor. He had not heard before about the one large candle which, shortly before sunset on Christmas Eve, the head of a household put in the principal window of his home, however humble, where it would remain lighted all night and, whatever the weather, left the front door wide open. Peter was told that the glimmering of these candles from the scattered farms all over the countryside was one of the most significant sights connected with an Irish Christmas and he was swift to recognize and appreciate its symbolism. It had the same underlying idea, he told Anne and Father Carroll, as the *posadas* of the Spanish-speaking people on both sides of the Atlantic, with whom he was familiar: for nine days groups of carolers went from door to door, seeking entrance in the name of the Holy Child Who had been born in a stable, because there was no room for His Mother and His foster Father at an inn; *posada* was the Spanish word for "inn" and the carolers took their name from that. The Irish candle and the open door was just another way, and a very lovely one, of showing that the Holy Family would be made welcome in every dwelling; and perhaps the widespread use of candles at Christmastime had come from it, just like so many other customs for which Ireland had never received due credit. At Cloneen, they would have the largest candle they could find and put it in the front window of the Chinese parlor, but, besides that, they would have candles of regular size in every window of the house. On Beacon Hill, Peter went on to say, they had carols and candles, too, lots and lots of both; and families like the Bradfords, who had lived there for generations, kept open house and invited the carolers to come in, whether or not they were strangers. Usually, there was snow in Boston at that time and the Hill sparkled with that and shone with candlelight and glowed with hospitality. At Cloneen they must do all they could to rival that wonderful festival and keep him from being homesick.

So candles were put in all the windows, not only of the mansion and the dower house, but of all the lodges and the farmhouse and Riordan's little stone house and Andy Farrell's quarters; and wreaths were hung on all windows and doors. In the mansion, the great hall and all the larger rooms were garlanded with laurel, and the mantels were banked with holly, and immense quantities of both laurel and holly were sent to Father Carroll for the church and the Mother Superior for the convent.

And still Peter was not satisfied: the question of a tree had not been raised at all yet and in many ways that seemed to him the most important of any.

"There must be a big one for the drawing room of the mansion and a smaller one for yours," he told Anne. "But shouldn't there be one in the servants' hall, too? And what about the lodges, the farmhouse, the stone house—all the places where we're sending candles and wreaths? Shouldn't we send trees, too?"

"The servants' hall, by all means. As far as I know, there's never been one there, but I think that's a gesture which would be very much appreciated by the staff. In some of the other cases, you've done so much already that I think they might be overpowered and, perhaps, a little puzzled. I don't think many of them ever had a Christmas tree or even heard about one."

"It's time they did. I'd better give another talk at the school. Of course, there *has* to be a tree there, with presents for all the children. In Germany, *every* family has a tree, even the very poorest."

"Peter, if you start trying to have a Christmas celebration that will include the customs of every country you've ever been to or can think of, it'll end in utter confusion. Anyway, I'm a little jealous you thought of Germany, just as you did when you were looking for a double desk, but haven't said a word about France! What about roast goose, as well as roast turkey for dinner? What about the extra seat at the table so there'd be a *place du pauvre*? What about the shoes on the hearthstone for *Père Noël* to fill? What about keeping away from the stables so that the animals may talk to each other during the midnight hour, in memory of those that surrounded the stable in Bethlehem? What about *Reveillon* after Midnight Mass?"

"Roast goose, as well as roast turkey, by all means. Suppose you take that up with Cook. I don't want to 'overpower' her, as you put it, and I've still got to break the news about chicken pie for breakfast. I skipped that at Thanksgiving—our second traditional day for having it at that time—because I didn't want to eat it alone and preferred an extra hour of sleep to celebrate a holiday, anyhow. But Janet would feel cheated if she didn't get it, so I shall rouse myself for her benefit. I'm all for the *place du pauvre,* as Americans have a counterpart for that, especially in country places; we try to make sure that anyone who might not have much of a Christmas, like a new doctor or a new clergyman, gets invited to join us; if there's anyone in a comparable category at Cloncoole, I'd like to know it. I meant to have stockings at the library mantel for Santa Claus to fill, but if you'd rather have shoes for *Père Noël* that's all right by me and I'm sure it will be for the others. I don't believe anyone is still *in* our stables at midnight, though the watchman, of course, is going the rounds; and, anyway, there weren't any horses in the stable at Bethlehem, were there, as far as we know? I'll warn him to steer clear of the barns for an hour if that doesn't make too much of a risk for the cows. The donkeys are all outdoors, so we'll trust they'll look after themselves."

He gazed at her with his most disarming smile before he made his one objection. "I hadn't said anything about making 'Christmas Gif'' a general handout, even though Letitia's sure to turn up in my room with a broad grin and an outstretched palm. So, with that omission from customs elsewhere, wouldn't you be willing to omit one that's French and skip *Reveillon*? It would keep you up pretty late and you'll already be tired, not only after Midnight Mass—if Dr. Carey lets you go to that—but after having all my guests to an early supper Christmas Eve, so that if any of them wish to receive Communion they may do so. It will be a wonderful way for them to begin their stay here and I'm very pleased you've thought of asking them. But I'm counting on you to preside over the goose at one end of my table and I hope you'll go straight to bed after Mass and stay there until it's time for Christmas dinner."

"And when are we going to see what *Père Noël* has brought?"

"We'll do that just before dinner. It won't take long, for those will be just fun presents. The really important ones will be under the tree and we'll open those after dinner."

"I see. Well, I suppose I can do without *Reveillon* for once, considering all the consolation prizes there are. But I wish you'd stop worrying about my getting overtired. I'm perfectly well."

"Yes. Right now. But you gave us one bad scare and I don't want another. In fact, the reason I set Wade to hanging up wreaths was because I thought you were doing too much reaching and standing on your feet too much. I'd be much happier if, from now on, you confined your efforts to tying up presents, which you can do sitting in a nice comfortable chair, with a table in front of you; and, even if you say you're perfectly well, there's something else I'm worried about, but I hadn't dared speak of it because you'd think such a remark not a delicate, but an indelicate attention. Have you, by any unfortunate chance, forgotten the solemn promise you made me about not restricting the size of your waist? You're not quite as thin as you were, which is all to the good, but otherwise you look about the same to me that you did in June. Where are you keeping this baby?"

To his relief, Anne laughed, though she flushed. "I haven't broken any solemn promises," she said. "Naturally, I lost quite a little weight while I wasn't keeping many meals down and I had to gain that back, before my clothes even fitted. Now, as you say, I've begun to gain weight and everything's been let out, whether you noticed the difference or not—Solange is very good about alterations of that kind. Presently, everything will be too tight and then it will all be discarded, probably for good, because I think I'd be justified in lightening my mourning a little, after the baby is born and, meanwhile, I'll soon be getting into draperies. I felt justified in taking off my heavy veil, so that the little girl who wondered how anyone could tell whether or not I was pretty could find out; and I've known some babies to be really frightened by very black clothes. . . . As to your other question, I'm not only keeping the baby where it ought to be, but it's been making its presence known for nearly a month now." Suddenly she looked more grave. "It's a strange feeling, this consciousness of carrying another life in your own. I'm honestly not unmindful that it's a great responsibility. I'm very conscious of it, Peter, even if it doesn't look that way to you. Please believe me. Please trust me."

She did not say any more on the subject and Peter found that he could not. He knew that, in speaking to Anne so intimately, he had come close to using the conversational prerogative of a husband and he must not run the risk of seeming so to trespass. He remembered hearing his brother-in-law say, jestingly, that he did not have a good night's sleep for more than four months before Sue's baby was born, because the little wretch kept kicking him; and a sensation of great loss, because he had not been lying close beside Anne every night and having this repeated assurance of his paternity, became mingled with his great yearning for her as his beloved. But he did not tell her so. He was thankful that, instead of taking offense at what he had said, as she might so easily and understandably have done, she had accepted his solicitude, both as a proof of his love and of his right to concern for their child. If no more unfortunate frictions arose between them, to develop further estrangement, he would be justified in hoping that, before long, Anne would confess that she returned his love.

Christmas came and went without any such confession or even any sign that it was near. Nevertheless, it was a period of such general good will that Peter knew he should not complain, even to himself, and he did not, until he was beset by new worries from a wholly unexpected quarter. The three McKeevers arrived twenty-four hours before the visitors from France, who were barely able to make Christmas Eve, and Peter was not sorry to have this time free for his Ulster relatives, who were eagerly planning to do as much shooting as they could crowd into their visit, much to Fagan's delight. Inevitably, Lady Susannah and Janet and the Polish prince would take over the center of the stage and it was fitting that the others should have his undivided attention first. This feeling was intensified when Janet proved to be in a state of exuberance to which her escape from school, the attendance of an eligible suitor and the festive atmosphere of her strange surroundings all contributed. Lady Susannah had frankly found the journey a tiring one and was glad to sit down and rest in the library before she went upstairs; but Janet, a dashing red figure, rushed joyously from room to room, trying to see everything at once, within minutes of her arrival. "You never told me it was so beautiful!" she exclaimed, almost accusingly, first to her grandmother and then to her brother. "Is your house as beautiful as this, Stefan?"

"It looks beautiful to me. I hope it will to you," the young Pole answered soberly. Peter had liked what little he had seen of him in London the previous June; now this liking was more than confirmed. Stefan entered easily and agreeably into the family picture and made a good impression on Anne and all the McKeevers during the course of the early supper by his share, which was a ready contribution, but at no time a dominant factor, in the pleasant conversation. Afterward, they all joked together over the arrangement of the shoes which *Père Noël* was to fill at the library fireplace. Then Anne returned to the dower house; Lady Susannah and Janet went upstairs to superintend Letitia's unpacking and deal with various mysterious parcels; and the McKeevers, who were not going to Midnight Mass, wanted to get rested for the shooting. Almost immediately thereafter, Stefan asked Peter, with becoming gravity, if this were not perhaps a propitious occasion for him to have a few words with his host on a confidential matter of great importance to him.

"I don't see how it would be possible to find a better one," Peter assured him. "Let's make ourselves comfortable by the fire while you tell me what's on your mind."

"I think you probably have guessed," Stefan answered, accepting the indicated chair and pausing politely.

"I'm sorry, I haven't. But I'm sure I'd be interested in anything you have to say."

"It didn't occur to you that, as your father is so far away, I might apply to you, as Janet's nearest available male relative, for permission to address your sister?"

Peter succeeded, not without difficulty, in answering with equal gravity. "No, it didn't. You see, American girls are taking these things into their own hands, more and more. I know that last June our parents felt Janet was too young to have a serious suitor—in fact, she was considered too young to go out socially at all, with the rest of the family, and it came as something of a shock when they found she'd seen quite a little of you after she happened to meet you. They more or less put her in my charge, but they didn't consider me much of a success as a chaperon; perhaps I'd have done better if I hadn't liked you so much, from the beginning. Anyway, as you know, they took her off to Italy, but when she wanted to stay in Paris, they were perfectly willing and they knew well enough by then what the score was. Besides, Granny Glover's been rooting for you from the beginning, so you've got nothing to worry about, as far as the family's concerned."

"Thank you. That is very reassuring."

"I can't answer quite so easily for Janet. As I told you, American girls—at least all those I know—tend to decide these things for themselves. They're not in the least like French girls, whose parents do the deciding for them."

He had not intended to let any bitterness creep into his voice in talking with this high-principled young man who was so deadly serious and so bent on leaning over backward to do right. Peter spoke again, hastily, hoping that his brief divergence from the subject at hand might go unnoticed.

"I know Janet likes you very much. If she didn't, she wouldn't have stayed in Paris on purpose to see you—because, of course, that's why she did stay, not because she was in the least interested in a French finishing school. She's never been much of a student, anyway. And I haven't a doubt that, besides liking you as a person, she is impressed by your title and flattered to think you're in love with her—after all, she's very young and you're a very desirable *parti*. But whether or not this all boils down to the fact that she's ready to become formally engaged to you and give up two or three years of probable belledom, I couldn't say."

"That is what I am afraid of, Peter—it is all right for me to call you Peter, isn't it? That even though the rest of the family, Lady Susannah especially, is kindly disposed toward me and will raise no objections to my suit, Janet herself does not want to be formally engaged. And that, of course, is what I want immediately. The day after Christmas is my saint's day and it would be such a wonderful time to announce the engagement! Then a wedding in the spring. I have hopes of returning to Warsaw, of serving my country in some capacity there instead of abroad for the next two or three years. I want to take Janet home with me when I go. She would be very warmly welcomed by the Polish nobility, because of its gratitude to the sept of the O'Tooles. The part played by Luke O'Toole in the rescue of

Princess Clementina, which made possible her marriage to James III, will never be forgotten. Personally, there is no one I need to consult. My parents are both dead and I was an only child. My estate is quite unencumbered. I have a house in Warsaw and one in the country. In style they are, naturally, quite different from this, but I believe they are comparable in size and importance. I can give Janet everything she could reasonably want and probably more than that materially. And I would do my very best to make her happy. I may perhaps mention that I am a devout Catholic and take marriage very seriously. Janet would have no rivals in my affections."

"I'd say she doesn't know how lucky she is. I'm with you and, if you like, I'll tell Janet so. How much good it will do, I don't know. She's not nearly as pretty as her sisters, but she's always had more beaux than the other two girls, though Sue's already married very well. There's an American author, whose work I've always liked, who describes one of his heroines by saying, 'She ain't pretty, but she's powerful pert.' That's Janet all over. She's powerful pert and that seems to go a long way with lots of men. It wouldn't with me, but that's neither here nor there."

Stefan rose and bowed rather formally. "You have been very kind," he said. "I am grateful for everything you have told me and I will go to my room now and say a few private prayers before going to Holy Mass. Most of them will center around Janet."

Peter had thought of asking Stefan to take a walk with him, to see the countryside as it would appear on this night of nights, with lighted candles in all the scattered farmhouses; but he was not sorry to find that he would be setting out alone. From what he had heard, he believed it would be a very moving sight and he had not been without some perturbation of spirit as he watched his guest depart. It was quite true that Janet did not know how lucky she was and, for this reason, she might let the opportunity for a really great marriage slip through her fingers. She enjoyed a lively give and take; it could be that the very propriety and solemnity of Stefan's approach would put her off. As her brother, who had unexpectedly assumed the position of her guardian, Peter wanted time to think the situation over by himself.

He had insisted that the tower must be numbered among the buildings where the door would stand open and a tall candle would burn brightly beside it; and, as he went past the old castle and saw that his instructions had been faithfully followed, he had the happy sensation that this ceased to be a ruin, that it was imbued with new life. Although he, as yet, had found no family record that confirmed such an impression, he still had a strong feeling that he was not the first of his race to visualize the tower's upper chamber—difficult of access, solitary on its story—as an ideal retreat in which to harbor his beloved. As he had told Anne, he hoped perhaps they might find in their bridal bower the tale which, so far, had eluded him, but which he felt so sure existed, and read it together by a light like the one that was burning there now, as Paolo and Francesca da Rimini had read the story of Lancelot and Guinevere together, but with joyous instead of tragic results.

The main lodge, which heretofore he had never been able to disassociate from the unrelieved darkness and the mournful sound of keening, which had marked his arrival at Cloneen, was now beaming with welcome and ringing with carols; and when he reached the bridge on the main road and looked back at the mansion, it was such a vision of radiance that he stood gazing at it for some moments, with a strange lump in his throat, before he went on to the village. Here he hesitated, tempted to join the jovial gathering at the crowded pub and finally deciding against it. He was still not sufficiently "one of their own" among the men who were roistering there; though he knew he had won their respect and their liking, he was still a "stranger" from their viewpoint. Possibly, in another year, it would be different. . . .

He went on up the hill and stopped again as his way took him past the old churchyard. The ruined chapel was roughly roofed over now and there was glass in some of the windows; the tinkers had done their work well and they were having a noisy celebration of their own in the caravans drawn up on a nearby side road. It would have been possible to have candles in this church, to proclaim that it, too, was no longer abandoned; and the tinkers would have welcomed him without the restraint of the men at the pub; maybe he had erred on the side of not having provided candles enough, or in showing himself more convivially inclined; but it was still solitude that he sought, still the scattered farmhouses that he most wanted to see.

When he left the churchyard behind him, he was facing other slopes, clustered around a little valley. They were higher than the one he was on and the dividing line between them and the starlit sky was hardly discernible, for they were much the same soft dark color.

Though the little lights on these were further and further apart, as they approached summits, every one had its beacon; a stranger, seeking shelter, would need no other guide than these. Gradually, the strains of the tinkers' concertinas grew fainter and finally were engulfed by distance. The land, lambent with the myriad of tiny gleams from the cottages on the hills, seemed hushed, as if in preparation for some outburst of joy that was still unsung; and there was a mystic loveliness about it which did not seem to come from candlelight alone. The simple faith in God, the good will toward fellow men which had caused humble people to open their doors and light their windows had created a glow of their own and given added luster to a transfigured landscape. This was not an Ireland of heartless landlords and vengeful peasants; neither was it an Ireland of a privileged few, nor of a cultured class, nor of the sceptic section of an insular dogmatism. It was the Ireland that mattered most, the Ireland which must, in the end, prevail.

Not quite conscious of how it had happened, Peter realized that he was on his knees, praying as he had never prayed in his life before: a prayer of thanksgiving for the Ireland he had seen that night; a prayer of supplication for guidance in the fulfillment of his part in its destiny.

After that night, the evil dreams ceased.

23

Peter's concern about Janet was increased next morning when, over the chicken pie, she began teasing her grandmother to let her stay in Ireland after New Year's for the purpose of being presented at the Viceregal Court. Lady Susannah tried, quite ineffectually, to squelch her.

"You're going to a ball at Shanapark Castle tomorrow night and it will be magnificent. The Slatterys entertain superbly. And you're going to another ball at the barracks in Cloncoole Wednesday night and military balls are always exciting, with all their red coats and gold braid and brass bands. That ought to be enough to satisfy you for a beginning. We have to start back on Friday, anyway. Your school reopens the morning after New Year's. We can't possibly stay in Ireland for that."

"I don't see why not. If I'm late getting back and Reverend Mother raises a fuss about it, I could go to some other school. Or I could stop going to school and have lessons at home, the way so many French girls do. I want to be presented."

"Next year."

"I probably won't be in Ireland next year. Oh, Granny, can't you see this is just the ideal time?"

"Well—" began Lady Susannah, visibly weakening. She liked to go to Viceregal balls herself and, after all, sisters were excused from deep mourning after six months. Peter cut in.

"Why should you want to be presented? That's giving official notice that you're a grown-up member of society, of suitable age to consider matrimony, isn't it? You've already taken things into your own hands, somewhat prematurely. You sneaked into grown-up society last June and you're already engaged or as good as engaged."

"I did not *sneak!* I had to do something to pass the time and I went to the Duchess of Radford's garden party quite *openly!* And I'm not engaged or even as good as engaged. Whoever said I was?"

"I certainly got that impression. How come you wanted Stefan to take this trip with you if you weren't?"

"He wanted very much to come and I wanted to be sure of somebody, didn't I? How could I tell what I'd find in Ireland with no parties here because of your mourning?"

"You knew Alec was going to be here. He isn't in mourning and he's very dependable."

"Alec!" Janet repeated scornfully. "He's been around for years, just like one of the family! You didn't expect me to get a thrill out of him, did you—or him out of me! And I didn't know about the Slatterys and the barracks until I got here. Now that I am here and it would mean staying only a few days more, I don't see why I shouldn't be presented and have the fun of wearing a train three yards long. It would be one more feather in my cap, if I did get engaged to someone, to say I did it in my first season. How can I say that if you won't let me have a first season?"

"You don't need any first season, Janet. You're way ahead of the game already."

"You mean, I would be, if I accepted Stefan, and I do like him a lot."

"Then you'd better accept him and give him a really merry Christmas. It would mean a great deal to him if you'd announce your engagement tomorrow. It's his saint's day, you know."

"And go to the Slatterys' ball as an *engaged* girl and miss half the fun? How can I tell whether or not I like Stefan better than anyone else unless I meet lots of other people? For instance, how do I know I wouldn't like Maurice de Briare better? You say yourself, Granny, that he's the most attractive young man you've met in ages. You know I'm dying for a chance to meet him. And Anne says she's sure her family would be delighted to have us spend a weekend with them any time we'd like to!"

So it was as Peter had feared, only worse than he had feared, for he had never thought of Maurice de Briare in connection with Janet. She would keep poor Stefan on tenterhooks while she first saw what Ireland had to offer and then, at the first favorable opportunity, she would head straight for Normandy. Having reasoned with her over chicken pie, he tried to dismiss her problems from his mind, but to no avail. Stefan had excused himself beforehand from coming to break-

226

fast, because he had hoped to begin the day with the good news which Peter would give him privately; and since there was no good news, Peter did not seek him out, though he waited patiently for such a summons. It was almost time to open the "fun" presents before they met and all Peter could say was, "Don't be too discouraged," before all the others were within hearing. Through all the activities of the morning, he kept thinking of Stefan's undeserved disappointment.

The "fun" presents were more of a success than Peter had dared to hope. Lady Susannah had brought perfume in dainty flacons and candied fruit in pretty boxes for Sandra, Anne and Janet; cuff links for Alec and cigars for Dermot, Peter and Stefan. Peter had contributed collars of Carrickmacross and Limerick lace for the ladies and initialled handkerchiefs for the men. Dermot McKeever had shown ingenuity in choosing various articles of Connemara marble—beads, brooches, bookends and paper weights—and himself had been given a Peterson pipe with tobacco to fill it. Anne's offering consisted of bog oak crosses for everyone, both male and female, and Stefan's of old Polish crucifixes had been a comparable one. They were all still arranging and discussing their presents and lauding the generosity of *Père Noël* when Wade came to announce dinner and the mood of merriment was sustained as they went on to the dining room.

Dinner was a regal feast, with turkey at Peter's end of the table and goose at Anne's and the spiced beef and baked ham suitably set forth on the sideboard. Peter managed to forget Janet's willfulness when he looked at Anne, dressed for the first time in black velvet, instead of the lusterless silk of conventional mourning and, also, for the first time—despite the skill with which the dress had been cut—showing unmistakable signs of her condition. After dinner, they all moved into the drawing room and Dermot McKeever played Santa Claus. *Père Noël* had been given credit for the presents in all the shoes clustered around the library fireplace, but Santa Claus flatly declined to accept a single attribute of generosity; the real donors must acknowledge their gifts. A beautiful white porcelain swan, with a chain of gold links around its neck, unlike the other offerings grouped underneath the tree, had not been gaily wrapped and beribboned, but allowed to dominate the scene; and Dermot picked up most of the packages that surrounded it before touching it and thereby gave it increasing prominence as it stood more nearly alone. He finally handed it to Anne, saying that someone had broken the rules—the tag on the swan gave her name, but not the donor's; no doubt, she would know how to deal with this anonymity. A dazzling background had been created for her by a length of ancient metallic brocade, mounted like a tapestry, which Stefan had brought her because "he was sure she would find the right place for it in her house and he had never felt it was suitably displayed in his"; and the diamond bracelets which had been Lady Susannah's gift were already glittering on Anne's white arms; but something undefinably charming about the swan seemed to make it still more outstanding. There was a moment of silence as everyone waited for her exclamation of delight; but she bent over, gathering the swan to her, and murmured her thanks for it, without looking at anybody, in a voice so low that she could hardly be heard. Almost immediately thereafter, the festive hubbub began again and, whispering to Alec, who was sitting beside her, that she had promised to pay a brief visit to the servants' hall, she slipped from the room, taking the swan with her.

When the presents had all been distributed, the company drifted apart: Lady Susannah and Peter, reminded of promises similar to Anne's, followed her to the servants' hall; Alec took the handsome new books his parents had given him to the library and started to leaf through them; the elder McKeevers decided to take a short brisk walk. Stefan went across the hall to the music room and opened the grand piano, to which no one had given a thought until then, and began to play a Chopin polonaise. He followed this with some of the *Songs without Words* and next, very proudly, with the *Minuet in G* by his fellow countryman Paderewski, who was just beginning to achieve fame and fortune. Afterward, he shifted to Christmas music, and presently the others returned from the various places to which they had gone and gathered around him to sing their favorite carols in the way that came most readily to them. As if by common consent, "Adeste Fideles" came first, English and French versions blending harmoniously with the original Latin. Next came "Silent Night" and it seemed equally natural to hear it in German on one side of the room and in English on the other. Anne followed this with:

> "*Minuit Chrétiens, c'est l'heure solennelle*
> *Où l'homme Dieu descendit jusqu'à nous. . . .*"

Lady Susannah immediately chimed in with:

> "O Holy Night, the stars are brightly shining
> It is the night of our dear Saviour's birth. . . ."

as Stefan played the air a second time. Peter contributed:

> "O little town of Bethlehem
>   How still we see thee lie. . . ."

and though that was new to the others, except for Lady Susannah and Alec, Stefan quickly picked out the air and it, too, struck a generally responsive feeling.

"It's remarkable, isn't it," Stefan said, running his fingers lightly over a series of chords, "how many different kinds of people, in many different countries, are moved by the same thoughts, in the same way, at a time sacred to them all? 'Stille Nacht' was composed by a village choirmaster and a parish priest, striving together to overcome the handicap of a broken-down organ. The French hymn was scribbled in a barroom by a lonely wastrel; and didn't I understand you to say, Peter, that 'O Little Town of Bethlehem' was written by a greatly beloved bishop in Boston?"

"Yes, that's so. And all these songs give you the feeling of a special kind of stillness, a special kind of brightness. I don't know whether the Irish have put it into a carol, too, but last night I had the sensation that Ireland itself was its own best carol."

"That's a wonderful way to express it, but there's an old Wexford carol which I think we ought to include in this songfest, even if it isn't the equal of the others." Lady Susannah rummaged in the music stand beside the piano and produced some yellowed sheets which she spread out before Stefan. He nodded and began to sing, acting at the same time as choirmaster.

> "Good people o'er this Christmas time
>   Consider well and bear in mind
>   What our Good God for us has done
>   In sending His beloved Son.
>
> "With Mary Holy we should pray
>   To God with love this Christmas Day;
>   In Bethlehem upon that morn
>   There was a blessed Messiah born."

When Stefan finally closed the piano, he was overwhelmed with compliments. Why hadn't he told them before he was such a skilled musician?

"It hadn't occurred to me to mention it," he replied with complete sincerity. "I'm very glad if I have been able to contribute a little something to the celebration when so much has been done for me, a complete stranger in your midst. I am happy to be here with you, not only because today is Christmas, but because tomorrow is my saint's day and it will be wonderful to have that the occasion of a family gathering, too."

"You mean your birthday?" Janet asked.

"Well, as it happens, it *is* my birthday. I believe my parents had considered naming me Noël when they realized what the approximate date of my birth was likely to be. Then, when the actual date was the day after Christmas, Stefan seemed a more logical choice. I have always been glad, for St. Stefan has always been one of my favorite saints. Naturally, I should like to begin the day by going to Holy Mass, if that would not inconvenience anyone."

He looked toward Janet, obviously hoping she would offer to go with him. But she either did not notice the glance or chose to disregard it. Lady Susannah spoke immediately.

"Of course, it won't inconvenience anyone and, as a matter of fact, I should like to go with you," she said warmly. "It's too bad we didn't know about this sooner or we would have tried to have some sort of a little celebration in your honor. I am afraid it may be too late for that now and I only hope that the way St. Stephen's Day is celebrated in this country won't be offensive to you. It's given over largely to 'Hunting the Wren' and to the 'Wren Boys.' Sometimes it takes rather crude forms. There are several legends to the effect that the wren is a bird of ill omen. One of these legends goes all the way back to the Druids, who esteemed the wren as the king of birds. The superstitious respect shown it gave offense to the first Christian missionaries and at their instigation it was hunted and killed by the peasants on Christmas Day and the next day—St. Stephen's Day. According to one account, it was carried about hung by the leg in two hoops, crossing each other at right angles; and a procession was made in every village of men, women and children, singing an Irish catch."

"But surely such a barbarous custom hasn't survived since the days of the Druids!" Stefan exclaimed in obvious horror.

"Probably it wouldn't have if another legend hadn't gained credence: at the last battle fought in the north of Ireland between the Protestants and the Papists, as they were called, a party of the Protestants would have been surprised, sleeping, by the Papist Irish if several wrens had not awakened them by pecking on their drums as the enemy was approaching and given them this much warning. Another version of the same story blames this episode on the invasion of the Danes. Anyhow, the wild Irish associated the wrens with betrayal, hated the poor little birds, called them the devil's servants and killed them whenever they could catch them. They taught their children to thrust them full of thorns and sometimes a whole parish would go running like madmen from hedge to hedge wren hunting."

She was conscious of the gentle Pole's recoil. "And do these hunts still take place?"

"Actually, to a certain extent, the ceremony of the 'Wren Bush' has succeeded it. The 'Bush' is composed of holly and ivy and trimmed with ribbons and feathers, and a bunch of these takes the place of the wren. This 'Bush' is borne from door to door by selected attendants and paraded in a picturesque procession. Sometimes young men and young girls take part in it and, if they become a courting couple on St. Stephen's Day, the courtship must be continued until Shrovetide. And sometimes there's a leader known as the Droleen (which is really the word for wren in Irish), who's very witty and quick at repartee. Very often, the amount of largesse such a group gets from the different houses it visits depends on his talents. It's a great distinction to be chosen as the Droleen, but he's expected to make good. Then other times the group is made up of just youngsters who are called 'the Bush Boys' or 'The Wren Boys' and who go from house to house carrying the decorated bush and singing their own special carols, for which they expect to be rewarded. You may be very sure they'll be here tomorrow."

"No doubt, I should find such processions very interesting," Stefan said with apparent relief, "provided I were not worrying about a poor little tortured bird. I hope a procession comes here which includes the young girls and the young men about to begin a promising courtship, which will last until Shrovetide. It might give Janet some very salutary ideas."

24

Fortunately, neither of the two processions which came to Cloneen the next day gave Stefan any reason to worry about a poor little tortured bird. The first group came fairly early in the morning and consisted solely of youngsters—the Bush Boys who, as Lady Susannah had predicted, carried their own special Bush decorated with gay ribbons and sang their own special carol:

> "The Wren—the Wren—the King of all birds
> On St. Stephen's Day was caught in the furze.
> Although he is little, his family is great;
> Come out, your honour, and give us a trate.
> Hurrah, me boys, Hurrah!
> I have a little box under me arm,
> A shilling or two will do it nor harm.
> A shilling or two is a great relief
> To the poor wren boys on a Christmas Eve.
> Hurrah, me boys, Hurrah!"

Stefan contributed so liberally to the Boys that he left them agape with surprise and pleasure and they insisted on singing an extra verse to show their gratitude:

> "The Wren—the Wren as you may see
> Is up for height on the holly tree,
> A bunch of ribbons by his side,
> And a little wren boy will be his guide.
> Hurrah, me boys, Hurrah!"

Stefan, however, was much more interested in the second group, made up of young girls and young men and led by their Droleen, who arrived later in the day, singing as they came:

> "Droleen—Droleen—where is your nest?
> 'Tis in the tree that I love best,

'Tis in the holly and ivy tree,
Where all the birds come singing to me.
Hurrah, me boys, Hurrah!
As I was going up the Slippery Dock,
I saw an old wren he was up on a rock,
I up with me stick and I hit him a lick
And I knocked him into a brandy shop.
Hurrah, me boys, Hurrah!"

This time, there were not only carols, but a great deal of merry give and take between the leader and his followers and jests at the expense of the courting couples; and Stefan was even more generous, claiming that it was not particularly the interests of the Wren he had at heart; the girls would need something for their trousseaux, the men would need more stock when they set up housekeeping. Nothing like this had ever happened to them before and they prolonged their visit to show their appreciation with more raillery and more singing. As they finally wound their way down the drive, their happy voices floated back to the hall where they had been received:

"God bless the Master of this house,
A golden chain around his neck,
And if he do be sick or whole,
The Lord have mercy on his soul.
Hurrah, me boys, Hurrah!"

"I was a little disturbed when your grandmother first told me about the way St. Stephen's Day is celebrated in Ireland," Stefan told Janet, linking his arm in hers and drawing her toward the music room. "But now I am quite reassured by the sight of all those nice young men and young girls pledged to each other, at least until Shrovetide. Don't you think their example is worth following?"

"Well—I might—that is, if it could be kept a secret."

"But that wouldn't be following their example at all: they're happy to go ranging from one estate to another all day long, letting everyone see them together, hearing their names coupled, accepting good wishes and congratulations."

"Stefan, you know how much I like you, but I don't want to hear my name coupled with anyone's—I mean, any one person's—just yet. I've told you that before."

"You told me that last summer in London. But when you decided to spend this winter in Paris, I couldn't help hoping—"

"Oh, I don't want you to give up hoping! In fact . . . why couldn't we just change things around a little and, instead of saying we'd be engaged at least until Shrovetide, we'd wait until Shrovetide and decide then about being engaged?"

"Of course, if that is the way you want it, Janet, that is the way it will have to be."

He spoke so quietly that Janet did not even notice his very reticence was a sign that she had hurt him almost past endurance and that he did not dare express himself more freely, lest he should betray the deepness of the wound. He went to the piano and began to play and remained there until it was time to dress for dinner. Cook had been alerted to the fact that this was an occasion for another feast and that, whereas cold turkey and cold ham and slices of left-over plum pudding were all very well for luncheon, there must not only be a birthday cake, but earlier courses equally festive in character. So there was a lobster chowder, which Letitia had learned to make in Boston, and there was pheasant, presented with all the suitable decorations, and mounds of quivering creams and jellies; and there were almost as many presents at Stefan's place as he had the day before, for Lady Susannah and Anne and Peter had all dug into their supply of treasures to give him something he would especially like. His health was drunk in champagne and he responded gracefully to Peter's toast and made nearly everyone feel that the day had been a very happy occasion. At all events, it did not occur to Janet to wonder if, perhaps, she had spoiled it. Her thoughts were centered on the ball at Shanapark Castle, for which she and Stefan and Alec were to start immediately after dinner, and she was rather in a hurry to be through with the toasting and presents and so on, of which there had been a good many already, and be on her way to the party.

The next morning Peter was just opening his door, ready to begin the day's work, when she came hurriedly down the corridor on the way to her own room. It was evident that, far from being ready to begin a new day, she was just bringing the previous one to a somewhat tardy close. She was still in her red tulle ball gown, which showed signs of rather hard wear, though it had been brand new when she left for Shanapark Castle the night before, and her hair was correspondingly disordered. Her expression, however, was jubilant, and when she saw Peter she came toward him in a rush.

"I never had such a marvelous time in all my life!" she exclaimed. "I knew it would be wonderful, but I didn't dream *how* wonderful.

234

I couldn't because I didn't know there *was* anything so wonderful. There was enough moonlight so that, as we drove up the carriageway, we could see the walls and the towers of the castle outlined against the sky, which was full of stars. All the windows in the castle had candles in them and the whole effect was just what I imagine fairyland would be like, if there were any such place as fairyland. All the great crystal chandeliers were candlelit, too, and there were huge roaring fires in all the fireplaces. There was no other light and the effect was magical. And to dance all night in a setting like that—well, I can't tell you what it did to me."

"Among other things, it caused you to rip several large tears in your skirt and, apparently, to lose a good many hairpins," Peter replied unsympathetically. "Who were you dancing with all this time?" he added, ungrammatically, but with some concern.

"Why, with everyone there, of course. The Honorable Vincent, who is the heir to all this, danced with me over and over again. He said he'd see me at the military ball tomorrow—no, it's tonight, isn't it?—and asked me to save at least six dances."

"I thought three were supposed to be the limit, unless you were engaged."

"Oh, if you're going to be stuffy and begrudge me a good time!" Janet said impatiently. Peter, already wearing riding breeches and carrying a crop, looked far too purposeful for such an early hour. In fact, the crop, instead of being tucked under his arm, was being used to beat a light tattoo on his boots as he talked; it thereby emphasized his criticisms and seemed like insult added to injury.

"Naturally, I was very thrilled with the Honorable Vincent and what he represents," she went on defiantly. "Did you know there are sixty bedrooms, each with its own dressing room, at Shanapark, and a whole succession of drawing rooms and—"

"And you began to feel that Cloneen, which you admired so much two nights ago, was hardly more than a shack?"

"No, certainly not, but Shanapark is even more exciting. I met lots of attractive men there. One of them told me he's a great friend of yours. His name is Lawrence Donovan. He's cute."

"*Cute!* He's almost as tall as I am and at least ten pounds heavier."

"Well, you know what I mean by cute. It's one of my favorite words to describe people I think are attractive. He's going to take me to see the Gypsies and get one of them to tell my fortune."

"If you're talking about the tinkers, they don't tell fortunes and

Larry is aware of that. They mend things. Just now they're doing a good job at the chapel. Please leave them alone."

"Why, you don't mind if I just go and *see* them, do you? Larry is coming to take me for a walk and we have to go somewhere. He's going to be at the military ball, too, and he asked me to save six dances. Obviously, I'll have to cut down somewhere, because I don't know how many dances there will be in all and I might meet someone who was even cuter."

"There's always that possibility. . . . How many dances did you have with Alec?"

"Only one. I wish you wouldn't keep harping on Alec."

"This is only the second time I've mentioned him and your answer hasn't been very satisfactory either time. I'd also like to know where did Stefan come in on all this?"

"Oh, he took me in to supper, the most gorgeous supper, served at little tables for six in an immense dining room. It was the Honorable Vincent's table and he asked me to sit there, but Stefan took me in and I had the supper dance with him. It seems that had been arranged beforehand."

"Is the supper dance the only one you had with Stefan?"

"No, I had two others, the first one and the last one. It seems that was taken for granted, also. But—"

"Janet, it's seven o'clock in the morning. I'm on my way to the stables and I think you'd better go to bed. I assume poor Granny had already sunk into hers before I caught sight of you coming down the hall. I don't know and, at this moment, don't much care just where and when you and Stefan parted; but as soon as you've had some sleep and I've done a few chores that are necessary to keep this place going, I want to have a little talk with you. No, not about the facts of life. I wouldn't be at all surprised if you had those all figured out long before Mother sent for you to come to her room and revealed a few of them to you with great delicacy, after carefully closing the door. But I'm not going to sit back and let you make a complete fool of yourself and hurt a fine man past endurance if I can help it. Run along now and try to keep out of mischief for at least a few hours by spending them in profound slumber."

He had not expected that Anne would come to the office that day; in fact, he had not counted on spending very much time there himself. But, to his pleased surprise, she appeared, unheralded, for lunch, listened with attentive interest to the accounts of the ball, which varied somewhat according to the teller, and then told him there was a matter she needed to discuss with him for a few minutes. As he had seen nothing amiss in his morning survey, he was puzzled and a little troubled by her suggestion. But when they were seated at the double desk, she smiled and shook her head before he could put his anxiety into words.

"Cloneen has never had such a merry Christmas, or Cloncoole or the tenantry, either," she said, "and the afterglow is almost as bright as the radiance itself."

"What's this urgent matter then?"

"First, I wanted to tell you how pleased I am with the swan and its golden chain—I mean, when I didn't have an audience for the thanks. To think that you remembered that lovely poem all this time! And the chain will make a beautiful belt, by and by. I measured it and found it's just twenty inches long. So I knew you'd thought of something else."

"Of course I did. I'm very glad you're pleased. Is there anything else?"

"Perhaps you'll feel it isn't my place to say anything else. But I wish you wouldn't be so hard on Janet. If you are, the result may be just the opposite from what you want."

"She doesn't know how fortunate she is," Peter said sharply, repeating the remark he had already made to Stefan. "And I can't stand seeing her make such a fool of herself," he went on, repeating the remark he had made to Janet. "Stefan's a fine man with a great position. She'll never have a chance like this again."

"A fine man and a great position aren't all a girl wants or needs if he doesn't happen to be the man for her."

"Then she ought to find that out before things have gone as far as they have between Stefan and Janet."

"Yes. But seventeen-year-old girls don't always find out everything they ought to know, as fast as they should. They can't. They're not worldly wise enough. And when they let someone else do the deciding for them, it's very hard for them later—when they do find out."

She had been more successful at keeping bitterness from her voice than he had in saying much the same thing to Stefan. Peter thought that, perhaps, in her case there was less bitterness to overcome. He hoped so.

"All right," he said. "I'll let her have her head. She's very much impressed with Shanapark, especially with the fact that it has sixty bedrooms, each with its own dressing room; and I think she has a rather mercenary eye on a young man who could supply her with all those, rather than being wrapt in bliss at the thought that she might be sharing one of them with him. Also, she thinks Lawrence Donovan is cute and has promised him six dances for tonight. Moreover, she's hell-bent to meet your cousin Maurice, whom she'll probably find cuter still. Heaven knows what she'll promise him. Meanwhile, we can only hope that Stefan won't find consolation in a ballet dancer before she sees the error of her ways. It's been known to happen."

25

Two days later they had all gone and the mansion seemed emptier than ever.

Dermot McKeever had enjoyed the shooting, as Mark Fagan predicted he would; but he did not feel he could leave his responsibilities at the factory to his foreman any longer, since the Christmas holidays were notoriously a time when even the most reliable subordinates went astray, unless controlled by a firm hand; and now that Alec was striving hard toward a partnership with his father, he said of his own accord that he felt his trip with Peter should represent his only holiday for the present. Their departure gave Lady Susannah a long-awaited chance to corner Peter and ask him some leading questions, which she managed to introduce as casual conversation.

"Apparently, you and Anne have buried the hatchet," she said pleasantly.

"There never was any hatchet," Peter replied shortly.

"Well, what *was* the matter then? She froze whenever she looked at you and even when anyone mentioned your name to her. You must have done something."

"I fell in love with her at first sight. Naturally, I didn't mention this to her when she had just become a widow because, whether you believe it or not, I try to observe the proprieties. But she sensed it, of course. I'm told that a woman always does know when a man's in love with her. So she put up all kinds of defensive armor. I tried to tell you that everything would be all right in time, but you wouldn't listen to me."

"And you consider that everything's all right now?"

"Well, as nearly so as I'd expect six months after her husband's death. I recognize that it's still too soon for courtship."

"You were worrying about Lawrence Donovan at one stage."

"Surprisingly enough, I've worried less since he came here to stay.

He didn't get very far with her, though not for want of trying. If you ask me, he lacks technique."

"I assure you, Maurice de Briare doesn't."

"I want to see that for myself. But it appears I'm to wait until July. At least, *he* isn't rushing his fences."

"And, meanwhile—"

"And, meanwhile, as I just said, I think things are going as well as can be expected. Of course, when you hear that remark made in a hospital, it may only mean that the patient hasn't actually stopped breathing, but I don't think the situation's quite as desperate as that. What do you say we talk about something else for a change?"

Stefan was due back at Galician headquarters in Paris the day after New Year's, so even if Lady Susannah had given in to Janet and consented to stay over, he would have been obliged to leave on the day originally set. However, in the end, Lady Susannah had been adamant: Janet must go back to school, and on time; if she still wanted to return to Ireland and be presented at the Viceregal Court the next year, no doubt it could be arranged; but by then she would probably be off on some other tangent.

"I was quite right, after all, when I said you were too young to know your own mind," she told Janet severely. "I'm almost sorry we came to Cloneen for Christmas, though it's meant a great deal to me in many ways. You would have said yes the minute Stefan asked you to marry him if it hadn't suddenly occurred to you that, given one more fling, you might find someone even more eligible. You haven't done that, because there *isn't* anyone more eligible. But you've found an Irish heir, who seems more glamorous to you because you've seen his enormous ancestral castle, which is probably much larger than he'll be able to keep up—there have been all sorts of rumors about the Slatterys' falling fortunes. And he has both a father and mother living, who have much more ambitious plans for him than marriage with an American girl—I've been hearing other rumors about an English duchess who's an heiress into the bargain. Besides the Honorable Vincent, you've met Lawrence Donovan, whom you insist on calling 'cute,' and who's giving you a rush, but who intends to marry Anne if he can possibly get her; and you're aching to meet Maurice de Briare, who has exactly the same intentions. You're wasting your time and, in addition, you've behaved very badly, not only to Stefan, whose conduct has been irreproachable, but in general. You've made yourself conspicuous, dancing too often with the same person; you invited Vincent and Lawrence to lunch without consulting anyone else beforehand. You've ignored Alec, who'd looked forward to seeing a good deal of you, and you've quarreled with your brother, who's always been much too good to you. You've neglected Anne, who's necessarily shut out from most of the merrymaking and who'd have enjoyed some nice quiet visits with you. You haven't shown any interest in going over the grounds and the outbuildings. You could have spent some time in doing that, instead of taking part in a hunt which you're not in the least fitted to do, and then streaking off to a hunt breakfast at the only time nothing special had been planned for you here. It won't do you any good to tease. We're starting back to Paris tomorrow."

Peter was not sorry to see them go. Janet, instead of being a source of pride to him, had been a thorn in the flesh. Lady Susannah, dear as she was to him, proved too inquisitive about his standing with Anne. Stefan, amiable and urbane to the last, finally became a source of irritation, too: why on earth, if he really wanted Janet, as there seemed to be no doubt that he did, couldn't he have asserted himself and told her that, if she would not consent to an announcement of their engagement on his saint's day, she might as well forget about him, because it was then or never, as far as he was concerned? Peter had not been unmoved by Anne's plea for Janet, but he did not think the former's argument was sound. In his mind, there was no valid comparison between her marriage to an elderly widower, at her parents' instigation, and a voluntary alliance between a silly young girl, who only wanted a chance to show off, and an accomplished and distinguished bachelor still in his twenties. As to the McKeevers, they could come back almost any time for a weekend; and probably he and they would get all the more out of a visit if no one else were around.

Yet the stillness of the house soon became oppressive to him and he was thankful for every occupation that took him out of it and for the presence of Rufus when he was in it; more and more work in the office chained him to his desk. He made his routine inspections everywhere and was careful not to slight the farm in favor of the stud again or to overlook the rightful claims which the gamekeeper had on his time. Though he spoke it imperfectly and was conscious of this, his Irish was improving; he could make himself understood in simple conversations, and the people with whom he talked were pleased at the effort he had made to communicate with them and did their part in bridging the gap between the words he knew and those he had not mastered. He could afford to laugh at his mistakes and encourage others to share in his drollery; and his offer of forthcoming prizes for the neatest cottages and the best crops among the tenants was already showing good results. All in all, since everything was going smoothly now, his visits, both on the estate and among the tenantry, could well be brief. On the other hand, he recognized more and more keenly how much he needed to learn about the financial management of all Anne's property and how little preparation he had for such complicated bookkeeping.

During January and February, Anne still came to the office most afternoons, unless the weather was really bad, by Irish standards, which meant very bad, indeed, by Peter's standards: the deep early darkness, the fierce relentless winds, the sudden driving rains, all seemed to him unsuitable for her to brave. It was he, sooner and more vehemently than Dr. Carey, who urged her to stay at home in "desperate" weather or let him send the carriage for her.

"I'm used to desperate weather, you know, Peter. And walking's supposed to be good for me."

"You might trip or something. Let me come and walk over with you and take you back. And why not come earlier—for lunch, instead of after lunch? Then the darkness wouldn't be one more thing for me to worry about."

"You're a constitutional worrier—if it isn't one thing, it's another. The days are beginning to get longer, anyway. But I will let you send the carriage for me in really bad weather and I might come to lunch —once a week."

This was a marked concession and he knew it. The time had long since passed when she would have been able to convince anyone that she disliked him, much less that she hated him; but nothing in her manner suggested anything warmer than congenial acquaintance, based on shared responsibilities. Though she had necessarily included him in her invitations, when she asked Lawrence Donovan to tea and all his house guests to supper, she had never invited him to have a meal with her at the dower house when they were by themselves; and she had never sent him a message, asking him to come to her there, instead of presenting herself faithfully and regularly at the office.

In early March, there was a long succession of inclement days and, for the first time, Dr. Carey objected to her working hours. "She gets very tired," he said. "She doesn't tell you and she'd be very angry if she knew I were; but she's so exhausted that, right after she gets back to the dower house from the mansion, she goes to bed and takes just a cup of soup for her supper. That in itself wouldn't do her any harm, for she gets enough food at other meals; but it shows that she's over-fatigued, because at other times she's ravenous. I'm not forbidding her to work with you, for I know she enjoys it and it's an advantage to the estate when she can. But I am advising against more than two or three hours in the office at a time and that no oftener than twice a week."

Anne had not been wholly correct in referring to Peter as a constitutional worrier, but there was some truth in what she said. The next afternoon he was more conscious than before of the deliberation with which she moved, the discomfort which caused her to keep shifting her position while seated and her lack of alertness in her survey of the material before them. As she closed her book, preparatory to departure, he reached over and took her hand.

"Couldn't you leave all this to your chosen representative for the next few weeks?" he inquired. "Wouldn't you really be glad to?"

"I—Peter, I wouldn't want you to think I was shirking."

"You know I'd never think that. What I do think is that your greatest responsibility, for the moment, lies somewhere else and that you ought to admit it."

"Well, if you put it that way."

She did not come again that week, nor did he hear from her until she sent him word that she would not be going to church because of the rough roads and unseasonable snow, though she felt very badly not to do so, as she would miss Mass on St. Patrick's Day as well as on Palm Sunday; but Father Carroll had supported Dr. Carey when the latter told her not to stir out of the dower house. Peter went to both these Masses and took her a shamrock from the first and palms from the second; and on St. Patrick's Day he went back to the village to attend the meeting which Lawrence Donovan had organized and at which he was to speak.

"Don't forget that Parnell has said, 'If I step out, Captain Moonlight will step in,'" he cautioned with the knowledge that this reminder would have special impact because of what had happened at Cloneen; and he developed skillfully from that point in favor of parliamentary reform and action. After the recital by the local brass band, which followed the address, the meeting adjourned amid scenes of great enthusiasm, and Peter invited Larry to return to Cloneen for a late lunch and a long talk.

"You certainly had your audience with you," Peter said enthusiastically when he and his guest had settled down in the library with port and cigars. He had said much the same thing already and had been puzzled because Larry did not seem to respond with much spirit. "I should think you'd be very much gratified."

"I'd be more gratified if I were also more encouraged. But the fact is, I'm afraid Parnell's power is being undermined."

"*Undermined!* In what way?"

"The way it was bound to be, sooner or later—by attacks on his private life. As long as these were only rumors, they did some damage, but not enough to worry about. Now that there isn't any question that these attacks are founded on fact and that he doesn't propose to silence them in the only possible way, the situation's bound to be serious— perhaps disastrous." Larry spoke with such concern that Peter realized his friend was deeply worried. However, as Larry did not go on to explain, Peter asked a direct question.

"What's the only possible way he could have silenced them?"

"Why, by cutting himself loose, completely loose, from Kitty O'Shea and everything connected with her," Larry exclaimed vehemently. "And what does he do instead? He absolutely refuses to listen to reason, as far as she's concerned. He uses her as his liaison officer with Gladstone! He lives at her house!"

"What do you mean, he lives at her house? He lives at Avondale, doesn't he?"

"Yes, when he's in Ireland. But that's very little when Parliament's in session. So he's become a permanent house guest at Elthan, the country estate that Kitty O'Shea's aunt has given her."

"She must be a person of some background, if country estates are part of the picture."

"Of course she's a person of some background—a great deal of background!" Larry was almost shouting now. "You've fallen into the general error of taking it for granted that she must be a hussy. It ought to be self-evident that no one like that could possibly have attracted Parnell."

"Well, perhaps it should have been self-evident, but it wasn't, as far as I am concerned. Nobody has ever come right out and told me anything about her before. All I've heard have been hints and innuendoes."

"All right, I'll tell you about her. Her grandfather, Sir Matthew Wood, was a famous Lord Mayor of London. Her father, Sir John Page Wood, was private chaplain and secretary to Queen Caroline and performed the last rites at the time of her death. Afterward, he was chaplain to the Dean of Sussex. Her mother was the daughter of an admiral and one of the Queen's personal attendants. Anthony Trollope and John Morley and John Constable were all great friends of her parents, and George Meredith comes regularly to read aloud to the bountiful aunt who lives on the same estate where she has given Kitty a house and an income to run it."

"It all sounds very impressive and cultured and so on, but English rather than Irish."

"Of course it's English! Kitty O'Shea has never been to Ireland in her life and if she's wise, she never will come here! Her maiden name was Katharine Wood and if she were going to change it, I wish to heaven it had been in a way that wouldn't make her sound Irish! That's one of the worst things about the whole affair—it's given rise to so much misunderstanding. Her husband's father was a responsible Dublin solicitor who wanted to give his son Willie, on whom he doted, every advantage—that is, to have him educated abroad and see that he got a captaincy in the Eighteenth Hussars. Eventually Willie sold his commission, made a failure of several other jobs, and finally entered Parliament. He's been a no-good all his life, but he has certain social graces and loves to give parties. His wife is a great asset to him as a hostess. When Parnell did not even answer a dinner invitation, she hunted him down at Westminster. She took her sister, Mrs. Steele, with her and drove up one day when the House was in session. Then she sent in her card with a request that he meet her in the Palace Yard."

"Just like that? And he came? You're sure you're not making this up as you go along, Larry? It's almost too good to be true."

"Unfortunately, it is true. He not only came promptly at her bidding, though he hadn't taken notice of any woman before as far as we can find out, but he explained that he hadn't answered her invitation to dinner because he hadn't opened his mail in some days—which actually is one of his habits. So then and there she invited him to another dinner and he accepted. At that moment, a white rose she had been wearing dropped from her bodice. Parnell picked it up and, instead of giving it back to her, raised it to his lips and then put it in his buttonhole. He has been wearing a white rose in his buttonhole ever since."

Larry's voice was by now strident with indignation. Peter answered rather gravely. "Then it was love at first sight."

"Personally, I've never taken much stock in that, but Parnell has certainly upset all my theories and those of a good many other people.

Presently, he accepted an invitation to make Elthan his headquarters whenever it would be convenient for him to do so. That invitation came from O'Shea himself. He wanted very much to be closely associated with Parnell and he certainly got his wish with a vengeance. If any husband ever deliberately made a cuckold of himself, O'Shea did. Apparently he and his wife have been more or less estranged, as far as marital intimacy goes, for a long time. But Kitty was useful to Willie, and Parnell could be, and if that meant a *ménage a trois*, he was more than agreeable to it."

"And how does Gladstone fit into this picture?"

"When the new Coercion Bill was being debated, Parnell was trying to establish some means of private communication with Gladstone. He couldn't approach him directly, since as far as the English were concerned, he was 'steeped to the lips in treason'; and he couldn't let the Irish know he was in communication with the enemy because he himself was under suspicion of capitulating in regard to the Kilmainham Treaty. So he hit on the idea of using Mrs. O'Shea as an intermediary. At his instigation, she wrote to Gladstone, introducing herself as a niece of Lord Haverly—another of her distinguished relatives that I forgot to mention before—and very adroitly suggested that he should see Parnell. Though Gladstone declined to do this, he agreed to meet her when she wrote him a second time and presently she was going back and forth between the two, taking him drafts, clauses and proposed amendments to bills affecting Ireland. Of course, he knew perfectly well what the relationship of Parnell and Kitty O'Shea must be, but the miserable old hypocrite will be the first to denounce Parnell when it suits him to do so!"

Larry had worked himself up to such a state of frenzy that Peter was not sorry when his excited friend abruptly took his departure, saying he must get back to Dublin and see what, if anything, could be rescued from the wreckage.

The house seemed emptier than ever after his guest had gone. Peter went to the Tenebrae alone on Holy Thursday, finding it extremely depressing, and to the early-morning service on Good Friday. Then he decided to put in the rest of the day studying the subject of the transportation of horses between Ireland and France—one of the many in which he lacked both personal knowledge and experience. The so-called bloodstock ships, which were used for this purpose, were private property and when not required by their owners were rented out to other persons.

The ship belonging to the Earl of Cloneen had not been needed, either by his stables or the De Briares, since the importation of Guillaume le Conquérant and Reine Mathilde, so it should have been rented regularly and this had not been done. Maurice had naturally felt that his responsibility for it was ended after he saw it safely tied up at the dock in Le Havre, because only a few days after he had returned to France with the horses he had brought back in exchange for Guillaume le Conquérant and Reine Mathilde, the old Earl died and the heir apparent became the logical person to carry out the widow's wishes. It was very rarely that Mr. MacAuliffe overlooked any item which he should have called to his client's attention, but in the confusion surrounding the Earl's death and the equally sudden adjustments that had taken place, it had entirely escaped his notice that the ship was unrented until a bill for wharfage had come in. He had then apologetically and belatedly called Peter's attention to the matter at the time when Anne was too ill to be consulted; and Peter's decision had been that he had so much on his hands, after the criminal raid of the Moonlighters, that it would be better to continue to pay wharfage until such time as he could give concentrated attention to the question. Now that time seemed to have arrived. But who should be approached? What price should be mentioned? For how long a time should the ship be available to an outsider? If Anne wanted to go home and give her parents the joy of seeing her and her baby, as soon as Dr. Carey announced it prudent for her to do so, she certainly had a right to such a trip; and in the course of it she would naturally select the horses she had not been able to choose at Christmastime, and Maurice would bring them over in July. The O'Toole bloodstock ship must be available then and, perhaps, since it had been idle this long, it would be better to continue to pay wharfage on it a few months more, rather than take a chance on some possibly unreliable lessee. Peter blamed himself because he had not thought of asking Larry's advice on St. Patrick's Day and this was no time to ask him to come back or to go away himself; and certainly it was an even worse time than September to ask Anne to straighten out an oversight which was not her fault and which would probably cause her distress.

Of course, he could write to De Briare, but no one had told him whether or not this fascinating Frenchman was a good linguist, in addition to being a skilled horseman and a charmer of ladies; and Peter was certainly not equal to writing a letter in French about anything that involved all the vocabulary necessary to deal with a bloodstock ship. He must go through all the records pertaining to previous trips and previous rentals and trust that, if some such records were in Normandy, there would be duplicates at Cloneen. But he must not be interrupted while he was trying to do it and gave strict orders to this effect. These orders were almost immediately disregarded.

"I know you said that you were not to be interrupted, sir, not on any account, but I thought, under the circumstances—"

"Is the house on fire?"

Peter tried to speak patiently and pleasantly, but this required an effort. It seemed impossible to give orders that were foolproof. There were always "circumstances" that, indubitably, warranted interruption.

"No, sir. But the Mistress has sent Solange over from the dower house with a note for you and Solange thought it might be urgent, because she couldn't help noticing that the Mistress was weeping while she wrote it."

As he spoke, Wade advanced toward Peter's loaded desk, silver salver in hand. The urgent note was a folded scrap of paper, so light that it had not really come to rest on the polished surface of the tray. Peter seized it before it could float off:

Dear Peter—he read with amazement—*Nothing is really the matter, but I am frightened. Please come and stay with me a little while. Anne.*

He jumped up, thrusting the note in his pocket; and, with a curt order to Rufus that the puppy must stay where he was, strode toward the door so rapidly that Wade did not have time to forestall him in opening it.

"Tell Solange I've already gone to Lady O'Toole," he called back to the astonished butler as he ran down the steps.

He did not slacken his pace until he reached the dower house and, finding the front door unlocked, he charged unannounced through the empty drawing room, library and dining room. He had never been upstairs and, under ordinary circumstances, it would not have occurred to him to go there uninvited, but certainly there must be something abnormal about the present circumstances. He mounted the stairs at the same pace that had marked his previous progress. Then, suddenly conscious of the fitness of things, he halted and called Anne's name. The answer was immediate.

"Oh, Peter, I'm so glad you came."

"Of course I came. But what on earth's the matter and where are you?"

"I'm in my room."

248

"Which is your room?"

"The last on the right. I'll meet you at the door."

She was standing at the open threshold, dressed in a soft white woollen robe, and when he put his arm around her, far from drawing away, she hid her face on his shoulder and clung to him trembling. Greatly puzzled, as well as deeply distressed, he raised one hand and gently stroked her unbound hair while he tried to think of something comforting and encouraging to say.

"Anne, you must tell me what's frightened you. I can't help you unless you do," he murmured ineptly.

"You've helped, just by coming," she whispered without raising her head.

"But you haven't wanted me to come before. You said—"

"Oh, I know what I said! But of course I wanted you—all the time. And now that any moment—"

"What's going to happen at any moment?" he asked, holding her closer and trying to suppress the evidence of his exultation at her confession that she had wanted him all the time.

"Why, the pains will start! And I'll be all alone."

"The pains?" he repeated stupidly.

"The pains of childbirth. You didn't suppose it was painless, did you?"

"No, of course not. But—"

"But, somehow, you didn't think of it primarily in terms of pain, did you? I didn't, either, until it drew so close. But ever since Dr. Carey told me that, at first, they'd come every fifteen minutes, not very bad, and then every ten and then every five, getting worse and then closer and closer together—pretty bad—I haven't been able to think of anything else."

"Why on earth should Dr. Carey have upset you by giving you a chance to worry about this so long beforehand? What was the use?"

"It *isn't* so long beforehand. I'm trying to explain it could happen any time now. The monthly nurse, Mrs. Hogan, arrived yesterday and has been bustling around ever since, getting things ready, as she put it. When I asked her, ready for what, she managed to give me the vague but horrible impression that it was a wonder any woman ever survived the agony she went through in having a child and that the nurse must be sure the deathbed was orderly. Probably she didn't mean to, but that was the effect she had on me. Anyway, I sent for Dr. Carey and asked him please to make things a little clearer and a little less frightening if he could. He wasn't trying to alarm me. He was trying to prepare me, so that I could face a long struggle without being frightened by that silly nurse, knowing that what was happening was perfectly normal—having all those spaced pains—and that when I couldn't stand them any longer, he would give me a whiff of chloroform—that there wasn't one chance in a thousand that they'd be fatal. I know I ought to suffer, to suffer terribly, bringing this child into the world. It's less than I deserve, just to suffer. I ought to die."

"And leave a motherless child? Of course you ought not to die, and of course you're not going to. Stop talking like that. Stop thinking like that. I'll have to shake some sense into you if you don't. My sister Sue had a baby last spring, and she said it wasn't nearly as bad as it was made out. I'll have a few words with that nurse myself."

"No, please don't. I should have been able to stand up to her, but somehow I couldn't before. But I will now. Oh, Peter, do you think I'm a terrible coward?"

"Of course I don't. You know I think you're the most wonderful girl in the world. And much too important a person to let a silly nurse upset you. Probably the doctor was right after all, telling you what was before you. And you can face it all right. I'm sorry you have to, but if that's part of having a baby, it must be worth it afterward. If it weren't, the human race would have come to an end a long time ago. . . . Look, now that I'm here at last, couldn't we sit down somewhere? On the *bergère*, perhaps?"

She lifted her head and nodded. The trembling had ceased and, though she was not actually smiling, her expression was controlled and she walked to the *bergère* with a firm step. When she and Peter were seated side by side, he took both her hands in his.

"Darling, you said something about being frightened because you'd be all alone when the pains started."

"Yes. Oh, that nurse will be here and Dr. Carey, too, as soon as I send for him. Mrs. Hogan is resting just now. She's entitled to a rest sometime every day. I purposely got rid of her this afternoon, so that I'd be sure to see you alone, and sent Maggie and Rory to their own quarters, but they're available at any moment I want them; Solange, too. However, that isn't the same as—"

"As having someone that belongs to you?"

"Yes."

"I belong to you. I'll stay with you."

"They won't let you."

"Who won't let me?"

"Why, the doctor and the nurse."

"Look, Dr. Carey and I understand each other pretty well. It won't make any difference whether or not the nurse understands me."

"But perhaps some other people, who might make a difference, could misunderstand."

"I guess we'll have to risk it. I'd rather do that than have you frightened because you were alone."

She did not answer instantly and he knew she was giving thought to his suggestion. "It's very important, isn't it, that no one should guess you care—especially—about this baby?" she asked after a pause.

"Yes," he answered reluctantly. "That's my part of the atonement you talk so much about. I'll never be able to acknowledge my own child."

"And that, until after my year of mourning is up—"

"You can't have an acknowledged suitor. Yes, that's very important, too."

"Well, if you stayed with me and saw that I was suffering, mightn't you accidentally say something that showed how much you cared about the baby and me?"

"I very well might."

"Then don't you see—you mustn't stay."

"I've seen right along that I shouldn't. But when I found that you wanted me to—that you were frightened—that seemed to matter more than anything else, loving you as I do."

"I do hope the baby'll be a girl," she whispered inconsequently.

"Why?"

"Because then if, by and by, you should have a son, he'd inherit the title from you, but you'd have it first."

"Darling, I've told you I don't care a rap about the title. Just the same, that's a lovely thing for you to say. There's just one slight change which would make it mean even more to me."

"What?"

"If, by and by, *we* should have a son."

"All right. If, by and by, we should have a son."

He bent over and kissed the hands he had been holding. Then he straightened up and looked her full in the face. She returned the look steadily.

"I'm not frightened any more," she said. "I'm sure I'm not going to die, but just in case I shouldn't have another chance very soon I'll tell you now that I love you just as much as you love me. But the pains have started. You must go."

26

He went no further than the library, where he found the lamps lighted and the fire burning and he had hardly settled down in the comfortable chair when Rory appeared with the tea table. Either Anne had guessed that he would not leave the house or preparations were being made for someone else—perhaps both suppositions were correct. Half an hour later Dr. Carey came in and Peter learned that this was the case.

"I thought I might find you here," the doctor said pleasantly. "Lady O'Toole just told me she had sent you a note, telling you she would like to see you, and it's quite natural, under those circumstances, that you'd wish to remain in the house, to be on hand in case an extra person might be useful for one reason or another or just to know how things were going without waiting for a message to be taken from one house to another. Obviously, you responded to the Countess in a way that was very cheering to her. I found her in better spirits than she has been for several days, though generally it's exactly the opposite with my patients when the pains start, and there's no doubt that hers have begun. Everything is perfectly normal and there isn't the slightest cause for anxiety. But labor is apt to be long, with a first baby. It's better that it should be, unless the mother becomes utterly exhausted. There's less danger of laceration in the earlier stages or the necessity of instruments at the end."

Peter winced, but managed to answer with suitable composure. "I'm glad you think it's all right for me to stay here. I know there's probably not one chance in a hundred that I could be of the slightest use, but I'd feel better to be on hand, just the same. . . . When you say labor is apt to be long, just what do you mean by that?"

"I won't frighten you by telling you how long I've known it to be. In this case, I'm very hopeful it won't be more than twenty-four hours at the outside."

"Twenty-four hours! All tonight and all day tomorrow! In dreadful pain!"

"The pain won't be really dreadful all that time. And, fortunately, we can use chloroform for the worst of it. When I first began to practice, most Irish doctors didn't like it or weren't sure just how to use it, so they were afraid of it. The world owes a great deal to Sir John Simpson and his royal patient."

"I thought it was Morton, a Boston dentist, who discovered anesthesia."

"Ether. The two discoveries came quite close together and both seem to have had equally efficacious and merciful results. In the United Kingdom we generally use chloroform, while American doctors generally use ether."

"Yes, I believe that's what my sister Sue took when her baby was born last spring. And, as I told Lady O'Toole, Sue said it wasn't half as bad as she expected."

Dr. Carey suppressed a smile. "How long after the baby was born did she tell you that?"

"I don't remember exactly. I was working hard on my finals at the Harvard Law School then and didn't get in to Boston as often as usual."

"By that time, she'd have forgotten a good deal. That's one of the few blessed aspects of childbirth. Mothers forget the worst of it very quickly as a rule. And fathers even more quickly, which isn't always such a good thing. A doctor who's nearly lost a patient and knows all too well what she's been through isn't very happy when he hears her husband's going to insist on exercising his marital rights again, as soon as he can get rid of the nurse. I actually did lose one of the loveliest ladies I've ever known that way—a second baby, ten months after the first, was fatal to her. . . . But I must stop talking shop, especially shop that has nothing to do with the present case. Shall we have some tea? I see everything's prepared to serve it at a moment's notice. Then I'll go home and make sure no emergencies have arisen that require my attention before I come back here for the night. I'll stop at the mansion and tell them you won't be there. Is there anything you'd like them to send you?"

"You mean you're going to leave the dower house now?"

"Yes. The Countess is only in her first stage and, unless I'm very much mistaken, she won't be out of it before midnight."

"What do you mean by her first stage?"

Dr. Carey began a brief clinical explanation, but soon saw that he was merely causing additional distress and gave up the attempt. "There's really nothing I can do for her at present and I've several patients who are desperately ill for whom I may be able to do something. Among them a frail woman who's approaching the crisis—the fifth day in pneumonia—and an old reprobate who celebrated St. Patrick's Day so immoderately that he toppled over on the hearthstone and was badly burned. I've no right to neglect them for her."

"Couldn't you call in another doctor to help you out?"

"I will if it will make you any happier. I asked the Countess, as soon as I knew she was pregnant, if she wouldn't like to have a specialist from Dublin handle the case. And she said she had perfect confidence in me. I believe you may have confidence, too. I assure you that the safe delivery of this baby, with as little suffering as possible to its mother, means just as much to me as it does to you."

That's all you know about it, Peter said to himself savagely, as he watched the doctor consume a hearty tea and take an unconcerned departure, while he himself choked over a single cup and let the scones grow cold without touching them. *You didn't take her and get her with child when she was married to another man and add mental and spiritual anguish over a mortal sin to all the physical agonies she's got to endure. You haven't lived near her, as a stranger, for nine months when you were almost crazy with love for her. You can eat and drink and go out to see other people to whom you feel you owe something, but I can't bear to see anyone, if I can't see her; there's no one to whom I owe anything. And what did you mean by telling me that story about brutal husbands? Have you guessed that I'm going to marry her as soon as her year of mourning is up and that when it comes to marital rights, I've waited and waited for them, all this long horrible winter, and I've taken it for granted I could exercise them as soon and as often as I wanted to, once I'm married to her? Well, that won't be just a month after this baby is born, it'll be three months or more; perhaps then it will be all right, if she isn't lacerated, if she isn't exhausted, if she hasn't been injured by instruments. If all that happened to her, perhaps she wouldn't want me anyway, perhaps she wouldn't be capable of passion, perhaps she'd just be "submitting" the way wives are supposed to do, however they feel, even if it's aversion to a man or fear of another pregnancy, so that they can keep their husbands from being unfaithful and give them as many children as they want. But that's a different kind of a marriage, that couldn't be Anne and me, because I'd never be unfaithful to her or objectionable to her; and she wouldn't be afraid of pregnancy, she'd want children, too. And even if there were times when she wasn't capable of passion, she'd know how desperately I needed her and she wouldn't ever turn me away; she'd always receive me freely and with loving kindness and she'd try not to let me know she was doing it without rapture. In a way, that would be a still greater sign of her love than if she felt the same need that I did; she wouldn't think of her bounty as submission and neither would I. I'd think of it as another proof that we belonged to each other, that her way of showing it just then was by utter compliance and mine was by glorying in it. Surely there are times like that in every marriage, when the man finds his fulfillment in domination and the woman finds hers in being dominated. They must become primitive male and female again, captor and captive. But such times wouldn't last, not with Anne and me. Presently, I'd overcome her lassitude by my vitality, I'd quicken her latent longing for me, and then she'd show me in a different way how much she loved me, how much she wanted me. . . .*

He was startled by some sound, he was not sure what, until he saw that a burning log had fallen on the hearthstone and that someone was replacing it on the fire. The lights in the library were lower now than they had been when he came in, so someone must have turned those down, too. With surprise, he saw that the man who had replaced the log and was now standing with a hand on his, Peter's, shoulder was Father Carroll. Peter started up in alarm.

"Is she worse?" he asked hoarsely. "Did they send for you to do whatever it is you might be needed for?"

"No, no," Father Carroll said cheerfully. "Nobody has sent for me. I happened to see Dr. Carey in the village and he told me he had been obliged to leave the dower house for awhile, but that you were here. So I thought I might come and keep you company while you ate your supper by and by. I've spoken to Rory about it and dispensed you from the Lenten fast. When I came in, something about your manner made me feel you were very upset. You were clenching and unclenching your fingers and muttering to yourself. Would it help if you told me what was the matter?"

"I'm afraid not. That is, it might. But I don't know that I can."

"Well, it was just a suggestion. I shan't be in the least offended if you don't act on it."

He smiled and drew up a chair opposite Peter's. "Perhaps I should be the one to do the talking," he said. "I've wanted for a long while to tell you how favorably you impressed me at the time of your uncle's funeral, but the right moment never seemed to come until now. I know that the lying-in-state and everything about the vault were strange and burdensome to you and that much of it must have been distasteful. You gave me confidence about the part you would play in the community."

"Thank you for saying that, Father. It means a lot to me."

"Then perhaps I may add that, in my opinion, your conduct in other ways has been irreproachable. I am referring, of course, to your attitude in regard to Lady O'Toole. Your manner toward her has always been one of the utmost devotion and respect, with no betrayal of any more ardent feeling."

This time, Peter did not answer.

"That represents, unless I am mistaken, a much greater and a much longer ordeal than the funeral," the priest said gently.

"Yes. Of course you're right. I've been in love with her since the first moment I saw her."

"But since her conduct has also been irreproachable, you had no reason to feel she returned your affection until she sent for you today?"

Peter hesitated. "Will it be all right if I just say that today she suddenly felt very much alone and she thought there would be no disloyalty to my uncle now if she turned to me?"

"Yes. That will be quite all right. Naturally you want to marry her?"

"Of course."

"And she wants to marry you?"

"I'm happy to say that I believe she does. But you disapprove?"

"Not in the least. In fact, Mr. MacAuliffe and Dr. Carey and I have all spoken of the matter and have all agreed that it would be suitable from every point of view. Much more suitable, indeed, than some other marriage that she might have considered making. It was inevitable that she would marry someone sometime."

"When I see Anne, may I tell her what you've said?"

"If you like. But again, unless I am mistaken, she already knows how I feel. Lady O'Toole and you don't regard me in quite the same light. This isn't a reproach. It's more natural for her to regard me as a family friend than it is for you. American Catholics and Irish Catholics often don't think of priests in the same way."

"But Anne is a French Catholic!"

"Yes. By birth. But now she's become quite naturalized. Perhaps you will be, too. For the moment, however, what you need is not a theological discussion, but light conversation about other things while we see what Rory has for you in the way of nourishing food."

The supper which Rory brought to the library was excellent and, far from choking over it, as he had over the tea, Peter did full justice to it. He was still lingering over his coffee when Dr. Carey came back to the house and willingly accepted a cup himself. He looked very tired and when Father Carroll asked him about the patients he had gone to see, he said very gravely that the frail woman with pneumonia had died, leaving a crippled husband with no near relative to care for him, but that the unwise celebrant at St. Patrick's Day who had suffered first-degree burns was getting along much better than could reasonably have been expected. "However, what you really want to know is how Lady O'Toole is doing," he added, forestalling Peter's inquiry. "It is just as I predicted—a perfectly normal process, but a very slow one. There are ways of hastening labor, but I'd rather not resort to them, unless I have to. She's very brave, so far. But if you should hear her cry out, later on, don't be alarmed, that would be normal, too."

He went out, closing the library door after him, and Peter winced again. He felt sure that Anne had ordered all the doors closed, between the place where he was sitting and the place where she was lying. For a long time the slight flicker of the flames was the only sound in the room and this was a soothing one. Though Peter would not have believed that he could possibly doze, he started up, realizing that he must have done so, when the door opened and Mr. MacAuliffe entered.

"Good morning," he said, speaking more softly than was his habit, but in no other way indicating that there was anything surprising about his presence. "I realized that it was almost time for Father to say Mass, so I thought I might come and keep you company while he was gone."

"How kind of you! But you don't mean to tell me that it's really morning? And that Dr. Carey hasn't been back here with a report since —what was it—midnight?"

"It's half past six," Father Carroll told him, "and evidently Dr. Carey hasn't felt it wise to leave Lady O'Toole again. You know he told you you could depend on him not to do so unless he was sure she didn't need him. I'll slip upstairs and see if I can find out anything. Then I do have to go to my church and my people. This is one of my busiest days. But I'll come back when I can if you'd like to have me."

"You know I would. And please hurry with that report, Father."

Since it was not possible to speak to either doctor or nurse immediately, the report was not made until ten minutes later. These minutes seemed like hours to Peter and the message, when it finally came, was anything but reassuring to him.

"I knocked on the bedroom door very gently and waited until Mrs. Hogan came out, so that she could whisper to me in the hall. She says the pains are coming very close together now and they're quite severe, but Lady O'Toole understands that she ought to keep fully conscious until it's nearly time for the child to come into the world, that if she had chloroform now she couldn't continue to help her delivery as much as she should. The baby is very large, but its position is correct and Dr. Carey still hopes and believes he can get by without instruments if Lady O'Toole can hold out a little longer and he thinks she can."

"What does he mean by a little longer?"

Peter's tone was one of anguish. Father Carroll and Mr. MacAuliffe exchanged glances.

"I'm afraid I can't tell you that because I don't know. But I've reported what Mrs. Hogan told me, word for word, and that was quite explicit. Moreover, I believe I'm right in saying there isn't anything to worry about. So far, everything is perfectly normal."

"Father, if I hear that once more, and also hear how much Anne is suffering, I won't be able to stand it."

"Not when Lady O'Toole is setting such a wonderful example of courage? Of course you will. . . . I've taken the liberty of waking Rory and telling him you and Mr. MacAuliffe could do with some early-morning tea. And I promise you I'll come back later in the day."

"Later in the day!"

"Well, later in the morning, as soon as I can leave the church. I suggest you send for your razor and a clean shirt if you don't want to go to the mansion long enough to shave and bathe. Actually, you'd feel much better afterward if you would and I'm sure you've plenty of time before the baby's born."

"I don't mean to be disrespectful, Father, but nothing you could say would make me feel more like staying just where I am."

Again the priest and the solicitor exchanged glances, but both felt too much sympathy for Peter's distracted state to argue with him. Mr. MacAuliffe undertook the sending of a message and, when Tim arrived with the requisite articles, Peter consented to leave the library long enough to make use of them. Then he slumped down again in the easy chair before the fire, a prey to reflections even more bitter than those which had obsessed him before Father Carroll freed him from them. If this were an easy, normal birth, what was a hard one? How could he ever think again of possessing this beloved woman without thinking also about the possible costs of such possession? He had dwelt with eager anticipation on the prospect of many children, no matter how close together they came, as sure that Anne would share this desire for fecundity as she would the passion which produced it. Now he could not believe that she would be able to receive him again without fear or that he would be able to take her again without sharing it. . . .

This time, it was a piercing cry that roused him from his harrowing revery—a cry which no closed doors could muffle and which echoed through the house, penetrating its silence. As Peter staggered to his feet the first cry was followed by another, more desperate than its predecessor, but speedily stifled. After that came utter stillness. Peter tore across the room and was halfway to the stairs when Father Carroll, re-entering the house at that moment, caught up with him and forced him back.

"My son, you mustn't try to go to her now. It's the last thing you should do."

"Stop holding me back. That silence can't mean but one thing. She's dead. I have a right to go to her now."

"She isn't dead. Peter, do you think I'd lie to you? She's drugged, at last. Carey must have had his reasons for not doing it sooner. Stand still and listen again. You'll hear something else in a minute."

The priest, surprisingly strong, was holding him by main force, saying the same thing over and over again, until Peter, who at first would not listen and then did not understand, finally grasped the import of the words. As he stopped struggling, he became conscious of another cry, utterly unlike any he had ever heard, small in volume, yet lusty and shrill, and somehow unmistakable as the first sound made by a newborn child.

"I think it will be all right for you to go upstairs in a few minutes, my son," Father Carroll said, "if you will stay in the sitting room until Dr. Carey comes to get you. Mr. MacAuliffe and I will await the good news in the library."

When Peter returned, accompanied by the doctor, he was carrying the baby. It was wrapped in a cashmere shawl, which covered it almost completely, but a fringe of soft black hair showed beyond the folds, as did a small wrinkled pink face with tightly closed eyes and tiny pink hands drawn up close to the little round chin. The cry which had heralded its entrance into the world was stilled; it was sound asleep. Peter held it with great care and gazed down on it with infinite love. In a voice which pride helped him to keep steady, he spoke to the faithful friends who had kept his vigil with him.

"I have the great honor," he said, "of presenting to you the eighth Earl of Cloneen, James Arthur Frederick O'Toole, the second."

PART FIVE

Late March, 1883,
to early May, 1883

Peter Bradford
of Boston,
Massachusetts

GRAINE TO FIONN

"There is one
For sight of whom I'd gladly spare
All! All the shining, golden world
Though such a bargain be unfair."

—The Second Book of
Irish Myths and Legends

27

It was the most beautiful day that Peter had ever known in Ireland.

There was not a cloud in the soft blue sky and, as he walked from the dower house to the mansion, he saw that, though it was early for these, there were actually a few fresh green leaves on some of the trees and that the lawns were banked with daffodils. Scillas and primroses were already budding in the walled garden where late snowdrops still lingered. The unseasonable snowstorm of Palm Sunday had not lasted long enough after all to do any serious damage. Peter could have sworn that there were no such signs of spring when he had crossed this same terrain twenty-four hours earlier. But then it had been raining hard; then he had been hurrying to Anne, who was frightened; then he had not heard the admission that she loved him and had wanted him all winter; then his son had not been born. Now why should the world not look different, since it was a different place?

Before he left the dower house, he had received the assurance that Anne was sleeping as peacefully as the baby, that none of the things which he had dreaded had happened to her: there had been no lacerations, there had been no instruments and, despite that one dreadful cry which had not been silenced, her worst sufferings had been brief and her physician had been justified in delaying the chloroform by the wonderful condition she was in now. She might very possibly sleep around the clock; if she did, the baby would be just as well off, for lactation did not usually begin sooner than that anyway; and when she woke, she would be refreshed, she would be happy, she would rejoice in her baby and very soon she would be able to receive a few brief visits. If she asked for Peter, there was no reason why he should not make one of them. . . . He was very sure that she would ask for him and that was among the countless reasons why he was so happy, as he walked along in the sunshine among the budding trees and the spring flowers.

The sound of many bells filled the air, and Peter suddenly remembered that this was Holy Saturday, that the bells which had been silent since the Tenebrae on Thursday night would, in any case, have begun to ring again after noon on what the Spaniards so rightly called the *sabado de gloria*. But surely more than the bell of the Catholic Church was ringing now. The bells in the Church of Ireland and the schoolhouse must be ringing, too. It was fitting that the church bells should hail the coming Resurrection of Our Lord; but those other bells were because all the friendly people at Cloneen and in the village were sharing the paean that rose from his heart and found expression with no conscious sacrilege, but with great reverence and thanksgiving in the words, "Unto us a child is born."

Of course, it was the doctor's reassuring words about Anne which had meant the most to him before he left the dower house. But Mr. MacAuliffe had also contributed greatly to his happiness.

"Naturally, you will be the baby's godfather," the solicitor said in a matter-of-fact way, as if there were no question about it; and Father Carroll nodded agreement.

Peter's heart gave another bound of joy. He had not thought of that. Even though he could not acknowledge the child as his son, as its godfather he would be entitled to many prerogatives, social as well as spiritual. He might logically have a voice in the boy's schooling, in the sports he enjoyed, in the travels he took. And presently, the addition of a legal verdict assured Peter that such supervision and companionship would be doubly safeguarded.

"Of course, the infant Earl must have a legal guardian."

"Not just his mother?"

"No, indeed. He must have a male guardian who should be appointed without delay. I will have the necessary documents prepared at once. Naturally you, as his Celtic next of kin, are the logical person to serve. I assume you will be glad to do so."

As his Celtic next of kin! His cousin, Mr. MacAuliffe meant, of course. Yes, it's true, there isn't any other male Celtic relative nearer. But this time Peter's heart, instead of bounding with joy, had seemed to turn over. *If they only knew, if I could only tell them,* he thought desperately. *But, of course, they mustn't ever, of course I can't ever.* It had been very hard, several times in the past twenty-four hours, for him to keep his voice steady. It was harder than ever now.

"Very glad. I suppose that's so, there are no nearer male relatives, unless we count Lady O'Toole's French family. But we should consult her, shouldn't we? She might wish to consider one of them."

"As I understand the situation, her father is already an elderly man, not in the best of health. He did not feel able to attend the late Earl's funeral, nor have his wife and elder daughter felt they should leave him, because of his infirmities, even to be at Cloneen for Lady O'Toole's confinement. Under those circumstances, he could hardly be counted on to undertake the active responsibilities of a guardian, even if his age expectancy were such as to make that feasible, which it is not. Lady O'Toole has no brothers and, though she has a male cousin, his relationship to the infant Earl is no closer than yours, if as close. Besides, it is very important that this child's upbringing should be thoroughly Irish, that there should be no foreign influence."

"And you could trust me to see that he had that, even though I'm half American—to all intents and purposes almost wholly American—so far?"

"We trust you completely, Peter."

"Then, if you're sure Lady O'Toole—"

Mr. MacAuliffe coughed, as he so often did when slightly embarrassed. "I took the liberty of consulting Lady O'Toole on this subject about a week ago," he said. "It would have been necessary to appoint a guardian for the baby even if it had been a girl, though of course that would not have had the supreme importance it does when the heir to the title is involved. And she took the initiative in saying that she desired you to be both godfather and guardian of the baby. So you see, Father Carroll and I are both well informed as to her wishes and now nothing remains but to carry them out."

"Except to discuss some details of the christening," Father Carroll added. "Perhaps it would be well to do that, too, before we separate. It seems particularly fitting that the infant Earl should be the first child baptized during Easter Week."

"During Easter Week?" Peter echoed with visible concern. "Why, Lady O'Toole won't even be out of bed by then!"

"No. But you'll find, when you talk with her, that she never expected to attend the christening. She knows it should take place as soon as possible after the baby's birth—at least, that's what we practice, as well as preach, in Ireland, though I realize that isn't the case everywhere. And perhaps you didn't know that the first child to be baptized with the newly blessed water is considered greatly privileged and especially fortunate."

"No, I didn't," Peter answered, still looking rather troubled. "But if Lady O'Toole feels that way about it, of course there's nothing more to be said. You could put it off long enough so that Lady Susannah and Janet would have time to get here, couldn't you? Say, until Thursday? I know Janet has been counting on being chosen as godmother and I assume there'll be some kind of a party at the house after the ceremony at the church. I'll need Lady Susannah to act as hostess for that, since Lady O'Toole can't."

"Well, Thursday would be quite feasible."

"What about supplementary godparents? Persons who'd be very pleased at the compliment of being asked? For instance, Prince Stefan Walewski, that nice Pole who was here at Christmastime, who I hope will eventually be my brother-in-law. And I think Lady O'Toole would like to invite her cousin Maurice—he didn't intend to come here until July, but he might change his mind and, if not, he could always be represented by proxy. And I thought of asking Lord Slattery and Sir Jonathan Dwyer."

"Prince Walewski, by all means. Poles are very devout by nature and this one would take the responsibility of sponsorship seriously. Frenchmen, on the contrary, have been known to consider themselves practicing Catholics if they are baptized in church, married in church and buried from a church, and if they go to confession twice a year before their semi-annual attendance at Mass and Communion. Well, that is a slight exaggeration, but you know what I mean. However, Lady O'Toole's cousin has always accompanied her to church when he has been at Cloneen, so I am willing to give him the benefit of the doubt as to what he does at other times. Lord Slattery is probably the most outstanding Catholic peer in Ireland, now that your uncle has died, and I understand he has been most cordial to you. So, such an invitation as you suggest would be very fitting. I'm sorry I can't approve one to Sir Jonathan."

"Why not? He's been very cordial to me, also."

"I know. And I believe he was baptized as a Catholic. But I've never seen him in church, and Lady Dwyer is a Protestant. Of course, you can invite them to the christening breakfast at the house. You may be very sure they'll understand why your invitation wasn't more inclusive and bear you no ill will. . . . Did you have any supplementary godmothers in mind?"

"No," said Peter, looking rather crestfallen. "Unless it might possibly be one of my other sisters, by proxy. I don't know that she'd measure up to your standards, either, but perhaps you'd take a chance."

"I'd be very glad to," Father Carroll said cordially. "And now that we've settled this much, I'll wait to go into some of the other details with you later on—there'll be plenty of time before Thursday. . . . Oh, here comes Rory with some appropriate refreshments for us. Of course, Wade will have some waiting for you when you reach the mansion. But I hope you can linger with us enough longer to join us in drinking to the health of the infant Earl and the Dowager Countess."

Peter had been happy to share the champagne which Rory, beaming broadly, had brought in, followed by Solange and Maggie, who were also beaming broadly and who had obviously spent the entire morning preparing hors d'oeuvres which were not only a work of art but a meal in themselves. Then Father Carroll had left to hear the Easter confessions of his parishioners and Dr. Carey had gone to treat the burned reprobate who was making a good recovery and look in on the crippled widower of the woman who had died of pneumonia and whose funeral must be planned for Monday. Peter had managed to ask Father Carroll, as they said good-by, if this would be a good time to start planning for that stained-glass window he wanted to put in the church to commemorate the previous earls of Cloneen. He had also managed, as he said good-by to Dr. Carey, to say he would like to be responsible for the expense of someone to stay with the crippled widower, until room could be made for him in the home of some hospitable family—or indefinitely, if that were necessary. Then Mr. MacAuliffe had agreed to take charge of dispatching the indicated telegrams and had said he would return for the signing of the necessary documents regarding the guardianship, as soon as these were ready, and Peter had started for home in the beautiful sunshine.

Up to this point, he had been conscious of no fatigue and he had walked with buoyancy, as well as joy, through the grounds. But as he mounted the steps of the mansion and Rufus came bounding out to meet him, he was suddenly very tired. Wade was waiting for him at the door, as Peter had known would be the case, and he also knew that he must not allow his weariness to cut the faithful old butler short, whatever the latter wanted to say to him. But he was far from guessing what trend the recital would take.

"We know you must be very tired, sir, and needing your rest and I'm not going to keep you long. You'll find everything ready for you in your room: your bed's opened and warmed, a fire's lighted, there's a good meal on a tray and a tubful of hot water. Tim's changed that every fifteen minutes ever since we knew it was almost time for you to come, so it would be just right when you did come. But before you go upstairs, there's just one thing I do want to say, sir, and it's in behalf of the whole staff, who've asked me to act as spokesman, as well as myself. We're very pleased and proud that there's an infant earl at the dower house and that his mother, our Mistress, is doing so well. With your permission, we're going to celebrate in the usual way on such occasions, with singing and dancing in the kitchen until a late hour. I've ordered a firkin of beer and with your permission, I'll take some whiskey and port wine from the cellar. Cook has prepared bread and ham and made a large cake with raisins. I took the liberty of telling the others it would be all right to go ahead and plan the celebration, because I knew you wouldn't be familiar with the custom and would be so weary you wouldn't want to be bothered with arrangements, so everything's under control and you'll be hearing the sounds of merriment very soon now. But this at least I must say, sir: if the baby had been a girl, there isn't one of us who wouldn't have been just as pleased and proud to have you for the heir as we are to have that blessed baby."

Only the consciousness that Tim's heroic efforts must not go unrewarded could have persuaded Peter to bathe, instead of tumbling into bed, as soon as he had flung off his clothes. But, afterward, he was glad he was scrubbed clean when he felt the freshness and warmth with which he was surrounded; and he reminded himself that if he were to set a good example to his son, he must lean over backwards in his observance of exemplary cleanliness. In five minutes he was sound asleep. But every now and then, through the long evening and the long night, he was roused briefly by the distant sound of a violin bow scraping, a drum beating, a whistle piping, of dancing feet and singing voices. This was a night of nights, not only for himself, but for everyone at Cloneen, for everyone in the village of Cloncoole. But why limit it there? Why not believe it might be a night of nights for everyone in Ireland?

28

Peter was not allowed to see Anne until Monday and then only briefly, as a special concession. By that time, plans for the christening were well advanced and it still troubled him to realize that she had not had more voice in these. It was bad enough, in his opinion, that she should not be present at the ceremony; the least they could do was to consult her about details. But Dr. Carey was adamant: she must have her first long sleep out before she had a visitor, and another good night's rest after that; she must have enough nourishment to make up for the meals she had skipped, and she would have to take this gradually; and in addition to the first measures to insure essential cleanliness, she would want to have a thorough bed bath. Peter came dangerously close to saying, "If I were her husband, you wouldn't make me wait until all that had happened, you'd let me see her at once for a few minutes; you'd know that would do her more good than all the sleep and food and freshening up that she could have." But, somehow, he managed to hold his peace and, at last, he was beside her, looking down at her with eyes of love, but finding that now he was with her he could not say any of the things he had meant to tell her, because his heart was too full for talk. It was she who spoke first.

"Aren't you pleased?" she asked.

"Pleased?"

"Yes, to see me looking so well. Or are you just surprised?"

As a matter of fact, he was surprised. Nothing about her suggested pain or exhaustion. This was perhaps partly because her bed linen and nightgown were so fresh and fragrant, her hair so neatly braided, her skin so clear. He had expected to find her deathly pale and, instead of that, the delicate color in her face was as lovely as he had ever seen it. Her eyes were bright, with no dark circles under them, and there was no mistaking the composure and happiness of her manner. It was hard to visualize her as the same woman who had clung to him in pain and fright only the Friday before.

"I am surprised," he admitted, "and, of course, 'pleased' isn't a strong enough word. I'm overjoyed."

"Then you're going to stop worrying right now, aren't you?"

"About what?"

"About my having babies. You can see for yourself that it doesn't amount to anything."

"I'm afraid I'm not going to agree to that. There were nearly twenty-four hours which are still pretty vivid in my mind."

"Only half of those were bad. In fact, only a few were very bad. And this was a first baby. The second one will be ever so much easier. As I hope to prove to you in due time."

It was true then, women did forget very quickly. He had not believed it before, but now she had almost convinced him—almost, but not quite—until she raised her arms and drew his face down to hers, with much the same gesture that she had made on the boat. He was uncertain whether or not she was as keenly aware of this as he was and he did not dare to ask her. The question and its answer might too easily lead to others, which it was wiser not to raise just then; and when they had kissed each other with great tenderness, she let her arms fall to her sides again, though she reached for his hand as he sat down near her bed.

"I think we were entitled to that one kiss," she said, rather gravely. "But I don't think we're entitled to any more until we don't have to make a secret of them. Do you?"

"No, I suppose not. But Father Carroll had already guessed—"

"That you wanted to marry me? Yes, of course. And it won't be any surprise to him that I want to marry you, though I suppose you didn't admit that. And probably he told you, in his opinion, the marriage would be very suitable and that Mr. MacAuliffe and Dr. Carey would feel the same way—a marriage sometime in late summer or early fall. But they wouldn't feel the same way if we cheated now, would they?"

"I'm afraid not. And I didn't intend to."

"Neither did I. But we did once, without intending to. And it would be dreadfully easy to do it again. So we mustn't risk it. Don't you agree?"

"I haven't any choice. But it was hard enough before I knew that you cared, too. Now it will be harder."

He could not keep the yearning from his voice. But Anne answered with cheerful composure.

"Yes, I was afraid that was what you would say. So I felt that was something we should settle right off—our course of conduct, I mean. As soon as I'd relieved your mind about having babies. Now let's talk about the christening."

"I'm not very happy about that. I'd much rather it didn't take place until you could be there. Lots of good Catholics don't have their babies baptized right away, unless they're sick or something. My sisters and I weren't, or my little nephew, either."

"Maybe. In Boston. But, Peter, this is Ireland. Father Carroll must have told you that I never expected to be at the christening. Lady Susannah will make a splendid hostess at the house. I'm so glad she and Janet can come. And I can have all the fun of planning with none of the work connected with carrying out the plans."

"I'm sorry to tell you that your plans needn't include any provision for Stefan."

"You don't mean to say he's declined to be one of the godfathers?"

"No, but his cable says that, to his great regret, it will have to be by proxy and that he's writing. The cable was addressed to me, though of course the invitation was sent in your name. The letter hasn't arrived yet. That will probably give his reasons for not coming. Perhaps we'd better not waste time trying to guess them, since that she-dragon of a nurse will be here to drive me out any minute and we've other matters to take up. . . . What about your family?"

"Well, what about them? You must have gathered by this time that neither my parents nor my sister ever go anywhere."

"Yes, I have. But, of course, I cabled them as soon as the baby was born. Then I sent a second cable, saying the christening would be on Thursday, that we hoped very much the De Briares would be represented. I thought 'represented' was a safe word. It can be interpreted almost any way you like."

"And have you had an answer?"

"Congratulations in answer to the first cable. A cable, addressed to you personally, has just come in. That may be an answer to the second one. Do you want to see it?"

"Yes, please."

He took the small buff envelope from his pocket and held it out to her, still unopened. She released her hand from his, with a lingering pressure, and took the cable. It was, as he had said, addressed to her personally, even to the extent of using her full title—an unusual proceeding for anyone in an economy-minded family. She looked at it curiously for a moment before she unfolded it and read:

> ENCHANTÉ D'ASSISTER AU BAPTÊME ENFANT DU MIRACLE. JE T'EMBRASSE TENDREMENT.
> TOUJOURS À TOI.

There was no signature. Anne tore the cable into small pieces and let them flutter down on the bed.

"There may have been an error in transmission," she said. "But I gather that my cousin Maurice will represent the De Briares at the christening. He's evidently changed his mind about not coming to Cloneen until July. . . . Why no, Mrs. Hogan, I didn't realize that the fifteen minutes were up and I'm sure that Mr. Bradford didn't, either. It simply can't be time for more nourishment."

274

29

Stefan's letter arrived in the Tuesday morning mail. Like the cable, it was addressed to Peter and he took it with him and handed it to Anne without comment, when he went to see her later in the day.

Dear Peter—she read—I was greatly pleased and touched by Lady O'Toole's suggestion that I might be one of the infant Earl's godfathers and, if you will stand proxy for me, I shall be honored to serve. I shall depend on you to tell her this. But I think I can explain to you better than I could to her, in a letter, why I feel I should not come to Cloneen at this time, since it is a matter more easily treated between two men— above all, two men who had expected to become brothers-in-law—than between a mere man and a great lady.

When I accompanied Lady Susannah and Janet to your house at Christmastime, I assumed it was as a recognized suitor, who needed only the authorization of her brother, acting in her father's absence, to become an accepted suitor. I not only wanted the engagement announced immediately, I had every reason, from Janet's attitude up to that time, to suppose that it could and would be. My saint's day seemed an ideal occasion. But because there was a great ball that night, at which Janet desired to shine as a belle, she declined to go as my betrothed. It was a presentation of which I mistakenly thought she would be proud, but which would have naturally prevented all other honourable men from paying her marked attentions and she was eager for such attentions. This, in itself, showed that she did not love me as much as I loved her, and her demeanor during the rest of our stay with you left no possible doubt of the fact that I could not count on her constancy.

Please do not feel that I am blaming her. I realize that I have not as arresting a personality as Lawrence Donovan, for instance, and that

I had no castle at hand with which to dazzle her. (She could hardly be expected to visualize one in a dim and distant place like Poland.) She is very young and it is natural that she should wish to be gay. As I have said, and I mean it most sincerely, it was my mistake to suppose that she was happy to consider me in the light of her future husband, instead of in the light of one among many admirers. Needless to say, I have not pressed my suit upon her since her return to Paris, though, when we have met, in the natural course of events, there has been no awkwardness. But I do not see how this could be avoided if we were fellow guests at your house and, above all, fellow sponsors at a baptism.

Lady Susannah, who I think is not entirely happy over the turn things have taken, has very kindly consented to convey my christening present to the infant Earl; also, Easter presents to Lady O'Toole, which I shall feel deeply honored if you and she will accept.

You have been kind enough to say, several times, that you liked me from the first moment of meeting. May I say that this feeling was reciprocal? It is possible that I may have a short holiday before I leave to take up my duties at my estate near Warsaw and, if this should prove to be the case, I should like very much to spend it with you, provided you are to be alone at the time. I will let you know, as soon as I know myself, when this holiday will come, and beg you to tell me quite candidly if the date is not convenient.

> *Faithfully yours,*
> *Stefan Walewski*

Anne laid down the letter and looked at Peter with distress. "You're afraid you were right and I was wrong about how Stefan would feel, aren't you?"

"Yes. But I shan't regard the situation as hopeless, until he's actually married to someone else. And he doesn't say anything that indicates another heart interest."

"And, as far as we know, Janet hasn't one, either. Anyway, she'll soon be able to tell us herself."

Lady Susannah, Janet and Maurice all arrived together later that same day, and Janet's preoccupation with Maurice was evident. To his regret, Peter found that he could not blame her: he had heard repeatedly that De Briare was "charming" but he had never succeeded in getting a detailed description of the man's looks. Now he began to understand why—it did not suffice to say that he was less powerfully built than most Normans, that his eyes were blue and his hair much the same color as Anne's; in fact, there was a definite family resemblance between them. His stature was not impressive and he would have seemed too slender for a man in his twenties if there had not been a suggestion of rapier steel in his slimness; he might be dangerous to affront and he would be almost certainly impossible to break. He was the personification of *bienséance* but it was a *bienséance* with both physical and spiritual force behind it. Peter had said of Lawrence Donovan that no one except a matinee idol should be so good looking; but he quickly realized that he could not classify Maurice de Briare, who was certainly equally handsome, as a matinee idol. Was it instead some medieval knight or even some valiant Norman saint? Peter could not quite place the image Maurice evoked, but it was a glorious one; and suddenly he remembered what Anne had told him about the special Mass at the Cathedral in Lisieux when a chorus of ten, dressed in hunters' pink, playing on hunters' horns and stationed in the choir, rendered the *Obyre-Tindare* music for the celebration of St. Hubert's Mass. *Now he had it!* St. Hubert, to whom a stag had appeared with a crucifix between its antlers and who had become a bishop with countless miracles to his credit. That was the great Norman Maurice called to mind. If Peter could have believed in reincarnation, it would have been easy to do so now.

For the moment, it was enough to understand that De Briare was indeed one of the most charming men he had ever met in his life and, if Janet were making most of the approaches, Maurice was certainly responding to them with great grace. He had gone immediately and by himself to see Anne, but his visit had been curtailed by the formidable Mrs. Hogan and, on his return from the dower house, he seemed quite willing to fall in with Janet's suggestion that they should stroll in the garden together. This left Lady Susannah free to speak her mind to Peter and there was no disagreement between them: Janet was making a complete fool of herself; she really did not deserve to be Jamie's godmother.

"And just wait until you see what Stefan has sent," Lady Susannah went on indignantly. As it was too late for Anne to receive more visitors that evening and it was her prerogative to open the tempting packages addressed to her, Peter decided to wait until he and Lady Susannah went to see her together the following morning and open all three at this time. Inside the wrappings of gilt paper were three embossed leather cases of exquisite workmanship which opened to disclose, in the first instance, a golden goblet, heavily encrusted with jewels; in the second, an enameled egg-shaped ornament, likewise heavily jeweled; and in the third, an ebony cane with a head of fine enamel on gold, studded with turquoises and rubies.

"The cup for Jamie belonged to Clementina, daughter of King John Sobieski, whose marriage to King James III Lucius O'Toole facilitated," Lady Susannah said drily. "He was the younger brother of Burke Andrew, the second Earl—you remember, they were both 'wild geese' who fought at the battle of the Boyne. How Stefan got hold of the cup I don't know, though I am sure quite honestly. He said he thought it was high time it should come to the O'Tooles. The present for Anne, on the contrary, is entirely modern—one of Fabergé's famous Easter eggs. I don't know who made the cane, but Stefan said it was one long carried by his uncle, who was Polish Ambassador to Russia, and that it was a present to him from the Czar, so it must be priceless, too. I hope you're not going to decline to accept these gifts."

"Why on earth should we?" Anne and Peter asked together.

"Well, the cup and the cane would be all right, of course," Lady Susannah admitted. "But I was afraid Anne might think the Fabergé was too valuable for her to accept as a personal present."

"I'm delighted to accept it. I can't think of any Easter present Stefan could have given me that would have pleased me more. I'm only sorry he felt he couldn't give it to me in person."

"Especially, since if he had been here, he could have kept Janet out of mischief?"

"I doubt it. Have she and Maurice gone riding together now? Yes, I thought so. She came and asked me for the same habit she borrowed for the hunt when she was here at Christmastime. It's one that was made for me when I was sixteen and it fits her very well. I'm a little taller than she is, but not enough to make a habit look too long, and I was pencil-slim, just as she is. . . . Did you bring plenty of *dragées* with you for the christening, *ma chère?*"

"Yes, more than plenty. And I'll go now and check with Mrs. Brennan and Cook, to make sure they're equally well supplied with everything they're supposed to provide. I assume there are all sorts of things you two want to discuss?"

"Nothing very vital," Peter said casually. "Everything seems to be running so smoothly that I was going to draw up an easy chair and ask Anne to tell me the end of a swan story she began long ago and never finished."

"Oh, if that's the case, I've a double reason to be on my way to the kitchen! I've been hearing those old swan stories all my life."

She stopped long enough to give one more lingering look at the presents from Stefan and then left, saying she would see Peter at lunch. He settled himself comfortably and looked expectantly at Anne.

"Do you really want me to tell you the rest of it now?"

"I do, indeed."

"It isn't very cheerful. I think they had reached Moyle's wild sea when I stopped telling you about them. There they were tossed from wave to wave and felt that no misery could be greater than the one they were enduring then. But worse was in store for them. A dreadful storm arose in which they were separated from each other and scattered across the surface of the fighting sea, so that none of them knew in what direction the others had been driven. Finola finally made her way to Carricknarone, which is called 'the rock of seals,' because it is there the seal people congregate when the weather is welcoming. But none was abroad at this time and there was still no sign of Finola's brothers. She had begun to lament them for dead when she saw a bedraggled white form in the distance and realized it was Conn. She plunged into the waves to rescue him and brought him safely to the rock, and shortly thereafter they saw Fiachra limping through the water and though it meant a mighty effort to bring him to them, they did so and placed him under the warmth of their wings. And soon thereafter, Aedh came back to them, not injured at all, but swimming proudly on the lip of the ocean, his head erect, his feathers dry and radiant. And after that, though they had many tribulations, they were never separated again."

"It's a beautiful story and becomes doubly beautiful because of the way you tell it. But surely there's more. Didn't they finally come home again?"

"Yes, though it was not a very joyful homecoming. One of St. Patrick's disciples, St. Caemhoch, heard their music and realized that it was the children of Lir, whom he had long sought, that were singing. So when he saw four swans lingering in the water close to the shore, he spoke to them, saying, 'Praise be to God that I have found you, for that is why I came here, having searched the coast from south to north. Come ashore now and trust me for I will end your enchantment.' They did as he bade them and suddenly the white feathery covering of the four swans began to fade and their shapes to alter before the eyes of all who were present on a bright summer day. Slowly they resumed human form, but alas! instead of the four golden bright happy children, who had been the pride and great love of their father so long before, they were now old and feeble. And they turned to Caemhoch and said, 'Oh friend and priest, help us and baptize us now ere we die. And bury us standing facing one another with our arms around each other as we so often stood when we were in the world before.' Then with the last remnants of their strength they sang a beautiful farewell song, and after Caemhoch had baptized them they sank down and died. But, as he looked up again, he saw above him a vision of four lovely children who gazed at him with immense joy. And he was filled with gladness because he knew that the children who had suffered so greatly on earth would suffer no more, but live in infinite and ever-lasting happiness."

"And this really is the end?"

"Yes, this really is the end. But I've left out a lot along the way. I didn't want to ramble on so long that I'd bore you."

"Bore me! Can't you go back and fill in some of the places you left out?"

"Not if you're going to get anything else done today and I imagine that, as usual, quite a number of things demand your attention. What made you think of this legend again?"

"Because of something I saw on the lake today."

"Our swan family? But the cygnets would be grown by now! You wouldn't recognize them."

"No, it wasn't our swan family. But perhaps it was the first step toward another swan family."

"What do you mean?"

"I saw a courtship. A lovely lady swan was receiving two suitors near the shore. She seemed quite indifferent to both—at least, she wasn't paying them the slightest attention. But they were preening themselves and gliding back and forth, keeping well within her range of vision. I stood and watched them, quite fascinated, for some minutes, but I was needed elsewhere and they were still showing off when I left. The lady swan certainly had a good chance to look her suitors over. I suppose she felt she had to choose very carefully, if it's true that swans mate for life."

"Yes, I suppose so. It's never a bad plan. And a lady should always simulate indifference as long as she can."

"I know that's the theory, but I don't believe it always works out for the best."

"You're still thinking about Stefan?"

"I can't help it."

"But Janet didn't pretend indifference to him. She just wasn't ready for monopoly."

"Then she should have made that clear to him sooner. As far as I'm concerned, I'll always be happy to remember that I knew you were in love with me almost as soon as I knew I was in love with you—and that was within an hour after we met."

Visits to Anne were still subject to abrupt termination by Mrs. Hogan, and Peter left the dower house feeling somewhat at loose ends. He had counted on having Maurice to himself for most of the day and he had several reasons for wishing to do so, not all of them disinterested. He was, therefore, greatly pleased when De Briare, of his own accord, said he had been hoping Peter would take him to the pleasure stables and the stud; at the former, he wanted to see his old friends; at the latter, he was naturally interested in the progress that had been made since the disaster of the previous autumn. He was cordially welcomed, first by Andy and his assistants and then by Riordan and his brother, and he was full of praise for the new mares and yearlings. When he and Peter returned to the office, after a leisurely tour of inspection, and were seated on either side of the double desk, it had been Peter's intention to begin their conversation with a discussion of the best procedure in regard to the bloodstock ship, still tied up at Le Havre; but Maurice forestalled him.

"I think you have been so wise to delay the purchase of a stallion until you could find exactly what you wanted and needed. I wonder if you'd accept a suggestion from me?"

"You know I'd be very grateful for it."

"Has Anne ever said anything to you about the two that we have at the Haras de Briare—a sire and his son, both steady prize winners?"

"No, I'm sure she hasn't. I couldn't have forgotten it, if she had."

"Well, she's had other things on her mind. But I've been wondering if, the next time the bloodstock ship makes the trip from Le Havre to Dublin, they shouldn't be in it."

"I'm not quite sure that I'm following you. We're hardly important enough to have two stallions here."

"But if you had the two I'm talking about, you'd soon become very important. You'd have one of the leading studs in Ireland."

"Yes, but—"

"*Mon cher,* I have a feeling that the place for the sire and son of whom I spoke is here at Cloneen. I should like you to bring them back yourself on the bloodstock ship after your visit to Normandy—for you'll be coming to Normandy soon now, will you not? In September at the latest? No, please do not say anything more just now, either to me or to anyone else. But think it over and later on let me know if I am not right, if that would not be the best arrangement."

The next morning was so bright and springlike that, by mutual consent, Peter and Maurice decided to walk to the church and meet at the porch the carriage in which Lady Susannah and Janet and Jamie would ride. Mrs. Hogan, out of courtesy, had been invited to go with them and hold the infant Earl until he was handed over to his godmother; but she was quite virulently Church of Ireland and would have nothing to do with the ceremony, even to this degree. Besides, she felt it was inviting pneumonia to keep a poor helpless baby out in the cold while all sorts of papist incantations were chanted. Peter had not been without some qualms himself about the exposure; but the balminess of the day had set his fears to rest. Lady Susannah, enchanted to have supplanted Mrs. Hogan, held Jamie during the drive; then, as they alighted from the carriage, Janet took him from her and, accompanied by Peter, walked up to the porch, followed by Maurice and Lord Slattery and Lady Susannah. Father Carroll was already waiting for them and began the prescribed questioning, to which Peter and Janet replied in unison. The baby lay quietly in Janet's arms through the exsufflation and the first imposition of hands, but began to stir as the blessed salt was put on his tongue. When the exorcism and final imposition of hands were completed, Father Carroll touched the baby with the end of his violet stole and, to Peter's great relief, they were finally admitted to the church, as he and Janet recited the Creed and the Lord's Prayer. A second exorcism came next and, after anointing the baby with oil, Father changed his violet stole to a white one and instructed the godparents to respond to a profession of faith.

By this time, Peter had begun to despair of hearing the words for which he had waited endlessly, but now, at long last, prompted by the sexton, he placed his hands on the baby and heard them: "James

Arthur Frederick, I baptize thee, in the name of the Father, and of the Son, and of the Holy Ghost." This, the exhausted godfather felt sure, must be the end of the service and he breathed a sigh of relief—only to find that the baby must be anointed with chrism, that a white linen cloth must be placed on its head and that he himself must hold a lighted candle while still another prayer was recited. Once again his hopes rose as he heard the words, "James Arthur Frederick, go in peace and the Lord be with thee"; and once again they fell when he found they could not leave the church until the baby's name, that of his parents and godparents had all been entered in the Parish Register!

By this time, Peter was quite ready to ride rather than walk to the mansion and gladly accepted a place in Lord Slattery's carriage, where he was promptly presented to the young English Duchess who was the Honorable Vincent's fiancée; *so Granny Glover had been right about that*, Peter said to himself, and he hoped that if Janet were going to make some sort of a scene in connection with it, it would not be until all the guests at the christening party had gone. Meanwhile, he was alert for anything that suggested trouble and he breathed a sign of relief when nothing happened to disquiet him. Everything had been very gala—a wonderful luncheon, magnums of champagne, pounds and pounds of *dragées*, a steady stream of telegrams and presents, people lingering for all sorts of reasons or none at all, as far as he could see. It was a long while before he was free to go to Anne.

He had seen neither Janet nor Maurice for some time, and after a glance around, to make sure he had not missed them somewhere in the spacious room, he shrugged his shoulders and started for the dower house. The younger generation had no manners, he told himself savagely, quite forgetting that De Briare, besides being generally considered the epitome of charm, was as old, if not older than he was, and that he and Janet certainly belonged to the same generation. It was not until hours later that he learned the young English Duchess to whom the Honorable Vincent was engaged and the devotion openly shown to her were a slap in the face, as far as Janet was concerned. She had retreated to her room, torn off her beautiful new dress and flung herself, weeping, on her bed. De Briare he found much sooner.

Peter went rapidly and joyously to the dower house and ran up the stairs. No matter how hard Mrs. Hogan tried to interfere with him, he proposed to stay with Anne long enough to tell her all about the christening. In his haste and excitement, he forgot to knock at her door before flinging it open. Anne was wearing a light jacket and was propped up by the pillows which were piled high behind her. Maurice de Briare was kneeling beside the bed, his head bowed over the hands which he was kissing. They were so absorbed in each other that neither heard the opening of the door or its quiet closing a moment later.

30

Peter went down the stairs much more slowly than he had mounted them and hesitated when he reached the foot. His first impulse had been to leave the house; but whatever lay behind the scene he had just involuntarily witnessed, he must go to see Anne sometime that afternoon or evening or have her and everyone else wondering and speculating as to why he had not done so. His second thought, if not actually sober, was at least more rational than his first; he had better go into the library and sit there quietly until he had thought things out for himself or until something had happened that, in itself, indicated what his next move should be.

The decision proved a wise one. The library was warm and still and, as always, seemed a friendly room. He sat down by the hearth and lighted a cigarette. Presently Rory came in to see if the fire needed mending and paused to ask the Master if he would not like tea or a drink.

"A drink would be very welcome. I was so busy seeing that the wants of my guests were well supplied that I didn't have a chance to get a really good one myself—not that Wade didn't try to look after me, but I couldn't take more than a sip or so before I was interrupted. It's often that way at your own party."

"Right you are, sir. I'll bring you a stiff drink straight away. Also, a small bundle that was brought here while you were at the breakfast, with the request I should put it into your hands as soon as you arrived."

"A small bundle? What kind of a bundle?"

Rory hesitated. "Well, sir, it's very neatly wrapped up, even if the paper is plain, and it's tied with string instead of ribbon, the way presents usually are. But I think it's a gift for the Mistress from someone who didn't venture to have it put with those at the big house and still didn't want to let the day go by without making a good-will offering of some kind."

"And do you know from whom this offering came?"

Again Rory hesitated. "It was Dan Foley brought the bundle, sir. He said his sister—Angie Sullivan, that is—had asked him to. I mistrust it's something she's knitted for the infant Earl. Very handy with her needle, Angie always was. I hope, sir, you'll feel you can take it to the Mistress."

"Of course I can. She'll be pleased and touched, just as I am. But now for that drink."

"Yes, sir. And after you've enjoyed it, perhaps you'd be willing to have a word with Mrs. Hogan. All afternoon, she's been asking to see you."

"Send her in at once if she's available. I'll have the drink afterward and try to recover from whatever new complaints she's ready to voice and the importunities of my guests at one and the same time."

Rory grinned and withdrew, ushering in Mrs. Hogan, who was bristling with indignation.

"I suppose you will insist on seeing her ladyship this evening, Mr. Bradford," she said belligerently. "But I hope you'll limit your call to five minutes. She's had far too much company already today. Lady Susannah and your sister and that Mr. Donovan bursting in and asking if he couldn't see her, too, while they were there! And, afterward, that French cousin of hers! All her rest periods upset, as well as the infant Earl's nap time and feeding time. He'll be howling his head off, the poor defenseless baby."

"The house seems very quiet to me. Wouldn't I hear him if he were crying? I certainly did the morning he was born."

"Well, for a wonder, he's sleeping just now, but he'll probably wake again at any moment and fret all night. And her ladyship's completely exhausted."

"She didn't seem to be when I looked in on her a few minutes ago. She was sitting up in bed and seemed quite able to do so. Monsieur de Briare was still with her, so I left them to themselves for a few moments. I believe he's leaving tomorrow with my grandmother and my sister and, naturally, Lady O'Toole wanted to give him messages for her parents and directions for the next shipment of horses. I'm about to have a drink and then I'll go and say goodnight to her. But you needn't worry; I won't stay long. I'm pretty tired myself."

Mrs. Hogan departed, looking, if anything, even more indignant than when she had come in, now that all the wind had been taken out of her sails. Peter heard Maurice going down the stairs and leaving the house, but decided to finish his drink before he went to see Anne. This time, he did not forget to knock and he could tell from the brevity of her welcome that she was, indeed, very tired. She was lying down again and, though she smiled and held out her hand, she was indisposed to talk.

"I've heard so much about the christening already that I'd rather have your version in the morning, if you don't mind," she said wearily. "But there's a question I've been meaning to ask you that I keep forgetting and, as I've just remembered it, I'll ask you now. Did you ever see the courting swans again?"

"I rather hoped you wouldn't ask."

"Why? I love to talk about swans."

"All right. We'll take that up in the morning, if you like, after we've exhausted the subject of the christening and listed all the presents that came to the big house so there'll be no mix-up in the thank-you notes. But there's one gift that was brought here this afternoon which I think I ought to give you right away. It's in a little bundle tied with a string. Shall I open it for you?"

"Please do, if you think I ought to have it right now and that wouldn't be too much trouble."

"It won't be any trouble at all."

He untied the string and folded back the paper so she could see what lay inside: a beautiful baby blanket of the finest wool, knitted in an intricate design. Peter lifted it up and handed it to Anne.

"From Angie Sullivan," he said, "with respectful good wishes to the infant Earl. That means a lot to all of us, Anne."

"I know it does. And it's all thanks to you."

"Nonsense. Anyway, I'm too tired to start an argument tonight. I'll never get over having to carry on without you, first through the complicated ceremony at the church and then through the party at the house which went on and on. But, considering your absence, I think everything went as well as could be expected, and I'm very happy that I could bring you this present at the end of it. Good night, darling, and God bless you."

Evidently she had forgotten they had agreed there should be no more caresses, for she raised her face for his kiss and then sank down among her pillows and closed her eyes. He did not think she was asleep when he left her, but he had the impression she wished him to believe that she was. The baby was still cradled in Mrs. Hogan's room, so there was no chance of seeing him and, as there was no point in lingering at the dower house, Peter went back to the mansion, intending to go straight to bed, only to find his grandmother waiting to waylay him in the Chinese parlor. She was obviously in a state of fury.

"Without saying a word to me, Janet got hold of Tim and sent him to the post office with a telegram for Stefan. If she'd only given it to Wade, he'd have known better than to let it go without consulting me first. But I suppose Tim took it for granted he must do whatever Janet told him to."

"What did she say in the telegram?"

"HAVE MISSED YOU VERY MUCH AT CLONEEN. STARTING BACK TO PARIS TOMORROW. LOOK FORWARD TO SEEING YOU ON ARRIVAL."

"I doubt if either Tim or the telegraph operator will read anything very indiscreet into that. And there's certainly nothing incriminating about it."

"It depends on how it's interpreted, doesn't it? To think that she should have so little pride! After the way she's treated him! It will serve her right if he doesn't come!"

"Quite true. We can only hope that, in this case, the quality of mercy won't be strained. Not that I think long suffering and an unlimited capacity to forgive on the part of a suitor are the best basis for a happy marriage. But I decline to worry over Janet any more and I advise you not to. I take it she's gone to bed? Why don't you do the same? I certainly shall, unless I find that Maurice is waiting for me in the library, which somehow I consider most unlikely."

Peter was right. Maurice was not waiting for him in the library and all farewells the following morning took a conventional form, though Janet was preternaturally subdued, Lady Susannah consumed with suppressed anger and anxiety and Maurice more urbane and attractive than ever. Peter saw them depart with even greater relief than he had watched the exodus at Christmastime; he welcomed help with his problems about the estate, but when it came to problems with Anne, he preferred to attempt the solution of those by himself.

He found her sitting up in bed, still looking rather tired, but eager to hear his account of the christening. When he had answered all her questions and made some comments on his own initiative, he rose to leave, but she detained him.

"You said you'd tell me about the courting swans this morning."

"I said, if you liked. I also told you I hoped you wouldn't ask."

"I do like."

"All right. But this is another story with a sad ending. After I witnessed the courting scene, I was sufficiently interested to keep looking for the indifferent lady and her suitors. Two days ago, one of the cobs was washed up on the shore—dead and badly mutilated. It's all very well to declare killing a swan or even injuring one a criminal offense; and, quite aside from questions of legality, I think they're very generally protected by a superstitious feeling about them among the people. But, after all, swans can't read."

"You think the other cob killed this one?"

"I don't think there's a doubt of it or that the victor is now enjoying wedded bliss with the lady, who's indifferent no longer. It's characteristic of your sex to like a winner."

"But not if he's a murderer!"

"Well, I don't know. Seems to me even that has happened. I certainly would have murder in my heart for anyone who tried to take you away from me."

"I hope you're not serious."

"Why?"

"Why, because I'm bound to have suitors, aren't I? That is, any woman—"

"That's right—any woman who looks like you. And I believe there's an old saying to the effect that, if one man wants to marry a woman, so do two others, at least. We'll let one of the others fight a duel with his rival, if he thinks it will do him any good. I'll just stand aside, if that's what you want me to do."

"And let the survivor of the duel have me?"

"Oh, no! But let him find out about the murder in my heart, so he wouldn't be too sure I might not commit it. And then it might occur to him that his suit was either dangerous or hopeless, or both, and he might stop hanging around. Besides, there's another angle to this: after a woman has told one man that she loves him as much as he loves her, she ought to do her share in discouraging other suitors. You did tell me that, the day before Jamie was born, and I had every reason to believe you meant it. Nothing you've said to me since has led me to believe you've changed your mind. Have you?"

"No."

"Then isn't the only reason we're not officially and openly engaged because that would be a lack of respect to my uncle's memory?"

"Yes."

"I thought so. I never thought you'd make the same kind of mistakes Janet has."

"Just what do you mean? Do you feel she's made another?"

"I think she's made a whole series of them. She's finally convinced it was you both Larry and Maurice wanted to marry, without finding out how little good that desire was going to do them. And, as you know, the Honorable Vincent brought his rich, ducal fiancée to the christening. So Janet went to her room and wept copiously for several hours and then she surreptitiously sent a cable to Stefan, telling him she'd missed him and hoped to see him as soon as she got back to Paris. Afterward, she confessed about the cable to Granny Glover, who's fit to be tied."

"But certainly you don't think Stefan will turn Janet down!"

"No. I think he'll go promptly to see her and propose to her again. As he's done so once and hasn't been actually turned down, being the sort he is, he'll feel in honor bound to repeat the proposal. And I think that, this time, she'll accept him without reservations. The engagement will be announced, practically to the sound of trumpets, and in June she'll have the most spectacular wedding Boston has ever witnessed. She'll be the Mistress of a vast Polish domain, she'll travel in luxury wherever and whenever she chooses, she'll be the Princess Walewska, she'll have a faithful and devoted husband. Perhaps she won't ever realize that anything is missing. But Stefan will never love her in the same way that he would have if their engagement had been announced on his saint's day, if she'd been presented at the Slatterys' ball as his fiancée. It would have been the proudest day of his life. And she made him sacrifice his pride, so that she could be the belle of the ball. I hope and believe you'll never ask a similar sacrifice of me. In the first place, I wouldn't make it. And in the second, I wouldn't ever feel the same toward you again."

"I shall never ask you to make a similar sacrifice," Anne said in a low voice. "Just the same, I made one grave and sad mistake. I agreed with you that we must do nothing that would seem disrespectful to your uncle's memory, that there could not be any open and official announcement of our engagement before June, at the earliest. But there is one person whom I should have told long ago, in confidence, that I was deeply in love with you and that I would marry you as soon as I decently could."

"One person? Not two?"

"No. I never gave Lawrence Donovan the slightest reason to suppose that I would accept him. You yourself saw, last fall, that he hadn't a chance and stopped being jealous of him. But it grieves me that you should have murder in your heart, as far as Maurice is concerned. Instead, he should have your profound sympathy and your profound respect. Because he did think, for a long time, that some day I would marry him. And it was only yesterday that I told him I never would, because I was going to marry you, instead."

So that was the meaning of the scene Peter had inadvertently witnessed: Maurice had not been making love to Anne, he had been kneeling before her as he accepted her verdict that his suit was hopeless. Peter tried to find the right words to answer her and found that they would not come, as so often happened when he was deeply moved.

"Almost the first question you asked me after you came to Cloneen was how I happened to marry a man old enough to be my grandfather," Anne went on, so quietly that he knew she realized what was the matter. "I wouldn't tell you then, but I'll tell you now: a childhood playmate and I had always been very fond of each other and suddenly my parents took alarm at this attachment. Perhaps they had reason to. It wasn't love, in the sense that you and I love each other, but maybe it might have developed into something like that. I don't know. Anyhow, there were two reasons why my parents thought marriage between this boy and me was out of the question. One was that neither of us had any money. The other was that we were second cousins. Of course, you know that I've been talking about Maurice."

"Yes," Peter said, still finding that it was hard to talk.

"If I hadn't been so young, maybe I could have held out. I'd have known that money is important, but that there are other things which matter more and I'd have looked into the matter of dispensations. Later, when a friend of my father's got one to marry his niece, so that the property could stay in the family, I did a lot of sober thinking. And then I found out how many kings and queens were *double* cousins! But at the moment I didn't know any of that and, obviously, Maurice didn't, either, or he would have tried to do something to help us out. Not that he could have. I suppose you know that, in France, you can't get married without the consent of your parents until you're twenty-five."

"No, I didn't."

"It's true. And it's a wonderful law—for parents!"

"Yes, I can see that. So what happened next?"

"Next, I noticed that your uncle, who'd been to visit us several times already, was looking at me in a different way. I don't mean different from Maurice—as a matter of fact, it was as nearly like the way Maurice looked at me as it could be, considering that your uncle was nearly seventy and that Maurice wasn't quite twenty. I mean, different from the way he'd looked at me before. And, presently, my mother told me that he wanted to marry me, that she and my father had been glad to give their consent and that it would be better if Maurice and I didn't see each other any more."

"You mean you weren't consulted at all?"

"*Consulted!* What are you thinking of? I was told how very fortunate I was and that I must try to deserve the honor that was shown me. I was terribly unhappy and I tried to see Maurice surreptitiously, but I was found out and the meeting was not only prevented but I was charged with being guilty of a very dishonorable act in attempting it; it seemed, if the Earl had learned of it, he would have been justified in withdrawing his suit. I hoped he *would* hear of it—in fact, I would have told him myself that I was in love with someone else, if I'd ever had a chance to speak to him alone. But, of course, great care was taken to see that I did not. I believe he would have understood, just as you've always believed he would have understood about you and me. But I was so very young and there were no other suitors in sight. . . ."

She paused and Peter knew that, with every word she spoke, the recital became harder. But when he begged her not to go on, she shook her head.

"No, this has been put off too long already. . . . I'm sure my parents would have been better pleased if your uncle had chosen my sister—in fact, I'm almost sure they tried to make him understand she was much better suited for him than I was. But when they found out it was hopeless to try to make him change his mind, they took fright at the thought he might go away uncommitted and said that, of course, they wanted him to follow his preference. Then there was a very formal little ceremony in the drawing room—I wasn't sent for until the end of it, after a lot of papers had been signed, a marriage settlement and a memorandum altering a will and so on. Your uncle kissed me on my forehead in the presence of my parents and gave me the ring that the Earls of Cloneen have always given their betrothed and said he would do his best to make me happy. He had to leave Lisieux for some unexplained reason the following day, and the day after that I was taken to Paris to get my trousseau. I had a superb wedding dress, really more suitable for a marriage ceremony in a cathedral than in a chapel, and a very elegant traveling dress and exquisite underclothes and negligees—that sort of thing. But very little else in the way of clothes. And I don't know where the money came from to buy that much, for everything must have been very expensive. I'd never had any *haute couture* clothes before and I would have been quite excited over them if I hadn't kept remembering why I was getting them. My mother assured me I could have as many more like them as I wanted, after I was married. And, of course, she was right about that. But it didn't help."

"Anne, you're not strong enough to tell a long story like this. You'll wear yourself out to no purpose, because it doesn't matter any more—"

"Oh, yes, it does. It wouldn't have if you hadn't talked about murder in your heart."

"I realize now I shouldn't have said that. I'm sorry, Anne."

"Sorry you *said* it! But you did feel that way, so I've got to go on. The next time your uncle came back to Lisieux we were married. We took the train for Paris that same afternoon and then we had dinner in our suite at the Meurice, which was beautifully decorated with flowers. But Solange and your uncle's old valet Sean were both with us, so I really didn't see him alone until he came into the room where I was in bed, wearing my most exquisite nightgown and waiting for him."

"Was that a shock to you? Didn't you know he would come?"

"Oh, no! I mean, oh, yes! That is, I knew he would come; my mother had explained that to me and told me I must do whatever he asked me to and let him do whatever he wanted to. But, somehow, it was a shock just the same, to find that he was actually there, that a man I'd never seen alone, who'd never kissed me, except on my forehead, until after the marriage ceremony, was getting into bed with me. Naturally, a girl can't grow up on a stud farm without learning something about how colts are bred. But she thinks of 'covering' in terms of mares and stallions, not of human beings. At least, I did. And I am afraid I showed how frightened I was, for I trembled all over, though I didn't cry out or try to draw away or anything like that."

"You poor child!"

"You're pitying me for the wrong reason, Peter."

"What on earth do you mean?"

293

"The marriage wasn't consummated—then or ever. Didn't you realize —that night on the boat?"

"My God, no! I'd thought, on the train, that there was something— well, actually virginal about you—and it puzzled me because, except for your slenderness, you didn't look like a very young girl and you were much too poised for one. By the time I came to your room on the boat, I only knew I wanted you, that I had to have you and that you were ready and eager for love. But that doesn't make what I did—or, anyhow, the way I did it—any more pardonable. What a fool I was, what a head-strong, brutal fool!"

"Peter, please don't feel this way about it! Don't you remember I told you then that I knew at last what it meant to be a woman? And that the only kind of a man a woman like me would want couldn't help taking her that way? I hope that after we're married, you'll always take me just as quickly and dominate me just as completely as you did then. I need to be sure, from the moment you touch me, that you have the power to possess me and that nothing will stop you from doing so as often and as forcefully as you want to."

"I'm afraid you don't realize how often that might be or how force-fully I could act. You'd better not encourage me to believe that you'd always welcome me."

"It's inconceivable to me that I won't always welcome you. But I want you to promise me that if I shouldn't seem to for some reason— if you were working very late or called out for some emergency and I was sleepy when you came to me; or if I seemed out of sorts or actually angry—you'd take me just the same. I'd never forgive you afterward if you didn't or if you denied yourself because you thought I was having babies too fast. I want to prove that I can have children—lots of chil-dren—that it isn't my fault I didn't have them long ago, just as I want you to prove that you can get me with child as often as you like and that you intend to."

"Anne, don't you realize you're very close to describing a relationship in which you justify a man for being violent and sensual and condemn-ing a woman to complete subservience?"

"I'm not! I'm describing a relationship between a young healthy man and woman passionately in love with each other. Don't you understand? If you don't treat me like that, I'll constantly be afraid that you can't get through to me! I was married to a man who desperately needed an heir and I was supposed to give him one. Besides, he loved me deeply, he wanted me for myself just as much as if he had been young, and I've told you the reason that I couldn't give him a child."

"And this was never accepted? Your family went on blaming you for not producing an heir?"

"Of course. But not my husband. At first, he was just baffled. He'd been assured by a doctor he'd scrupulously consulted that his health was excellent, that his age was no impediment to normal married life. He couldn't believe that doctor was altogether mistaken; he couldn't bring himself to acknowledge defeat—he was always kind and tender and gentle, but it was so sad, so pathetic for him."

"And such hell for you! Why don't you say it?"

"I can't! I won't! But perhaps you'll understand now why my marriage to you has to be the way I've tried to describe it. Also, why I seemed so 'virginal' to you when we met on the train and why I must have seemed like that to Maurice, too, until the last time he was here. Then he saw, right away, that there'd been a change. It must have showed in my face. But of course he didn't guess what had caused it. He didn't dream I'd been unfaithful to my husband. He thought the marriage had been consummated at last. And all along, he'd known it should be, but somehow he couldn't help being glad that it hadn't been. He couldn't help looking forward to a bride who was—I mean, who wasn't—" .

Then suddenly she was crying, crying bitterly and convulsively. Peter reached over and gathered her into his arms.

"I'm not forgetting our pact, forbidding premature love-making," he said soothingly. "But this is one time I've got to feel you close to me while I'm talking to you, so there can't be any possibility of misunderstanding between us. I know you're not deliberately trying to make me more ashamed of myself than I was already for having said there was murder in my heart toward Maurice or for having felt that way. You don't need to. You're trying to tell me, aren't you, that though a head-strong fool like me couldn't wait even twenty-four hours for you when I fell in love with you, that a fine man like Maurice waited patiently all these years? That he believed as soon as you were free, which, in the nature of things, would be only a matter of time, you would marry him? But that, meanwhile, not a word of love passed between you, though he felt as sure of yours as he did of his own?"

"Yes, that's what I mean."

"So that, when he was invited to the christening, he felt justified in asking you not if you would marry him, but when you would marry him? That it didn't seem necessary to wait any longer to ask that question?"

"Yes, that's what I mean," she said again.

"So when he told me he expected to see me in Normandy next summer, he meant I'd be coming to your wedding with him?"

"Yes, of course."

"And he presented a very strong case for himself, as well he might. The perfect house he'd kept ready and waiting for you, your unity of background and interest, your youthful attachment, his complete faithfulness?"

"Yes, but you see I was able to present a case that was even stronger. I told him."

"You told him that you fell in love with me at first sight, that it was very different from the love you'd felt for him?"

"Yes, but that wasn't enough to make him give me up. He said my feeling for a complete stranger must have been just a *coup de foudre*, which is what you called it once yourself; but he added that an infatuation like that wouldn't last, because it had nothing behind it like what he and I had shared, nothing ahead of it like what we could still share at the *Haras du Lieu Plaisant*. So next I told him that I'd hoped it wouldn't, that I'd done everything I could to kill it, partly on his account and partly because I knew it had been sinful for me to fall so passionately in love with anyone as I had with you. He simply smiled at the idea I would do anything sinful. I had to tell him everything before he would admit you had a stronger claim on me than he had. But he did admit it and he understands."

"You told him *everything?*"

"Yes. So now there's one person who shares our secret and it's as safe with him as it is with God. He knows that my first sight of you wasn't at Cloneen after your uncle died, that it was on the Irish Mail. And what happened on the mailboat. And that Jamie is your child."

31

Peter could not remember when the weather had been worse. After a succession of mild days, many of them sunny, longer and brighter than any he could remember in Ireland, it was unseasonably cold for early May and the chill was intensified by a persistent downpour. He had ordered fires lighted in the grates of all the rooms that were in use, both in the mansion and in the dower house, and had given strict instructions that these were to be kept going night and day in the nursery and the Mistress's rooms, though elsewhere they might be carefully banked at bedtime. His plans for the installation of hot-air furnaces in the basements, with open registers in every room, set aside when he found it was impractical to have them installed during the winter months, were taking new form again, along with plans for two real bathrooms; he was resolved that, as soon as summer had really come, the work should not be put off another moment. Fireplaces were wonderful from the viewpoint of making a room seem cheerful and homelike, as a focal point for the effective grouping of furniture and as an auxiliary means of raising the temperature. As a solitary means of providing sufficient heat during cold weather, in Peter's opinion, they were no more effective in Ireland than in New England.

So far, he was his own secretary, as far as correspondence was concerned, and had taken over Anne's as well since the birth of the baby, except for the little personal notes that she enjoyed writing herself; but it was clear to him that he would soon need to have help with letters, as well as more with accounts, now that she did not work with him on these. Danahy was willing but slow and there was always a backlog on Peter's desk. He spent more and more time in the office, trying to cope with it; the result was that he did not devote quite as much time as he knew he should to the supervision of grounds and stables, and nowhere nearly as much time as he would have liked to spend with Anne and Jamie. She was coming downstairs for her lunch now and it was understood that he would generally take his with her, because that was a suitable time to go over matters that required her attention. Directly after lunch, she went for a short drive, when the weather was pleasant, and since there were other matters which required consultation *sur place*, it was also considered suitable that Peter should accompany her occasionally on these outings. But, so far, she was forbidden to go over the stairs more than once a day and, after her drive, she took a long rest and then had tea in her upstairs sitting room. Mrs. Hogan had departed, regretted by no one, and a very superior nanny, Nora Mulhall, had taken her place. This was Nanny's supper hour and the time that Peter longed especially to be with Anne. A supplementary cradle had been placed in the sitting room, so that if she chose, Anne could watch over Jamie during this interval, instead of having Solange do it in the bedroom. Almost invariably, Anne did so choose. Rufus lay contentedly beside the cradle. The tea table, surmounted by a softly singing kettle, was set close to the fire and invitingly spread with hot scones, thin slices of buttered bread, jam, marmalade and fruit cake. The baby, who had slept most of the day, was generally awake by now, but lay quietly until tea was over, occasionally turning his head slightly from side to side or moving his arms a little, but otherwise motionless, as well as silent. Then his movements gradually became more animated. At first there was only a slight stirring; then he began to beat the air with his fists and gurgle intermittently. If Anne paid no attention to the gurgle, it would change to a whimper and then to a lusty howl. At this point Peter, if he were there, could pick Jamie up and give him to Anne, who would draw away from the tea table to a rocking chair and hold him in her arms while she nursed him. She never wore black upstairs any more; she came in from her bedroom robed in soft white wools, or white silk with a faint sheen or white crepe de chine veiled with lace. Peter had never seen a woman whose loveliness compared to hers, as she sat in the firelight holding her baby. By and by, satiated and sleepy, he would be taken back to the cradle by her bed for the night. If Peter were there, he could carry him into the bedroom and straighten the smooth sheets and warm blankets that covered him and lean over to kiss his son, when no one could see him.

"It almost seems as if we were married already, doesn't it, when we're together like this?" Anne asked one evening when Peter came back to her after lingering a few minutes in the bedroom beside the cradle.

"Yes—except for one thing, but that's a rather important one."

"Yes?"

"If we were married, I wouldn't leave you at this point, as I've got to do now. I'd stay all night—every night."

"It won't be long now, Peter."

"It seems damn long to me already."

He kissed Jamie, secretly, but he never kissed Anne. They both knew that such a kiss would be dangerous. Peter tried to tell himself that he had a great deal and that he should be thankful for what he had: he was assured of Anne's love; she had come triumphantly through the ordeal of childbirth and was able to nurse their baby; both were blooming with health. The child he could never acknowledge would grow into a fine strapping boy and become a strong handsome man, and Peter himself would have the privilege not only of seeing, but of guiding this development. And there would be other children whom he could acknowledge, who would pass for half-brothers and half-sisters of this one, but who really would be his own. Yes, there was a great deal that Peter should be thankful for. But as he sat in his office, drafting a letter about furnaces and bathrooms and closing his consciousness to the backlog of accounts, which he still did not understand very well, he could not suppress his uncontrollable longing for Anne.

He had lived continently ever since his one night of love; he would never be unfaithful to Anne no matter how long he had to wait for her and, as she had said, that actually would not be very long now. They had talked of a quiet wedding in September, but perhaps that could be advanced to August. Certainly, he ought to be able to hold out until then. If they continued to sit together, evening after evening, in the friendly firelight, their baby between them, the rest of the world dismissed? He knew that he could not. He would tell Anne so at lunch the next day and she would understand. Later on, they would work together in the office, they would ride together about the grounds; it would not be like the intimacy of the little sitting room, it would provide much less of a temptation. It would also mean seeing much less of the baby. But that could not be helped.

With a sense of his own unworthiness, Peter compared his relentless urgency with Maurice de Briare's long years of self-control and ultimate uncomplaining self-sacrifice. The French cousin was a man of finer fiber than the American interloper and Peter recognized this; and he not infrequently asked himself how he could compensate in other ways for the qualities Maurice had and he lacked. In his moments of deepest discouragement, he even went so far as to feel that he never could, that Anne, no less than Maurice, was being sacrificed. This, of course, was not true; her love for Peter had been as instantaneous, as passionate and as enduring as his for her. She had told him the truth when she had said that only a man like him—a man intensely virile, a man of driving determination—could give her fulfillment. She would find it, as he did, in his inflexible possession of her, and the more completely he enthralled her, the greater would be the glory he gave her. She had meant every word she said when she told him what she hoped their marriage relationship would be—one of passionate intensity. He never would make a demand of her to which she would not joyously respond; but neither would she ever be able to forget that she had once gladly given herself to him before marriage.

Peter had never felt the same deep remorse that Anne had for this first fulfillment of mutual desire. He had been wholly sincere in telling her that he had not once thought of her as a light-o'-love, that he had known then, as surely as he did now, that she was the one woman in the world for him and that he had grieved bitterly because they could not be married immediately. But he knew, as well as she did, that a second illicit interlude would be unworthy of their love. If he tried to anticipate the rapture of their wedding night, she would be justified in feeling that what he had done was unforgivable. So he must not allow her to provide him with opportunities which he would not be strong enough to resist.

He pushed aside the sheets covered with estimates representing the cost for modern plumbing and heating, which seemed more staggering every time he looked at them, and picked up a communication which had given him so much pleasure when he received it the day before that he had purposely kept it where he could reread it from time to time. It bore the letterhead of the Kildare Street Club in Dublin and read:

Sir,

I have the honour to inform you that at a meeting of the Committee of the Kildare Street Club, held yesterday, you were elected a member of the Club.

The Chairman of the Committee has directed me to express the hope that you may be willing to join and, in that happy event, I am to ask you to be good enough to fill in the enclosed Bankers Order, and return it to me at your convenience.

> *I am, Sir,*
> *Your obedient servant,*
> *John Mitchell, Secretary*

If this invitation had reached him after Anne had given birth to a baby girl, Peter would have been afraid, probably with reason, that it had been indicated as a suitable gesture toward the new Earl of Cloneen. Under the circumstances, however, he knew it was a tribute to him personally. It had a great deal of meaning since it was addressed to Peter Bradford.

He was distracted from his pleasant perusal of the missive before him by the sound of a carriage coming up the drive and stopping before the entrance. He was expecting no visitors and, when he went to the window, he saw that the vehicle which had halted was the only one for hire at the station and not a private trap or coach. Its passenger, whose back was turned to Peter, was paying the driver and evidently instructing him to deal with the baggage, for the man dismounted and, reaching inside the sidecar, drew out two large valises and started staggering up the steps with them. The rain was falling in torrents and both passenger and driver had the collars of their coats turned up. But after a moment of bewilderment and incredulity, Peter recognized his father in the former, just as the bell announcing this unforeseen and unexplained arrival sounded through the house. He rushed to the door and flung it open, stretching out his hand to grasp his visitor's, and silenced Rufus, who was barking loudly.

"For God's sake, where did you come from?" he gasped. "If you wired, the telegram must have gone astray. I'm awfully sorry you weren't properly met and all that!"

"I didn't wire," the elder Bradford responded drily, detaching his hand from his son's and shaking himself free from his dripping coat and hat, which he threw on the nearest chair, where they sent rivulets flowing to the floor. "I wanted to surprise you," he added, still drily.

"Well, you certainly have." Peter picked up the wet garments and handed them to Wade, who had appeared as promptly as was humanly possible, but not in time to forestall the first moment of awkwardness. "My father has come to pay us a visit, Wade," Peter went on, hoping to sound as if it were the most natural thing in the world for Mr. Bradford to arrive in this manner and fearing that it did not. "Please take these things to the kitchen and get them dried. And get a fire lighted in the room I had when I first came here myself, as soon as you carry these bags up there. Incidentally, Mr. Bradford will prefer to do his own unpacking. . . . When you came, I was in the office, Father," he continued, turning back to his visitor, "just here to the right of the entrance. Perhaps you'll join me there for a drink before you go any further. You look as if you needed one and it's nice and warm in there."

"I can't say as much for this hall," Mr. Bradford observed, shivering. "You don't mean to tell me you haven't got a furnace in this great ark?"

"No, we haven't yet. Furnaces present rather a novelty in Ireland. But we will have one before another winter. In fact, I was writing a letter on that very subject when I heard you coming. . . . What'll you have to drink?"

"Scotch, if there is such a thing in an Irish house, and not luke-warm, either. With ice in it, unless I'm asking for an impossibility."

"There's plenty of Scotch and almost anything else you'd care to name. I understand the O'Tooles have rather prided themselves on their good cellar. And, believe it or not, there's ice, too, as a concession to me. We get it at the fishmonger's. . . . Scotch and soda for two, please, Wade. And wait a minute—what about something to eat with your drink, Father?"

"Well, I believe you've had some experience with Irish trains your-self, so you know I haven't had anything since I left Queenstown. I had to spend the night there, as your grandmother did when she came, because we docked so late. Terrible hotel. Cold as a tomb, like your hall. And they woke me up this morning to give me early tea. That was bad enough, but just to add insult to injury, the hot water was in an open pitcher. I was surprised it didn't freeze over before I could drink the mixture."

"I'm afraid your first impressions haven't been very favorable. But we'll do our best to correct them by making you comfortable here. . . . Sandwiches with the Scotch, please, Wade."

"Very good, sir. And may I say it's greatly honored we are to have your father come to visit Cloneen and we'll all do our best to make him feel he's welcome."

Wade bowed and withdrew, carrying the wet garments over his arm and a bag in each hand, without any sign of strain or surprise. *He stood up to that better than I did*, Peter said to himself, *but then he isn't so new at his job*. "Do come in and sit down, Father. I think you'll like that chair."

Mr. Bradford consented to enter the office and seat himself, still shivering noticeably, though Peter immediately threw a log of wood on the turf fire. The visitor glanced around the office appraisingly and it was obvious he saw nothing in it that excited his admiration. As his gaze rested on the overloaded, untidy desk, he smiled wryly.

"It looks as if you had too much work to do or couldn't manage to handle it. Which is it?"

"A little of both, I'm afraid. Of course, I've had no experience in managing an estate of any kind, much less a big Irish estate. I've a good lawyer and a good land agent to help me, but even so I can't seem to keep abreast of everything. Especially as Lady O'Toole hasn't been able to help, too, lately."

"Was she actually ever of any help?"

"She certainly was. She had a very practical upbringing, like most French girls. And she'll soon be working with me again. She's come along finely since the birth of her baby."

There was a discreet knock at the door and Wade entered with a well-laden tray, which recalled to Peter the one with which he had been greeted on his own arrival. They might have a climate to which outsiders had difficulty in adjusting themselves, and they might not have been swift to appreciate modern conveniences, but when it came to the amenities, he would challenge anyone to surpass the Irish. He was gratified to see that, determined as his father seemed to take a very dim view of everything, the latter could not possibly fail to appreciate the food and drink now set before him and the elegance with which it was presented. He stopped shivering, accepted a glass containing very little soda, plenty of ice and some rare old whiskey and himself selected several sandwiches in quick succession from the tempting array available. For a few moments he ate and drank in silence and with obvious satisfaction. Then, on his own initiative, he began to explain his presence.

"I told you I wanted to surprise you," he said. "That was because I wanted to find you the way you really live, every day, not when you have things fixed up for company, with a regular reception committee and all that sort of thing. And I did. I found you in the office of a bitterly cold house, late in the afternoon, struggling with work you don't know how to do and ought not to be trying to do. You must be crazy if you think I'll let you go on doing it. You say Lady O'Toole's made a good recovery since the birth of her baby, that she's had a very practical upbringing and that she really knows how to take hold. With the help of the excellent lawyer and land agent you mentioned, she ought to be able to resume her responsibilities almost any time now. And they *are* her responsibilities, you know, not yours. I have naturally acquainted myself with the terms of the old Earl's will and he certainly left everything he could to her—a little more than he should have, in my opinion, since he believed, when he wrote it, that you were his heir. Since you're not, since the birth of this posthumous son of his frees you from any obligation, there's not the slightest reason why you should stay here any longer. I've come to take you home."

32

Peter lived to be thankful that he was so stunned by this calm announcement of authority that he was unable to word the angrily rebellious retort that choked him. By the time he recovered his voice, he realized the disastrous folly of making such an answer.

"Well, we don't have to start for the United States tonight, do we?" he asked with attempted facetiousness, which was more successful than he had dared to hope. "It's raining pretty hard and you've had quite a trip already. Why don't we have a good dinner and a quiet evening and talk things over?" He glanced at the clock. "Meanwhile, what about tea at the dower house with Lady O'Toole? I think you'd enjoy meeting her. I generally go over about this time to report on the results of the day's activities. I'll send a note, asking her if I can't bring you with me. I'm sure she'd be delighted to have you, but just as a matter of form, I think I ought to ask her."

"Can't you even bring your father to tea without asking permission from her royal highness?"

Again, Peter fought down a furious retort. "Of course I could, under normal circumstances. But she isn't very strong yet and it seems more courteous to ask."

"All right. Just as you say. I confess I'm rather curious to see this young woman that your grandmother and your sister consider such a paragon."

"Surprisingly enough, you might agree with them. Anyhow, we'll find out."

Peter turned to the desk, scribbled a few lines and rang for Wade. "Please send Tim to the dower house with this note for the Mistress and tell him to wait for an answer," he said to the butler. "And Ryan'd better bring the brougham around. My father and I may want it."

"You mean to tell me you've got so soft that you take a carriage to go from one house to another on the same grounds?"

"I don't when I'm by myself. But then I've got used to the rain. I even rather like it. But I know you hate it. And as Letitia would say, the dower house is a far piece from here. . . . Let me just pick up these papers and lock a drawer or two and then I'll be through here for the day. I hate to begin the next one with a littered desk. If you don't think it will spoil your tea, why don't you have another drink while I'm doing my housekeeping?"

"I never noticed that good liquor spoiled anything. And I'll say this for your whiskey, it's the best."

Bradford helped himself to more and settled back in his chair, watching his son with covert attention and deciding that the boy had changed a good deal in less than a year and that he was bound to admit to himself that the change was for the better. Peter's clothes and the way he wore them were different and so was the way he sat and stood and moved; but the change went deeper than that. He had come to man's estate. Peter had left Boston a well-mannered, attractive, easy-going youngster, even-tempered unless he were driven too far, and then explosive; he had been good at sports, but less outstanding as a student: a three-letter man at both Milton and Harvard, he had gone through college and the law school with academic adequacy but with no particular distinction; and the popularity which had assured his prompt election to the Hasty Pudding and the Fly had marked him as belonging to gilded youth, but had not pointed to the brilliant legal future which a place on the editorial staff of the *Review* could have done. He had never been called upon to assume responsibility and there had been nothing about him to suggest any aptitude for it; but despite the untidiness of his desk, which had made such an unfavorable impression, and the fact that a good executive should have finished his work earlier in the day, he was obviously in control of the situation at Cloneen. He gave orders civilly, but concisely and, while those that his father had heard were about trivial matters, there was no doubt in Bradford's mind that more important commissions would be accepted without question as authoritative. What was more, Peter had declined to be overridden about sending a message to the Countess and had failed to take umbrage, or at least to show it, when accused of being soft. He had not only matured, he had developed to a rather surprising and, perhaps, an inconvenient degree. He certainly was not going to

306

take orders from anyone else, and it might even be hard to make him change his mind about anything once it was made up. . . .

Wade knocked and came in with a small folded note, which he presented ceremoniously on a silver salver. After reading it, Peter looked up with a smile.

"It's all right, Father. Lady O'Toole would be delighted to have us both for tea and I think I have everything here shipshape. I see our chariot at the door—let's be off. Come along, Rufus."

By the time they reached the entrance, Wade was waiting there with an umbrella and Ryan had the door of the brougham open. There was no doubt of it, Peter got excellent service. As they rode down the driveway, Bradford could not fail to observe the scrupulously well-kept condition of the grounds, which even the rain could not obscure. At the dower house, they were admitted by Solange, wearing a crisp, frilled apron over her well-cut black silk uniform and a crisp, frilled cap with long black satin streamers. As she stepped aside to let the visitors pass, Anne came down the stairs.

Peter had never seen her when she looked so regal. She was wearing black velvet, instead of the lusterless silk of conventional mourning, as she had done only once before since the Earl's death and that had been for the Christmas feast; but now her low-cut dress was closely molded to a perfect figure and the skirt fell to the floor in long graceful folds. Around her throat was a necklace of ancient workmanship and the gems with which it was set caught the light as she moved; while spanning her waist was the golden chain, the first and last links meeting with a precision that accentuated the size Peter had stipulated and which seemed to him more alluring than ever. Her hair was piled high on her head and had something of the same glitter as the stones and the belt. She came without haste, smiling but not speaking until she had almost reached the bottom of the stairs.

"What a delightful surprise!" she said then; and, as soon as she was close enough, held out a hand in welcome. "And how kind of you to come at once to see me when you must be very tired after your long journey, besides having a thousand things to talk over with Peter. Such a dreadful day, too! Do come into the library, where there is a nice warm fire and tell me about your voyage. I'm sure you are a very good sailor, but at this time of year there are so often very bad storms. Did you escape them?"

She had me talking about myself before I knew what I was doing, Bradford thought resentfully, as he and Peter walked back to the big

307

house, *and then somehow I kept right on. I didn't get a word out of her about her own plans and she didn't even suggest showing me her baby. Most young mothers would have done that first of all. I don't understand how she guessed I didn't want to see the kid that's done Peter out of his title—not that I wanted him to have it, but after all it was his by rights.* Bradford was doing some very serious thinking, but he did not feel like talking, and evidently Peter realized this for he was silent, too. The rain had stopped and the evening light was very pleasant. "Well, I have to admit your grandmother and your sister have some grounds for their enthusiasm about the Countess," he said at last. "I don't know when I've seen a more beautiful woman or a pleasanter one. You're not in love with her by any chance, are you?"

"Of course," Peter said lightly. "I couldn't very well help it, could I, when everyone else is? It wouldn't do for me to be the exception to the rule."

It was going to be harder than he had expected to get the boy away, Bradford reflected with continued resentment. Boy! Peter wasn't a boy any longer! He was a man with a mind of his own, and his mind was probably made up in a way his father wouldn't like. There had been no chance to talk with his son privately the evening of his arrival because, just as they got back to the big house, Peter announced that they were having guests for dinner—of course, if he had dreamed his father was coming, he'd have called off the weekly game of whist that he played with the priest and the doctor and the solicitor. But it was so late when his unexpected visitor from Boston arrived that he felt it wouldn't be very courteous. He thought his prospective guests rather looked forward to this diversion, as indeed he did himself—it had made a welcome break in the monotony of life during the long dark winter and, now that spring had come at last, it was a more-or-less established habit. Bradford was obliged to say that he would be glad to meet Peter's friends, though he was sorry to disrupt the game of whist by making a fifth to the party. Oh, that could be taken care of quite easily, Peter assured him, if his father would like to play. They would have two tables instead of one. He would send Ryan with a message to the Hermitage, which was only a few miles away, and he was sure some of the Tyrrells who lived there would be delighted to join them. They all played well and some of them were sure to be free. However, as a matter of fact, he was sure that the company originally invited would much rather have a chance to talk with his house guest than to play whist, which they could do at any time. His father could not have failed to notice how much Lady O'Toole enjoyed his conversation.

Bradford decided in favor of the smaller party and found that he, too, enjoyed the conversation. Father Carroll had studied for the priesthood in Salamanca as well as Dublin, Dr. Carey had taken a postgraduate course at a medical school in Edinburgh after serving his internship at Dr. Stevens' Hospital in Dublin. Both had kept in touch with the outside world much better than Bradford would have expected for men living in a small village, some distance from any good-sized city. As for MacAuliffe, Bradford was not slow in sizing him up as a very able solicitor; in fact, he regretfully admitted to himself that he would prefer not to be placed in a position where he would be obliged to argue a question of legal importance with this provincial Irishman. Meanwhile, he did enjoy a discussion of the political picture, both in Ireland and elsewhere, and found the divergence of views expressed stimulating rather than irritating.

The dinner was excellent and there was ice water at Bradford's place, so a complaint that he was prepared to make was stilled before he could voice it. And Peter was right: the O'Tooles had reason to be proud of their cellar if the wines served that night were a fair sample of what it contained. Then there was that bottle of excellent port, hospitably set forth afterward in the library, as well as whiskey and soda—all conducive to further conversation. Like most Bostonians, Bradford was by no means unfamiliar with the political picture in Ireland; he strongly suspected that his mother-in-law, Lady Susannah, had subscribed liberally to Fenian bonds, though he preferred, as a lawyer who practiced what he preached, to ignore the possibility that anyone in his household was helping to promote a revolutionary movement. On the other hand, he was equally indignant because many American citizens had been arrested and imprisoned under the Coercion Act of 1881 without being brought to trial and he had added his very considerable influence and prestige to the agitation for their release. He knew that this law was labeled by the English government as "The Protection for Person and Property Bill" and that it had been branded by Parnell in the House of Commons as "cruel, wicked, wretched and degrading"; but he had never heard it discussed by men who had the same intimate acquaintance with its conception and development as his fellow guests. At the moment, Ireland was held tightly in its clamp; however, it had a term of only three years and then the battle against it would be renewed. Meanwhile, Parnell was wisely biding his time.

"I'm sorry our friend Larry Donovan isn't here tonight, Father," Peter said, as he noticed Bradford's unfeigned interest in the subject of the bill. "He's one of Parnell's closest assistants. He could have told you more about the prospects of a possible repeal than any of us can. If I'd only known you were coming, I'd have made a point of asking him here. He comes and goes all the time, helping me with the stud, so just as likely as not he'll turn up by tomorrow, anyway. If he doesn't and you'd like to see him, I'll send him a wire."

"I'm very much afraid that by the time the bill expires, Mr. Parnell may not be able to help Ireland as much as he has in the past," Father Carroll said gravely.

"Really?" Bradford asked incredulously. "I thought his star was in the ascendant."

"And so it was—until very recently. But I doubt if it is any more, even though it has not fallen yet."

"I did hear some rumors about a love affair. That isn't really serious, is it?"

"As far as the Church is concerned, it is very serious," Father Carroll said, still more gravely. "Ireland lost a God-given opportunity when it failed to give Daniel O'Connell more powerful support. We owe the Catholic Emancipation Act largely to his efforts, and he founded the Repeal Association on the same lines. True, times changed between the eighteen twenties and the eighteen forties. But if there had been no dissension within the Association itself, he might still have prevailed and Ireland would not be dependent today on a leader who himself breaks the rules of both God and man."

"However, you're not intimating, are you, that the Church would condemn a man whose public life is not only blameless but inspired, because of some reflection on his private life?"

"It could have no choice."

"Even if that meant not only his destruction, but everything he stood for? A free Ireland?"

It was Peter who spoke this time, and when Father Carroll looked at him sorrowfully, without making an immediate answer, he went on impetuously.

"I haven't succeeded in rationalizing Irish moral standards," he said. "When you go to St. Patrick's Cathedral, you're shown with pride the brass lozenge that marks the tomb of one of Dean Swift's two mistresses *en titre* beside his own. If you go to the opera at Covent Garden, either you hear *Tristan and Isolde*, which is most in vogue just now, or everyone around you is saying that what you're hearing can't compare with that; and Isolde is just our old friend Iseult, the Irish princess for whom Chapelizod is proudly named, who drank a love potion with the emissary whom King Mark of Cornwall had sent to fetch his bride and then and there decided Tristan was her man and she would have him, even if she died for it—quite along the same lines as Francesca da Rimini and Paolo, whom we were brought up to believe were so very wicked. And then, among the earlier Irish stories—but I won't enlarge on that. And going all the way back to still more ancient history, what about David? He not only wrote the psalms, which have found and kept an important place in both the Bible and the liturgy of the Church, he fell so deeply in love with Bathsheba that he brought about her husband's death, in order to marry her, and didn't wait until this arrangement was completed before going in unto her, as the Bible so graphically puts it, and getting her with child."

"While pointing out the inconsistencies in Irish standards, you're certainly making a very strong case in favor of leniency toward a certain kind of sinner," Mr. MacAuliffe remarked, "and using rather famous persons as examples; but probably it would be safer not to come any closer to the present with those. . . . Have you been interested in following the trial of the Invincibles, Mr. Bradford? We're expecting a verdict any day now."

Although no one had a word of defense for the Invincibles, there was considerable difference of opinion about the conduct of the trial, and by the time the party broke up Bradford was in no mood to argue with anyone, certainly not with this strange, self-assured young man who was his son. He was yawning when he went up the long stairs and was glad to find his bed already turned down and his night clothes laid out for him; and though he pushed aside the hot stoneware bottle that was ensconced between the sheets, its delicious warmth was the last thing of which he was conscious before he fell into a deep and peaceful slumber.

When he waked, the sun was pouring into the room, for he had flung back the carefully drawn curtains as he opened his window for the night, and now he looked out on a peaceful scene. Peter, who had accompanied him to his room when he came up the night before, had shown him the bell he was to ring when he wanted a fire and bath water the next morning; and his summons was almost instantly answered by Tim. A cheerful blaze was soon crackling on the hearth and steam was rising from the hip tub set in front of it.

"The Master said you wouldn't be wanting early-morning tea, sir," Tim said respectfully when his preparations for the guest's comfort were complete. "And that he thought you'd be wanting your breakfast in the dining room. But if you were to prefer it here, sir, I'll have it up in no time at all."

"No, my son's right. I don't like breakfast in my room."

"Then shall I tell Cook you'll be coming down in about half an hour, sir? Or perhaps a little more than that? The Master likes to allow forty minutes, unless there's some reason why he needs to hurry."

"Oh, he does, does he? That's something new. Well, I can make it in half an hour all right."

To his chagrin, Bradford found that forty minutes would have been better after all. It took an uncommonly long time to sharpen his razor, change his cuff links, shift his wallet and keys from the dinner clothes he had worn the night before to the suit he intended to wear that morning and find a clean handkerchief in the jumbled contents of his bag. Then he was such an ungodly distance from the dining room— that long corridor outside his bedchamber, that endless flight of stairs, that vast hall! But there was nothing about Wade's demeanor or about the breakfast itself to suggest that he was overdue.

"The Master asked me to tell you, sir," Wade said, as he filled Mr. Bradford's glass with ice water, "that he thought of asking you to take an early ride with him, it's such a fine day and all. But when Tim told him you hadn't rung, he thought it better not to disturb you. He'll be back any minute now, unless something's delayed him at the stables."

"He rides every morning, does he?"

"Oh yes, sir. He takes Rufus with him and goes through the stables and the stud and afterward to the pastures. But everything's running smoothly now, thanks to his wonderful management, if I may say so, sir. What we'd have done without him, I don't know."

Mr. Bradford nodded without answering and thus put a stop to further conversation. He felt disinclined to hear anything more that would confirm his growing fear that Peter would be hard to dislodge. But he attacked his food with relish. To his amazement, the meal was almost a replica of what he would have had on Beacon Hill: there were neatly halved oranges to begin with, there were eggs which had been cooked exactly four minutes, there were piping hot muffins, there was cream for the strong coffee, there was a small steak embedded in fried potatoes and, finally, there were griddle cakes with maple syrup. It was while he was doing full justice to this last course that his son came in with a cheery "Good morning."

"Sorry I couldn't make it a little earlier, Father," he said, sitting down and drawing the coffee pot toward him. "We've got an especially important confinement at the stud this morning and I had to see how things were going—satisfactorily, I'm glad to say, so far."

It was quite true that Peter had been to the stud, but in mentioning the "confinement case" as the reason for his delay in coming to the breakfast table, he was by no means telling the whole story. When Edward Bradford announced, the day before, that he had come to take Peter home, he had been overheard by Wade, on his way to the office to remove a tray; and Wade, overcome with anxiety, had gone straight to the servants' hall with a story of impending disaster. Before the dinner party was over, the bad news had been carried to the stables, the stud, the farm and the lodges and the next morning, at every turn that he took, Peter had been stopped by pleas for reassurance, all of them patently sincere, some eloquent, two or three very touching. He had thanked everyone for the loyalty and good will evinced by these protests against any plan for departure and assured one and all that there was really nothing to be anxious about; but he could not keep his father waiting indefinitely and he had been as brief as was consistent with courtesy in his replies. The result was that he had not succeeded in setting fears to rest and several times these had been repeated from the same source. When he finally managed to break away and was on the point of entering the house by a side door, he was stopped once again, this time by a short shabby man he did not recognize, who was standing, hat in hand, an expression of abject misery on his thin face.

"If you please, sir—" the stranger began, and something in his manner made Peter realize he must stop and listen. "It ain't true, what they're saying, be it, sir?"

"I'm not sure I know what you mean," Peter replied, though, as a matter of fact, he thought he was.

"That your father wants you to go back to Boston."

"Yes, that's true."

"But you won't go, will you, sir? He says he's come to take you home, and this is your home. We're your people. You can't leave us now. If you do, we'll feel the blame is on us. Me, anyway. Me and my family and my friends."

"I'm not blaming anybody. It's natural for my father to think of Boston as my home, and for me to do so. I'll be glad to talk to you about it some other time but he's waiting for me now."

"Yes, sir, if you'll just say before you go that you won't leave Cloneen. Maybe you didn't place me, sir. I'm Dan Foley, Angie Sullivan's brother. I swear to you, if you'll only stay, we'll make it up to you."

It was fifteen minutes after this that Peter entered the dining room, giving his abbreviated version of the delay and fearing that his voice did not sound natural as he did so.

"I hope Wade has looked after you all right. I knew you wouldn't like a row of dishes on the sideboard, with no one to help you pick and choose among them and finally ending up with kidneys and kippered herring, any better than you'd like early-morning tea."

"You were right, and this is the first breakfast I ever had, in either Ireland or England, when cold toast on a rack wasn't the only kind of bread offered me. You must have done some effective missionary work in the kitchen."

Peter laughed. "Come now, you must have had cold brown bread, as well as cold toast, offered you in Ireland. It's one up on England in that respect. And I can't take credit for the missionary work in the kitchen. Solange began it and Letitia went on with it. Tomorrow, you can have croissants or popovers or doughnuts or all three. The only missionary work I can take credit for is in regard to the ice water and the cream in the coffee. . . . Would you care to have a look at the grounds with me after you've satisfied the pangs of hunger? You'll never get a more beautiful day."

"Without doubt, it'll be the only one this month when the sun shines for more than a few minutes at a time," Mr. Bradford retorted. "But what I really want is to have a good long talk with you. I thought I made that clear, when I told you, as soon as I got here, that I'd come to take you home. But you managed to see that I didn't get a word alone with you most of yesterday afternoon and all of yesterday evening. Before you try any more tricks on me, I propose to speak my mind."

"I'm not thinking of trying to play tricks on you. As you know, you took me completely by surprise, not only with your visit, but with its purpose. I did think it was just as well that I shouldn't make an immediate answer to your announcement about taking me home, because I was afraid it wouldn't be very well considered. But it's also true that I had planned to take tea with Lady O'Toole and have guests here for dinner, and I couldn't courteously change these plans at the last moment. My plans for today are only tentative and those that I have can

314

be very quickly altered. If you'll excuse me for fifteen minutes so that I can look in at the stud again while you have a cigar, I'll meet you in the office and do my best to see that we're not interrupted, though I can't promise. It's just nine o'clock. We generally have lunch at one-thirty. Do you think four hours will give you enough time for everything urgent you need to say to me?"

There was no doubt about it, this Peter Bradford was not the same Peter Bradford from whom his father had parted complacently the previous June. The latter was hardly seated when the door of the office opened abruptly and a dark unkempt man shouted excitedly, "Lucy Locket's dropped her foal, sir, the finest little filly I ever saw!"

"Good. I'll be back there as soon as I can. Meanwhile, just carry on in the usual way."

"You don't mean to say that ragamuffin is one of your employees?" Bradford demanded as the door slammed after Riordan's retreating figure. "Why, he looks like a Gypsy."

Peter laughed. "And for a very good reason. He is one—at least, by heredity. Also, he's a superb studmaster and it's very seldom that he looks disheveled, much less dirty; but we've been a little worried about that maternity case I mentioned before and he was so excited because mother and child are at last doing as well as could be expected that he couldn't take time to get cleaned up before coming to tell me the good news—or even to knock. Now that everything's all right, we won't be interrupted again. Perhaps in the end it will help out if I speak my piece, or at least part of it, first. Because now, I *can* make a well-considered answer. And that answer, to put it bluntly, is that I haven't the least idea of leaving Ireland and that there is nothing you or anyone else could say to me that would make me change my mind."

"That's a great way to talk to your father."

"I'm sorry. I don't mean to be disrespectful and I'm very grateful to you for all you've done for me. I don't see how any boy could have had a pleasanter home and a better education and more advantages generally than you gave me. But, if I may say so, you didn't talk to me yesterday as I would have expected you to talk to a son twenty-five years old, who's never done anything to disgrace you. You talked to me as if I were a headstrong youngster who'd got to be brought to heel by mandatory measures."

"That's insolent—and ridiculous."

"It isn't meant to be. But I don't think you've quite grasped my position here. I'm new at the job and I've a lot to learn. Milton and Harvard teach a good many valuable things, but not how to run an Irish country estate. However, I'm willing to learn how to do that and I *am* learning. I'm not a sort of upper servant, as you inferred yesterday—perhaps, by now, you've seen enough of me in action to gather that. I'm the Master here and recognized as such. I propose to go on being the Master until that baby you weren't interested in seeing is old enough to take over. Then I'll gladly step aside for him. Meanwhile, I'm his godfather and his legal guardian and I intend to serve his best interests as well as I can."

"Suppose the beautiful Countess should marry again? Isn't that more than likely?"

To his father's surprise and somewhat to his annoyance, Peter smiled. "I suppose it is," he said quietly.

"Then wouldn't her husband be the Master here? Wouldn't he become the baby's legal guardian?"

"Undoubtedly."

"You don't seem to be very much worried about it," Bradford remarked with increased irritation. "Didn't you know her second marriage is as good as arranged?"

"I wouldn't go so far as to say arranged."

"Don't split hairs like that!" Bradford exclaimed, his voice rising almost to a shout. "You know there's nothing that makes me madder! Naturally, they can't come right out and say anything until the year of mourning they set such store by is up. But just as soon as it is, Maurice de Briare will make a formal request for the Countess's hand. As a rich young widow, she's in a very different position from that of a penniless young girl. De Briare will have not only her parents' approval but their blessing. They're as anxious now to further the match as they were to prevent it five years ago. And what could be more logical, I'd like to know? That baby, whom you quite rightly said I wasn't interested in seeing, is the heir to both properties and Maurice de Briare wouldn't have to give money another thought as long as he lived."

Bradford had become so excited over his own declamation that he had paid no attention to the way in which it was received. If he had, he might have taken warning by something in his son's face.

"Where did you hear about this logical arrangement?" Peter asked.

"Why, your grandmother was the first person to speak of it. You know she went to Normandy on purpose to make the De Briares' acquaintance before the rest of us went home in September. And she came back saying she thought Maurice de Briare was the most attractive young man she'd seen since she could remember and that, of course, none of the objections that the Countess's parents made to a match between two penniless youngsters would hold up now that she was a rich widow—unless it were the question of consanguinity, and it would be easy enough to get a dispensation to take care of that."

"And this is all she said? That the Countess's parents wouldn't object any longer if a dispensation could be arranged?"

"Well, isn't it easy enough to go on from that point? There's no question that the Countess and Maurice had been so much attached to each other when they were in their teens that the girl was married off in a hurry to prevent their attachment from going any further. What makes you think it never went any further? Wouldn't it be natural for the Countess to look forward to a second marriage with a man her own age and her own nationality, especially one whom she would have married in the first place if the cards hadn't been stacked against her? De Briare hasn't married anyone else and he's been going back and forth with the Norman horses at intervals ever since his cousin's marriage took place. In fact, he brought the last two over in June, didn't he? The end of June?"

"Just what are you trying to say?"

"Nothing much further, unless I completely lose my temper and I'm pretty close to it. You're my only son and I've counted on you to carry on my name and my position, both social and legal. You know that, you've known it for a long time. But when I try to remind you of your normal obligations, you fly off the handle and say that nothing either I or anyone else can say will make you stir out of Ireland. You're an outsider and you always will be. The time will come when you'll miss the places and the people that you grew up among; you'll long for them bitterly. You won't always be perfectly contented to stay on in this place which doesn't belong to you and never will, acting as its administrator because you're the godfather and guardian of another man's child and you propose to do right by it. You don't give a thought to the possibility that this man may come along and throw you out almost any time now."

"Will you say that again please?" Peter said so quietly that his father sounded all the louder as he answered.

"My God, Peter, here you were bragging a few minutes ago about being twenty-five as if that meant you knew almost all there was to know about human nature! Do you really believe that a man seventy-four years old, who'd been childless through two marriages, would suddenly become potent enough to beget a healthy baby? And do you really believe that a man like Maurice de Briare wouldn't take advantage of a situation that was made to order for him? He'd be less than human if he didn't and so would anyone who blamed him. If that baby isn't his, it ought to have been!"

As he halted, breathless with anger and excitement, he was conscious of a strange stillness in the room which his raucous voice had filled. The silence hung between himself and his son like a menacing presence and when he tried to break it, he found he could not. He had to wait for Peter to do this and it took Peter a long time. The charge of illegitimacy, which he had dreaded ever since he learned Anne was pregnant, had come at last, and not from any of the quarters which he had originally feared might raise it or at least suspect it. The family solicitor, the family physician and the family confessor had all accepted Anne's baby as her husband's without a question. Peter did not believe that there was even an unvoiced question in the mind of any one of the three—to them, Anne was so far above suspicion that they would never associate her with any act of disloyalty. Now his father had opened the closed question. It lay with Peter to close it again, this time forever.

"I'm afraid you're overlooking two or three vital facts," he said at last. "The most important one is Anne's character. If you think she would have carried on a surreptitious love affair with her cousin, during her husband's lifetime, you're not as good a judge of women as you like to pretend. The second factor is her husband's character. He'd have been instinctively jealous of any younger man, particularly a former suitor, who showed the slightest sign of improper attentions to his wife. And, if Maurice de Briare came here as often as you think, James Arthur Frederick O'Toole would have had plenty of chances to observe such signs. I strongly recommend that you read his will more carefully; it will show you pretty clearly what he thought of his wife, if I can't. Incidentally, before he married Anne, he took the precaution of getting expert medical advice. His doctor encouraged him to hope for an heir and the tragedy is that he didn't live to see it. The last factor I'd like you to consider is Maurice de Briare's character. I admire him more than any man I know. He came here to the christening, as I believe you know. I had no trouble gathering that he was still in love with Anne and nobody needed to point out to me how logical a marriage between them would be. But that was where two other supplementary factors entered in. The first of these is that Anne wasn't in love with

318

Maurice any more, if she ever was in the real sense of the word. The second is that she's in love with me. She's promised to marry me in September. I don't think we need to discuss the possibility of my return to Boston with you any further."

Inevitably, the parting between father and son was hard on both. Edward Bradford said he would prefer to go to the station alone and Peter did not try to overpersuade him. But when the carriage was at the door, he returned to the study, where Peter had gone back to work while Bradford packed, and haltingly asked two or three questions which on the face of them seemed trivial, but which were underlined with pathos.

"Since you've really decided to stay on here, wouldn't you like some of your things sent to you? I mean the cups you've won, your winning oars, your diplomas and certificates of membership in clubs, things like that. They'd look well in this room and—well, they'd be pleasant reminders of things you've done."

"Thanks, Father, but I don't believe you'd better. Somehow, I don't think they'd fit in here and, honestly, I don't need any reminders. I shan't forget those things."

"It was just a thought. You'll come back to Boston once in awhile, won't you? Not to stay long, I understand now you wouldn't do that. But to class reunions and so on. Perhaps to vote, since you can keep your American citizenship. Of course, you could bring your wife with you."

"Yes, of course, I could and I know she'd like to come—after the baby gets old enough to come with us. Unless there's another one by then that she can't leave. We're hoping for a large family."

"I'll understand about that, too. But there isn't anything final about this good-by, is there, Peter? Because of some of the things I said?"

"Of course not. We Bradfords all lose our tempers and say things we don't mean every so often, don't we? You must come back and see more of the place whenever you feel like it. And bring Mother with you. Perhaps you'd both come to my wedding. Naturally, it will be a very quiet one, but Anne and I would both be very glad to have you."

"I'll tell your mother and let you know. I think she'd like to come."

"Fine. Give her my love."

"I will. Good-by, Peter, and good luck."

"Here they say, 'God bless,' when they say good-by."

"All right. God bless."

After his father had left, Peter stood for a long time at the window without really seeing what he was looking at and, eventually, he realized that, of course, he could not see anything because the pleasant twilight had faded into darkness while he stood there, already yearning for the things his father told him he would be bound to miss and seeing those very clearly. It was night again and, suddenly, he was very lonely. Rufus had come and looked up at him questioningly and then lain down beside him; but this time it did not help. If he could have gone to Anne, that would have helped, but he had promised her that he would not try to see her again at night until they were married and he must keep this promise. Besides, he must not depend on Anne or anyone else to help him through the lonely times or over the hard places. He had also promised that she and all those others could depend on him and he must keep that promise, too. And that was not enough. "All those others," so far, meant only his priest and his solicitor, his tenants and retainers. His children—both the one that he could not acknowledge and those he still hoped to have—would be Irish, for all that their mother was born French and he American; in what sort of an Ireland would they grow up, if he limited himself to removing the curse of landlordism only from his own tenants, if he used his wealth and ingenuity only to repair the wreckage he could see around him? If it were true—and Peter deeply feared it was—that Parnell's inspired dedication to Ireland could not, in the eyes of the Church, counterbalance his love for a woman who was another man's wife, what would happen when the "uncrowned king" of Ireland was dethroned and there was no one to take his place in fighting her battles? Donovan was vehemently devoted to her cause; but he lacked in depth of vision what he possessed in eagerness of purpose. Healy was brilliant, but for some reason Peter had distrusted him from their first meeting at the Mansion House, far from standing by his chief in his hour of need, he might be the first among the traitors. Gladstone must have been well aware of the relationship between Kitty O'Shea and Charles Parnell from the moment he accepted her as their regular liaison officer; but Peter had always felt that the Prime Minister would pretend, with hypocritical horror, that this came as a terrific shock whenever it best suited him to humiliate and then destroy Parnell by doing so. Many others whom Peter hardly knew by name as yet would do the same; and then Parnell's own sad prophecy of chaos and violence would be fulfilled.

Up to now, Peter had been so deeply involved in trying to cope with his immediate obligations that he could excuse himself for not being better prepared to cope with the problems of Ireland as his adopted country. But after he and Anne were married, after the stud was functioning as a practical asset to the estate, after he was no longer a "stranger" in the community, he would not be justified in doing so. He must be ready and able to do his part in helping to make Ireland a better homeland, not only for his own children, but for all the children in the country. The time might conceivably come, during his life, when she could and would achieve her independence; if that happened, but only then, would he consider that he should no longer remain an American citizen, but become a citizen of a free Ireland which he had helped to create.

He knew that all this would mean endless study, endless preparation, endless activity, endless patience and endless faith. He could not waste time thinking about such personal matters as loneliness when so much was at stake. He turned away from the window, lighted the lamp and went back to work.

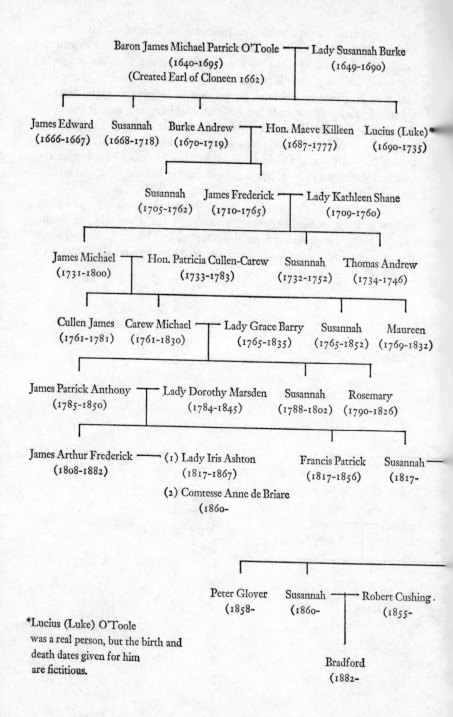

Baron James Michael Patrick O'Toole
(1640-1695)
(Created Earl of Cloneen 1662)
— Lady Susannah Burke
(1649-1690)

James Edward
(1666-1667)

Susannah
(1668-1718)

Burke Andrew
(1670-1719)
— Hon. Maeve Killeen
(1687-1777)

Lucius (Luke)*
(1690-1735)

Susannah
(1705-1762)

James Frederick
(1710-1765)
— Lady Kathleen Shane
(1709-1760)

James Michael
(1731-1800)
— Hon. Patricia Cullen-Carew
(1733-1783)

Susannah
(1732-1752)

Thomas Andrew
(1734-1746)

Cullen James
(1761-1781)

Carew Michael
(1761-1830)
— Lady Grace Barry
(1765-1835)

Susannah
(1765-1852)

Maureen
(1769-1832)

James Patrick Anthony
(1785-1850)
— Lady Dorothy Marsden
(1784-1845)

Susannah
(1788-1802)

Rosemary
(1790-1826)

James Arthur Frederick
(1808-1882)
— (1) Lady Iris Ashton
(1817-1867)
(2) Comtesse Anne de Briare
(1860-

Francis Patrick
(1817-1856)

Susannah
(1817-

Peter Glover
(1858-

Susannah
(1860-
— Robert Cushing
(1855-

Bradford
(1882-

*Lucius (Luke) O'Toole
was a real person, but the birth and
death dates given for him
are fictitious.

Genealogical Chart

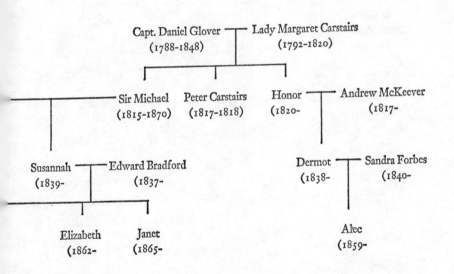

Capt. Daniel Glover ——— Lady Margaret Carstairs
(1788-1848)   (1792-1820)

Sir Michael   Peter Carstairs   Honor ——— Andrew McKeever
(1815-1870)   (1817-1818)   (1820-   (1817-

Susannah ——— Edward Bradford   Dermot ——— Sandra Forbes
(1839-   (1837-   (1838-   (1840-

Elizabeth   Janet   Alec
(1862-   (1865-   (1859-

Bibliography

Bibliography

HISTORY

A History of Ireland. Edmund Curtis, M.A., Litt. D. London: Methuen, 1936.

A History of Irish Catholicism. Vol. V. General Editor, Patrick J. Corish. Dublin and Melbourne: M. H. Gill & Son, Ltd.

A Short History of the Irish People. Part II—1603 to Modern Times. Mary Hayden, M.A., and George A. Moonan, B.L. Dublin: Educational Company of Ireland. London: Longmans, Green, 1927.

Donegal Annual, Journal of the County Donegal Historical Society. Vol. IV, No. 1, 1958; Vol. I, 1964; and Vol. VI, No. 2, 1965.

Irish Journal. Heinrich Böll. Translated from the German by Leila Vennewitz. New York: McGraw-Hill Book Company, 1967.

Ireland, from the Flight of the Earls to Grattan's Parliament, 1607-1782. Compiled and edited by James Carty. Dublin: C. J. Fallon. Chester Springs, Pennsylvania: Dufour, 3d ed., 1957.

Ireland, from Grattan's Parliament to the Great Famine, 1783-1850. Compiled and edited by James Carty. Dublin: C. J. Fallon. Chester Springs, Pennsylvania: Dufour, 3d ed., 1957.

Ireland, from the Great Famine to the Treaty, 1851-1921. Compiled and edited by James Carty. Dublin: C. J. Fallon. Chester Springs, Pennsylvania: Dufour, 2d ed., 1958.

Irish Families, Their Names, Arms and Origins. Edward MacLysaght, Litt. D., M.R.I.A. Illustrated by Myra Maguire. Dublin: Hodges & Figgis & Co., Ltd. New York: Barnes & Noble, 1957.

Titles and Forms of Address. London: Adam and Charles Black, 1967.

New Ireland Political Sketches and Personal Reminiscences of Thirty Years of Irish Public Life. A. M. Sullivan. Glasgow: Cameron, Ferguson & Co.

Tales of the West of Ireland. Edited by Gertrude M. Horgan. Dublin: The Dolmen Press.

The Course of Irish History. Edited by Dr. T. W. Moody and Dr. F. X. Martin. Cork, Ireland: The Mercier Press.

J

The Fanad Patriots. Full Authentic Story of the Killing of Lord Leitrim. April, 1878. Derry, Northern Ireland: McKinney & O'Callaghan.

The Great Northern Railway of Ireland. Edward M. Patterson. Lingfield, Surrey: The Oakwood Press.

The Lough Swilly Railway. Edward M. Patterson, D.Sc., M.R.I.A. Dawlish: David & Charles. London: Macdonald, 1964.

The Story of a Great Man and a Fatal Flaw—The Parnell Tragedy. Jules Abels. New York: The Macmillan Company. Ontario: Collier-Macmillan Canada, Ltd., 1966.

Scenes of Edwardian Life. Sir Charles Petrie, C.B.E., M.A. (Oxon), F. R. Historical Society. London: Constable & Company, Ltd., 1965.

The Ill Starred Stewarts. Mabel Dodge Holmes. New York: The Vantage Press.

Scotland's Royal Line. Grant Richardson Francis. London: J. Murray.

Survivors of the Armada. Evelyn Hardy. London: Constable & Company, Ltd., 1966.

Realities of Irish Life. W. Steuart Trench. London: Macgibbon & Kee, Ltd., 1966.

Ireland, Harbinger of the Middle Ages. Ludwig Bieler. London: Oxford University Press, 1963.

The Making of Modern Ireland, 1603-1923. J. C. Beckett. New York: Alfred A. Knopf, 1966.

The Church in Early Irish Society. Kathleen Hughes. Cornell University Press, 1966.

Ireland. Joe McCarthy and the Editors of *Life.* Time Incorporated, 1964.

NOVELS

Clementia. A. E. W. Mason. London: Methuen & Company, Ltd.

Never Call It Loving. Dorothy Eden. New York: Coward-McCann, Inc., 1966.

The Heat of the Sun. Sean O'Faolain. London: Rupert Hart-Davis, 1966.

The First Day of Friday. Honor Tracy. New York: Random House.

DRAMA

A View on Vanessa. Sybil Le Brocquy. Dublin: The Dolmen Press, 1967.

The Invincibles. Frank O'Connor and Hugh Hunt.

Juno and the Paycock. Sean O'Casey. London: Macmillan, 1948.

Pictures in the Hallway. Sean O'Casey. London: Macmillan.

The Plough and the Stars. Sean O'Casey. London: Macmillan, 1948.

The Complete Authentic Texts of Boucicault's Three Irish Plays, "The Colleen Bawn," "Arrah na Pogue," and "The Shaughraun." Edited by David Krause. Dublin: The Dolmen Press, 1966.

TRAVEL AND GUIDE

Enjoying Ireland, What to See and Where to Go. William F. Kehoe and Constance Kehoe. New York: Devin-Adair Company.

Facts from Gweedore with Useful Hints to Donegal Tourists. Compiled from notes by Lord George Hill, M.R.I.A. Dublin: Philip Dixon Hardy & Sons, 1845.

Gweedore. A pamphlet first published in 1868. Worcester: Phillips & Probert, Ltd.

Highways and Byways in Donegal and Antrim. Stephen Gwynn. With illustrations by Hugh Thomson. London: Macmillan & Company, Ltd., 1899.

In Search of Ireland. H. V. Morton. London: Methuen & Company, Ltd., 1959.

Irish International Airlines—Aer Lingus—Complete Ireland. Edited by Reginald J. W. Hammond. A Ward Lock Red Guide.

Londonderry Official Guide. Issued by the Authority of the City and County Borough of Londonderry and published and printed by Tradepress, Belfast, North Ireland.

Mévagh Down the Years; A History of Carrigart, Downings, Glen and the Surrounding District. Leslie W. Lucas. Bray, County Wicklow: The Record Press, Ltd.

Railway Magazine for December, 1966. Published by Tothill Press, Ltd., for the Proprietors National Trade Press, Ltd., 1966, London.

The Reactionaries. John Harrison. New York: Schocken Books.

The Yeats Country. Compiled by Sheelah Kirby. Dublin: A Dolmen Press book, 1962.

Thoor Ballylee—Home of William Butler Yeats. Dublin: The Dolmen Press.

The Remarkable Irish; Chronicle of a Land, a Culture, a Mystique. Marc Bence-Jones. New York: David McKay Company, Inc., 1966.

The Strange Death of Lord Castlereagh. H. Montgomery Hyde. Icon Book, Ltd.

Signpost. W. G. McMinnies. London: E. J. Larby, Limited, 1965.

Castles of the Old World. Robert P. Long. East Meadow, New York: Robert P. Long, 1966.

Dublin, in the Age of William Butler Yeats and James Joyce. Richard M. Kain. University of Oklahoma Press, 1962.

BIOGRAPHY AND AUTOBIOGRAPHY

Cadenus. Sybil Le Brocquy. Dublin: The Dolmen Press, 1962.

Seventy Years Young. Elizabeth, Countess of Fingall. London and Glasgow: Collins.

Victorian Scandal. A Biography of the Right Honourable Gentleman Sir Charles Dilke. Roy Jenkins. New York: Chilmark Press, 1965.

Stella's Birthdays. Jonathan Swift. Edited with a commentary by Sybil Le Brocquy. Dublin: Dolmen Editions.

Autobiographies. W. B. Yeats. London: Macmillan & Company, Ltd., 1961.

Experiences of an Irish R.M. Edith O. Somerville and "Martin Ross." London: J. M. Dean & Sons, Ltd., 1956.

Charles Stewart Parnell. His Love Story and Political Life. Katherine O'Shea (Mrs. Charles Stewart Parnell). London, Toronto and Melbourne: Cassell and Company, Ltd., 1914.

Parnell. Joan Haslip. London: Cobden-Sanderson, 1936.

Parnell. St. John Ervine. London: Ernest Benn, Ltd., 1925.

Charles Stewart Parnell, a Memoir. John Howard Parnell. London: Constable & Company, Ltd., 1916.

Manners and Morals in the Age of Optimism, 1848-1914. James Laver. New York: Harper & Row, 1966.

Long Shadows, Memoirs of Shane Leslie. John Murray. London: John Murray, 1966.

Coole. Lady Gregory. Privately published by the Cuala Press, Dublin, 1931.

Mountain Year. Michael J. Murphy. Dublin: The Dolmen Press, 1964.

POEMS AND LEGENDS

Collected Poems of W. B. Yeats. London: Macmillan & Company, Ltd., 1950.

Love Poems of the Irish. A Selection by Sean Lucy. Cork, Ireland: Mercier.

The First Book of Irish Myths and Legends. Eoin Neeson. Cork, Ireland: Mercier.

The Second Book of Irish Myths and Legends. Eoin Neeson. Cork, Ireland: Mercier.

Romantic Donegal, Its Songs, Poetry and Ballads. Harry Percival Swan. Belfast: Carter Publications, Ltd.

The Poet's Circuits. Padraic Colum. London: Oxford University Press, 1960.

The Midnight Court. Bryan Merriman. Translated into English [from Irish] by David Marcus. Dublin: The Dolmen Press, 1953 and 1967.

Irish Ghost Stories. Patrick Byrne. Cork: The Mercier Press.

HORSES

The Whitbread Book of Horses. London: Stanley Paul & Company, Ltd., 1962.

The Morgan Horse. Jeannie Mellin. Brattleboro, Vermont: The Stephen Greene Press.

Cavalcade of American Horses. Pers Crowell. New York, London, Toronto: McGraw-Hill Book Company, 1957.

Early Myopia. Allan Forbes. Privately Printed.

The History and Romance of the Horse. Arthur Vernon. Garden City, New York: Halcyon House.

Wild Sports of the West, with Legendary Tales and Local Sketches. W. B. Maxwell. London: Richard Bentley, 1832.

The Morgan Horse Magazine. Issues for March, May and July 1966. The Official Publication of The Morgan Horse Club, West Hartford, Connecticut.

FRENCH

Les Hôtels de l'Île Saint-Louis de la Cité, de l'Université et du Luxembourg. George Pillement. Editions Bellenaud.

CUISINE

Recipes from Ireland, Traditional and Modern. Frances Mayville Budin. New York: Taplinger Publishing Company, 1966.

About the Author

FRANCES PARKINSON KEYES, author of many best-selling novels, was born at the University of Virginia, where her father headed the Greek Department; but she grew up in Europe, Boston and at her mother's ancestral home, the Oxbow, in Newbury, Vermont. At eighteen, she married "Harry" Keyes, a rising political figure; and though their early married life was spent at Pine Grove Farm, Haverhill, New Hampshire, her husband's profession eventually took them to Washington and the United States Senate. Mrs. Keyes' career as a novelist and a commentator on the political and social scene, both at home and abroad, began almost simultaneously. Since her husband's death, Mrs. Keyes has maintained her ties in Washington and New England. While continuing to travel extensively, she spends part of every year at Beauregard House in New Orleans, which she has restored to its erstwhile glory. *The Heritage*, with its scene in Ireland, is her fiftieth book.

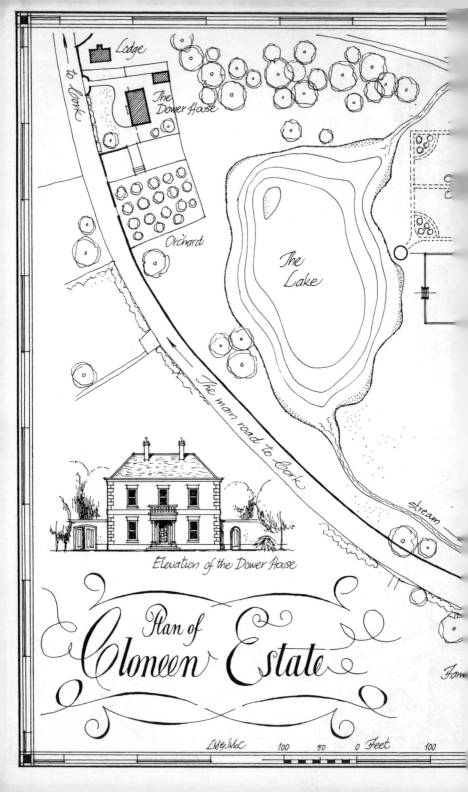

Lodge

The
Dower House

to Cork

Orchard

The
Lake

The main road to Cork

stream

Elevation of the Dower House

Plan of
Cloneen Estate

LM & JMcC   100   50   0 Feet   100